DELUDED YOUR SAILORS

A NOVEL

MICHELLE BUTLER HALLETT

| | | Canada | Newfoundland Labrador |

We gratefully acknowledge the financial support of the Canada Council for the Arts, the Government of Canada through the Canada Book Fund (CBF), and the Government of Newfoundland and Labrador through the Department of Tourism, Culture and Recreation for our publishing program.

Cover Design by Todd Manning
Layout by Joanne Snook-Hann
Printed on acid-free paper

Published by
KILLICK PRESS
an imprint of CREATIVE BOOK PUBLISHING
a Transcontinental Inc. associated company
P.O. Box 8660, Stn. A
St. John's, Newfoundland and Labrador A1B 3T7

Printed in Canada by:
TRANSCONTINENTAL INC.

Library and Archives Canada Cataloguing in Publication

Butler Hallett, Michelle
Deluded your sailors / Michelle Butler Hallett.

ISBN 978-1-897174-77-7

I. Title.

PS8603.U855D44 2011   C813'.6   C2011-905322-5

DELUDED YOUR SAILORS

A NOVEL

MICHELLE
BUTLER
HALLETT

killick press
an imprint of Creative Publishers

St. John's, Newfoundland and Labrador
2011

Sky Waves is a dynamic and shape-shifting work that redefines the project of storytelling, which complicates oral/aural tradition... both raucously funny and deeply troubling as it delves courageously into Newfoundland's many-faced identity. *Sky Waves* mobilises the cinematic: we find ourselves investing personally in each character, trying to hold on to them in memory until they reappear, potentially in another time, another place. The elusive characters are nevertheless compelling, for their radio silences are punctuated with our developing relationship with them: we yearn for their return from the past or future, hoping that they might give us the key to the novel, a desire *Sky Waves* intentionally never satisfies. When they do come to the fore, they are painfully bright and neurotic, sharp with wit and experience, and even malice. Others are cast in warm soft-focus, threatening to retreat into the past before we get what we want from them; dead before they can speak for themselves, their loss haunts us like a voice we can't quite make out. When we do, Butler Hallett's characters come to life actively, fighting for air time. Their humour betrays generations of pain, and yet their pains are so incredibly human that frequently we can't help but laugh. – *Maple Tree Literary Supplement*

Butler Hallett is not afraid to take chances with genre or format. The convolutions in the plotlines are clarified by writing that is imaginative and uncluttered... there are scenes of violence, psychological descent and physical degradation that are frank and unflinching. At the same time, Butler Hallett is often very funny. – *The Telegram*

DOUBLE-BLIND, *shortlisted for the 2007 Sunburst Award*

Butler Hallett's own weapons are subtly deployed in this convincing human drama. Her characters are thorough and striking, and her book is replete with aspects of horror, mystery, and hospital thriller, while transcending the conventions of mere genre. The descriptions of medical procedures are impressive in their detail, but the book avoids 'going textbook' on the reader. In fact, Butler Hallett's voice often surprisingly, pleasantly veers to the poetic. The Vietnam vets are described as 'each rotting in his own illness.' Giving electroconvulsive therapy to one terrified kid, Bozeman discovers, within the child's psyche, 'some brittle landscape, hard fruit on the ground.' Both Bozeman and Hallett dare to go beyond the accepted – in both cases, to impressively terrifying results. – *Quill and Quire*

Double-blind is wonderfully original while chillingly based in history. It really shook us up. Through the chronically self-deceived mind of the narrator, the novel delves into profound questions of ethics in a morally ambiguous world, and comes up with tragically ironic answers. The writing is incredibly layered, with metaphor and symbol perfectly balanced against the hard neutrality of scientific language. – Sunburst Award Jury.

Skill and confidence... economy and power. – *Books in Canada*

THE SHADOW SIDE OF GRACE

A rich and demanding read... Butler Hallett seems often to be creating from a subliminal place, riding on intuition, unencumbered by the counsel of editors. – *The Globe and Mail*

Draws from all of her influences to create a genre that is truly her own. – *The Calgary Herald*

Her characters speak from the margins of society, or of their own sanity... her writing is succinct and taut, her topics both universal and so offbeat as to be genuinely original, and her manner spare and unsparing. – *The Telegram*

Your men was not crazy, your men was not mad
Your men was not deep in despair-o
I deluded your sailors as well as yourself
I'm a maiden again on the shore, shore, shore
I'm a maiden again on the shore.

– 'Maid on the Shore,'
folk song,
as sung by The Once.

Another one for Michael Thompson – dead, but I keep wanting
to show you how this one worked out.

And another one for you, David, husband and friend,
scant return on all your love.

ACTS OF FOLLY

Everything is Bulls**t = $$$

Phil Churchill, *Anything is Possible*

1) OPENING REMARKS

January 5, 2009, as made at the Tourism, Culture and Recreation Department Breakfast, by Assistant Deputy Minister Chris Jackman, St. John's, Republic of Newfoundland and Labrador.

I got bacon on me tie, just a minute. Is the mic on? Good morning, me gaffers. Let me welcome you all back from a generous and what I hope was a restful Christmas and / or holiday season break. The government of the Republic of Newfoundland and Labrador supports employment equity and diversity. I should add we respect all religions, regardless of where they do or do not go to church.

As our doors are knocked on by the new year, I rest assured we all see the need to embrace the upcoming challenges as regards putting a fine polish on the incoming tourism experience.

All tourism is cultural. Whether tourists actually come out and say they want cultural tourism, the Republic's rich and unique culture and heritage are always a part of a visitor's experience. It certainly isn't the weather that brings them here, except inasmuch as the weather informs our culture. Because all tourism is cultural, all cultural industry must keep tourism in mind. In these days of changing energy supplies and fickle international markets, at least we will always have ourselves. To market our authenticity and create the best possible tourism experience, we must think, act, and feel that authentic experience. History is a resource as much as nickel, oil, copper or gold. Dig it up, refine it, and put it to market. The joy of tourism and culture, however, lies in the realities of host's privileges. When it comes to nickel and oil, we cannot tell the markets what they need when. They tell us. But when it comes to marketing our culture, we can tell the tourists, those wonderful end-consumers, what they need and want. By hosting tourists to our culture, we can focus their experience and, in the end, generate more revenue. The key to all of this is to always think of the lucrative tourism market and thereby always present the culture and heritage of this republic in the manner most appropriate.

New project and sustaining funding guidelines will be available by the fall of this year. In the meantime, funding applications for cultural endeavours need to be decided on a case-by-case basis for best fairness within the boundaries of budget. By working patiently within these fences now, we can best ensure that no layoffs or cutbacks will be necessary this fiscal year.

Anyways, I hope everyone enjoyed their breakfast as much as I did. I'm sure I'll see ya later up on deck.

—You don't have to forgive him.

So her psychiatrist said.

Nichole Wright, hiding her face behind curtains of long hair, twisted and destroyed a tissue. —All this time I've felt guilty about even accusing him in my head, never mind out loud, then thinking I owe at least the hard work and duty of forgiving him, it's just – hard.

—Owe whom?

Nichole pretended to study the muted landscape Dr Miller had hung on the wall: placid pond, smooth rocks, white birch. No cracked boulders, no deranged black spruce. *All the better for calming the crazies like me.* In truth, Nichole examined her distorted reflection in the glass laid over the painting: eyes wide like a child's after a visit to a fairground haunted house, face lined like an old whore's after a dead night. *Yeah. Whore. You heard me. Take it away, Robertson Davies, you and yer spooky Canadian identity questions: Hoo-er ya? Newfoundland version: Whore you at all, hey? Who owns you?*

The glass over the painting reflected back a somewhat overweight woman wearing rectangle-framed glasses, that particular shape and style ubiquitous in 2009. Subtle makeup softened what Newfoundland English called a right hard-lookin face, that face made all the harder from years of grotesque weight loss and weight gain – of bingeing and purging. Her thinned-out teeth, enamel translucent at the biting edge, betrayed that lovely little habit. Not beautiful, oh no; Nichole took great care to avoid *beautiful.*

Not ugly, though.

And no whore.

So pretty. Can't keep my eyes off ya. Come sit in my lap, ya pretty thing. Shh...

—Nichole, you don't owe anyone. You are the injured party.

Experienced, white-haired, physically strong but pale, as though he bled in secret, Dwayne Miller looked to be drowning in compassion and quite unaware of it, a happy child dog-paddling in water maybe six inches over his head and watching the bubbles rise.

Not accepting, not believing Miller's words, lies the norm, after all, Nichole gave a nod. So easy to lie, to ooze past the chasm between the desired reality and the dirty truth. —But how much of it do I even know? I mean, I know it, somewhere, yet I don't, because I can't pin down the memories. How can I not know what I know? What if I'm accusing these men falsely? Holes. My memory's holed. Not like those things you simply don't remember, but like someone stove in your skull and shoved out great ragged chunks.

Dr Miller spoke some more, reminding Nichole that her symptoms read like a bulleted list in a textbook, that her damaged memory and roughed-up storyline could only be called common. Normal to refuse knowledge and belief, to create an historical naught. Not. Knot.

—Cherry trees. He liked to pose me nude in front of this one particular cherry tree, all young and spindly. Wild cherries, little things, more pit than fruit, suck off all the fruit and skin and spit out the seeds. I'd gorge on them, pack my mouth and cheeks so full I didn't dare speak, because then I might choke. I'd dance with that tree, when no one could see me, lead it, like it stood rooted to be my passive partner. Later, I scrawbed into the bark of it with a soup spoon. Broke off its branches. Flung them into the woods. Likely a half dozen more cherry trees there, yes now, a whole forest of cherry trees, all from one beat-up sapling. All my fault.

—None of this is your fault, Nichole.

—Sanded me down just fine for getting tangled up with that Foxe fucker, didn't it?

—Re-victimization. It's another common pattern.

—Is there a peel-and-stick label standing by for everything I've gone through?

Dwayne Miller sighed, very tired. Tired of how often he had these conversations with patients. He'd not been raised Catholic, but some days he wished he'd instead become a priest who could give absolution after hearing confessions, those rituals looking easier than these long struggles to heal. That's why he studied medicine, wasn't it, to heal? *Right, a priest.* At least he'd corrected Nichole's prescriptions; some fool colleague had done harm, writing Nichole up for lithium. —Re-victimization is part of what happened when Almayer Foxe stalked and attacked you. Because of your past, you'd been groomed, so to speak, to respond a particular way to a predator's overtures.

—Then it *is* my fault.

Not that Nichole spoke loudly enough for anyone to hear.

Dr Miller kept talking. —I wish medicine better understood the predators. Then we might treat and heal someone like your grandfather, too.

—Heal *him*? I want him staked down to a bog and left for the rats and the crows and fuckin starved stray dogs! You hear me?

—I hear you. Keep speaking.

—I want him to suffer! I want him to feel the pain and the humiliation and the dirt, the fuckin *dirt* soakin into his soul and stainin him forever!

—And why do you want that?

Don't drop your Gs, don't aspirate your vowels, always speak nicely. —Because he hurt me. And he had no right to.

A few moments of quiet. Miller asked if Nichole still meditated.

—When I can get my mind settled down.

—Binge-eating?

—Now and then.

—Purging?

—Not as much.

—And are you testifying at Foxe's trial?

—No fucking way.

Her own worst enemy, some days. —Nichole, I wonder –

—I don't have to forgive him. You said so.

—I was referring to your grandfather, but –

—All the same to me. One abuser, two abusers, three abusers, four. I am not looking at Almayer Foxe ever again; it's as simple as that. Besides, I just got this play commission from the Allied Cultural and Heritage Enterprises for the Settlement 250 celebrations out in Port au Mal. TCR money and two hundred and fifty years of white European history, all you can eat. I've got a fair bit of research to do, so I just won't be able to go to court.

—Are you afraid?

Nichole glared at him. Dignity vanished as if on her breath, and she hunched her shoulders and sank in her chair, a sneer ageing and deforming her face, while her voice fell into the tones of an old-school moneyed townie: disgust and entitlement.

—Fuck fear.

She stood up calmly, wrapping her pashmina scarf round her shoulders and slipping on her long coat. A clean and simple authority radiated from her. —I think our time's up today, and the waiting room is busy. I'd better go.

—Reception will call you with your next appointment time. Prescriptions good?

Nichole's smile transformed the snotty troll who'd just said *Fuck fear*. —Fine. Everything's fine.

Boots clicking on the hard floor, she departed.

After completing his notes, Dr Miller emerged from his office to call his next patient. A busy waiting room, yes – he shared it with two other psychiatrists – but the clock told him Nichole's hour still had fifteen minutes left.

Not the first time she's done that.

3) LIVE DOCUMENTS

Crazy cunt.

Evan Rideout sighed; dust motes danced. Harsh winter sunlight – tormented, quickened by old windows that seemed to melt and spill, dull panes thicker at the bottom, glass refusing gravity yet surrendering, beautiful – galled his eyes. His recent ex-girlfriend, had she heard his thoughts, would have punched his upper arm hard enough to leave a mark. *Rightly so,* Evan told himself, rubbing the imaginary wound. *Where do I get off thinkin about a nice old lady like Mrs O'Dea in words like that? Grandfather would tear a strip off me, too.*

Mrs Rebecca O'Dea laid a china plate of cookies and squares on the table, directly under Evan's nose. Date squares, lemon squares, snowballs and those waxed chocolate mice with the crispy rice and peanut butter centres, Evan's favourite, tottered and slid, only saved in the end by the friction of the paper doily beneath them.

—Last time I saw those letters, wait now, yes, up in the attic. I remember, because John barked his head off a ceiling beam so hard he nearly crashed down into the kitchen. The attic's almost directly overhead.

Chewing an entire chocolate mouse at once, Evan dutifully glanced up at the low ceiling.

Mrs O'Dea nudged the teapot closet to Evan. —You'll hear me lumbering up there in a moment. Pour yourself some tea once it's steeped, and have another square. It's not every day I get company, especially polite young men who look so smart in their Republic Parks uniforms.

He'd worn the Parks uniform so Mrs O'Dea wouldn't think he'd come from Rare Documents. Born and raised in Newfoundland, and not terribly young – he'd recently lost an argument with forty-three – Evan understood the etiquette: refuse a cookie, square or, worst of all, a cup of tea, and you'd spark in your hostess a steadily hotting-up frenzied quest for something you would deign to accept, take, eat. Hard times, days of common and private starvation, lurked in living memories. Supermarkets and regular imports had cosseted everyone into expectations of quick plenty, when in truth a ferry disruption of a mere three days would cause visible shortages. Offers of sweets and

8

tea, then and now, translated into offers of shelter, common decency and love. Translated, too, into status, ambition and lies.

Evan just stopped himself from answering *Yes, Nan,* like a child. —Thank you, Mrs O'Dea.

Moisture beaded the chocolate mice. Mrs O'Dea, Evan reflected, had likely just fetched the sweets from a tray in her deep freeze, trays kept handy for company. Evan's grandmother had always disliked having company over. Company meant shoes in the front porch, perked coffee in the front room, and a madness of J-Cloths the day before. Friends, by contrast, piled in the back door, drank ready tea in the kitchen and confessed happily to the state, my dear, the absolute *state* of their own houses.

Evan listened to Mrs O'Dea climb a far-off ladder and then tread slowly over the attic floor, almost certainly wiser and more careful than her husband about where now she stood, crawling through insulation and dust for a local boy from the other side of the bay. Certainly not for Rare Docs. And not for Evan. For Evan's boss, Assistant Deputy Minister of Tourism, Culture and Recreation, Chris Jackman, or, to Mrs O'Dea, always and forever Larry Jackman's boy.

She cried out.

Evan nearly squashed a lemon square between his forefinger and thumb. —You all right, Mrs O'Dea?

No answer.

Evan scowled. *Be Jackman's fault if Mrs O'Dea breaks her hip up there. Yes, you, Chris Jackman, you Ritalined pork-barrellin skeet. How in the name of Jesus did I let you suck me into doin your dirty work? Heritage and culture – no. You promised to help me fast-track my grandfather into a Home, skip past those Jesus wait-list lotteries.*

The house had a smell to it, familiar and frightening: must and foust and baby powder and damp wood and copper, hidden decrepitude, as if some moist corpse all washed and dressed in Sunday best, watch and fob, high collar and waistcoat, soaked that crumbling wall and would soon rupture it, plummet to the floor and release a mushroom cloud of dust from his hands, and –

Evan's belt cut into his belly as he leant forward to pick up his third cookie. He sat back, considering the expense of his tailored Republic Parks uniform and how Tourism, Culture and Recreation had issued memos denying replacement before two years' wear on all uniform pieces, maternity excepted, and decided to stop for coffee but not doughnuts on the drive back to St John's.

Least this house doesn't smell like Nan's, all glassy piss and kerosene, her and that Mason jar full of kidney stones. Don't know how Pop stood it. Misses it now.

High above Evan, Mrs O'Dea opened and closed something, probably a trunk, muttered, and crawled carefully back to the attic ladder.

Chris Jackman's voice, deliberately slumming into dialect: *Evan, me ol cock, dart out to Riordan's Back for me and see what Mrs O'Dea is after thinkin she's found for Settlement 250, some letters, been in her family since the year dot. She said she's after hidin them from the Rare Docs crowd. Some glad I seconded you from Republic Parks. Beats collectin the dole all winter, hey b'y?*

Mrs O'Dea stood before Evan, clutching something precious to her chest. —Are you all right, Mr Rideout? You looked so angry just then. Have another cookie. Or should I pour you some tea?

She carefully placed the treasure – a flattened and decapitated cat, perhaps – on a lavender armchair still wrapt in clear plastic. Then she poured tea into china cups patterned with lush blue roses nearly the same hue as her eyes. Veins and knuckles interrupted the soft skin on the backs of her hands.

—I don't know what he was thinking, telephoning me on a Sunday morning during mass. At first I couldn't figure out the message on my machine, but then when Chris said he was Larry's boy, it all came rushing back. I hadn't heard from him since he took it on himself to create all those Living History Displays. Remember those? Couldn't sweep a floor in a bay for the LHDs there for a while. Even got my father-in-law involved, though I don't think Ange, God rest his soul, really liked it. I remember, Larry's boy propped Ange on a rocking chair, up on a little stage all roped off like those line-ups at the bank, made Ange act like he was mending a net, but a brand new net, bright green. But I think what really got to Ange was the woodstove, chimney pipe just jutting towards the ceiling, connected to nothing.

Silence. Evan strived to mark it with the answer Mrs O'Dea wanted. He failed. —Like how Riordan's Back isn't even on Google Maps?

Mrs O'Dea sipped her tea, quite loudly. —Did you say you draw cartoons on Signal Hill?

—I'm the military animator for Signal Hill. In tourist season. I look after the Tattoo, re-enactments of fife and drum drill with

10

the Royal Newfoundland Regiment of Foot. I supervise the weapons and look after historical accuracy in costume and drill. Sometimes I do consultin for the Admiral's Rooms. Over the winter I'm assistin Mr Jackman with the Settlement 250 initiative.

—Settlement 250, yes. VOIC Radio hasn't shut up about it, and Reverend Winslow over at Prevenient Grace in Port au Mal – I must remember to bring him some cookies, he's getting thin – he wants to organize a protest group to just leave all the old history alone if the arts crowd from town can't promise to interpret it properly. Sure, the whole works is still a year off. Though lots of people out this way haven't got much time for the arts crowd. Even John – my husband, I mean – even John's been asking me about it, and he's in the Estuary Home with Alzheimer's.

—You're a long way out. Estuary's in St John's.

—The dementia beds are all full out here. Did I hear right that some young girl from town is supposed to come out here to write the play for us?

—Nichole Wright. Friend of mine.

—Is she anything to the Port au Mal Wrights? Good. That's not so bad then, not the same as some perfect stranger come digging for his own reasons. But it's my John you and Larry's boy need to thank, really. John's the one who insisted we keep the Captain's papers all these years. Poor Captain Wright.

Jackman, for fuck's sake, you told me... —So these letters haven't been in your family for generations?

—Lord, no. John got these letters and the pelt bag off Captain Wright on one of his foggy days, no, wait now, what did he call them? Storm days. Nothing to do with the weather. Captain Wright, I mean. One of his sons went on to found VOIC, did you know that? But the storm day: 1947, dampest old draughty winter day, Captain Wright criss-crossing the bay a dozen or more times, pressing old rags and scraps and broken lamps on people willy-nilly. The winter before that he coppied ice pans barefoot, carting a big slut kettle. How he didn't slip and drown, I'll never know. God looks after His fools, I allow. You haven't started your tea. But then I suppose you want to look at what the captain left us.

—I should wash my hands before I touch it.

—Kitchen sink is right over there. Sugar or milk in your tea?

I don't want any friggin tea. That's why I didn't pour any. I hate tea. —Plain is fine, thank you.

11

—John now, John, I couldn't get him to give up the sugar in his tea to save his life. Him diabetic, too. How many times was I after saying...

No longer listening, Evan carefully washed and dried his hands, then tugged on white cotton archivist's gloves. He stood over the lavender good chair and studied the treasure: a flat bag, almost an envelope, made from seal fur and fastened by a loop of leather over a piece of bone, rather long piece of bone, a strong finger and tapered nail, pointing...

Only flipper bone, ya fool.

The seal bone reminded him of his ex, all waxed, zaftig and dyed. *She really looks after herself, that one,* his grandfather had observed, over and over. She filed her strong nails to a lovely almond shape, and she'd taken Evan's comparison of her lying prone and post-coital to a harp seal basking on a rock completely the wrong way.

Mrs O'Dea's cup clinked against the saucer. —Aren't you going to open it?

Not a malicious dig or demand but an expectant reminder, as though Evan just missed a crucial step in a ceremony.

Evan gently lifted the leather loop from round the seal bone. Nothing crumbled.

—I was after John for years to bring that into the university. Then Rare Docs came looking, but no way would I let them take it. I wouldn't even let them in the porch, told them I had no artifacts whatsoever. Young men in suits with name tags, honestly. As if I'm going to address some boy in his twenties as 'Mr'.

Papers. Very old. Thready handwriting, the spill and the scratch of a quill, iron-gall ink faded to that old brown, a feminine hand, sentences criss-crossed, half the text perpendicular to the other half, some words ruint by folds, but most decipherable to the trained and patient eye. To Evan's eye. Squinting, Evan took hard care not to breathe on the paper.

—Can you actually read that writing? John and I could never make head nor tail out of it.

—I studied with a professor in Salem a few years ago. Massachusetts. He taught me all about eighteenth-century spelling and penmanship.

Date, date... 1745? Blisterin third-degree royal-arsed fuck. I got a letter here addressed to some Cannard dude in Port au Mal in

12

1745. I'm gonna come in my pants. Wait. Settlement 250 presumes 1760, 250 years of settlement to 2010. We got the wrong date. We got the whole fuckin thing wrong. Wait –

March 14th, 1745. From Newman Head, Merchant, Salem, Massachusetts. To John Cannard, lately of Bristol, residing now in Port au Mal, Newfoundland.

Sir: I knew both Captain Finn and Captain Cleasby. Captain Matthew Finn, for so we in Salem knew him, sometimes also Kit Finn, being a Christopher as well as a Matthew...

Evan grinned, getting quite warm. Not just a letter, this, but also an answer. Meaning the first letter pre-dated this one. Meaning, given shipping times, settlement of Port au Mal dated at least to mid or late 1744. At the very least.

Alarmed, Mrs O'Dea put down her tea. —Goodness, sit down. You look like you're about to faint or – oh my.

No slight bit embarrassed by the hard-on now poking the pleats of his Republic Parks uniform pants, Evan sat. He even drank some tea, medicinally, just to steady his nerves.

17-fuckin-45.

Mrs O'Dea held out the plate of cookies. —Date square?

Evan's drive back to St John's, rendered all steamed-up misery by snow showers, horrid early dusk, lap-spilt coffee, chargeless iPod, staticky VOIC radio signal, and the sudden death of the car heater, kept him from swiping his timecard back in at Tourism, Culture and Recreation until almost 5:30. With any luck, Chris Jackman had already left for his weekly supper at the Prime Minister's house – the weekly supper about which he regularly briefed his staff and tweeted to his followers.

Fluorescent lights spread greasy cold glare over the dozens and dozens of cubicles crammed together on TCR's huge open floor. Years before, uncounted secretaries had typed and answered phones and crossed their legs behind desk modesty panels. Now the floor housed the much-expanded department's workforce – the gaffers, as Jackman called them. Behind closed doors, other Assistant Deputy Ministers just used the words 'cattle' and 'stalls.' Evan, a

13

seasonally-seconded temp, had been lucky to get a cubicle. A few committee heads and the Assistant Deputy Ministers, those happy few, worked in tiny Venetian-blinded offices lining the east wall, scheming and competing to stand ready when the Minister called one of them up to fill the empty role of Deputy Minister. They kept their office doors closed. The Minister himself rarely graced the department, but two executive assistants regularly dusted and vacuumed his cavernous office. Much as Evan disliked swelling Jackman's head still further, he must agree: in Tourism, Culture and Recreation, at least, the Assistant Deputy Ministers did most of the work.

Evan followed his memory-thread to his cubicle. Faux St John's street signs marked the pathways: St Clare, Water, Elizabeth, Duckworth, Harbourside, Beck's Cove, Clift's-Baird's Cove, LeMarchant, even George. The little corridors intersected like the handwritten sentences from 1745. Not corridors, truth told, nor pathways. Most people called them lanes, despite Chris Jackman's several memos instructing staff to refer to the paths as drungs. *If the Department of Tourism, Culture and Recreation of the Republic of Newfoundland and Labrador does not use authentic Newfoundland English, then who will? We here at government cannot allow Newfoundland English to go on state-sanctioned life-support the way that Irish Gaelic did.* Evan had chuckled when first reading the memo and almost shared his thoughts with Jackman, but then the pathologically busy ADM would likely take Evan's sauce for a rallying cry: *What once they spoke we speak?*

Evan's cubicle, three desks left of the intersection of Harvey and LeMarchant, housed a small desk, one antiquated laptop, a refurbished olive green rotary dial telephone, one framed photo of himself in eighteenth-century Royal Newfoundland Regiment uniform and bearskin hat doing the grip-and-grin with the PM, and one wobbly four-caster chair stained with beige splashes.

Evan had just planted his arse in said wobbly chair when Chris Jackman Kilroyed over the facing cubicle wall. —Any mummers lowed in? Piss yourself, Rideout?

—Coffee, potholes and winter. Deadly combination. When are you gonna get that stretch of highway paved?

—Not my department. Potholes are worse than moose, some days. Get anythin from Mrs O'Dea we could turn into dinner theatre for the tourists? You're hidin somethin from me.

Lying, Evan said no. Once last year he'd joined a poker game with Jackman, justifiably confident he'd win a little. He planned to hold back, truth told, so he wouldn't piss Jackman off. But Chris Jackman, one of those men gifted with calculation and frightening sight, murdered the lot of them. Since that costly night, Evan had worked to better hide his thoughts from Jackman. Another X for failure on the calendar today.

Chris Jackman's thinning fair hair wisped up dead straight as he ducked out of sight. Evan sighed, turned round in his chair and faced the cubicle entrance. Jackman leapt into the cubicle, too joyful to care that Evan had anticipated him. —I know that face, Rideout. Either you're after givin birth to a turd thick as your fist, or you found somethin really good out there.

—I just want to authenticate – gimme that Jesus briefcase!

—Ah-ah-ah, don't you talk to your boss like that.

—Jackman, put on these cotton gloves first, will ya? The oils from your fingers can damage the papers.

—Oil? Don't be talkin. I got some writer tryna pin me down for an interview about *Sea Sentry*. That rig went down almost twenty-five years ago. Why can't we just leave it the hell alone? It's disturbin a deep grave, sure.

Evan nodded. *Your father's grave.*

—Ev, how old is this at all?

—Eighteenth-century, I think.

—Wha, Victorian?

—Seventeen hundreds. I'll bring those papers to the Admiral's Rooms tomorrow, see what the head curator can tell me.

—Yes, and then lock them away and get them registered at Rare Docs. Hang on, Rare Docs is after movin again. I think they're in the old Professor Danielle rink. With any luck it'll be too cold there for a fire.

—So I'll be out most of the day.

—No can do, Ev. It's all hands on deck here tomorrow. ACHE Board meetin tomorrow night, on top of everythin else. I need you there takin the minutes.

—About that: should the assistant to the non-votin government rep really be the one takin minutes?

—I can't write fast enough. And Jesus, Lewis Wright's the secretary. I'm not sure he can sign a cheque before sundown even if he starts at the crack of dawn. VOIC Radio boardroom, up to the station on Kenmount Road, seven o'clock sharp.

—I thought the Wrights sold VOIC years ago.

—Wolf Broadcastin bought it, chain from Canada, bad as Tim Hortons or mildew on the bathroom ceilin. But they rent out the board room, solid revenue stream. And we're lucky to get that boardroom. Jesus, we got no infrastructure in this city, and every time a developer tables a plan, the city denies it for not comin in line with the proper heritage look. Bad enough the government's spread all over St John's. Now I got the arts crowd cryin about how we had to close down the Hall for asbestos and mould. I can't even find a room to get a committee together, and now these friggin actors are comin at me, whinin they got nowhere to go play make-believe. And Seth Seabright, that nuisance, I don't know who he thinks he is, but he delivered a petition to me this afternoon, by hand, if you please, leanin there behind the media scrum, his dirty old boot sole flat against the antique wall. Jesus. I gotta go. PM's expectin me. Republic's work is never done.

And Chris Jackman tossed the briefcase back onto Evan's desk, knocking over the framed photo and a cup of coffee left over from the previous week. The briefcase flapped open, and the packet from Mrs O'Dea slid out. Stale coffee marked with fronds of curdled cream flowed and just missed the sealskin.

Allied Cultural and Heritage Enterprises
Board of Directors Meeting
Thursday 10 Feb 2009
VOIC Radio Network board room, Kenmount Road

Present at Kenmount Road:
Dorinda Masterson, President
Johnny Malone, Vice-President/Avalon Peninsula Representative
Lewis Wright, Secretary/Treasurer
Chris Jackman, Government Representative (non-voting)
Evan Rideout, Assistant to Mr Jackman (taking minutes)

Present via conference call:
Linda Gillingham, Eastern/Central Representative
Cissy Dawe, Western/Labrador Representative

Meeting called to order at 7:05pm by ACHE President Dorinda Masterson.

Motion to adopt the agenda. Cissy so moved. Lewis seconded it.

Motion to adopt the minutes from the last meeting. Johnny so moved. Lewis seconded. Linda Gillingham noted three typos on page 8 of 12. Motion to adopt the minutes with changes to fix typos. Linda so moved. Lewis seconded.
ACTION ITEM: Evan Rideout to fix typos.

SETTLEMENT 250
Johnny delivered his report on the involvement of businesses from St John's to Trinity chiming in to become a part of Settlement 250, next year's festival commemorating 250 years of settlement of the Port au Mal region of Conception Bay.

Chris Jackman reminded the board of the considerable government funding for this project and the need for accountability and transparency for all projects applying for said funding. He said that Settlement 250 is expected to attract many ex-pats and tourists as the Republic of NL continues to roll out its extensive Cultural Tourism Blueprint. He reported that relevant materials and literature have been distributed internationally, penetrating markets in Canada, the United States, Scandinavia, Australia and New Zealand, as well as Ireland, England, Scotland, Wales, France and Germany. He noted that significant online presence has also been developed and launched, including Web 2.0 interactive sites and messaging boards. Follow-ups are planned. Chris expressed the opinion that it would be really nice if we could meet our tourist quota this year.

Dorinda expressed concern that the tourist quota, already a problematic concept, seems a bit high.

Chris replied there can be no industry growth without extra effort from all those involved.

Cissy commented there is little interest in Settlement 250 west of Trinity, and that the initiative offers nothing to the western half of the island or to Labrador. Linda agreed.

Chris explained that Settlement 250 should be thought of as a homecoming summer festival on steroids, baptised with offshore oil, and that if Settlement 250 performs as expected, it will set a funding precedent for other regions.

Lewis asked if there is a list of projects and funding levels. Chris replied there is no such list as of this time, but the initiative is just getting started out the gate in the slush.

Dorinda asked Chris for an update on the theatrical idea he wishes ACHE to administrate. Chris reminded the Board of their previous motion to hire a writer to take on the necessary research and writing to produce a tourist-appropriate play for Settlement 250. He stated that it was best not to hire a big name, as remuneration will be limited by funding parameters and budget commitments. He noted that an emerging writer would be grateful to benefit from exposure and connection with Settlement 250, and ACHE's supporting an emerging writer would also in turn cast a good reflection on ACHE.

Lewis commented that this makes the third meeting where this point has been discussed. He stated that he contacted novelist Nichole Wright, who expressed interest in taking the commission. He said Nichole is his cousin and has family roots in Port au Mal.

Dorinda and Evan discussed Nichole's novel. Dorinda expressed her approval of commissioning Nichole Wright.

ACTION ITEM: Lewis will continue to liaise with Nichole on behalf of ACHE re researching and writing a play based on the history of Port au Mal area for the Settlement 250 initiative. He will report regularly to the Board.

BUSINESS ARISING

Cissy commented that the western part of the island and Labrador feel neglected by TCR. Linda agreed and asked about funding plans about eastern, central and the south coast. Vigorous discussion.

Johnny stated that Cissy's lengthy concerns should be added to the agenda for the next meeting, and that a report specifying the complaints would be useful. Johnny added that he requested Cissy take the latter action at the last two board meetings. Vigorous discussion.

ACTION ITEM: Cissy and Linda to prepare a report citing their regions' concerns. Report to be circulated to the board before the next meeting and added to the agenda for that meeting.

Johnny moved to adjourn the meeting because of worsening weather and deteriorating driving conditions. Chris seconded. Dorinda commented that a motion to adjourn needs no second. Meeting adjourned.

4) BIG WHITE PHONE

Dreams hissing with wasps and sleep battered as ballicatter, Nichole Wright, alone, struggled to stay awake. She felt sick – plagued – with the stale hangover of old abuse and the newer stink of the Almayer Foxe trial. Foxe had arrived in Newfoundland in the mid-1970s, running from a mucky past and hurriedly making up a name after catching sight of a book title. Faux-posh English accent eliciting enormous respect in post-colonial Newfoundland, Foxe quickly settled into broadcasting, a career he enjoyed. His social status eased his three hobbies: tea-blending, health scams, and serial seduction-for-blackmail. Over the decades, the few victims who spoke to police, braving the revelation of extremely compromising photographs, faced questions of chastity, vanity, and consent. Surely the women had allowed the alleged photographer to see them in such a state. Surely the women had enough sense to know they could not possibly be models, despite this photographer's alleged promise to break them into the business. And, my dear, who's going to believe someone like Almayer Foxe is up to things like that? That's not the half of it. That dried up old hag of a journalist, Rose Fahey, who fucked off to Canada first chance she got? She came back and decided to play Foxe's game. Starved for a story idea, was she? Lowering herself like that.

Rose Fahey stole Foxe's new digital camera that night, the camera's memory card crammed with dated photos of other women, the most recent being Nichole Wright. That heavy theft, plus a painfully detailed statement, got a search warrant and an arrest. Tardy justice toiled. The crown ruled the stolen camera inadmissible and set a trial date. Three complainants: Rose Fahey, Evelyn Lockyear, Nichole Wright. And delay after delay.

He said she said. Ya knows, now.

Nichole needed to disappear. Light out for the territories. Just fucking *drive*. Ice cream shop: large milkshake. Burger stand: globular patty between a baker's fog bun, and onion rings. Different ice cream shop: a second milkshake, sweet, creamy, undemanding, and sucked back. Convenience store: two big bags of potato chips, a few candy bars from the 2 for $1.29 boxes, and a half-litre tub of frozen dessert topping. Pass the beer fridge. No, no worries there, for Nichole had given up drinking, quite in control, thank you.

The bender lasted about two hours. Hardly sated, just numbed and suddenly relieved, Nichole took a few experimental breaths, closed her copy of *Pilgrim's Progress*, spinecracked and splayed where Appolyon crossed the field – all hideous and proud, fish scales glittering – and paced steadily to her bathroom. She ignored the cat but then changed her mind, turning back and speaking gently to the pussens, yes, the sweet old cat, darling killer, beautiful beast. Nichole led the cat to the kitchen, where she opened a can of something fishy and forked it down to mush on a saucer. The cat ate, noisily. Nichole inhaled the scent, shut her eyes, and resumed her ritual walk to the bathroom – practically a walk down the aisle, oh yes. No cameras, no grandfather, no Foxe. Just her own fingers. First inserting two glycerine suppositories high up her rectum, then receiving a wash of soap and madhot water, finally working down her throat to tickle the gag reflex she'd nicknamed Lovelace.

Kneeling at the toilet.

Winter and rough weather played merry hell with the plumbing; the water in the bowl rocked, rose and fell.

Harder, deeper.

Just a little further, knuckles past tonsils, gag once, gag twice – heave it outta ya, girl, heave it out –

Vomit spattered back onto Nichole's face and shut eyelids; she'd long ago learnt one must purge blind.

Dig deep, deeper –

Breathe, girl, breathe, good, good girl.

Leaning her right cheek on the toilet seat, Nichole gasped and shook, spat, gasped again. She groped for tissue and wiped bile from her lips and chin. Bits of tissue stuck to her mouth. She examined her production. Slick globs – oh, look, an oil spill – floated round the bowl. Chunky mush of potato chips, sticky and somewhat-chewed Turkish delight, curdling milk and ice cream, soothing once but all acid burn now, and yep, found the burger.

Another thrust down the throat. Cramps already. Glycerine maddened her colon, then sweat and that curious, most unpleasant sensation she might vomit excrement – flush, flush again, rinse her mouth, sit on the toilet, and sweet, sweet relief. *Let's get you all cleaned up down there, Nichole.* Like the cat with a hairball. The expanding pressure beneath her ribs: gone. Released. Swirling now towards the sewer pipe exit directly into St John's Harbour, Godspeed. Perfectly natural. And just fine, so long as she kept control of it. She'd always kept control. Never said a word.

Nichole supported herself on the vanity, stood up and looked in the mirror. She ran cold water until she seemed to smell the reeds from the bottom of Windsor Lake, then splashed it on her face. Nichole Laika Wright, aged 38, green eyes bloodshot, too-long hair sweated up, only surviving child of Stephen and Una Wright, the others lost to crib death, a particular problem for the Wrights. Yes, one of *those* Wrights, the over-reaching high-achieving risk-addicted business crowd connected for years to VOIC Radio, some days drowning in paralytic sadness and so desperate to *feel* that they'd seek out grand projects and heavy tasks and so self-medicate with pressure, deadlines and adrenaline. Not Nichole, though. Just an all-round failure there, as lost some days as a stray dog shot into space. Even the answering machine said so.

'Hello! This is your captain speaking. You've just won a cruise holiday! Please call us back within the next hour to confirm your credit card number, and soon you'll be on your way to the sunny seas.'

'Nichole, Evan Rideout. Can you come in to the Admiral's Rooms early tomorrow and look after the *Lady Voter* exhibit? I've got to meet Chris Jackman again over at Tourism, Culture and Recreation.'

'Nicky? It's your mother. Remember me? Pick up. Oh, for God's sake, I don't even know why I try to talk to you some days.'

'Hi, Nichole. It's Callie Best, Claire's mom. I found a photo album today from when you two were in school, looks like grades three to nine. Let me know when you want to come get it.'

I can't!

Photo albums meant proofs of the past and hard, sweet memories of Claire who just fucking died. Just died. Four years ago, come April. Four years?

'Ms Wright, this is Reverend Elias Winslow of the Church of Prevenient Grace at the End of Things in Port au Mal. You may remember selling me some land last year. I'm calling on behalf of HARC, the Historical Accuracy Reproduction Committee, and as a personal favour, to caution you against overly rigorous research. No one wishes to see government time and funds wasted on careless digging. I would be happy to direct you further.'

Nichole, electrolytes wrecked, tottered and grasped a short bookcase. —The fuck?

'Might I add: "There is no prince that will thus lightly lose his subjects, neither will I as yet lose you; but since you complain of my wages, be content to go back, and what our country will afford I do here promise to give you." '

I need to sit down.

'I trust you will be in touch soon.'

The answering machine clicked off.

This Reverend Winslow had quoted *Pilgrim's Progress* at her. Quoted from the very page she'd just marked.

—I hear all this *after* I've done the b-p? That's hardly fair.

Cat rubbing her ankles, Nichole hauled herself onto the couch, picked up remotes and flicked on the television and DVD player. *Star Trek* lulled her. Over the hissing racket of the poorly costumed Gorn fighting Captain Kirk, she heard Claire Furey chanting their rainy-day rhyme:

Little Sally Saucer, sitting in the water
Rise up, Sally, and wipe away your tears.
Turn to the east side, turn to the west side,
Turn to the very side that you like best!

That game, best played round a puddle, sometimes enticed Claire's grandfather to come outside, back when Claire and her mother lived with him. Nichole adored Claire's grandfather, only later coming to understand that Claire's Poppy had another name: Jack Best, architect of Newfoundland and Labrador's 'responsible independence' and the republic's first prime minister. Nichole's grandfather, retired civil servant William Wright, always asked about Claire's Poppy in a strange way, like he hoped something bad had happened to him. Poppy Best liked to teach the girls games: Blind Man's Bluff, Freeze Tag, and a complicated variant on hopscotch:

Marlow, Marlow, Marlow bright,
How many miles to Babylon?
Threescore and ten.
Can I get there by candlelight?
Aye, if your legs be as long as the light,
But take care of the old grey witch at the roadside.

Jack Best, in his mid seventies, would then pretend to be the old grey witch and chase two pre-school girls round a huge backyard. Grand fun.

William Wright did not play such transparent games. Bring on the old grey witch, for, by comparison, she be harmless. Nichole still could not speak of most of what William Wright had done to her. Memories surfaced in pieces, timedulled, barely recognizable, unlabelled little movies so disconnected from the rest of her that they could not possibly be true, just compelling, hypnotic, and tyrannical. Simplistic, when narrated, crassly symbolic: *He treated me like I was special – thought it meant some kind of love – he took me across a pond to a storage shed – out on a yacht, him and some other old men, singing that rant and roar song, endless –*

The answering machine beeped.

'Ms Wright, Reverend Winslow. I came across this verse and thought of you: "Thou shalt no more be termed Forsaken; neither shall thy land be termed Desolate; but thou shalt be called Hepzibah and thy land Beulah..." '

Stand there, now: pretty girl against the summer landscape.

Captain Kirk hove a cardboard rock at the Gorn. Nichole listened to Reverend Winslow, knowing the telephone had not rung.

'I have known your family for many years, Ms Wright, tilled the thin soil those roots penetrate. Did you know some plants will break rocks? And the barrens, Ms Wright: your cousin, Lewis, dreams he's crucified on the barrens. Moss and bog, worn rocks white and dead as the moon, everlasting wind eating his eyes, his skin, finally his bones. Nailed to a bent starrigan. Caribou run past, fog hiding them. Stains in the blood haunt him. You need me. Whatever it takes to jig yourselves free of dark water, hey, my dear.'

I am not your fucking 'dear.'

The cat kneaded Nichole's lower belly, purred. The Gorn hissed and growled.

And – God love him – Reverend Winslow sang. He clearly had a thing for Bunyan.

'Who would true valour see,
Let him come hither;
One here will constant be,
Come wind, come weather.

24

There's no discouragement
Shall make him once relent
His first avowed intent
To be a pilgrim.'

Nichole compared the Reverend's performance of the song to
Maddy Prior's and found the Reverend wanting.

'Addicted to risk, anything to crack your calloused shell and
allow feeling in. And out. You'd better come and see me.'

Nichole forced herself to stand. Then she staggered back to
the bathroom, the vomiting involuntary now. And hard. Ribbons
of thick yellow bile landed in the water.

Reverend Winslow's telephone-dusty voice changed timbre as
it emerged from the toilet bowl. 'And here is the chasm between
the official version and what really happened.'

The nurses at the old Janeway Children's Hospital, helping six-
year-old Nichole after a disastrous bout of seasickness and
something else: *Let's get you cleaned up down there.*

Winslow continued as Nichole retched. 'What really happened?
Tell us what happened. The full story. All of it.'

Omnipotent, condescending aliens complimented Captain
Kirk for showing mercy. Nichole grabbed the word, spoke it to
Winslow, her grandfather and his friends that day out on the yacht,
Almayer Foxe, the toilet bowl: —Mercy.

'Come see me. I dare you.'

Galled mouth burning, Nichole recognized that begging
mercy from the toilet bowl marked the first time she had spoken of
the abuse outside her psychiatrist's office.

She smiled.

Because she hadn't swallowed; she'd spit.

5) 'WHERE ONCE'

Lewis Wright fingered the two-pronged electrical cord wrapped in green, yellow and brown threads. An elegance missing today, when cords lay exposed to their dull plastic casing. *Fabric-wrapped electrical cords. Almost an argyle going here. Why must we lose beauty for the uniform goo coating transmission lines – electricity, telephones, radio, internet? Do we dip communication into a toxic bog? And why must perching birds die?*

Carefully re-sealing the box containing what his brother, Matt, called the Ghostometer, Lewis Wright blew greying blond hair out of his green eyes and winced at the stiffness in his lower back. His father, Thomas, suffered stiffness in knees, hips and sacroiliac joints but dismissed it as simple age and happily swallowed glucosamine and seal oil. Yet Thomas lost mobility. He lost height, too, a good inch over the last year. During a photo op at the Admiral's Rooms, when they opened the radio exhibit, Lewis met Matt's eyes over their father's head. Taller than Skipper, whose voice could still frighten them? Nonsense.

Lewis sang as he gently hoisted boxes and crates, folk songs on sighs, hardly knowing he did so.

—'I will die, I will die, this young captain did cry, if I can't get that maid from the shore... ' Familiar, beloved topography: his father's attic. Old portraits, clothes, radio gear, talismans of his grandfather, Robert Wright, who'd founded VOIC Radio. Lewis had never known his grandfather, except though stories and photos. Despite chairing the Royal Republic Historical Society of Newfoundland and Labrador, Lewis had cared only sporadically about his father's attic. Until a few months ago. Not long after Thanksgiving. When the fluoxetine took root in his brain.

—'Then she took his broad sword instead of an oar and paddled her way to the shore, shore, shore, and paddled her way to the shore.'

Depressed? Me? I don't feel depressed. Separate, maybe. Detached. Not in the world with the rest of you. Lonely, yes, sometimes. But no, not depressed. I came to see you about my insomnia, Doctor. Runs in the family. I'm afraid I'll start drinking too much just to get a decent night's sleep. I keep counting the dots in my ceiling tiles and mentally drawing lines between them to form new constellations.

—'It's of a pretty female, as you may understand, her mind been bent for rambling into some foreign land.'

Pills? Prozac? I don't know about that. I think I can pull myself up by my – you know, I've never seen a bootstrap.

Lewis cradled the old ledger in his elbow and sneezed over his shoulder. He knelt down, placed the ledger on top of the Ghostometer box, pulled on archivist's white cotton gloves, and turned over several pages: stains, mildew, decay, and many notes and tallies. On the left-hand side, opposing counts of rope and salt, strange handwriting.

Cast away. A castaway for fourteen years in this settlement of thin-stilted draughty shacks perched (and praying not to slip) upon this stone leviathan, this lonely rock sheared and broken out of the sea, up out of the sea: Lucifer's fist shaken at God. Thrown off, unwanted seed. Fourteen damned years, God far away, past fog and strange sky.

Lewis touched the old inkstains.

He suddenly cared nothing for the rarely acknowledged and forbidden Ghostometer beneath the ledger. The apparatus supposedly broadcast to the aether – to the dead. Or so the smudged 1930s magazine article buried in the box with it claimed. Teenaged Lewis had set it up one rainy afternoon, wire antenna, extension cords, Tesla coil and all, his brother Matt protesting but never really refusing to help. The final touch: Lew connected the apparatus to a reel-to-reel. The tape rolled, recorded Lew's callout: *CQ, CQ, calling all stations, CQ, this is Lewis Wright, please acknowledge, over.* The boys heard no answer. The house's fuse box melted. The tape, however, when played back, gave up disturbing signals: *Acknowledged ... hear me? Glasses fell... hear me?* The chief engineer at VOIC erased the tape, for Lew's own good, he felt. God only knew where that signal originated. Disturbing, yes. Terrifying once. Perhaps the Prozac softened Lewis's instincts, rendered him happy, passive, and numb mush for predators, like that dream, runt spruce, rocks and fogbound caribou –

—Lew?

His father's voice.

—Lewis, what in the name of God are you doin up there?

—Digging, Skipper. I'll be down in a minute.

Thomas Wright, seventy-something, broad-shouldered and dressed like Oscar Goldman on his way to Studio 54, hauled himself up the silly ladder to the attic and looked at his son's knees.

27

Then he glanced at the Ghostometer crate – they'd only discussed the apparatus once, both men embarrassed, intrigued – and finally, up at his son's green eyes, so like his own.

—But you're all right, Lew?

Not hangin from a rafter? Not suckin a gun?

Lewis had spit-warmed a .303 once but got interrupted. His father, who'd been making breakfast in the next room, did not know that, but he'd not have been surprised to find out.

—I'm fine, Skipper.

Thomas scowled at the dusty boxes. —This old stuff.

—Should be in a museum.

—Where's the sense in lookin backward?

—Fine words from a man on the board of directors for Rare Documents. Sometimes it helps you figure out where you're going.

Thomas changed tack, as he often did when potentially losing an argument. —You still takin all those old pills?

Secret boxes and hidden portraits, Prozac and Ativan; *'old stuff,' 'old pills' – what's the difference?* Lewis dropped his gaze. Could it be normal for a grown man to fear his father still, normal to crave his father's approval the way he craved air? —It does me good.

—Witch doctors and mad scientists scrapin money out of you.

Lewis dared himself to look at his father again and caught a glint in the older man's eyes. A plea? No, the simple strength of a man who needed no doctors, no stuff and no pills, and who sure as hellfire knew what a bootstrap looked like, never you mind what he crammed in the attic.

Thomas rubbed his lower back. —I had a dream this mornin that's got me right in the rats. The minister out in Port au Mal at that old church. I used to dream of him whenever I got sick enough for a fever, or back when you were all banged up after you crashed your Cessna. He kept tellin me all this old stuff, but I couldn't make head nor tail out of it.

Lewis studied his father and worried a bit; Thomas must be upset to use so much dialect.

—He spoke to you in the dream?

—Valour and pilgrims. Just foolishness.

—Skipper? Mind if I let Nichole look at this old ledger? You remember Nichole. Stephen's daughter, used to write ad copy at the station.

28

—Never mind that. What ledger are you talkin about?

—The one you were thinking of giving to Rare Docs for their new collection. At the reunion?

—Tell her to be careful with it. And I want it back in time.

—Good, good.

—There'll be people at that reunion I literally haven't spoken to or set eyes on for years, Lew. Decades. Grown children I've never met. My sister and that leech she married moved away after she took the chafin pan to my head at that banquet. You remember that? No, you were still small. My other sister died so young. Nothin would have kept me from spoilin her children. Libby. Never mind that now. I've got an appointment with an orthopaedic surgeon tomorrow, right down in the deepest bowels of the General Hospital. Can you come with me? I don't want to worry your brother. I just don't want anyone worryin. I – I'm not accustomed to...

To being afraid. Lewis nodded.

—Yes, b'y, I'll come with you.

6) DIRTY DEEDS

Not flashback this time but memory, visited willingly: a hospital room in April of 2005.

Green curtains, frayed and holey, hid nothing, gave no sanctuary as Nichole argued with a doctor named Swift. —I can't be bipolar. Depressed, sure, but I'm not manic. I'm creative.

—Many bipolar patients experience delusions of heightened creativity and intelligence with manic episodes.

—My novel's a delusion, is it?

—Is it published?

—Not yet.

—Then it's a product of one.

—I'll be sure to get my publisher to add a delusion clause to the contract. Look, I'm crazy, yeah, I admit that, good-crazy most days, but I am not manic.

—You'll come to see it in time.

While she waited for that particular revelation, Nichole took up bad habits the way a toddler might throw a tantrum. Cigarettes beloved and abandoned, though she still craved the spongy filter between her lips, the nicotine smack to her sludgy morning brain. No more cocaine, though. *Cocaine got me in enough trouble (what a great pun, yes, girl, dart down to see the Morgentaler crowd) back in university, happy happy happy.* Nichole wondered if the coke hadn't corroded bits of her brain. Very little excited Nichole anymore, and she longed to feel. Dr Miller connected the numbness to her chronic post-traumatic stress disorder; *repeated strain and dread affect the neural pathways and can literally re-wire the brain.* Antidepressants helped, a bit, but this hole... Sometimes she saw herself as one of those wretchedly obese people whose skin fused to their blankets and chairs, whose bodies become one with previous comforts that now galled. Hidden wounds festered, and nothing could reach them. Happy? Some stimulant, please. Some shade of the flame of being alive. Espresso mixed with cereal milk helped ease her off the cigarettes but then greasily led to three double americanos a day, then three before lunch. The caffeine burnt her stomach and duodenum until only rice pudding digested easily. *Leave it to me to abuse the polite and respectable drugs. Well brought up, that Wright girl.* Fortune smiled, and Nichole obtained a fine supply of Boost and Ensure when cleaning out Claire's apartment. Odd time, that, Claire not quite dead but not coming home, waiting for a transfer to palliative care, so tired – sick to death, even – of IVs and feeding tubes. Light a smoke, light the whole pack, light a candle. Nichole cleaning out the apartment with Callie, Claire's mother. Claire's various illnesses while growing up and Nichole tutoring her when she missed school. Claire's neglected work wardrobe, blouses and skirts balled up and tossed to the back of the closet when she quit VOIC. Claire's corner cupboard crammed with loose tea, three full shelves of it. Nichole and Callie laughed, and Claire not even dead yet. (Eat, eat something, anything, chips, damn I'm out of rice pudding, raw pasta noise and crunch *cram* the mouth and chew, chew and chew and chew so your jaws ache molars crack til it all hurts so bad because you deserve this hurt you rancid worthless slut you deserve it even the pain of knowing and losing Claire but you see this pain you can control just cram chew chew chew and swallow gulp it down, always swallow – Claire – food explodes in your gut throw it up fingers down there *throw it up* –)

No bingeing on tranqs, though. Nichole no longer longed to die.

Just wished it all didn't hurt so much.

Asleep now, this tedious night in February 2009, head on a towel spread over the toilet lid, she dreamt of the Church of Prevenient Grace at the End of Things. Nichole hadn't gone near Prevenient Grace since the late 1970s, when the pastor frightened her with a sermon on the sins of the fathers, but in her dream she remembered it quite well. Sharplined, cold and dark, no electric lights, no heat. Deny the flesh and sharpen the soul. An apocalyptic church, this Prevenient Grace at the End of Things, though mysteriously inconsistent, for The End Had Come, right on schedule, back in 1974. Blissfully ignorant, mankind suffered on, denied even the grace of oblivion, as Reverend Winslow answered when pressed.

Reverend Elias Winslow. That voice tonight through the phone and the plumbing – finally, a name for the voice that tried to preach though the hissing in her stupid nightmare, and damn it if that dream hadn't slopped over into the recurring abortion dream – Nichole seeking her foetus as it cried weakly from within a misplaced box, Nichole finding the box, opening it, releasing a swarm of wasps.

She woke. Reverend Winslow, collar and robe and patient eyes, stood by her bathroom vanity, coaxing Nichole to seek paths to God through tangled starrigan and tuckamore, bogs and rocks, traps and snares. Then he helped her stand up and totter to her bed. She suddenly felt very weak, feverish, like that time she brewed pneumonia and coughed up phlegm gone the hues of old photographs, sepia and grey. Spruce needle tea, a great steaming mug of it, Reverend Winslow holding it near Nichole's mouth and coaxing her to drink it. *Make you feel better.* Nichole arched her face away: *I don't drink, no, gave it up.* Winslow gently guided the cup to Nichole's lips again: *It's only spruce tea. I would not poison you, not when you have such talent for poisoning yourself. Drink the tea. Only tea. Shhh.*

At the Prevenient Grace rectory in Port au Mal, Elias Winslow woke – eyelids dusty, chest sweaty – worried. Quite worried.

No storm surge, no loud teenagers: then what just woke him? *Purpose mislaid.*

The handle of the sailmaker's secret knife left marks in his grasping hand.

Winslow eased himself out from under his bed – he slept curled up on the wooden floor – and caught the scent of spruce needle tea. Twice that night he'd offered troubled dreamers spruce needle tea: Seth Seabright and Nichole Wright. In the past he'd guided dreaming Seabrights to bottled messages and hanging nets, Wrights to cold barrens and jagged rocks. But why? Dust clots stuck to his dry lips. One good thing, at least: he remembered how to make spruce tea. Other old recipes had crawled off and died, bones and shades of them rattling round Winslow's skull in forgotten orbits, but he could still grasp the memory of spruce tea if he stood tall enough, if he reached.

Am I not supposed to torment these people instead of giving them tea?

Small wonder I hardly sleep.

Driving the hard road to Port au Mal, Lewis Wright spoke over a VOIC report on upcoming ceremonies to mark the sinking of *Sea Sentry.* —So that's why I want you to have the ledger. It's from Port au Mal: that much I know. The writing looks old, and the ink has gone that rusty brown colour. But I need it back before the family reunion. You know about that, right?

—A ghastly idea.

—Good, good. I haven't spoken to some of our cousins since – you know about that big rift when Skipper took over the station there after Grandfather crashed his plane? His sister, my Aunt Marie, she and her husband took Skipper to court, to get their share. All about money and memory, that was. Never quite understood it, myself. So be extra-careful with that ledger. We wouldn't want to get Skipper upset.

—I glanced at it this morning before we left St John's. Lewis, that ledger is a major find. I found dates in there well before 1760. *Before.*

—Keep that to yourself for now.

—It's right there on the page.

—Maybe so, but a lot of work's after going into Settlement 250. We've got to respect the date they've given us.

—Lewis!

—By the way, your book, a novel, right? Is that fiction or history?

—Fiction, Lew. A novel by definition is fiction. Mine's got history in it.

—But it's made up?

—Yes.

—The play won't be made up. That'll be simple history. She patted the ledger. —Simple.

—That reminds me. The ACHE Board wants me to pass a message on to you. Whoever else gets cast –

—I'm not looking after casting. That's the director's job.

—Don't shoot the messenger, Nichole. Whoever else gets cast, someone named Seth Seabright has to get a good part.

—Why?

—Some arts-work quota scheme, tied into the government money. Actors' Queue, they call it. Seabright's next in line.

—Does he want to be in the play?

—Beggars can't be choosers. You ever dream about Prevenient Grace, Nichole?

—Mind the bumps, Lewis.

—Only ginger ale. That won't stain my upholstery.

—No, just my jeans.

—Good, good. I've always laughed at the name of it. Church of Prevenient Grace at the End of Things. I think it was the first

33

place I ever felt sad. Truly sad, I mean. Up til then I'd just felt lost, or numb, like when a snowstorm traps you in the woods.

—You crashed a plane once yourself, didn't you?

Nichole hoped the taboo utterance would silence Lewis; she'd never known him so talky. Truth and memory should put him back in his place.

Fuck, I can't believe I just did that. Total power-tripping, dirty Wright trick.

But Lewis only chuckled. —Long time ago now. Except I got out of it, unlike Grandfather. Banged myself up pretty bad, injured my brain. Not even twenty when I did that. Taking flying lessons out in Gander with the Americans. I signed up under a false name and put my brother down as next-of-kin. Didn't dare tell Skipper. He'd have put the kibosh on that right quick, right damn quick.

Nichole's vision blurred: fir, spruce, pine, ponds, barrens.

—Because of what happened to his father?

—Grandfather was only in his early fifties. Looking for a lost youngster. No one ever figured precisely what killed him, because there was hardly a mark on the body, apart from a few bruises. He had a bad heart, but he'd also lost his glasses, blind as a stump without them, so he couldn't read the gauges. Engine cut out that day, too. Skipper wouldn't even let me and Matt play with remote control planes. Someone gave us a matching set one Christmas, but Skipper took them away. Then I started building my own. I must be talking your ear off. Stomach any better? You said you were throwing up last night.

—I'm just not used to hearing you talk. You're still nervous and jumpy and all that, but you're not the same Lewis Wright I worked with at VOIC.

Lewis almost said *No more am I*; instead, he swerved to avoid a moose. The car skidded off the shoulder into a snowcrammed ditch. The moose clopped across the road, rustled through trees and snow, disappeared.

It's caribou in my dream.

Both Wrights blinked, sniffed, cleared throats, and loosened their locked seatbelts. Each turned to the other and spoke at the same moment.

—You all right?

—Fine.

Lewis cracked his knuckles. —Good, good. You scoot over here in the driver's seat, and I'll get out and push. Can't keep Reverend Winslow waiting.

Nearly lost to unaided vision, the ceiling reached through dun to heaven, and the pews' edges looked straight enough to be sharp. The windows, iced-over and Protestant-plain, further dulled the winter daylight. Far past the windows, down on the stony shore, sat the flattened boulder locals called The Devil's Couch. Nichole had reclined there once, suffering the breakdown that cannot be called a breakdown, because we don't use that word anymore, Nichole.

The Church of Prevenient Grace at the End of Things.

Nichole shuddered. —Still no heat or light in here. And that smell, Lewis. You catch that? Old smell. Smell of old things, I mean.

—Probably smelled like this when Grandfather crashed his plane. Good, good, Reverend, hello.

Black shirt, white collar, black pants, dark eyes, thick brown hair shot through with grey and white and rather long hair for a man his age, whatever his age might be: the Reverend Elias Winslow. Something leather-bound hung off his belt, near his right hip. —Welcome to the Church of Prevenient Grace at the End of Things. Did you have an appointment?

—Reverend Winslow, this is my cousin, Nichole Wright. I spoke to you about her on the phone. I believe you bought some land from her. Nichole, this is Reverend Elias Winslow. We're here to speak with you about Settlement 250 and all that old stuff.

A soft and pale hand took Nichole's bony one. —Ms Wright, nice to meet you.

—Spruce tea. I've been here before. So were you. A long time ago. I remember your voice.

Reverend Winslow gently pressed her knuckles, her bulimic's calluses. —Look no further for the hearth. The old hearth out on the plot. I watched you kick the turned-up ground. We started digging last fall. I'm sorry to say I allowed the hearth to be bulldozed, for I'd no idea of its true age. A mistake I shall not repeat, I promise.

Nichole snatched her hand away and bumped into the edge of a pew. —You're confusing me with someone else.

Lewis dipped his chin to his chest. —I remember that hearth. Nichole, do you? Out here, summers, touching the old stones and mortar, and someone even carved a man right in the back, man wearing a hat and stooped under a sack. Is that what you were looking for?

—When?

—Visited that hearth every day, the summer I spent out here with Aunt Ellen.

—God, Aunt Ellen. Three steps shy of being the Bearded Lady.

—No need to be cruel, Nichole. I'm sure she had more important things to think about than her looks.

Reverend Winslow met Nichole's hard gaze. —Do you have a question, my child?

—Were you out here in the late 1970s?

Winslow took a step closer to Nichole, his waxy face smooth, as if he shaved with Uriel's sword and then splashed his cheeks with plaster. —I am deeply rooted in this community. Now, Lewis, why did you come here?

—Haah...

Nichole also tried to explain. —The snow and the frozen mud, the highway, then the moose – I just –

My God. I dreamt this years ago. Dreamt I stood in this church after seeing mink pelts stretched and pinioned on a cross made of spruce boughs.

Reverend Winslow smiled.

Lewis chewed the insides of his cheeks. Nothing in the Prozac handout from the pharmacy had prepared him for this meeting.

—As I said on the phone, Nichole is researching this history of Port au Mal. Settlement 250.

Reverend Winslow smiled some more.

Nichole glanced at Lewis, then back at Winslow. —Tell me, Reverend, will you be getting this old church declared a heritage site once you build the new one?

—We'll just tear it down.

—You must be planning some serious upgrades. Electricity, maybe?

—Candles and lamps suffice. Fire is God's light.

Wind beat the windows, hard, but the glass held fast. The strong draughts narrowed to chills and invaded through cracks. As usual.

Note to self: brain Lewis for dragging me out here. Not that much would spill out his ears – wow, they really stick out.

—Haah, right. Yes. Reverend, I hear you're heading up a committee to help the project.

—The Historical Accuracy and Representation Committee. More to oversee and guide.

—HARC, good, good. What can you tell us of the settlement history out here?

—The first white European settlers arrived in 1760, of course, hence Settlement 250 next year.

—The other night, when I was cleaning out my father's attic–

—You belong to Thomas Wright, correct?

—Yes. Me and my brother, Matt. When I was cleaning out my father's attic –

—Give your father my regards. I've not seen him for decades.

Enough of this. Nichole cleared her throat. —Lewis found a ledger with handwriting and tallies and dates preceding 1760. The writer's name is John Cannard, and he notes living out here in Port au Mal *before* 1760.

Winslow looked directly at Lewis, not Nichole.—How did this Mr Cannard get here?

Nichole answered, voice getting louder. —Shipwrecked.

As Winslow seemed not to hear Nichole, Lewis repeated it. —Shipwrecked, Reverend.

—And literate? How convenient, a Newfoundland Crusoe. Even an amateur historian must see how that is not very likely.

—He wasn't alone. He writes about other people, where we make it out.

—Old handwriting is notoriously tricky. I expect the curlicues deceived you, dear. Port au Mal's settlement records start, quite clearly, in 1760.

—Reverend, we had Hayman and his *Quodlibets* over in Harbour Grace from 1718-28, then our first Naval governor in 1729, yet there is no mention of Port au Mal until 1760? Are you quite certain of that?

—So many of our written records were lost in those Rare Documents fires. Did you come with a spiritual question, Nichole?

—Cannard's Point? Lacey's Lookout?

—Place names around here for which there are no written records prior to 1790. Even that record notes the names are traditional, despite there being no Cannards and no Laceys here. I'm sorry, but this is normally when I write my sermons.

Outside, shards of snow scraping their faces in a minus ten windchill, Nichole and Lewis sighed in unison.

—Not worth beating our heads off this wall, Nichole. Let's just get back to what the ACHE Board originally said.

Nichole answered as she climbed in the car, so Lewis could almost pretend he did not hear her. But she said it, and he heard it: —Not fuckin likely.

Pleased her voice could not be easily heard in the crowded restaurant, Nichole dipped a piece of sushi into soy sauce. —Then he tells me I've got to cast some Seabright guy. ACHE is pushing me around left, right, and centre. And I'm just writing the damn thing, not directing it.   ·

Evan fell out of his admiration for Nichole's use of chopsticks at the name Seabright. He pushed the last of the seared tuna, her favourite, onto her plate. —Seth Seabright? That little hurricane? He crashed the Tattoo last summer. At least, I think it was him. Just a rehearsal, thank God, with no audience. I got them doin a full drill when boyo leaps over a chain fence and joins in. Thinks he's fuckin Danny Kaye with the knights in *The Court Jester*, dancin in formation with them, marchin a perfect drill. God love them, they didn't miss a step, them in full dress kit and bearskin hats with this force of chaos mockin them. I lost it. Not just because he was interruptin practice, and not just because he was makin fun of history and all the work the Tattoo was after doin, but because we had live fuckin firearms on the go. And I'll be honest with you, Nichole, what pissed me off the most was the beauty of it. He did a good job. Outta fuckin nowhere.

Nichole passed Evan a new set of chopsticks to replace the ones he'd just snapped.

—You sure it was Seabright?

—No. Whoever it was took off before I could get to him. I bawled out *Halt* so much I lost my voice for the rest of the week. I finally got the whole regiment at attention when boyo leaps like someone set fire to him. The b'ys told me afterward that whoever it was stank of sweat and piss and gin.

—Charming.

Evan accepted the bill from the anxious waiter. —Looked like Seabright. I saw him in a play once. Place is gettin crowded. Still up for that drive?

Somewhere in the inconveniently and stubbornly historical Petty Harbour – where old houses seemed to look down in anger at the upstart paved road, the road itself a cowpath – Nichole mentioned the ledger. —Would you take a look at it, see if it's genuine?

—What'd you say the dates were?

—Before 1760. Cannard began –

Evan quickly pulled off to the dangerously narrow shoulder, coasting to a stop just left of a graveyard and church. He loomed over her. —*John* Cannard?

Nichole immediately felt for the door lever and yanked it to escape. The engaged power locks imprisoned her but also kept her from falling out. —Evan, let me out of this car.

Evan followed Nichole's glance downward. Sure enough, an erection starting. — Nichole, wait, I'm not – I'm sorry. I just get so excited – I mean –

—I'll scream. And I will drive my keys so far into your eyes –

—No! It's not like that. I'm not like that. I just – the ledger, sweetheart, the ledger. Just listen to me. Okay? Y'all right?

Nichole slowed her breathing, put her keys back in her pocket. —Sorry, Ev. This is my first time trying to date since – I dunno, are we dating? I mean –

—Two friends gone out for supper is what we are.

—The ledger. The ledger. Right. Now, 2009, this is 2009. Yeah, John Cannard. The ink's gone brown.

Evan kept his voice low and calm. —Iron-gall, most likely. Pigment comes from galls on trees, these cyst-things on leaf buds: wasp eggs. Goes down blue-black and fades to that rusty brown. No blotters back then, so they'd sprinkle sand or grit to dry the ink.

—Fear in a handful of dust?

—Those letters I picked up in Riordan's Back, dated 1745? Written *to* John Cannard of Port au Mal.

While Nichole took this in, a slight flush colouring her upper chest, Evan squirmed against his snug jeans.

Then Nichole smiled at him. —Can I see those letters?

Nichole tugged on archivist's gloves and tried not to flinch as Evan tied back her coarse and brittle hair. —Ev, I'm sorry. It's a big deal for me to let someone touch me from behind.

Not sure what she meant, Evan refrained from leaning round to kiss her on the cheek. —You've got nice hair.

Nichole said nothing to that, but she could hardly leave the ragged silence alone. *Keep cool, girl. Evan's no Almayer Foxe. Too late to pop a tranq now with these gloves on, anyway.* —Nice table. I like the lines, all straight and clean.

—Great-grandfather made that. Back before all those chrome dinette sets from Canada took off. I just need to get the letters from my room. Then we can spread them out here. If you hear another voice, that's just my grandfather, True Rideout. He lives here. He and Nan reared me, and now I'm lookin after him. Funny how it turns out. If he says anythin to you – yeah, he's not at his best anymore. But more than likely he's gone to bed for the night. I'll be right back.

Nichole stretched out her gloved hands. —I feel like a lady who lunches. When can I wear white shoes?

Laughing over his shoulder and wincing at his messy bed, Evan gently shifted dirty laundry to a spot in front of his glass-doored bookcase, a gift from his grandfather a few years ago. *Where the hell did I put my briefcase?*

—Who's out there?

A beautiful bass voice, like that of his hero, Johnny Cash, came from True Rideout. He stood in the unlit hallway, thinly dressed and cold but tall and still muscular. Evan had his build. True had forgotten something before going to bed, some crucial step. Both the forgetting and his recognition of the forgetting deeply irritated him. Now, on his way to investigate noises in the night, he'd forgotten yet something else. Not his teeth: sticking them in his gob when stalking burglars would just be vanity. Not his glasses: he only needed them for reading. Evan would know what he'd forgotten. Except Evan had gone out. And by the sounds of it, some brazen fool now ransacked Evan's room.

—Right here, Pop. In my room. Sorry if I woke ya.

True Rideout could not guess who spoke just then, because Evan had gone out. That fact remained, and True clung to it. —By the Jesus...

Evan got to his knees from lying on the floor to peek under his bed. A sudden scent that belonged on Signal Hill with the Tattoo, not at the back of Evan's head: gunmetal.

—Twelve-gauge, laddybuck. Not gonna try your home invasion shit on me.

Evan kept still while his balls crawled up his throat. Kneeling back-on to his grandfather, he could see the old man's muddy reflection in the glass doors of the bookcase. —Pop, put the gun down.

—Terrorizin old people, pawin for either bit of money or jewellery for your little habit. The crystal meth, is it?

—Pop –

—You're some God damned lucky my grandson Evan isn't home. Just the two of us, but we're some team. Or maybe you're not lucky. Because he'd talk me out of this.

Can't risk turnin around. Use the childhood word. —Poppy?

Confusion ruint True's face. He nearly dropped the twelve-gauge. —Evan? When did you get home?

—Give me that, now.

—I thought somebody's after gettin in the house.

Hands slick, Evan cracked the barrel. *Jesus, it's loaded. Somethin else I got to hide.* —Just me, Pop. No one else has got a key.

—Don't need no key if you're hard up enough.

Evan pocketed the shells, peered down the barrel and then locked the trigger. He studied his grandfather, this big man who had snared, fished and hunted his own food, built his own house, who sold almost everything and moved to St John's to look after young Evan. Who now stood disoriented but pleased in ratty boxer shorts and a stained undershirt. Evan took his own bathrobe off the hook by the door and helped his grandfather into it. —Can I get ya a cup of tea before you go back to bed?

True followed his grandson to the kitchen, where the comfortably old wallpaper nearly made him tell the story the day he put it up. Instead he caught himself (*mind slippin like summer tires on black ice*), nodded a hello to the woman wearing a ponytail and white gloves (*Avon lady, I spose*) and finally remembered some of what he'd meant to tell Evan all day. —I needs a ride over to Mrs Dunphy's house tomorrow night.

Evan recalled being a young teenager: *Pop, you're some good to drive me everywhere.*

Day'll come when it's you drivin me.

—Mrs Dunphy's, very good. What time?

—Eight o'clock, I wants to be there. And I needs some oh what do you call them, those doohickeys, birdhouses and whatnot, splinters and paint, you know – Popsicle sticks. Buildin her somethin.

Evan replaced the shotgun in the hall closet and took out the box of remaining shells.

—Out of Popsicle sticks?

—It shines when it's got the juice. You knows what I means. *Don't do this to me, Pop. You're all I got.* —Shines with the juice?

—You plugs it into the wall.

From the kitchen, Nichole suggested the noun. —Lamp?

—That's it. Gonna build her a Popsicle stick lamp. Tis all Popsicle sticks at her place, b'y, ashtrays, flowerpots, you name it. But she got no lamp.

—I'll get you some at the craft store. You gonna shave before you go this time?

—Go where?

—Mrs Dunphy's.

—Jeannie, right. I needs some of them – those wooden – stir coffee with them, great big toothpicks.

—Popsicle sticks?

—That's them. Wonder if she'll let me kiss her goodnight. Anyway, I'm gone to bed.

—Take your tea, Pop.

—Good night, missus. Good luck sellin the Avon.

Nichole smiled at True Rideout – beautifully, Evan thought.

—Thank you, sir. Good night.

Evan waited until he heard True's bedroom door close.

—Thank *you*, Nichole.

—Is his name Truman?

—Just True. He had three sisters, Faith, Hope, and Charity. Here's the pelt bag.

—I keep expecting the papers to be brittle or damp. But they're almost creamy.

—Sealskin's a tough shield.

March 14th, 1745. From Newman Head, Merchant, Salem, Massachusetts. To John Cannard, lately of Bristol, residing now Port au Mal, Newfoundland.

Sir: I knew both Captain Finn and Captain Cleasby. Captain Matthew Finn, for so we in Salem knew him, sometimes also Kit Finn, being a Christopher as well as a Matthew, stands in my memory as a fine and capable captain who offended none, at least, none who matter.

Evan liked the new pretty shine to Nichole's eyes.

—Ev, I think it's a match. How many John Cannards in Port au Mal could there be? And Newman Head is a treasure all by himself – look, his daughter wrote this for him. This is all –

—What I want to know is, who the hell are Captain Finn and Captain Cleasby?

—And the settlement story. It's all wrong. This can all go into the play – but HARC and Rare Documents – God, we keep losing all the records.

—No. Rare Docs keeps losin them. I'm convinced they've got a firebug workin for them. Two retro-fitted, climate-controlled libraries don't burn down by accident. And now they've got half the republic lookin down at their shoes in shame, while they go on pillage. No amount of fire gives them the right to go snappin up whatever diaries, letters and photos they can get their hands on and then lock them away under glass. I wouldn't trust that crowd with last week's supermarket flyer. And TCR doesn't bat an eye. So this is what I'm after doin. My boss – you've met Chris Jackman, and you know what a dick he can be – he knows I got these letters, and he's supposed to officially notify Rare Docs of their existence. He delegates that task to his assistant, which would be me. Once Rare Docs actually finds out about the letters, they'll want a rough catalogue of those letters from a TCR Officer. Which would also be me. So I'd like to think that until Jackman smartens up, and that'll be about three minutes before the Rapture by my reckonin, you've got research time.

Days and nights of caffeinated reading and writing, of deliciously busy oblivion? —I'm there.

—Not yet, you're not. Somethin else you need to know – hang on. Pop, y'all right?

Evan and Nichole listened to the sounds of someone rustling, then falling, in a closet.

—Pop?

—Don't worry about me.

Evan smiled grimly. —No, b'y, I won't worry a bit. Now then, Ms Nichole Laika Wright, you anythin to the VOIC crowd of Wrights, or wha? Who owns you?

—You know perfectly well.

—I also know perfectly well that your uncle or cousin or whatever he is, Thomas Wright, will officially present that ledger to Chris Jackman at your family reunion in September.

—I'm not going to any family reunion.

—The ledger is.

—But I need it. For the play. And this letter. And because it proves that – oh, for fuck's sake. Thomas Wright wants to make a big fuss over giving it to Rare Docs, and it'll get locked under a clear box.

—Clear? Heaven forbid. That ledger's goin to be part of a dozen grip-and-grin photos and will then be locked in a friggin safe. No general access.

True Rideout crashed around a closet some more, then padded down the hall towards the kitchen.

Nichole blew loose hair out of her eyes; it only got tangled in her eyelashes. —And besides, the truth is dead?

—Sweetheart, you wanna go kamikaze against bureaucrats? Be my guest.

—We can't just pretend the ledger doesn't exist. That's lies and –

WHACK

Evan screamed, last nerve gone. Nichole jumped up. True Rideout chuckled and pointed to the hakapik he'd just driven into the sealskin, and the table. —Now that, me sons, is how ya gets it done.

As Evan got his grandfather back to bed, Nichole, hands trembling, gently tidied the letters. Then she eyed the pelt bag, wondering how best to rescue it.

She couldn't budge the hakapik.

7) THE SAILMAKER'S SECRET KNIFE
Feb 15-16, 2009, Port au Mal and St John's.

After waking well before dawn and blowing dust from his fingertips, Elias Winslow wrote his sermon on a laptop, his typewriter-trained fingers giving hard abuse to the computer's soft keyboard. He did not know when he might deliver this sermon.

The serpentine path a lone woman may follow, this woman already an interloper on our righteous community, a woman tainted by sins of the flesh, even bound to those sins and only then, escape impossible, did she taste the gall – the serpentine path of the songs of the flesh, the desire to wrestle with history as though it were an angel sent by the Lord, to then change that history and thereby bind it to the twistings of irresponsible imagination; to defy reason, courtesy and good counsel and persist in this desire, worsening it by associating with the deliberately ungodly, with a man of deplorable family and upbringing, they leaving together talking of alcohol – alcohol, my brethren, do you recall our long battle to declare this community free of that substance which further impedes the self and gives over to flesh, the law of sin? And where hides redemption? When one recognizes the laws of flesh and sin ...

Elias minimized that window and maximized voic.com.

Sudden Death Delays Foxe Trial
Another delay in the upcoming trial of former broadcaster Almayer Foxe has been called, after the sudden death of a woman who was to testify. Fifty-four-year-old Evelyn Lockyear was found dead in her car last week. Police say the cause of death is carbon monoxide poisoning. Almayer Foxe faces multiple charges of uttering threats, forcible confinement, assault and sexual assault.

Elias tapped the LCD laptop screen, creating brief and tiny puddles beneath the name Foxe. As he did this, Nichole Wright dreamt she drew a very old knife, sharp blade, chipped onyx handle, and used it in murderous self-defence. Relished using it. Elias nodded. Patting the knife on his belt, he then decided to take a walk.

When not infusing the dreams of others, Elias himself dreamt of spying the midnight sun through a window at the end of a long corridor. Might he finish his days in Iceland? Or Russia? Somewhere cold, yes, he did rest reasonably sure of that, and *aurora borealis* would light the way. No midnight sun for Newfoundland, so he must rendezvous with the right light, as in his memories: swirling walls of blue and green fire, black sky, black rocks, black water. Someone whispered the land's names, Nitassinan, Markland, Lavrador, Labrador, Nunatsiavut. *Munus splendidum mox explebitur;* the splendid task will soon be fulfilled. Elias Winslow, not created of Labrador but assigned there and left to find his way, bore his own splendid task. If he could just recollect the task's precise details...

Chanting disrupted his meditations and jolted Elias back to the ground. Sometimes he forgot himself and travelled long distances very quickly, skimming over the woods, his threads of energy wisping round spruce and fir like fog. Increasingly he got caught in streetlights. Not that anyone could wholly see him in that state, but an observant groundwalker who rarely blinked might catch a silhouette in the beam.

Settling behind trees on the edge of a small field, Elias listened to the chanting and quickly figured out who mocked the old dances this time. Every fifteen years or so, roughly since the mid-1920s, a clot of adolescents dared one another to meet in this field in darkness and – well, get up to devilment. Small town boredom and hereditary rites of passage: *My cousin, right, when she turned 14, she said there's, like, this ritual everyone's got to try in the graveyard.*

Only three of them tonight. Two girls and a boy, maybe fourteen. Pentagrams, a little altar, and three inuksuit. No animal blood staining the snow this time, just incense burning on the inuksuit heads.

One of the girls cracked her gum and fixed her hat.

Bonnets, cloche hats, salt and pepper caps, berets, toques, hoods, and now those Andean hats with long and untied strings. Minutes pass in hat fashion: clogged time freed. Spruce gum to sugarless cinnamon. Can I put that in a sermon?

Gum Girl rolled her eyes at the boy in the group. —Kev b'y, I've told you I don't know how many times, you can't draw down the moon unless the moon is full. Moon's gone stale, now.

—And I told *you* we shoulda done this back on the ninth, but no, you said we had to wait til the weather got fit, because freezin drizzle rots your hair.

—Whatever. But there's no use in drawing down a sliver of the moon, because then we'd only get a sliver of the experience, and that sliver would be exponentially equivalent to the relative size of the moon meshed into our experience.

—Wha?

The other girl, consulting a book by flashlight, giggled.

—Drawin down the moon means you invite the triple goddess into your body so she can be made incarnate. Think you can handle bein female, Kev?

The joke flatlined. No one spoke. Incense wafted, cheap sticks from the strip mall, Elias noticed, ten for a dollar, Dragon's Blood or Queen of the Night or some other sharp stink fit for Frangina Murphy – Frangina, with the green and blue Mohawk, that one – and her briny spare bedroom, where she entertained.

Book Girl stood up. —This is about our heritage. Our history as women. Human beings, I mean. No one's trying to exclude you, Kev. This is about defying the Burning Time. Lots of people in this little shithole of a bay would try to burn us at the stake if they caught us at this. And it's harmless, right? It's not like we're conjuring up demons.

Elias nodded. *Smart girl. Still, enough is enough. That incense is nauseating me.*

Filling the diverse alveoli of his weakening lungs – such frailty a ragged scar on his corporeal design – Winslow stood up and slowly sighed the air back out. The effort exhausted his body; he might need to cancel tomorrow's pastoral visits.

Kev felt it first. —B'ys, it's gettin some cold.

Gum cracked. —We're not b'ys, Kev b'y.

Book Girl looked up from lighting fresh incense. —'B'ys' is gender-neutral and inclusive. I don't – whoa, that's a wicked sea fog coming in. Did you see that?

Elias Winslow's hallucinogenic breath tangled perceptions. Kev suffered sudden deep cold, as though infected with thousands of parasites made of ice which then stung and thrashed beneath his skin, the formication of broken glaciers. Gum Girl collapsed to her knees and sobbed, convinced oxygen no longer existed. Stubborn Book Girl gazed round, sought and found the origin of their misery: the grey form of that old Reverend Winslow spreading his wings – *wings?* – and striding towards her, his mouth in a deliberate *o*. Her animal brain took over; paralyzing brainstem dread captured fight-or-flight and turned it cannibal. Book Girl moaned and fainted. Kev and Gum Girl ran.

Elias unsheathed the old knife: oh yes, the sharpened blade, the chipped onyx handle. Atom by atom, he strained to become too, too solid flesh, and steadily picked his way across the meadow. He reached the inuksuit and the unconscious girl, snuffed the burning incense with his fingertips and held the sticks as he might hold a bouquet of flowers. Then he cracked them and tucked the pieces into a pocket. Book Girl's freckles smudged her moonlit face. Elias smiled. *You deserve better friends. But you're not the one. I'm not supposed to give the knife to you.* Kneeling at the inuksuit, Elias gently scraped away ash and defilement from the balanced rocks. *Red iron ore. Be red ochre next. Young people today –*

As Elias scraped, an inuksuk toppled onto Book Girl's head.

Elias kept still, waited for Book Girl to moan or move or cry out after those dull smacks. Those little rocks were hardly enough to harm her, except that he'd harmed her first. Groundwalkers most receptive to the truth of Elias and his brothers often suffered from the encounter. Sometimes just shock, sometimes lasting illness. Sometimes, death.

Thready pulse.

Damn!

Elias leapt, only partially ready. Feet weighting him, he crashed into the trees at the edge of the field. Then he remembered the knife. Drawing his deepest breath since falling off an ice pan in February of eighteen-twenty-something, Elias leapt back to the rocks and the blood, found a steady pulse in Book Girl's neck, retrieved his mercifully unstained knife, then leapt once more, hard this time, hard and high over the trees – but tumbled, hurtled and spun through the sparkling aether like a drunk groundwalker drowning. He thudded to the ground near the rectory's back door. Those nuisance needs of the flesh, pain and fatigue, would gnaw him the rest of the night. Too spent to brush away dirt, leaning against doorjambs and walls, Elias got himself to his room and crawled beneath his bed.

48

What does this mean? What does this mean?
I'm getting old.

Eight months shy of a haircut and apparently terrified of a razor, Seth Seabright spat on the floor of the Port au Mal Loyal Orange Lodge and lit a cigarette. He ran his thumb over his fancy Zippo lighter before tucking it in a pocket. His blue eyes looked dull and tired. —Dorinda Masterson told me auditions were goin ahead today on some kinda priority basis, and now you're tellin me this play won't happen til next *year*. What the fuck am I out here now for?

Still carsick, and now chilled after waiting two hours for actors to show up – Seth the first – Nichole took a deep breath before replying. She'd heard that Seth Seabright could be brusque, slightly paranoid and generally hard to get along with, but she hadn't expected blunt questions and choice profanity before mutual introductions. —It gets staged next year as a tie-in with Settlement 250, and Dorinda Masterson told me –

—This play your idea?

—Not really. I –

—Then who do I speak to? I don't want to go talkin to Dorinda again, that lovely Cleopatra's grip of hers notwithstandin. I thought that vintage HILF was hooked up with that Gabe Furey fellah.

—HILF?

—Hag I Like to Fuck.

—Charming.

—Who's the playwright? Can ya tell me that?

—I am. At least, I'm working on it.

—Not even fuckin written yet? Jesus. When are ya drivin me back to town?

—Excuse me?

—What'd you say your name was?

—I didn't. Nichole Wright.

—Nichole, right. I mean – listen, I hitched a ride out to here. Port au Mal is not exactly on the highway. Walked from St John's to Seal Cove. You ever walk that distance?

—Just –

—When you've walked halfway from St John's to the arse end of Conception Bay to audition for a play that's not even fuckin written yet, then we'll talk. For now, just tell me when you're drivin me back to town.

Nichole chewed the inside of her bottom lip and studied the dart scoreboards on the walls. *Time to pull that snotty God-peering-down-from-the-mount-Wright face.* Not too difficult, as Nichole stood taller than Seth, for a start. She cocked her chin, let her glasses slide down her nose, dropped her jaw, lolled judgemental eyes over Seth's long hair and beard, and cranked her townie accent.

—And you are?

Seth studied Nichole, willing himself not to avert his own eyes from her deep-set green ones. He thought a moment, blew smoke away from her face and extended his hand. —Seth Seabright. And before you ask, yes, I'm one of those Seabrights.

—I'm one of those Wrights, myself.

—The VOIC Wrights?

—Guilty as charged.

—Ever think of changin your name?

—Everyone'd still know. And I'd probably have some cousin I've never met hunt me to the corner of some dilapidated cabin and heave me down the gullet of a whale for denying my sacred Wright heritage.

—Cracked as my crowd. 'Seabright' is no Catholic name; I'm pretty sure one of them fuckin stole it. You need a smoke? I saw you lookin.

—Thanks, no.

—Listen, that was bullshit about walkin from St John's to Seal Cove, but I did hitch out here. Can you give me a ride back?

—Sure. You know you're getting paid for this audition, right? Actors' Queue and TCR's funding rules say we've got to get some local amateur talent at least trying out, and the ACHE Board figured getting some professionals from town out here might encourage local support.

—I'm not from town. Can I see whatever part of the script you got done?

—You want to audition from the script?

—It'd be nice. Kinda hoped to see the script in advance, to tell ya the truth. Who's buddy in the dog collar outside?

—Reverend Winslow. He runs the Church of Prevenient Grace at the End of Things.

—You drive all the way out here for church?

—Believe me, I am not one of his flock.

—He's lookin at ya like you are.

50

Nichole gave Seth the thin manuscript and peered through the grimy window. Elias Winslow caught her eye and strode to the door. Before Nichole could explain Winslow any further, the minister stood in the doorway, dark against the scarce daylight.

—Ms Wright. I might have guessed. Are you going ahead with those try-outs today?

—Yes, we –

—Excuse me, young man, but all public buildings are smoke-free.

Not raising his eyes from Nichole's script, Seth crushed the ember of his fresh cigarette between thumb and forefinger, the same way Winslow had extinguished the graveyard incense.

Elias Winslow walked towards them, and the old wooden door slammed shut. —Ms Wright, you surprise me today. But then you aren't a part of this community, so perhaps I should take that into account. Has it occurred to you, within your little bubble of defiance and pride, to wonder why no one else has shown up?

Slap Nichole Day, is it? Nichole sicced the Wright face on Reverend Winslow, though she had to push her glasses back up first.

—Enlighten me, Reverend.

Quietly, but not so quietly Seth could not hear: —You suffer from powerful and genetic need for humbling. God have mercy on your arrogant Wright soul.

Winslow looked at Seth next. Doubtless another wayward lamb sent to try his patience and irritate mute memories. *Damnation, hellfire and demons' wings, what I am supposed to remember about this one? A Seabright?*

Then he spoke at his normal volume. —A young girl died here last night. She's some of our best talent, and she was going to audition today, Ms Wright.

—I'm sorry. I had to no idea.

—So show a little respect. I am very disappointed in you, Ms Wright, but perhaps I should have expected no better. When one dies in Port au Mal, Mr Seabright, we are all diminished, for we are a true community. Yes, I know who you are, you and your filthy books. I need a bath every time I see your covers in a store.

Rolling the script into a cylinder and tucking it into his back pocket, Seth locked eyes with Winslow. —Don't get out shoppin much, do ya? Diminished, Jesus, and a clod be washed away. If I were John Donne, I'd invite you out back for a word of prayer.

Dust motes thickened the air.

Seth hooked his thumbs in the front pocket of his jeans, gently nudging the knife case on his belt. Reverend Winslow copied his posturing.

Chill spread tentacles like a virus in Nichole's blood. *Knife-fight in the Orange Lodge, great. New folk song'll come out of this, yet.* She dropped her brittle Wright certainty. —Reverend Winslow, I can re-schedule the community auditions, but Mr Seabright is a professional actor on a schedule, and he needs to go ahead today.

Winslow ignored her and spoke to Seth. —You recognized John Donne. Very good. It seems you've managed to cram in some poetry between fights and fornications. Can you actually recite any?

The saint's medal around Seth's neck flashed in the light. —Jeez b'y, I dunno. Any particular poetry you wanna hear? I do all right with the seventeenth century. Let me fall to my knees for ya.

So when my days of impotence approach,
And I'm by pox and wine's unlucky chance
Driven from the pleasing billows of debauch,
On the dull shore of lazy temperance –

Hang on, now, Rev, there's more. Not polite to leave in the middle of a performance.

I'll tell of whores attacked, their lords at home,
Bawds' quarters beaten up, and fortress won,
Windows demolished, watches overcome,
And handsome ills by my contrivance done.
Nor shall our love-fits, Chloris, be forgot,
When each the well-looked linkboy strove t'enjoy,
And the best kiss was the deciding lot:
Whether the boy fucked you, or I the boy.

Knees obviously paining him, Seth walked over and slapped Winslow on the shoulder.

—John Wilmot, Second Earl of Rochester. Right noble, that is, and you loved it. Tell the truth, now.

Winslow said nothing. Nichole's jaw worked as she kept her laughter in.

Seth took the script out of his pocket and looked at Nichole.

—From the top?

Act one. Scene one, Port au Mal, Newfoundland. John Cannard, an Englishman in his late 50s, sits writing.

CANNARD: Port au Mal, October 10, 1761. So, trapped on this pinned chart as the corrections made in another man's hand be trapped between two coursing lines of mould, like clews, one larboard and one starboard; so trapped I draw my finger lightly over the coast of Massachusetts, of the bays round Salem (for so this chart be titled, Waters of Salem), stir up gales as I once stirred coffee, thoughtlessly, in Bristol with Runciman – another country, and me another man. And which stranger, then –

Winslow tore the script from Seth's hands. —No! Making a whore of history. Changing dates willy-nilly, destroying the true story of this place. Misleading tourists, heaven help us. Imaginary muck that will besmirch the name of Port au Mal and the good people who live here –

Seth giggled. —Besmirch?

—You shall learn. Both of you. You may not – must not – play with history.

Elias Winslow threw the script at Nichole's feet and departed, quietly enough.

Nichole sagged against the wall.—God. He wears me out.

—Nothin like some dusty old porn to get people to back right the fuck off. You should read Rochester in the bath. Do ya the world of good. Where'd you come up with that Cannard fellah?

—That bit's verbatim from a ledger my cousin found in his father's attic. It seems to match up old letters a friend of mine found out here. Letters from Salem.

Seth picked up the script. —Strict history, then. So what's his Most Reverend Holy-Rollerness Supervillain gettin on with?

—The letters seem to indicate English settlement in this area before 1760.

Seth stopped lighting his cigarette, quite serious. —He the same Winslow who started the whole Settlement 250 thing?

Nichole nodded.

—Dorinda's into Settlement 250 up to her tits, too. Jesus, Nichole, there's fuckin millions on the go here, and that's just

what's on the books, never mind what's stashed in the pork-barrels.
Stakeholders, they call themselves. Stake through the heart is what
they need. You all right? You wanna get a drink?

    *No, I want a two-litre pail of ice cream, a big bag of chips, and
my own toilet.* —We'd have to go to Harbour Grace. Port au Mal's
dry.

    —Ain't that the fuckin truth.

8) BOWGRACE
July 3, 2009, St John's.

Gabriel Furey – that Gabe Furey fellah, as Seth Seabright called him – lived in Dorinda Masterson's basement apartment. Dorinda had been sweet on Gabriel since both were in their twenties but drifted away when she heard he'd not only shacked up but had a baby on the way. Now, each nearing sixty, they lived in the same house, assumed by many to be a couple, but no: separate doors and separate keys. Gabriel settled into a calm relief, making no move on Dorinda and believing she would make no move on him.

Gabriel had grown up in the Christian Brothers' St Raphael's Home for Boys, and he treasured both the concept and the reality of personal space. St Raph's had left marks predictably tragic and tragically predictable. When younger – dyslexic and usually drunk – Gabriel could not hold down what other men called a real job. He managed to fall in love with the prime minister's daughter, Callie Best. They had a daughter, Claire, but Gabriel remembered very little of Claire as a youngster. However, he did remember drunkenly studying Claire one evening the way paedophiles had once studied him. Monsters' hands not only bruised but stained him, tainted his heart and mind? The nightmares graced that fear with flesh and bone. Would he ooze poison? Touch his daughter like that?

No fuckin way.

So he'd run.

1979.

Claire had been young, but not so young that she forgot him, old enough and young enough to blame herself. Gabriel left a note to Callie, trying to say he'd felt smothered, that he needed to be an artist. Bullshit, but semi-plausible bullshit. Gabriel the janitor, Gabriel the rent-a-cop, he got the means to sculpt and paint and send some money home. He also kinda lied about his citizenship – his mother had been Canadian – getting several Canada Council grants after sweet-talking various women into filling out the forms for him. The City of Ottawa commissioned a statue, installed it on Sparks Street. Gabriel had called it *Sea Angel*. Then someone in the NDP asked him for a sculpture of Louis Riel, which he delivered, Riel life-size and looking at the ground, hesitant, but the sculpture had gone missing and remained so. When Gabriel returned to Newfoundland in 2005, he met Claire by accident, or at least without planning to, and a little late. Already sick then, Claire died within a few months. Watching this, Gabriel talked to Callie about the real reason he'd left. Callie – *God love ya, girl* – had guessed the most of it. But she wanted nothing to do with him. Gabriel listened – his turn. Callie had endured derision and then silence from her father for living common-law with Gabriel. Then Gabriel had beaten her and abandoned her, left her with a girl to raise on her own. The forces of Gabriel's past had strung him up and yanked him about, fed his demons. Callie knew that, but she said *What the hell was I to you, a fish to split and splay out in the sun? A blow-up doll that made breakfast?* He couldn't answer.

At their daughter's deathbed, Callie and Gabriel spoke civilly, shared tears. That was all.

Life continued to surprise him. A few years ago, Dorinda Masterson offered her basement apartment to him rent-free. Homeless, he'd quickly agreed. He'd sold some paintings and sculptures, gotten some commissions, and taught drawing workshops at the Penitentiary, much to the disgust of several politicians. He started to dry out. He sometimes had to accept Dorinda's invitations to supper or go hungry, but he had a bed. Four walls and a roof. Electricity for the kettle, and heat in winter. A draughty mock-up of heaven, he called it, privately. Now he also had a commission from the Admiral's Rooms for the *Peril on the Sea* exhibit. And more loose tea than he knew what to do with. Someone – probably Dorinda, but possibly Claire's friend, Nichole Wright – had signed him up for three different tea-of-the-month clubs, a mystifying gift. His damaged taste buds, rotburnt from drink and cigarettes, took in very few of the promises on the packets.

I am not worth the effort.

So, on this summer afternoon, pot of tea made and forgotten, apartment draped with spattered plastic sheeting, fingers caked with clay, Gabriel worked smaller studies for his *Sea Sentry* piece. He felt free and clean, playing in the mud like a youngster. Happy.

Dorinda Masterson knocked on the apartment door, noise lost to John Lennon, cranked up loud.

Porthole. Slightly skew; water will flood through here.

—Gabriel?

Fuck off, I'm workin. Oh, Dory. —Wha?

—I just got back from the ACHE board meeting. A total fiasco. The woman we've commissioned to write the play is really upset and ... can I come in?

Gabriel turned down Lennon's plea and opened the door.

—You own the place, Dory. I'm just the stray you took in.

—Do you have to be like that? Oh, my God.

—Yeah, bit of clay on the go. Excuse the mess.

—I thought you were doing this at the studio.

—The main piece, yes. These are just studies. I'm tryna figure out how to get this a decent size without havin it weigh forty fuckin pounds. That blows up, it'll take the kiln with it. You want a cup of tea? Pot's gone cold. Jesus, is that the time? Dory, honey, I'm sorry, but I'm after forgettin to meet Nichole at Mahon's Galley for tea.

—Nichole, who?

—No need to say it like that. Just that one, Nichole Wright, Claire's friend.

Nichole Wright? Jesus, this town is too small. —Here, take my rig.

Gabriel accepted the key and kissed Dorinda on the cheek. She smiled as his stubble gently scraped her. Then she watched his sweet little arse animate his tight jeans as he loped up the stairs. She started to climb the stairs herself, head rattling with the ACHE meeting, with Nichole Wright's understandable dismay at TCR's new Tourist Friendly Arts Template – Dory's vigorous opposition to the template officially noted in the minutes, her moving to ram the TFAT up Chris Jackman's arse unrecorded.

She'd stepped in clay without noticing.

She slipped and fell.

The sound of her right ankle breaking sickened her nearly as much as the pain. Below her: Gabriel's apartment and, somewhere past the clay, his telephone. Above: her part of the house, and, somewhere on the kitchen counter, probably near her grandmother's china teapot, her cell phone. *Nan might get out the bar of soap if she heard me curse like this.* Yes, Nan who had slipped on the stairs...

Dory yelled. —These very God damned stairs, in this very God damned Official Heritage House. Twisted Jesus in the garden, that hurts!

She tried to stand, but bearing weight proved impossible, and balance eluded her. She collapsed, smacking her chin off the edge of a step, cutting her lip and chipping a tooth. Feminism long ago liberated her tongue, but she still kept one word in storage, for special occasions. She howled it now.

—Fuck! Gabe? Gabriel, can you hear me?

Ignition.

Adjusting the driver's seat and the rear-view mirror, Gabriel tried to puzzle out why accepting favours from Dory felt like accepting charity when she probably loved him. *Does she?* He backed out of the driveway, straining to see past the various old trees, turned south.

Dorinda listened to Gabriel drive off.

Assess, Dory, use your brain. Wiggle your toes. Good. Feeling in both legs. Good. Yes, damn strong feeling in the broken ankle. Roll over, gently, gently. Good. Get my breath back. Gabriel won't be long – oh right, sit on my arse and wait, Dorinda, Dorinda, let down your hair. Bracing her hands against the step, Dorinda pushed herself arse-first up to the next step. She rested a moment, heaved again, and repeated this exercise eight times until she sat in the main porch. The door to her part of the house lay ajar. *Just another few scoots...* And Dorinda banged her temple off a radiator. Dizzy, she leaned against the wall a moment, resumed her journey. Kitchen. Success. Dorinda got to her knees, grabbed the counter and hauled herself up, caught the cell phone and slipped again, this time smacking the pointiest part of her right cheekbone against granite. Wrenching her back to avoid bearing weight on her ankle, Dorinda descended in jerks, landing on her left hip. Eyesight blurred with angry tears, she flipped open her phone and pushed the hotkey for 911.

Nichole tried to keep her voice quiet, but her words pattered quickly. She knew she sounded manic. *Lithium, oh, lithium, oh, have you met lithium.* —And then I report to the ACHE Board of Directors, and it turns out not one of them has read the outline I e-mailed them because they're all too busy freaking out over Seth Seabright being cast, when it was them all along who told me to cast him. And now it turns out he's Actors' Queue all right, but not TFAT –

—Tea fat?

—Tourist. Friendly. Arts. Template. Remember all that stink over Seabright's last play, language and whatever, and how he got invited to Toronto and flew up on the NL-Canada Tourism Ambassador Program, but then couldn't stage the show once he got there because they couldn't understand his accent?

—Bit more to it than that, I heard. That young fellah came out drunk to the dress rehearsal and took a piss on stage. I saw that play here, just before TCR closed down the Hall. Really good.

—I am *never* gonna get this done! Now ACHE needs a new draft per TFAT submitted to a committee at TCR so they can study it before granting funding approval. I might not even get paid for this. I've worked my arse off drafting this play, and they just feed me some line about tourism. On top of that, they're all upset because they think I've changed the dates, that I'm making up my own play and defying the mandate. But I'm not. Port au Mal had settlement before 1760. I've got written proof. I can't just ignore it.

—You'd think the ACHE crowd could take a little creative license of their own and realize the history they started with is wrong.

—Incomplete, at least.

—You want my advice, ducky? Fuck TFAT, and fuck Settlement 250.

Nichole sat back hard in her chair. —All the money's tied up in Settlement 250.

—If you don't mind me askin, what did you do with that load of money you got from that land sale? Didn't some church buy a few acres off you?

Nichole blushed. —Church of Prevenient Grace out in Port au Mal. Land my grandfather Wright left me. I took the money just before I decided to go off the lithium, and that fucked me up, because I shouldn't have been on that shit in the first place. I got to feeling the money was dirty, so I gave it away.

Gabriel stared at her a moment, then laughed. —Who'd ya give it to?

—Women's shelters. Spent a few dollars on some new clothes; my weight goes up and down. I just – hated having that money.

—The day I left St Raphael's, the brother in charge gave me fifty dollars.

—But you didn't spend it.

—I most certainly did. Twas either that or starve, now, wasn't it?

—I never thought of it that way.

They finished their tea in a mostly comfortable silence, and then Gabriel decided he should get back to work. As he pushed his chair back, Nichole flushed and paled.

—Y'all right, ducky?

—Do you think I should testify against Almayer Foxe?

—You should be testifyin against the likes of that with a birch junk. Studded with nails.

—Like telling a roomful of strangers is going to make this better. I don't want to. I just – can't.

Gabriel tried to say *I know* but failed, throat too tight. He passed Nichole a napkin. As he'd once drunkenly passed crying Claire a napkin, when she sat across from him in a dark little pub, angry, betrayed and already sick. *Shouldn't be me doin this. Not right. Where's your father to, Nichole?*

Claire had thrown her tea in Gabriel's face.

Nichole blew her nose and made a mess of it. —The worst of it's – my parents won't even – my mother asked me how I could let Foxe –

—You didn't *let* him do anythin. Nichole, look at me. Nichole. You are not the criminal here. This Foxe prick, he's goin to prison regardless of what you say. Question is for how long, and where. You don't participate, don't tell your story, then maybe enough years get knocked off his sentence that he strolls out of HMP next summer. Because you hide the past.

—*My* past!

—I know, ducky. And he fucked with it. Not just your past, either.

Another silence.

—I'm sorry, Gabriel. You need to get back to work. I can see the clay under your nails.

—I looked into the whole St Raphael's record a while ago. Brother who fucked with me?

—Yeah?

—Never charged. Should be dead by now, though.

They both got to their feet.

—Chin up, ducky. You'll make somethin of this yet. Somethin beautiful. Reach deep down inside ya and haul it out.

Gabriel kissed Nichole on the cheek and hurried out to the street.

Hungry for supper, Nichole strode east on Water Street as though heading into a storm. She caught her reflection in a bank's window – not hard to tell she'd been crying. Taking her tiny iPod Shuffle from the neckline of her dress, she thumbed through her playlist, stopping when the driver of a car which had right-of-way barmped. There she stood, middle of the crosswalk at McBride's Hill, against the light. She darted to the sidewalk, twisting her ankle slightly on her heeled sandals, and decided to accept whatever tune came next: Laurie Anderson, 'One Beautiful Evening.' Eyes down, she resumed her stride, noticing she'd only polished the toenails of her left foot. Sparkling silver, hardly a summer colour; go for a peach or a coral, her mother had advised, something neutral, something nice. *Nice*, like the hazardous sandals, a birthday gift from her mother.

Looking up from her feet, Nichole caught sight of a sandwich board sign with photocopied posters for upcoming concerts. A little higher: a greasy doorway, through which Seth Seabright fell arse-first onto the sidewalk, long beard and hair stuck off like the birch broom, the one in the fits. Just beyond Seth, outside a café: bikers in their fifties and sixties, all denim, new leather chaps, beer guts, sugar-free skim lattés and gold credit cards. A few glanced over at Seth but said nothing.

As Nichole took her earbuds out and slung them round her neck, the wind carried scraps of sound off from the Tattoo's extra evening performance on Signal Hill: Evan Rideout bawling orders, gunfire. —Seth, you all right?

Seth blinked, bit off a fingernail so hard the quick bled, got to his feet with vicious speed and shouted at the pub. —You can't fuckin treat me like that!

A badly-toupéed man, Seth's height in his platform shoes, stuck his face through the doorway. —Seabright, you got thirty seconds to get out of my sight before I call the Constab. Jesus, b'y, you could crawl to the lockup faster than the coppers could get here, but the lockup's where you're headed, guaranteed.

Though she'd later question the wisdom of it, Nichole spoke up. —Excuse me. Yes, hello, I am addressing you. Mr Seabright is with me. Is there a problem?

The toupéed man – a dreadful hairpiece, hybrid of a Beatles moptop and that Three Stooges bowl cut – tilted his head back to view Nichole. Grey hairs, long and coarse, poked out his ears and nose. His down-townie voice, vague belligerence and vaguer Irish, knotted up in Nichole's head. The latté bikers all watched now, enjoying this bit of dinner theatre.

—The problem, Miss, is that young Seabright is drunk and disorderly.

Seth wiped spittle from his mouth, but most of it frothed and stuck to his beard. —Begged ya to cut me off, ya scabby cunt.

—Nothin I'd like better some days, my son, though I expect there ain't much there.

—No fuckin son of yours.

—Well, thank Christ for small mercies. And if he's with you, Miss – it is 'Miss,' right? – then where might you have been for the last few hours while your date got shitfaced?

—He's not my date.

Seth noticed Nichole. —Do I know you?

—Then how is he with you? Answer me that.

Letting the family manner infest her face and voice, Nichole burnt her ancestors for fuel. *Damn, this is too easy some days.* Shoulders back, tits out, hips even, she hurled stretched-out vowels like a mace and chain. She did not shout; she projected and enunciated like a stage actor, a radio announcer, a discreetly-beaten upper-class wife in turn berating a servant.

—Perhaps you are hard of hearing, my man, or perhaps I have not made myself clear. Seth Seabright is with me, so there is certainly no need to bother the Constabulary. We will leave your establishment, as, for the life of me, I cannot see any reason to step inside. My feet would stick to the floor and so rend me Daphne and tree. Seth, let's go.

Bikers chuckled. *Missus is the feisty one, all dolled up.* Toupée Man withered, confused.

Seth followed Nichole up the first few steps of Rendell's Lane, steps that led up towards Duckworth Street. —Bet ya I can climb these faster than you.

—Seth, listen –

He somehow raced up the crumbling steps, knocking into an old steel-banded trash basket and setting yellowjacket wasps to angry defence. Ducking the wasps, he tripped in an empty India

62

Ale box rotting quietly outside a dark little pub, a literal hole in the wall – and Official Historic Site – called The Wrecking Ball. Crumpling the picture of the Newfoundland dog as he squat the beer box in his fall, Seth cursed indecipherably, picked up the box and pitched it back down towards Water Street. It clocked Nichole upside the head. Seth, horrified in the manner of a tiny schoolboy who's just talked back to a nun, stared at Nichole for maybe half a second and bolted. Yellowjackets hissed over to Nichole, drawn by the sweet scent of the beer box.

Nichole stood on blackened stone, steady, still, and quite thoroughly ticked.

Enough of this.

—Seabright!

She chased him – not that she knew what she'd do if she caught him – finding him on Duckworth, hands crammed in his pockets, staring across the street at the boarded-up Hall.

Seth spoke first. —I can't believe that's still closed. Here we are, whorin out our culture, pitcher plant, I spose, drown the tourists and eat them, and TCR won't pony up their share of the fundin to refurbish the Hall. We got no theatre space, except what we keeps rentin from the fuckin schools. Have we met?

—You just threw a box at me.

Seth bolted across the street this time, enjoying the long honks on the horn from drivers. He stood now at the base of the barricaded and condemned wooden steps leading up to the Hall, raised his arms and shouted to the sky. —We got no fuckin theatre!

Checking traffic first, Nichole jaywalked safely across Duckworth and touched Seth's shoulder. —You might need to lie down.

—I prefers to stand. But not tonight, I'll never get it up. Got no money left, anyway.

—Charming. How did I get tangled up with you?

—And you are?

—Nichole Wright. We met out in Port au Mal for that Settlement 250 play. I was getting ready to drive you to Harbour Grace for a drink before going back to town, but then you hooked up with the skank with the green and blue hair.

—I remembers that. You fucked off and abandoned me out in some rancid bedroom with, Jesus, what was her name – Frangina

63

Murphy. Not dry at her place. And me after thinkin we were in Harbour Grace.

—I did not abandon you! You slithered off with that woman of your own free will.

—I slithered, did I? She tasted some good. I remembers that much. Fuckin bedbugs, though.

—Seth!

—Wha?

He staggered and fell, landing once more on his arse. For just a moment, his eyes reminded Nichole of Gabriel's, but that sudden hell-flame of self-knowledge and recognition sputtered out. He ignored Nichole's offer to help him up and once more stood with speed and grace.

—I gotta git. But we've met. I know we've met.

He walked away from her slowly, backwards. Then he ran across Duckworth again and ducked behind a brick outcrop. Angry drivers accelerated, running the red light. Nichole walked quickly to the intersection, waited half of forever for the light to change, crossed legally and still nearly got hit by a car, then made it to the brick outcrop.

No Seth. Just yellowjackets and garbage bins.

Fine.

Nichole continued east on Duckworth Street. She wanted to look at the old house on Prescott Street where Claire's apartment had been, wanted to see the house one last time before it got torn down.

A knocked-down wall: tar paper, floorboards. *Already?* Claire's apartment exposed to winter and rough weather, to the heat of the sun. The cramped afterthought of a bathroom and its stained clawfoot tub designed for much shorter ancestors or perhaps hobbits. The dark kitchenette. The front room where she'd painted and sketched, kneeling sometimes on the hardwood floor.

Seth, meantime, took stock. Satched cigarette butts and rotten fruit, cups from smoothies and iced coffees, cans from cola and energy drinks, and six, count em, six used condoms, wasps everywhere, all of it sticky, all of it sweet, rotting, but sweet: good enough. Squatting down on some bare ground behind garbage bins, Seth decided to take a short nap. Consciousness and time departed. A wharf rat, a good eighteen inches, peeked round a bin, sat upright and sniffed the slumped human: harmless, for now. As

Seth's body relaxed, his feet lolled. He immediately dreamt of the hanging net and kicked, disturbing an underground wasps' nest. His patched canvas sneakers gave no defence against the first few stings. He kicked again, then jumped up, wide awake now, backing awkwardly against the bins, desperate to stand and run. A cloud of wasps, hundreds he thought, stung him, up his jeans and down his shirt, crisscrossing his hair and beard and nearly every centimetre of exposed skin. He lurched out to the sidewalk and straight into a strip club poster taped to a utility pole. The wasps stung and stung. Ready to spew, Seth fell to his bad knees, suddenly remembering how they'd ached earlier in the day, and cursed himself for his clumsiness – now he'd need to patch the jeans. He tried to call for help, but, as he inhaled, wasps flew into his mouth. Prying and spitting some out, he got one good breath and bellowed the first word that came to him.

—Nichole!

Nichole, coming out of the coffee shop on the opposite corner, ran over the crosswalk to the convulsing Seth. Seeing the wasps, she poured her bottle of water over Seth's head. Then she called on her cell phone for an ambulance, getting stung on her hands and arms. No drivers stopped. A pedestrian, a man in his fifties – bitter and grey and squint-eyed, one fight-damaged ear pierced, disgusted that God had not seen fit to propel him to fame, money and easy lays – offered Nichole some advice.

—Nice girl like you, with them gold earrings and fancy sandals: young Seabright isn't worth your time. Leave that little alkie to sleep it off, me trout.

—I'm no 'girl.'

—Fuck you, then. Only tryna help. Jesus, where are all the wasps comin from?

—I fell on the stairs!

—Ms Masterson –

—*Dr* Masterson.

—Sorry.

—I teach English, Cultural Studies and Women's Studies at the university. You're a resident, right?

The young ER doc brushed a loose spiral of red hair out of her blue eyes and tucked it back into her purple headband. Dorinda scowled, but not with pain. Fair skin, blue eyes, red hair: Dorinda used to pray every night from ages six to twelve to wake up the next morning with blue eyes and red hair. The skin she'd leave up to God. Today, complexion mottled by tans and cigarettes, coarse hair fried by colours and bleaches, breasts sagging and belly soft, Dorinda felt ugly, deeply ugly, before the younger woman. So, her father's warning had come true? Her father the stevedore and carpenter who'd rather take a nap than pick up a book, what did he know about justice and hard work, she'd thought. *Now Dory, no good can come of you screamin and whinin about this women's lib foolishness. Full-on anger never changed nothin for the better. It's a start, but even the unions can't work on just anger. And on top of that, anger makes you ugly on the inside, darlin. No man wants to marry that kind of ugly.* And now, her father long dead and suddenly missed, she sat on a hospital cot, battered by accident and nauseous on painkillers, too damn tired for anger, just empty, hollow, anger having sustained her so long.

—That morphine didn't last.

—I can't give you any more yet. You're still full of ketamine from where we re-set your ankle.

—Oh my God, there's a wasp in here. I can't stand wasps.

—We've got a patient down the hall who fell onto a nest. We put him in isolation, but some wasps got through. We'll be killing wasps all night.

—Jesus, Jesus! Is it on me?

—No, it flew off. Are you allergic to stings, Dr Masterson?

Dorinda shut her eyes hard enough to scrunch up her face.

—Just afraid.

—About your injuries. I know the nurses have already asked you. But –

—I fell on the stairs.

—Yes, it says so here in the notes. Do you know why I decided to become a doctor? Because of all the nights I sat in the emergency room down at St Clare's with my mother after Dad had taken his fists to her.

—Look, I –

—Do you know how many doctors asked my mother if someone had beaten her? Guess. None. Not a single one even asked.

—I'm very sorry.

—Who beat you?

—No one.

—My mother said she walked into doors or fell down stairs. I tried launching myself down the stairs once, so I could get bruises in my face like hers, and then we could both say we fell down the stairs.

—Technically, I fell up the stairs.

—Were you pushed?

—No. Gabriel had just left.

—Who's Gabriel?

—The man who – my tenant.

—Are you in a relationship?

—Now listen –

—Did Gabriel beat you or push you down the stairs?

—No!

The resident thought a moment, then told Dorinda she had a visitor waiting, a Mr Furey.

—Would you like me or a nurse to stay in the room?

—For the last time, Gabriel didn't hurt me. I don't think he could.

—You can't be too careful. Here's a card with a number to call if you change your mind. I'll go arrange for your crutches.

She left, and a few moments later, Gabriel rushed in. —Jesus, Dory, you look like someone shoved ya down the stairs. Y'all right, or wha?

Dorinda rested her forehead on her hand and cried. Gabriel rolled up a magazine and quickly, capably, whacked two wasps to death.

Fresh from a binge and preparing to purge, Nichole decided first to call the hospital and check on Seth. She'd been barred from staying in the ER with him, not being immediate family, so she figured this time she'd lie if necessary. *Lie, and say what? 'Sister' is no good. 'Some chick he thought was a hooker,' yeah, go with that. 'Cousin' is the best you can do, and even that's a stretch.*

Why do you even care?

She caught her fierce reflection in the mirror as she laid out her purging tools. The stiffened welts on her hands and forearms made this difficult. She recalled a nurse's advice that her own stings might make her sick and sleepy later.

Should market this as a kit in a pretty box, like a tampon multi-pack. It's entirely possible to die from wasp venom. I care because I care. Isn't that enough?

The phone rang.

How to make a boy call? Either get in the shower or get ready for the private and oh-so-intimate ritual of purge-o-rama.

Rang again.

Tip #3: Before you stick your fingers in and out your throat, drink, like, omg, TONS of salt water... or, like, go inhale the North Atlantic, you big fat failure bitch... and like, binge on smooth foods, right? Stringy stuff like beef gets caught in the drain.

Three rings. *Fucking hell.* Nichole threw the canister of salt into the sink and ran for the phone. —Hello?

—I think I remember.

—Hello?

—Out in the graveyard, with the incense. I didn't mean it. Nichole?

—Who is this?

—I am no longer sure. I've so long gone a-roving that my legs fell off, out there in the lamplight. Do you remember lying on top of *Newsbird's* heaped wreckage?

Newsbird, the little yellow Tiger Moth her great-uncle had loved to fly, had crashed while looking for a girl lost in the deep woods near Port au Mal. Little Sally Saucer, crack goes the breakdown: a few years ago, Nichole drove out to Port au Mal, burning like a fat fire with need and desire to rebuild that plane, make art out of it. So many plans. An elderly man, white hair, white beard, aglow it seemed at the time, talked to her politely, talked her down, called an ambulance but got a hearse. *Charming.* That hallucination earned a Thorazine weekend, but then how else had she gotten to the hospital?

—Nichole, do you remember?

—Reverend Winslow?

Elias Winslow sighed. —Dust on my teeth. Dust closes in. I think I've fallen.

—Are you hurt?

—Could you come?

—Reverend Winslow, my hands – you're a two-hour drive away.

Silence.

68

—Is there someone else I can call for you, Reverend, someone in the area?

—I think I've fallen. But I can't remember. Do you remember? I know you remember the fierce dream of the knife, how you fought.

The two litres or so of ice milk in Nichole's stomach swished and gurgled. She'd soon lose her purging window. —Damn, I got the order wrong, anyway. Salt water first.

—What about salt water? Nichole? Can you come see me?

—Do you need an ambulance?

—No. I need to talk to you.

Nichole suddenly heard in Winslow's voice what she'd seen in Gabriel's eyes, Seth's eyes, in Claire's eyes as she lay dying.

—I'll be leaving in five minutes, Reverend.

Darkness and coyotes made the rectory seem even smaller. Nichole expected the darkness, despite the electrical wires connected to the little house. The coyotes, brazen but quiet, almost encircling the rectory, surprised her. Slowly retreating as she got closer, the coyotes acted as a wayward escort. Their eyes reflected back her headlight beams, and they seemed to gesture with their heads to the fog in the bay.

Keys spiking between her fingers and reinforcing her fist, Nichole walked like a Wright: head up, shoulders back, stride long. Oh, such purpose. She felt sleepy.

Reverend Winslow spoke from his doorway; he seemed to fill the entire space and yet cringe at the same time. —I am happy to see you.

Compelled yet free, much as she'd felt when Seth landed at her feet on Water Street – just walk away, no, just try to help – Nichole touched Winslow on the shoulder. His boniness shocked her, but at least he felt warm. —And I'm happy to see you're all right.

He led her inside, to the blue glow of his laptop. The only electrically powered item in the rectory, the laptop hummed very loudly. No clock, refrigerator or baseboard heater competed. Accepting an invitation to sit down, Nichole recognized that the laptop sat on the hearth of a crumbling chimney. Old and sour clothes padded the hard seat of the wooden armchair. Dust flew with each human movement, and as Nichole's eyes adjusted to the dark, she saw Elias Winslow wipe the space immediately before his face the way he might wipe an obscured window. Then he clicked an object free of his belt and gave it to Nichole.

A very old knife.

—Dear girl, what happened to your hands?

—Why are you giving me a knife?

—Ever been to sea, Nichole?

She snorted. Yes now, twenty-first century Newfoundlander raised in the city on Canadian and American television, Toronto, Bangor and Detroit. No dialect allowed in the house, fish rarely eaten, let alone ever handled. Out on the water every day, sure. Cue Frank Zappa: townie girl, she's a townie girl. —I get seasick.

—Answer my question.

Just like a kitten a-gnawin fresh fish. We'll rant and we'll roar...
—Once, my grandfather Wright took me out, for a treat. Because I behaved so nicely. Some friend of his had a yacht. Just him and a bunch of other old men.

Socks rolled down. Dirty nails and bad breath. I got so sick. Kept crying and swallowing back the snot. Only made it worse. But that's all.

(Let's get you cleaned up down there, Nichole)

—Can you remember, Nichole?

—No.

—Do you remember, Nichole.

(on deck and below) —No!

—Will you remember?

—Reverend Winslow, I'm really tired, and I drove all the way out here from town –

—Why do you think you dreamt of this knife?

Nichole turned the knife over in her palm, trying to see it better by the laptop's light. Here, in the dark with some strange and quite likely crazy dude sporting a robe of God, it seemed safe to speak.

—Because I had to defend myself. Been fucked-over.

—A nice girl from a family like yours?

Nichole gagged.

Reverend Winslow stood behind her now, holding back her long hair as she leant forward to vomit. Not old bile and curdled ice milk but a clump of old wounded flesh, needles of pine and spruce, and something shiny. Whitish liquid oozed from it, formed a puddle.

70

Elias Winslow drew an old blanket round Nichole's shoulders. —It's a bezoar. A combination of things you've swallowed but couldn't digest. People once thought them antidotes for all poisons. That one is very old; it has wanted to come up for some time.

Yellowjackets hissed, unseen; Nichole wondered if they'd stuck to her clothes. Gasping, she swatted round her head and finally spoke. —Feel like I just heaved up a rock.

—Very well done, my dear. Now tell me. And be honest. Why did you come out here?

—Not to puke on your fireplace, I promise. I guess because you sounded so sad.

—I think I fell. And then I got lost in a creation story. They're happening all the time. It's no trouble at all to trip and fall face-first into one. I hope I get this right. It began like this. I screamed it. Yes: I watched him to pry her fingers loose from the edge of his kayak, and he spoke through tears. 'For all that is sacred, daughter, I beg thee, plead with thee, let go. Rape, yes, I believe thee, and I do not blame thee, but thy hunger trails famine behind it. I cannot save thee. Must not.' And suddenly I screamed 'Let go!' And I fell. Face-first.

My boneblade knife broke – not the one I gave you, no, I stole that from Finn – and mangled his daughter's fingers – *my* daughter's fingers. We murmured to her how the cold salt water would soon numb her past all caring. But her strength, her weight, her fingers, tipping us – did she want to drown me, her own father? The mercy of cold. Her pregnant belly knocked the kayak, but her remaining fingers strained to right it.

My daughter, my beautiful, loyal, violated or willingly ruined daughter, would not drown me, though I would drown her. Seven fingers gone, floating on the grey waves. And on those waves, from the torn muscle and cracked bone of severed fingers, trickled many spheres, tiny and dark, first dull, then glittering. She moaned, just once, as salt water washed over her nine ragged stumps. I, her father, eyed the distance between my blade and her remaining finger. Ice sparkled in her long hair, long and strung out like the night sky, phosphorescence imitating starlight.

One finger.

One daughter. Monstrously pregnant. By a dog, some said. She was so hungry.

The wind quickened. Each sphere – millions of them now – grew, strained, burst like an infected cell spewing a virus, like a star gone supernova. Light and particle and wave, all at the one time, and then thousands of animals running and swimming and flying. Then creatures like me, airless, winged, tailed, naked and confused, spinning, slowly at first, like individual storms seen from far above, then faster. Out here, far from shore, a father dark with honour and murder: I saw it. I remember. Glass shattered, as it would thousands of years later when I dropped a compass.

I slashed and cursed then, afraid of her. I sang to her. I called her a whore. The hairless winged ones spun round us, more of them than stars, however blasphemous the observation, and I grew wings again. It hurt. But as a father, I felt the slap of the water and saved no one. Fortunate Abraham.

And then my daughter smiled and let go.

I spun again, nearly out of pain. *Aurora borealis* shimmered, beckoned me. I felt like wave and particle at once and wanted clarity. So I stretched out and touched snow.

Fell.

The wings clung to my back, tight as lichen. Barefoot on tundra, on ice floes, arm stretched to the sky, I begged God to take me back. Instead, as I bent over in the cold, I hardened. Muscle, blood and skin. Bonecage.

I finished falling.

Bogs. Barrens. Where I – not born, just made aware. Have You not granted me this defiance? Will? Do You not therefore beg me to defy You? I can leap across oceans and do not drown, because time and bones knit.

Now I steal. Back to the island – when did You bring me here? I did not choose to come here myself. An island, crusted round with nennorluks and kraken and fish and gulls?

I stole the sailmaker's secret knife. You hear me? I *stole* it. Because You, o Merciful One, banished me here with Your beloved.

And you, Nichole, your melancholy crowd of Wrights? The first one arrived here in 1750, quite some time before I could fully materialize as a man. I watched John Cannard, watched your Wrights. Fingering that stolen knife and sucking it some nights, the knife and its intertwined players, and that strange woman with her one swollen breast. I stole her knife and drank her misplaced light and anger before I thinned out like fog, because – no! I will *not* die, not yet. This morning I tottered round my parlour, arms warped out like black spruce branches, because I wanted to spin. Why do I study this Nichole girl? What was my name before I chose 'Elias Winslow'?

Assigned. Assigned to the last of the Wrights. Very good. I shall do battle with Nichole Wright. I must. No, no, this is stupid.

I will, I will, I will.

How shall I greet her?

Reverend Winslow's voice eddied out, and his chin fell to his chest. Nichole watched him a moment, making reasonably sure he'd fallen asleep before placing the blanket warming her shoulders around his. The invisible yellowjackets had gone quiet; the only hiss came from the waves on the near shore. The bezoar still leaked.

How shall you greet me? I think you just did.

Winslow took a deep breath and shifted in his chair. —I hope I've explained myself.

Nichole would have stifled the whole scene – she had a talent for stifling scenes, strangling the newborn breath out of them (*whore, murdering failure whore*) – except she touched the bezoar. Pricked her finger on a pine needle.

Winslow chuckled. —Waiting to fall asleep for a hundred years?

Nichole sucked the drop of blood from her skin and looked into Winslow's eyes. *Why did I ever fear you?*

—Nichole, could you please help me take off my shirt?

And why the hell don't I have the sense to fear you now?

Hand stiff, she lifted his robes up over his head, revealing a white shirt and brown pants, size small, at most. So thin.

Shirt unbuttoned, Elias Winslow shrugged. As he bent forward a bit, the laptop light shone on the tight and translucent skin of his shoulders. Beneath his skin, something the colours of lichen but the shape of many feathers and dormant wasps subtly rippled.

Winslow wept and smiled. —I've fallen. Not Lucifer. Just one of thousands. Struggle and defy. I fell.

—I believe you.

Nichole watched relief take Winslow like an intravenous narcotic taking a pain-wracked patient: rough and artificial grace, but acceptable.

—Say it again.

—I believe you.

He giggled. —Then I didn't make it up. Do you remember, Nichole? Here. Hold the knife. Hold my hand; I'm so cold. Hold it. Warm me. Are you afraid of heights?

—No. I'm afraid of falling.

This made Winslow laugh so hard he nearly collapsed, unable to breathe. Eventually he settled, and a strange strength infused his grip. —Leap the chasms? Not sure I can still fly. Not sure I still remember.

Squeezing Winslow's hand back, Nichole could think of only one thing to say. —Leap.

Wings fluttered beneath his thin skin as Winslow shifted in the chair. —We'd better start with the letters old Captain Wright kept. Poor Captain Wright, slow madness there. You look like him, you know. What else have we got? Dissenters' New World offspring, and then that ledger Lewis found – yes, I know all about John Wesley Morgan Cannard, the failed divinity student. I watched his hair streak white as though comets cut paths there. Time's light tricks me. And of course he'd no inkling where once I stood.

ACTS OF FEVER

I ain't gotta tear
I ain't gotta light
I ain't gotta time or a place
I wish for tomorrow
But its truths are all bound
To the never-ending escape

Blair Harvey, 'Bury My Body in the Pines,'
GutterBeGutted, 2006.

9) WINDROSE
March 14, 1745 (old style), Salem, Massachusetts.

—Cocksure ingenuity sails more cargoes than timidity and fear, and capital, sir, gushes out my hands like hard-drove rainwater. Rarely do I dry out. A man earns my respect. I give it not freely. Yet we must be civil with one another, for civility is good business.

Old words. Comfortable as a favourite waistcoat – and this morning mumbled at the hearth as Salem merchant Newman Head, belly and shoulders rounded, cursed the fog and stoked the fire. Then he adjusted his wig, the scalp hair beneath gone patchy and gull-grey. Smoke wafted past the grate and obscured the stones and the one small poppet leaning there before dissipating over the white tiles of the floor. Wood, once, that floor, young Newman kneeling to holystone it smooth for his infants' hands and feet. Now, as the flames rose, brilliant white tiles glowed into Newman's dim eyes. Trinkets of other lands – his clay teapots and nesting boxes, paintings, rugs, cups, India ink that smelled of camphor and patchouli, a tiny compass set within gold-inlaid filigree – declared him successful. Light streamed through many large windows and helped fade the portrait of his dead wife. The poppet sat posed, expectant. Bones creaking, Head reached for the little doll, remembering the origin. He'd sewn it, decades ago, cutting the form out of a flour sack, then stuffing the sack with barley and tea. He'd given it to his daughter, Rachel. She, in turn, had given it to her daughter.

Janet's poppet now.

Tell me not of patience under God, Peabody. I call the Angel of Death a thief!

The old serving-woman quietly placed breakfast on the large table, and Head pretended not to hear her. Once she left the room, he walked over to his plate, chose some meat from it, and decided to pick up his coffee. He would sit in the armchair by the fire, rather than alone and small at his table. A square of grey linen distracted him. Hardly a napkin – not like the beautiful ones Rachel had embroidered with windroses – and hardly fit to place on the brilliant white table cloth. No: touch told him paper, a sealed letter, damp and stained. Addressed to... no matter. It had fallen to his table and therefore must be meant for his eyes.

Later, his daughter gently shook his shoulder. —Did you not sleep last night, Father?

Head watched Rachel stoke the fire and wondered how long he'd been dozing. Somehow he'd voyaged from table to armchair, still holding the letter. Ink blurred between his fingers.

He'd slept badly for much of his life. Insomnia helped him keep watch at sea, and as a young father. He'd check on his infants throughout the nights, passing them to his wife for suckling. Persons, he'd tell himself, little persons in the dark, their futures a mystery, the night sky contained in one little pupil. He once argued with his friend Reverend Thomas Peabody, burying a third, that infants were proof of the damp and sometimes filthy grandeur of grace. Peabody hardly knew what to say to that, so he'd smiled. Head always loosened his children's swaddling clothes; the sight of their tiny bodies bound straight deeply unsettled him. Quarrels with his wife whenever he untied infant Rachel from her standing stool and permitted her to crawl as she pleased: *Our daughter on all fours as a beast? Newman Head, what folly is this?* Rachel had permitted her Janet to crawl, too. Rachel had swaddled her infants tightly, as her mother-in-law insisted. Of Rachel's three babies so far, only Janet had survived longer than a few weeks – very like her mother.

Strands of Rachel's hair escaped the pins.

Not white, surely, not yet.

—Father?

Head straightened his back and passed his daughter the letter.

—Pick the stitching for me, gosling.

Shifting some more, Head thought of his former business partner, and onetime friend, Jericho Gosse. His memory got stuck: an afternoon in 1733 when Gosse explained Head's reluctance to discuss a sloop called *Kittiwayke* with the Royal Navy's Captain Cleasby. *See, I got no reason to lie and deceive you gentlemen. He does.*

Rachel opened the envelope.—Tis from someone in Newfoundland, one John Cannard. 'Lately of Cannard and Son Bristol Atlantic Shipping, now residing after shipwreck in 1719 in Port au Mal, Newfoundland.'

—I care not for artificial mystery, gosling.

—'Sir: in 1734, *Kittiwayke* wracked herself off Port au Mal' –

—*Kittiwayke*'s come home at last. Give over that letter. At once.

—Father, do not grasp so. Smoke – what burns?

Scent guiding him, Head shoved his daughter aside. A spark had jumped the grate and scorched the dry poppet's face, and a tiny flame took hold. Head quickly mashed the doll against his chest, burning a hole in his waistcoat. Then he sat back down, holding the poppet out at arm's length to inspect for damage.

—Janet's dolly. Once yours, gosling. Blackmarkt now. A revenant.

Rachel wanted to take the poppet and hide it permanently, even destroy it – *ha, bury it?* – but felt she would be cruel to do so. She placed it on the shelf near the compass. —Tis only a doll.

No, Peabody, I shall not guard my words! Tell me not of patience under God, sir. I call the Angel of Death a thief! I should know, I should know.

Rachel forced her eyes back to the letter.—'Owner of *Kittiwayke*, Salem, Massachusetts, *in re* the late Captain Finn *et cetera*' – who brought this to you?

—Gosling, please, just read it.

—'From John Morgan Cannard, lately of Cannard and Son Bristol Atlantic Shipping, now residing after shipwreck in 1719 in Port au Mal, Newfoundland. November 2, 1744. Sir: in 1734, a sloop out of Salem, called *Kittiwayke*, wracked herself upon the pointed rocks off Port au Mal, precisely where my own vessel ran foul, these rocks named by the inhabitants The Fire Rocks, or sunkers. *Kittiwayke* was trying to elude *Dauntless*, a Royal Navy frigate. Pray, sir, what know you of Captain Finn, variously called by the Christian names Kit or Matt, and the sloop *Kittiwayke*?

I can tell you how Captain Finn fared on board *Dauntless* not long after the wrack. At the time, I received stern enquiries from Captain Cleasby of *Dauntless* regarding the history and proclivities of Captain Finn, enquiries which, naturally enough, Cleasby found me unable to satisfy. These events being old and distant, I no longer dread the return of Cleasby, *Dauntless* or any other Naval spectre. Therefore, I beg you: share with me any knowledge of Captain Finn you may possess, for I sleep but little, and my long memory, so incomplete, troubles me. Understand that my own enquiries come prodded by neither malice nor justice but simple curiosity. Grateful and indebted for whatever lines you may throw my way, I remain, your humble servant, John Cannard.' Father, you've gone the colour of old linen.

—This will ruin me.

—All involved lie bony dead. Father, you must not get excited.

—Think on it, and use that ingenuity God saw fit to grace you
with. That braying ass Cleasby put in here at Salem, he and that
redheaded Lieutenant Kelly – aye, no names slip my knots. No
good may come of this.

—Cannard insists he seeks no kind of justice –

Newman Head spat the word. —Justice? For Matt Finn? See
now, tis plain writ: Matt Finn died on board *Dauntless*. Such
knowledge galls worse than none at all. Better Finn drowned. Done
in, I know it, by Cleasby's hand, or perhaps his boot –

—Oh, settle yourself. Captain Cleasby and Lieutenant Kelly
were men of dim moral sight but hardly murderers. I am certain –

—Certain?

—*Certain*, Father, that Cleasby and Kelly treated Finn with
every due courtesy. Finn was likely injured, cut or broken in the
wrack, and that injury led to his death. You must answer this Mr
Cannard. Dictate to me. For with your eyes –

—Sauce me not, woman.

—No sauce but cold meat. Whom may you trust, Father, with
such correspondence? Your secretary? Should I run down to the
dock and fetch a ropewalker? Surely he'd say naught of molasses
and the past. I shall use the India ink.

—Indeed, you shall not. Iron-gall is good enough for this.

The first quill broke. Rachel took up another.

March 14th, 1745. From Newman Head, Merchant, Salem,
Massachusetts. To John Cannard, lately of Bristol, residing now in
Port au Mal, Newfoundland.

Sir: I knew both Captain Finn and Captain Cleasby. Captain
Matthew Finn, for so we in Salem knew him, sometimes also Kit
Finn, being a Christopher as well as a Matthew, stands in my
memory as a fine and capable captain who offended none, at least,
none who matter. I welcomed him as a guest at my table, and I am
most irritated to read in your blunt missive of Finn's death. You
might have done me the truth more kindly, sir.

I often hired Captain Finn, as did a cartel of my fellow
merchants. Finn's death exposes a great loss of seamanship and
good sense. But as I may not question the wind, so I may not
question the decisions of our Maker. Ownership of *Kittiwayke*

broke down thusly: I at thirty percent, and Captain Finn at forty percent. The rest we freighted out. The late and childless Jericho Gosse was *Kittiwayke*'s first majority-owner. He designed her, too, and oversaw her construction. Gosse would charge harder and higher rates to ship cargo on *Kittiwayke*, claiming *Kittiwayke*'s fine construction and lead bum justified the increases. I hardly dispute that Gosse designed strong and tidy vessels, that being his only success beyond emptying pitchers.

My heart, sir, bends like damp timber to think of *Kittiwayke* wrecked on the rocks and of Captain Finn so sore pressed. I beg you, sir, to tell me what you know.

10) THE RELICS
FROM JOHN CANNARD'S LEDGER, OCTOBER 10, 1760 (OLD STYLE), PORT AU MAL.

...tired; so, trapped on this pinned chart as the corrections made in another man's hand be trapped between two coursing lines of mould, like clews, one larboard and one starboard; so, trapped, I draw my finger lightly over the coast of Massachusetts, of the bays round Salem (for so this chart be titled, Waters of Salem) and stir up gales as I once stirred coffee, thoughtlessly, in Bristol with Runciman – another country, and me another man. And which stranger, then, marked the first corrections to this chart?

Thus from Salem, where I sent my letters enquiring after *Kittiwayke* and her history, and where arrived the navy ship *Dauntless* to seek a prodigal and a thief. I drag my finger to the spot on my table where Newfoundland should be, were this chart large enough. A missing Newfoundland. Would I'd missed it, and all these bitter collisions.

Come to inheritance after the death of my older brother James in 1719 and suddenly no more angry at being cast the second son, I did permit myself be tasked to voyage on King's business to this mess of fish guts and rocks settled in tiny snatches, as though God–

Does it not suffice that I keep him in food and gear? Good God, he'd waken Lucifer with that denting fist, bring us barren waters, the sea as much a desert of cold salt as any plain of hot sand when the fish hide. Aurelius Jackman at my door, so named for his silly mother's paternity, though how a Devon tenant came to the burden of 'Aurelius' remains a dull mystery. At least I know this Aurelius Jackman at my door be no flesh of mine. Nancy Truscott, later my wife in the manner of this place, witnessed Aurelius' birth in 1717. She cheered his obscured face: born with the caul, he was, a most fortunate sign. Once Jackman became a man and took to wife a Simms girl and fathered three sons, he fancied himself my equal, coming uninvited and unannounced to the Hall (a dwelling Admiral Lacey, fever of determined settlement on him, had built separate from his fishing rooms) to, of all things, talk. *Converse*, he meant; *discourse*, he desired: he accomplished only talk. He does so still, all manner of subjects, and I catch myself unlocking such treasures as I had packed in my young brain before taking

81

departure (though to look back remains the worst mistake, for it feeds my bad dreams). Aurelius Jackman in turn speaks to me of what he did witness or heard upon his visits to Harbour Grace, visits increasingly made on my behalf. Harbour Grace, once my most fervent desire, is now a spot I visit but annually of necessity, for I find no appeal or truth in Jackman's description of its worldliness. *Tis a major port, Mr Cannard.* No; my Bristol is that.

Jackman might be pleasant enough company when he deigns to show courtesy and sense. Other times he stumbles past my door when I am writing the tallies or elsewise far from a fit and proper state of mind. One evening, he mocked me, gently at first, gently, so I knew not the fire'd been lit until I smelled the smoke come up between my toes, this unlettered fisherman casting me as a heretic whom he might pluck from the flames everlasting of my own pride. I'd erred before, confessing to Aurelius Jackman I felt forgotten by God. He'd laughed.

The fishermen here be much occupied with fog and the patterns wind marks on the surface of the sea. On foggy days I wheeze, for I never got my lungs' strength back after the wrack. I did marvel, before my first whole winter in Newfoundland, at the bravery of fishing in fog. So I remarked on it to Tom Truscott, my wife Nancy's first husband. 'Course we go out in the fog,' he told me, brazen and dark. 'We like to eat.'

Cast away. A castaway for fourteen years in this settlement of thin-stilted draughty shacks perched (and praying not to slip) upon this stone leviathan, this lonely rock sheared and broken out of the sea, up out of the sea: Lucifer's fist, shaken at God. Thrown off, unwanted seed. Fourteen damned years, God far away, past fog and strange sky.

I did be trapped in this Port au Mal fourteen years when *Dauntless* pursued *Kittiwayke* through the narrows. 'Sunkers out there,' Tom Truscott liked to observe, with annoying frequency, nodding at dozens of rocks that broke the water at low tide. I knew those sunkers. They can bugger a compass senseless. Some devious mineral sparkles in threads through the rocks, Lucifer's embroidery, and near these rocks not even simplest cork and needle could point out the truth. Tis a strictly local phenomenon, for none suffers such trouble navigating near Harbour Grace. My little brig, *Bonny Jane*: her tortured compass needle jerked east, west, east southeast, and west again until wrenched north to circle widdershins as we squinted at charts in maddened lamplight. So we met the sunkers.

Relics of *Kittiwayke* fouled the nets and washed ashore for years after she sank. Aurelius Jackman, gifted with a preternatural attraction to flotsam, often discovered pieces between rocks. Newman Head's several letters, perhaps most helpful, now lie safe and bound together in Admiral Lacey's old trunk. I witnessed but a flash of the story myself, a scene illuminated as if by lightning over a bog; my memories do not suffice.

I owe debt as well to the first lieutenant on board *Dauntless*, John Kelly, who died in my bed of pneumonia. Kelly possessed knowledge which must, he begged me, reach England.

So, trapped, aged an ancient sixty-seven, I sit with a scrap of sail, a splinter of mast, letters from Salem and a dead man's notes. I need the winter nights already promised me to plot this particular course, which I shall mark on the old time, for I dislike the new calendar and its fuss over twelve days. The players be: myself; a spymaster named Runciman; Captain Finn out of Salem; Captain Cleasby and Lieutenant Kelly of the Royal Navy; some agents; a female; a bag of gold; old charts and a useless compass. The story began, as does much in this life, by accident.

The accident occurred at the Bristol docks in late 1718, March month. I expect I did be there.

11) DRINK THAT LIGHT

Ignition: the silly and sacred *fwhoom* as Robbie Pike lit the torch and the torch took the flame. Ann, dressed in shirt and breeches, long hair tied back in a plait, breathed deeply and got the scents of pitch and rot layered over the dank stink of the Avon. Pike and Ann worked the riverside, this major shipping route giving plenty of business. Pike, her guardian since, well, always, kissed the top of her head and playfully cursed the moon. Such a team, Pike and Ann, she so quick and smart in her disguise, he waiting to carry out the rougher work. Under Pike, Ann got nearly enough to eat and usually a place behind a wall to sleep. Robbie Pike had known Ann's mother, and he'd made her a promise: —I'll look after your Ann. I swear, by all the stars in the sky and all the tears in the sea, that girl shan't work the trade whilst I live.

A story to cling to, like a blanket. Ann liked the story and often asked to hear it.

—What did she die of, Pike?

—Fevers and regrets, but even then, all she cared after was you.

Torchlight and shadows made Pike's skin and eyes yellower, his hair and beard darker. He'd trained Ann to pass as a boy on the streets because boys seemed to have a marginally easier time of it. How he and Ann would manage when paps and hips erupted, he'd got no idea. For now, Ann worked as a glymjack, or a linkboy, one of those youngsters who bears a torch and guides a man's way though a city at night. The darker the night, the better the business. Glymjacks sometimes partnered with larger thieves, making a walk at night a calculated risk. Alone and unlit, you risked getting robbed. Following a glymjack, you also risked getting robbed. Not all linkboys led a man to trouble, but many did. With light, you might escape. With luck, the linkboy led you to your destination. Linkboys could also make extra money with their hands and mouths. Pike did not expect this of Ann.

Prettier linkboys sometimes disappeared.

Target in sight, Ann blew life onto the torch's flame and darted out of shadow.

—Glymjack, sir? Light the way and guide the walk, just one farthing.

The customer paid readily. He stood straight and easy, broad in the shoulders but thin in the legs, arm muscles forcing his sleeves taut. A sailor, almost certainly. He fingered his left ear, covering it then with most of his hand, and leaned down to look the glymjack in the eye.

—Ever heard the story of why a sailor drives rings through his ears? Sharpens the eyesight.

The sailor yanked his hand away from his ear. The scar had been cauterized, healing clean. The bottom third of the ear was gone.

—No truth to it. Got that sliced off in a fight, and I see fine. Should like to know who sliced it off? Man who tried to cheat me.

Failing to back away before he could clamp a hand on her shoulder, Ann tried to bring the relationship to some shade of normal.

—Where to, sir?

—Let me look on you a minute longer and mark those green eyes. Be feverish? No, forehead's cool. Such a sweet face. So sweet and complete. Better fall and burn in hell for your pretty face than drown in the shitten gutter in the dark, hey? Can you sing as we walk? A second farthing in it.

Ann accepted the extra cash, swallowing little pricks of fear. *Two farthings, don't run from two farthings ...* Pike should be quite pleased.

—What song then, sir?

—Can you sing 'Lizie Wan'? My ship's docked near the Cannard and Son warehouse. Do you feel no cold?

Even close to the flame and certain of her path, she felt the cold. First glymjack lesson Pike taught her: how to poach warmth and light the way. He'd told her a story about Lucifer falling from heaven and stealing fire on the way and then giving it to mankind. Jesus hunted Lucifer down and saw him nailed to a rock so birds could eat out his liver every day, except clever Lucifer substituted a lesser devil and carried on to rule over hell. Ann always imagined seagulls tormenting the demon, first with their racket and then with their beaks, but she'd yet to see a good rock to set the scene. Another of Lucifer's tricks: to draw heat from the fire without setting oneself alight. Slippery one, that.

Ann's torch only brief defiance, a little standard of need against fertile shadows and noise, she led her customer along a shortcut.

Five times the night before, as she had many nights, Ann had led her customers to Robbie Pike, who hit them, aye, but just a love-tap to the head – no stove-in skulls here, no ambitions to murder. Clotted blood over the ear and a headache be all. A matter of a deathbed promise to a clapped-out whore, aged eighteen. A matter of study, of pace-counting by daylight. A matter of getting something to eat.

—Tis so? Fuckin little liar.

Expectation in the customer's voice: he'd spotted the trap. Ann swooped the torchlight at him and darted off some more, trying to confuse him, tempt him away from Pike.

Does ragged-ear see in the dark?

—Follow me and my hot green eyes, hey? Hey? My pretty face be over here. Over here.

She'd never heard Pike say *Jesus* that way before, hoarse and deep in the throat.

Someone fell.

Ann waved her torch again, desperate for sight. Robbie Pike twitched in a puddle.

Run –

The sailor's hands missed her neck and shoulders but just caught her plait. He jerked her back, and she dropped the torch. It rolled against a wall, burning low.

—Flick those pretty eyes and lead me to ruin? I'll teach you hard lessons against that. And I'll hear that song, too.

He taught. She knew.

She weighed maybe fifty pounds, mere feathers for him. Skull smacked off the wall twice, three times, hard fingers prying and blunt – split, rent – by all the stars in the sky and by all the tears in the sea.

Footsteps and torchlight. Still behind Ann, the sailor reached round and snapped back one of her fingers, breaking it. His words seeped as he crammed her into his ditty bag. —Pretty little boy-gift, thrown across my path by maybe God Himself. Who be I to argue with God? Screw your eyes tight shut and let not one whisper get past those lips. Keep stiller than death or get more of it, hear me? Little thief. Little gift. Keep still.

12) DEAD RECKONING
MARCH 1718-20, AS TOLD JUNE 1734 TO LIEUTENANT JOHN KELLY, RN, BY CAPTAIN CHRISTOPHER MATTHEW FINN.

How came I to this? Sit down, then, Lieutenant, and look at me, eye to eye, sir, for you'll notice I cannot stand. I wonder I speak to you at all. Bound, now, I see naught left to lose. Here's adieu to all sorrow and care, hey?

The pox had ruint his face, aye, but his voice echoing out that barrel chest would persuade Lucifer he hadn't fallen. Blinded with it, too, and in bad pain. But still looked after me, in his fashion. He walked right delicately for a big man. Captain George Walters, master of *Bonaventure Walters*, and full owner, too. The man answered only to himself. Think on it. Bearing up under all the fuckery, gall and torment of being at sea not for your captain, not for the sake of the crew, but for your own self. Once the fuss of me being aboard calmed down, he told me stories, but the only ones he knew fell out of his own life. He'd been a navy man once, he told me, pressed near the docks, sea-legs giving him away. When he argued, a midshipman not half his height whacked him on the head. Good blow to the head can be quite useful.

His face had gone all lumpy with flesh and skin, though 'lumpy' hardly be the best word, all of a cause that lumps hardly live. These did. They grew and they twitched, and sometimes I'd be awake – he'd slung me a wooden hammock in his quarters, a hanging crib, to keep me safe – I'd be awake, slush lamp burning away, watching him sleep. The lumps suffered little fits of their own, independent of the rest of him. The fits often woke him up. He'd got this truly spectacular lump just left of his nose, and the bloat of it ate up that side of his face. His right eye bulged right out his head, droopy like an old pap. I figured that eye would slip free of its socket any minute. And if that eye deserted, I'd have asked to peek in the hole.

Likely just another lump waiting in there.

Decline, right? Man and ship. Easy enough to deny, and he helped the denial along with the proper good pay. He could do that, writing up all profits and losses in his own ink. He liked to please the devils he knew, because he feared what new men would steal from him. Old hands, the lot of them working *Bonaventure Walters*.

It got rainy the night I came on board *Bon Wally*. Galls me still. That raggedy-eared dog-fucker, Ned Coltman. Soon as he could, he crammed me and his ditty bag deep into his big sea chest, and locked it. I nearly smothered in there, sucking at canvas and wood. I could trust Coltman, aye, trust him to choke and bugger me. Captain Walters caught him at it early on, out to sea, and warned Coltman he'd ruin me as surely as he'd ruin a dog by beating it too much.

Walters, I loved the way he talked, even just the sound of his voice. I did. I loved him, the way a drowning man loves a floating plank. No, Lieutenant, tis important, and if you wish to learn a single half-fact about that lost God damned gold and how you and me came to be sitting here, then you will listen. Tis you who did beg me to tell, you'll recall.

Atthey told me about the night I came on board, Captain Walters yarring like it would cure him.

'Stow the salt pork with the purser, no stow the purser, Atthey get that canvas rolled. Sail boy? God, Gabriel and Saint Peter, not this voyage, we only go to Christiania, for to lay in lumber and tin. Tennant, bring me the manifest before – Clinch, when – Jesus, stop stumbling, or I'll cuff ya up to London, the stink – Morris. Morris! Grimes, Tennant wants to discuss the victuals with you. Pass the word for Morris. Devil-sent carpenter, he'll ruin me missed nail by missed nail. For want of a nail – Morris, I tell you again, repair the damned rung. Body will kill himself climbing down that demented companionway. For the love of God, Gabriel and Saint Peter, men, I know tis dark, but which of ye let the whores on board? Get! Coltman, come aboard at last, have ya? God forbid we attempt to sail without the charms of Ned Coltman. Stow that ditty bag below and haul arse back up on deck before I find a reason to slice off your other ear and make you a present of a matched set. Aye, Rattlebags, what now? Finch the coffee-merchant desires a word with me? Now? Tell that rotten begone peddler to – has he? Devil take him. Atthey, I've not got one fraction of a moment for your worry. Finch, Japheth Finch, coffee-merchant, merchant of coffee. At your service. A delight to see you again, good as fire at night, especially when neither of us owes the other. Norway, I'm bound, Christiania, bit of tin, bit of lumber, got the buyers all queued up and wound round the corner. No, not one coffee bean in sight. Short-shipped ten pounds? Sweet profit there. A merchant of your

88

standing? Now what man would be so foolish as to try and cheat the likes of Japheth Finch? Aye, Coltman with part the ear gone, he ships with me, calls me captain. Look now, what me men get at ashore be their own concern, not mine, not yours. A linkboy led you past an alley – Finch, set me straight. Since when be buggery a moral quake for you? That whore, Jane Wilkes, will not – aye, Jane does be very sweet, and pretty, finest mouth of many, and I hear she'll flog if that be your taste, but then you never did join the navy. Be that as – I imply naught, Finch. I state outright. Oh, bugger the linkboy. Dozens more like him spawned daily. Sneaking glymjacks be not worth the blood they tax off their mothers comin into the world. No doubt he took a fright, if twas his first time, maybe cried and then cherished a new rubbing-knot in his heart because he suddenly enjoys the ancient risk of his profession. My men's shore leave has precisely what to do with coffee? Outraged at me wilful blindness? Ten pounds short-shipped, I'd be outraged, too. Ah, Morris, my cherished carpenter, come join this happy parley with Finch. I be aware we got no coffee on board. I be just explaining to Finch the waste, the almost tragic and heart-rending waste, tragic if not so common, of men left unemployed – Atthey, fix not your pissburnt eyes on me, or I'll see you sewed up in your own sailcloth still alive! Finch, do you not agree? Why take on new men when the old work twice as hard in fear of an empty belly and solitude in the cold? Other commanders must go a-beggin to take out a bummary on their vessels, bitter mortgages, never paid for mounting interest. Aye, other masters must go a-beggin, sir, while I might sheathe my ship's pretty bum in gold. But lead must suffice when tis all the market can bear. One day I shall quit this toil and freely spend my age in comfort. Tis just south of destiny. So might you. Comfort of jingling coins. Will that conclude our business tonight, Japheth Finch, coffee-merchant and merchant of coffee? Mistaken, aye, no doubt, light being tricky and shadows being deep. Do keep hold of your health – tangled in the what, now? Rattlebags, help Finch remove himself from the course lines. And why do they lie slack and not made up? Get them neat round the belaying pins. Every time Finch comes on board… aye, my best to your missus, too. And Jane. Godspeed, God be with you, good riddance. Bloodless poxwalker, mind crumbled, gone to arsenic. Coltman! For peace and pity's sake, stop buggering boys in the street. Boatswain. Boatswain! What name did his mother steal for him? Boatswain, see to the lines. Rattlebags, make us ready. I want us taking departure within the hour, free of trouble, full and by. The boatswain, his name slipping me like that?'

Christopher Atthey found me and later on loaned me his name. No man on board called *him* 'Kit.' Besides, we already carried a 'Ki,' Ezekiah Rattlebags. Tis just as well Atthey remained Atthey so I might be Kit. I figured out pretty quick I needed to throw 'Ann' overboard.

Named or not, I nearly did go overboard myself, as Atthey told it. 'Secrets crack like the wood of a ship surrounding them,' he said. All of a cause that Coltman glowed smug longer than usual after shore, Atthey set to looking. Coltman's sea-chest being tucked well beyond the reach of a slush lamp, Atthey missed it twice, even on his determined walkthroughs.

I loved Christopher Atthey, too, but I did not recognize that for a long time. Atthey wanted to watch over me, but I got afraid. Because Pike got killed all of a cause of watching over me. So I strangled my good feelings. Pike said my mother strangled her other infants, she being a whore and babies being a nuisance, but not me. Never me. I got no memory of her.

Secrets, then. Atthey and Rattlebags sought out any happy secret Coltman might have tucked away for later that could only harden into trouble. Another walkthrough, dodging hammocks and sleeping shipmates – sleeping good as death at sea, deaf to all but bells. They respected Atthey on *Bonaventure Walters*. He'd sailed with Walters ten years, and with other masters many years before that, and he lost no strength to his white hairs. He'd stop fights, jump right in, if one of his sharp looks didn't work first. Years of receiving strange confidences on night watches – Atthey decided he knew men nearly as well as God Himself. And he knew that ship.

I must tell you his prayer: God grant me a full belly and dull voyage.

Atthey heard me sucking air at the sea-chest hinge and mollyrigged open the lock. I'd not got much struggle left in me when Atthey moved that lid. Blue at the lips, he told me, fists clenched right up to my face, rest of me curled up tight as a burnt corpse. Ever seen such a thing? A man burnt to death looks like he's fighting, or ducking a blow.

I remember sucking fresh air, dragging it into myself. Thought I'd drown. My broken finger pained hard and my arse and jaws ached for days. But once I got the air in, I fought in Atthey's arms, even when I saw his two whole ears. He set me down at the companionway, and I climbed it like a monkey. On deck then, overcast and dull, I had to shut my eyes, even that dim light too much. My hips and knees bent and swayed, right easy, like some dance revealed itself in my blood. A man said 'Jesus' like Pike did just before he died. Someone else, not Coltman, said 'What in hell be that pretty thing at here?' Another one called my mouth very sweet. I smelled the pitch still on my fingers, and I got my eyes open. We stood stern. Coltman and another man stood fore, backs to us. Two masts, square-rigged, bowsprit pointing well above the horizon and then smacking down off the waves. Men keeping right still as they tried to decide if they saw me or not.

Atthey spoke then, his voice rough, like he'd drunk broken glass. He stuttered, too, had a hard time with it, agonies on C, K, G and W, though he usually spoke fluent to me. I will not mimic him. He asked which of them saw me dragged aboard, and his disgust scared me all of a cause I thought he aimed it at me. I stepped away from him, but I could hardly decide where to stand, all these lines and pins and men not a pace away, and the wind cutting right through me. I shook.

Atthey cut the meat even smaller. 'Out with it. Which of ye knew the secret boy?'

Coltman, they all muttered, only Coltman'd be so dirty. Discussion, too, of night and fog and the captain's fierce hurry to leave.

Rattlebags, officer of the watch, emerged up the companionway. Hair like frayed rope, he had, though some of it curled. Dark blue eyes, too, not the least touch cold. This Rattlebags looked at me, and I looked at him, and then he looked to Atthey, who scowled so great I feared him more. Rattlebags did be the first mate, but Atthey gave the order.

'Captain must be told. At once. And you be the man to do it.'

Rattlebags cursed.

Years later Con Pilgrim told me how Moses likely stammered and needed his Aaron to speak for him. At first I couldn't see how this Aaron would know what Moses needed to say. I expect if Pilgrim did sit with us now, and I fell mute, he could speak to you my mind.

Ever see a butcher's yard? The guts out back, all the waste and blood and sawdust? A particular worm thrives there. It leaps, sir, being six to eight inches, leaps and dives into the newer muck, eats its fill, leaps again. My heart be that butcher's yard.

Truly, you'd not refuse me a drink? Look at me.

I thank you for your assistance, Mr Kelly.

Some of them talking of me, some of them talking of anything else, those brave men of *Bonaventure Walters* carried on with their duties whilst I, under the escort of Rattlebags, travelled below to see the captain.

Compact little thing, *Bon Wally*. Collier, first, so all square-bummed, which cramped up the captain's cabin, though it did be still all luxury compared to the men's quarters. Rattlebags had to rap the door pretty hard and then beg the captain's pardon at least a dozen times. And my first glimpse of that poxy bloat-king nearly set in stone my belief that monsters sailed the seas. His first glimpse of me likely sparked the thought that linkboys were vermin that walked upright and plagued men. Given that linkboys be poorly thought of, and given that I stood totally uninvited and most unwanted in his private quarters, he should have demanded I disappear. I dare say he wished to.

Instead, he rubbed his forehead and his jaw, nerve pain shooting up and down his face, and sighed. 'Rattlebags, what in the name of God, Gabriel and Saint Peter have ya got there?'

'A boy, sir,' said the loyal Rattlebags.

'And how are we supposed to feed a boy? Do you know what the purser will be after saying to me, the whining about tallies and totals I got to put up with now? For the whole blessed voyage?'

'Aye, sir,' said careful Rattlebags.

'Do you think Finch's pawky fuss meant something?'

'I wouldn't know, sir, for the noise he made,' said honest Rattlebags.

'How did he get aboard? Hey? Answer me that, Rattlebags.'

I answered him. 'In a ditty-bag, sir.'

Neither of them knew what to say to that. After a moment's thought, they both ordered me to speak up. Then they both ordered me be silent. Finally, Captain Walters buttoned his greatcoat – warmest thing I ever saw, all the proper wool and the big collar, worth a fortune – and ordered us back on deck, he to follow. We ganged along, Walters slipping on the companionway and cursing the carpenter, until we stood once more in open air and dull daylight. Coltman by now stood stiff and innocent as the mast.

Captain Walters skipped formalities and beginnings and just bawled it out. 'Did not one of ye hear the noise? See that ditty-bag squirm?'

Mumbles of 'No, sir,' 'No, captain,' Coltman mumbling loudest of all. He spoke like an honest man. His little gift, that. He even feigned concern when looking me up and down, and then he gave me a nod and a wink as though trying to cheer me up.

Try to hold both these ideas in your head at once, for tis like balancing a scale without touching it. This man murdered, buggered and abducted all in the one evening, most likely planning a second casual and tidying-up murder, and yet he smiled so handsomely, shone with the angels' own innocence. Truth split for me there. I knew what he'd done, yet I also knew he'd done naught. I knew what pained me, and I also knew naught could possibly pain me.

So Atthey the sailmaker bound up my broken finger and got me some warm clothes. Right quick about it, too, big needle tearing through canvas and even a few scraps of wool. Needle and palm. First lesson for me: how to sew up canvas. Seeing that, Walters told Atthey he'd got his wish, got his sail-boy after all.

Except I didn't piss in the lee. Not about to piss in a scupper, either. Atthey noticed that right quick and gave me orders not to hide below each and every time nature tickled me. Then he stopped, and not because his speech got stogged. He guessed. Rattlebags figured it out next. I doubt Coltman ever did, doubt he cared: a hole is a hole. Rattlebags and Atthey, though, right exasperated with me, then pitying me. I caught Rattlebags asking Atthey 'Well, Jesus, now what do we do?'

I cared naught for this debate. I needed to layer my heart with leather, the way Atthey leathered his palms to protect them from the driving needle. Besides, I ate three times a day on *Bon Wally*, and Rattlebags and Atthey slipped me biscuit to keep in my pockets. Slept warm, too, wooden box opened up and rigged like a hammock, little crib in the captain's cabin. He tucked blankets round me sometimes.

So I became Kit. The captain's kitten.

Eyes nearly gone, Captain Walters would lean on me, and I'd count out the paces of his own ship – eight, nine, turn left – me quite content to burrow into my new work. But that troublesome and loving old sailmaker would not lie down and be content. I expect Atthey hoped for a few more men to join him and Rattlebags, hoped for a true council of war. He tried his best.

I'd not long come off watch, being much used as a messenger and general scutboy – ever try to clean a slush lamp? Free a while, and beat out, I made my crib ready quietly so's not to wake the captain, who slept a lot but never very well. A heavy knock on the door made us both sigh, and in shuffled Atthey and Rattlebags, for once not studying the floor before looking full on the captain. Pale Rattlebags suddenly could not speak, and he widened his eyes at Atthey in dumbshow. Aye, make the man who stutters break the silence. Walters ordered them take their stares elsewhere, preferably overboard. That caused Rattlebags to clear this throat, but it was Atthey who spoke. As he formed his first word, carefully, he lifted his right foot and pointed his toes, like a drum-major on parade. Then he kedged his other foot into line with the first. Walters giggled at that. A dreadful noise. More and more he laughed like a youngster caught tormenting a cat. Then he leant on me, big hand right heavy.

Walters told them to speak freely, and Atthey drew a deep breath. And stuttered. Walters wondered out loud if Atthey might ever speak freely, and the sailmaker hissed at that. Rattlebags giggled then, just like Walters, and I hated him for it. Finally, Atthey stood as tall as he could at sea and eventually said 'We be concerned about the kitten, sir.'

Captain Walters rolled his eyes, a jelly-sight. He said 'As I've already promised ye both, we shall return this little Kit to the Bristol docks when we ourselves, ship and all, return to the Bristol docks.'

Atthey spat. 'And when will that be?'

'Plot our course,' said Captain Walters, all easy benevolence. 'But oh, I forget you be no artist, Atthey, no literate navigator: Christopher Atthey, his mark. Mr Rattlebags can plot and navigate. He knows the course. Mr Rattlebags, tell Mr Atthey roughly when we expect to put in at Bristol.'

Rattlebags shifted his weight, a stupid and disastrous move that pitched him headlong for the captain's bolted-down desk. He broke his fall with his face, quite deliberately, I believe. When he landed at my feet, this great long splinter pierced his cheek, but his hands, curled up right close to his face – well, he had to protect his hands. We all waited calmly, knees and hips bending with the swell, while Rattlebags righted himself and worked the splinter out of his face. The canvas snapped in luff, and we rolled hard, causing Rattlebags to yell 'Dowse, dowse, ye fools.' He tugged out that splinter, and I wonder now at the roughness of that deck. Did Walters allow no holystone? Rattlebags held the splinter against the dull window's scant light, studied the bits of his flesh stuck to it, and then flicked the thing away. 'Bristol,' he said, 'does be a way's off yet.'

Atthey said 'Kitten'll be a rock round our necks in Bristol. By Jesus, Walters, I promise you that murdering pirates execute the man who steals a brat and hauls him to sea. Yet we stand here all an act.'

'Hardly pirates,' said Captain Walters, 'just men of business. Civilized men of business with cargo due. And what's there been of uncivilized behaviour here? In this room?'

Atthey flushed a dark red beneath old sunburns. 'Not you, sir. But Kit, Kit, you see, tis no simple matter of – you know. You *know*.'

'What I know, Atthey,' said Captain Walters, 'is this: the kitten first appeared – as far as I'm concerned was birthed – some days ago. Should there be a man in Bristol who cares – rare man, rare man – that this dockside linkboy tripped aboard a departing merchantman – for all we know, ran loose off his proper master and stowed away – '

'Forced on board,' Atthey snapped, quite fluent. 'And we got to see Coltman answers for that.'

But Walters easily spoke over him. 'For all we know, stowed away, then I shall buy the man who cares about Kit – or Coltman – a mug of strong ale and see he gets to toast his cloven hooves at the fireside, for, mark me, Atthey, no such man exists. And we still got cargo due.'

Atthey talked back to the captain like never before. 'So keep watch and tend the rigging, for all be well?'

Before Walters could answer, I tugged straight the canvas jacket Atthey'd made for me and said 'Be no matter I stay on board.'

Not one of them made me an answer.

I figured they'd not heard me, so I said it again. 'Be no matter I stay on board, being already here and working hard as the rest of ye. I be alone, none left on land worrying. So tis no matter. Not even to you, Mr Atthey.'

The poor mender took a step back at that. At quite some risk, he'd gathered courage for both Rattlebags and himself to confront the captain, even though such deviance sank ships. I frightened Atthey, he told me later, not just with my plain words, but with my calm face and feverish eyes. My words and face said one thing, my posture and eyes another, and he could no more understand me than he could a man screaming into the wind.

Rattlebags shuffled toward the door, touching Atthey's arm to guide him away, but Atthey threw his final weapon.

'Ask your kitten why he dunna piss in the lee!'

I stared down his hard betrayal, hating him.

Captain Walters gave this naked declaration a little thought, his voice quiet and soft when he finally spoke. 'Boy, girl, devil or Christ-child, my answer remains. This be a merchantman, not a coach-and six. Resume your duties.'

Atthey tried so hard to answer that his face screwed up on one side, and he made noises like a trapped rat. Walters, pretending first to look at something important on his desk, peeked up at Rattlebags and grinned. 'Listen to him. He'll be telling me how to sail me ship next. Ye pair of besotted fools, fretting over a docksider squeezed out some slut gone bald for the lues. Atthey, my man, do you live?'

'I will, sir,' Atthey finally got out.

'Will, what?'

'Tell you how to sail your ship, sir. When necessary.'

Captain Walters' fist smashed Atthey's nose just as fast as Robbie Pike used to tap a skull. 'You, Mr Atthey,' said Walters, 'you with your pissburnt eyes and your crippled tongue, you will tell me how?' Walters struck Atthey at the base of his neck then, and the mender crumpled to his knees, blood leaking between the fingers of his cupped hands. 'You, some holy fool of a sail-maker, can tell me naught, naught of any worth in this world, for the tale be only as strong as the teller.' Now Walters boxed his ears and kicked him. 'Here, a black windrose for your ribs, and here be black pence for your eyes!' Out of breath, Walters quelled. Then he helped Atthey sit up so he'd not choke on his own blood. 'Sway starboard,' he told Atthey, 'easy, easy. English oak, you be. Take my word: when time and tide permit, all will be made right.'

I stayed behind Captain Walters that time, for he did not touch my shoulder and signal me to count the paces. No, I remained in that ugly place, trying to help Rattlebags get Atthey to his feet. Atthey shook us both off.

Game and prize revealed in my standing around, Coltman said naught of the new sail-boy, certainly said naught to me, just looked. Hard, smirking. So much can be forgiven an able seaman, and by God, Coltman could probably sail *Bon Wally* by himself. Even Atthey said I could learn much seamanship from Coltman, just not safely. Atthey warned of something else, too, the truth in that warning all tucked in and bigger than one little merchantman.

'Now that you be numbered amongst us, Coltman will be more choosy, if not outright careful for once. Aye, we all know what he gets at with boys, just as we all know the colour of the hairs on one another's balls. Canna escape much at sea, little kitten. So look behind you. In any dark spot might hide one who'd do you harm. We got a few dark spots on board *Bon Wally*. But you need to watch on deck, too. Scattered man's got the fear ripped out of him, and he, your true enemy, will strike and wreck you in broad fucking daylight. Conny me, Kit? Understand? Daylight, hiding so close you might spit on him. He be the enemy of all of us on board, too, because the captain dunna see him. So he takes what pleases him, knowing the captain dunna see.'

The most of that made no sense to me at all, and I admitted so, but Atthey refused to explain any further. Quicker than squalls, he tied a bowline in a short length of gasket rope and waited for me to do the same. Bloody knots. Pilgrim can tie the most beautiful ones, all purpose and strength, but I need to think through the simple bowline. Atthey so patient with me: 'Learn the bowline, and you'll need no other knot.' Took me weeks to learn to tie a bowline.

The same day Atthey warned me about dark spots and daylight, I asked for a knife.

He laughed. 'So you might add murder to your sins?'

'So I might be safe,' I said. Then I grabbed his words. 'Safe from one who would strike me in daylight.'

'Nicely looped. No.'

'I'll be safer.'

'You'll only feel safer.'

But the first time I tied the dog-fucking bowline proper, Mr Atthey have me a knife with a gorgeous black handle to it. He said

97

it came from a far-off land. And then he and Rattlebags showed me how to use it, a little slashing dance. Oh, Coltman got nervous, seeing that. I slept better, knife beneath my head. On watch, I hung it down my shirt off a smart lanyard Atthey'd made for me.

The storm got us about two days outside Christiania. Coltman, God's born sailor, smelled the coming roughery before anyone else. I knew about bad weather – on land. Good as naked to the wind some nights, but at least the ground beneath me kept still. Usually cold on *Bon Wally*, but that night I got the proper bone-rotting chills while still abed. My feet were like numb stumps. Couldn't feel the deck beneath them as I counted the paces for Walters. Little pockets of air hit us, mad weather gods, some warm, some cool, and one, I swear, mad hot. All slapping rain and hard wind on deck. Captain Walters could not even hear me count. The men looked like walruses, all wrapped up, but they moved with the tidy speed of little hard bugs. Rattlebags screeched orders in the helmsman's ear, almost kissing him to do it. The wind tore it all up. Atthey, Coltman and two others had gotten aloft and furled canvas, but the canvas fought back. (When Con Pilgrim told me the story of Jacob wrestling with the angel, I saw angels made of sailcloth.) Meantime the jibsails and lines flapped and snapped, soaked, fit to flay the hide off a live bull. Then Coltman lost his grip. He'd got the other hand tight round a gasket, but that gasket did not fully bind the sail. It only wrapped round part way and ended loose. I thought that dog-fucker would fall and shatter, and his brains and guts would make the deck even more slippery. Ned Coltman, nuisance to the last. But Atthey caught him. Steadied him enough so he could fling his loose arm over the spar and haul himself back to the footlines.

But the jibsails. I'd been sent out the bowsprit on steady days, and I knew how to furl. I glanced behind me: Rattlebags shouted and Captain Walters paced about, grabbing hold of lines as if he could see them. Catching Atthey's eye, and Coltman's, I lurched and squat down, hands and feet suddenly on fire, the feeling back. I crept up to the bowsprit. Danger's bliss.

Of course I fell. Jesus, Lieutenant, did you not hear me say 'storm'?

Atthey caught me, by the clothes and by the hair, his second rescue that night. He screamed right in my ear about being a stupid whelp, and what good was a knife when I threw myself at death?

We both fell against the fiferail, me smacking my head off a belaying pin. The last of the daylight gave in. The rain changed to sleet then, and snow, even as it fell. Far colder than ice, those waves gashing the deck. Hills and mountains of salt water, plains and valleys. Rattlebags at the helm now, we yawed hard, starboard gunwales kissing the ravenous water. The boatswain tried to drag me to the charthouse, but we pitched again, and I slid away. Then Coltman took the helm, and Rattlebags, weeping and cursing, bawled at the captain, who screamed back, gesturing at the empty space near his right hand, the space where I should have been. Rattlebags sighted me then, crouched low, and dragged me to the charthouse.

'Too thinly dressed for heavy weather,' he shouted. 'Stay here.'

Lamplight danced as I tried to keep my balance and decipher the weighted-down charts. All squiggles and lines to me then, incomprehensible art, only the krakens and the four winds making the least bit of sense. I curled myself into a little ball in a corner.

The storm eased. I returned to the deck. Colder breezes now, much colder, and the water looked beaten smooth. The clouds raced, and ice chunks bobbed. Atthey, helmsman now, eased us back on course. The carpenter nursed two broken fingers, and I bound them the way Atthey had tied mine. The carpenter healed up fine, after. Captain Walters stood fore with Rattlebags, inspecting damage. The boatswain leaned on the charthouse wall, cheeks green and lips blue. A rough time. But Coltman, ha, he took my shoulder like the captain did and leaned down so I could not shrug him off or escape his speech.

'I promised to teach you plaindealing. Recall that? This storm tonight, I should have died, should have pitched headlong from the mainmast to die at your feet. But Atthey saved me. Think on it, little kitten. I did not die tonight for the same reason I found and took you.' Rattlebags sighted Coltman talking to me, frowned and strode toward us. Coltman lifted his hand from me. 'Meant to be,' he said, giving me the nod and the wink and then tending to a loose line. I'd completely forgotten my lanyard and knife.

Atthey called me over. Smiling but breathing hard, he nodded toward the sails, all rounded out in the wind. 'Full and by, Kit, full and by. Graceful canvas, no luff, no shiver. Unlike you. Afraid now, with the storm over? No shame in it. Be plenty of men afraid of a storm. Be shaking all over myself, save I've got the wheel. See Morris there, got that fine tremble? Poor bastard's in pain, too.

Nice work, your binding his fingers; I saw that. Rattlebags and the boatswain, see how they cross their arms? That's for the fear they forgot to feel. Best cure for storms, this is, sailing full and by, when God in His grace allows. Feel those winds? Naught else like those fair beating winds after roughery. Fit to lift you up like some little bird. A kittiwake, you, the smallest one but hunting the furthest out to sea. On fair beating winds. I promise you, we'll die a dry death yet.'

Atthey died the following forenoon watch. Starboard bow, he stood, skin the colour of a seagull's wing or fog late in the day. I was aft, for he'd set me to practice my stitching and bowlines, and I oozed catarrh. He stopped. Just stopped. Then his mouth hitched up on the right, like he'd gotten stuck on a word, and he took three steps sidewise. Those three steps, no good dance. I stood up and drew breath to call Rattlebags, who worked at fixing the mainmast. Atthey fell. Over the side. I ran fore and got to the bow in time to see Atthey's descent. Atthey, living still, paddled but quickly lost his strength. He sank feet first, eyes up, hands curled near his shoulders as though ready to hoist himself over a spar. Ice chunks keeled deep, and Atthey's body caught on one and then slipped below.

Passing ancient rocks and more conifers than the men of England got hairs on their heads, we made Christiania the following night. Much like coming at Newfoundland. Rattlebags asked permission to scandalize the rigging and thereby show we mourned. Captain Walters assented so quickly that his words got tangled up. The cargo kept us busy, and I had to help lift on top of running messages, *Bon Wally* being short good as two hands with the carpenter's fingers fresh broke.

I hardly believe I've spoke all this to you when I've told no other man of Coltman. Not even our shared employer, though that canny owl likely guessed.

Ned Coltman caught me staring at the Christiania docks there maybe our third day. He leaned close and asked if I wanted to starve on a foreign street or pay little fees for the privilege of staying on board. I said naught to that dog-fucker. Rattlebags intervened; he often did. Soon Rattlebags set me half a dozen long tasks, all a way of keeping me close by.

'I failed Atthey,' he said to me.

As we took departure from Norway, Rattlebags set me to counting ice-strays. He said, 'Can't help thinking some great berg mourns her wandered strays.' He taught me my letters that voyage back, and if I did a lesson well, he'd tell me a story. Don't remember most of them. One night he told a story about names. 'Be calling you just Kit from now on,' he began. 'Kit from Christopher. Aye, thought that might please you. You'll find much power in names, Kit, and loss, and foolishness. My surname, Rattlebags, be bad enough, but my Christian name before it sounds like a mistake: Ezekiah. My poor mother, what was she thinking? Never get lost in a crowd now, will I, straggle-headed Ki Rattlebags? I hope the boatswain in the story remembers to call me by name. He hardly bothers with a name, just calls. And one mustn't miss his call. Tis a story I heard a long time ago. Ancient days, now.

'Sailor man, he's got a few scarce hours to call his own, and he spends them crawling along a strange shore, his ship putting in for water. And his ship's well in sight, so he relaxes, for the vigilance and the watches have worn him out. Seashells in easy sight, too, all pearly rainbows, just begging him to pick them up and warm them in his hands. The sun beats down on our sailor man, but a fair breeze tempers the heat. He picks up more of the shells, and some shiny rocks, and a piece of driftwood. Sailor-man gets desperate. He wants to steal all those shells and rocks and stray wood from that sunlit beach, stuff it all under his clothes and haul it aboard, but he knows, you see, he *knows* that once he snatches the pretty things from the beach he'll never see their colours again. Already the sun's dried the rocks he took, and they're gone dull. He brings his spilling handfuls up to his face but nearly drops them, because all he can smell is the death of what once lived. And his ship's ready to depart. Sailor-man, he's all taken by his pretty things like they was wife and children. Boatswain calls, calls him by name, threatens to tie his arms and legs and bundle him aboard like a sheep, because the ship needs him.'

Rattlebags tucked loose hair behind his ears, and I asked him what the sailor-man did.

'Story never says,' Rattlebags told me. 'Frightens me sometimes, like the nennorluk tales.'

Lieutenant, I must ask your assistance again. Explanations dry me out.

Truly, I thank you.

Know you the nennorluk? It comes from these waters, just further north. 'The nennorluk,' Rattlebags told me, 'is worse than

101

the kraken. I know, because a Labrador Eskimo once told me of it. Some Englishman befriended him and taught him proper language, persuaded him to cross the sea and be a living prize of brave exploration. The Englishman died of the bloody flux not a week out. How many ways at all can a man die at sea? So this Labrador man, he landed in Plymouth, speaking some English. The rest of his story he drew. Could make some fine sketches, that man. Black eyes. Black hair down to his waist, beautiful as a woman's. Cheekbones like an adze. Told me of the nennorluk in words and pictures. His own father saw it. The thing surfaced, shedding ice pans and rolling a berg. (Harsh voice, the nennorluk has, worse than thunder, and when the Labrador man made the noise for me, the other men in the tavern called him a devil.) Spreading the folds in its skin out, like sails, it climbed up to the shore. Think on it, Kit: it walks the sea-bottom til it comes ashore to eat men. Fast as fire, the Labrador man said, faster than their white bears. When the Eskimos first saw the Spaniards' sails, they thought the nennorluk had come.

'Two moons, your eyes. Nennorluk, oh my, tis the likes of the foolishness I'd burn Atthey's patience with. He'd get all angry and sneer at me, tell me I both thought too much and not enough. Did I tell you my dream about going home? I hate it, and I keep trying to change it, but it always ends the same. I'd got a long shore leave, so I walked days and days to my parents' house. Gone, they were. Moved, lost, dead? No one knew, and I knew no one. I could walk through that house with my eyes closed, yet no one remembered the name Rattlebags. And I had to turn round and walk back to my ship.'

Some four days passed before he told me another story.

Bon Wally and her first mate learnt me good lessons. How to hide right where people think they can see, how to listen, how to furl and how to climb. Captain Walters said I looked like a ferret, slipping in and out of sight, only I'd got more teeth. 'Slowly, Kit. A man'd think the devil himself stalked you, hooves scraping the floor and tail hissing through the dust.'

I learnt to be useful, so that by our return to Bristol, neither Walters nor Rattlebags would wish to see me go. Solo glymjacking be risky. I'd be ate in no time, the likes of Coltman not near rare enough. Like the hunting animals, they are, all with slightly different appetites, and God didn't see fit to give them a smell. But three meals a day and a blind captain needing his own glymjack? I sailed with them almost two years. Crew changed, but Walters, Rattlebags, Coltman and I remained. After Christiania, we returned to Bristol, traded cargo, and set for Harbour Grace, Newfoundland.

Walters got blinder, and Rattlebags quietly commanded that ship. We pretended not to notice. I often caught Rattlebags praying in the starboard bow. He didn't look like he prayed, standing there with his hands crammed in his pockets, but as *Bon Wally* and the swell danced him, he muttered questions at the sky. So I took to listening. Not that tis always easy to hear a private conversation on deck, but Rattlebags needed to hear his own words, so now he spoke them clear. He called himself a proud dissenter cursed with questions, asked about heavy cargo and why he deserved it. He never asked God to solve the problem of the cargo, whatever twas, but submitted to it, saying 'Tis Thy plan and Thy need. But please, tell me why.'

Captain Walters got a bit touched there towards the end, no question, but Rattlebags had the harder time of it. Walters kept thinking we all wanted to disobey him. He could hardly stay awake, let alone stand upright. He left navigation and command more and more to Rattlebags, but poor Rattlebags needed to sleep, too. Coltman helped, but Coltman could not read a chart. I could; Rattlebags had seen to that. One day Rattlebags got feverish, and by the next watch he lay splayed out with the flux. Captain Walters stumped on deck, and he didn't know whether to yarr or lead. All he wanted was to sleep.

We veered off course in no time. I made frequent excuse to leave the deck – muttering about flux and having shared some scrap off Rattlebags' plate – to sneak a study of the charts. We'd deviated badly. The water offered no check, no guidance, and the helmsman obeyed the captain. Rattlebags felt it, felt *Bon Wally* strain and shift. He tried to get out of his hammock and come on deck, but he fell and cut his face again, other cheek this time. He'd got himself part way to the charthouse when I met him.

'Tell captain I beg a word.'

After much persuasion, I got Walters below. By now Rattlebags had made the charthouse. Dizzy, squinting, and newly sharp-boned in the slush lamp's greasy light, Rattlebags begged for answers. 'Sir, why did we change course?'

'We've done no such thing,' said Captain Walters.

Rattlebags looked to me, and I nodded, right subtle, but Captain Walters, still touching my shoulder, felt the movement. 'Kit, what be this, collusion? Rattlebags, get back to your hammock.'

'Aye, sir, hammock,' said Rattlebags, first glancing at the chart notes. He read the plotted course to the captain and asked if we sailed it.

'I just told you we sail it,' said Captain Walters. 'Now get below.'

Rattlebags returned to his hammock, and Captain Walters and I got back on deck. Not too long after, Rattlebags peered out the charthouse. I lied to Captain Walters about some foolishness Coltman did not commit, for a change, and Walters strode fore, ready to lace into him. I figured that would keep them both busy and leave Rattlebags the room to whisper corrections to the helmsman. But Walters turned his path in the bow and wound back toward the helm on the larboard side, standing a moment directly between Rattlebags and the charthouse. The wind, crooked that night, changing in gusts and then changing back, carried the sick-smell from Rattlebags to Walters.

'Mr Rattlebags,' said the captain.

Oh, that bitter honourific. Each man on *Bon Wally* knew the boom fell when Walters mocked them with 'Mr.'

'Mr Rattlebags,' the captain said again, 'be there some trouble with the course I set?'

Sighing, Rattlebags answered no.

'Be there something wrong below to force you up here then, against my orders?'

'Only this, sir: the charts lie askew. One of the rocks weighting a corner slipped. I advised the helmsman as you looked busy fore.'

'I smell shit and lies,' said Captain Walters. 'Will *you* now tell me how to sail my ship?'

None of us looked at Walters and Rattlebags, not directly. The captain's face-lumps flushed dark red, and he took a ragged breath. I did not want Rattlebags to be English oak, like Atthey. I wanted him to strike some sense into the old fool, but I knew he must take the blows. A shame it needed to be done before the men.

Rattlebags answered 'No, sir.'

'So get below.'

Rattlebags tried again to tell the captain we needed to change course, but Walters just repeated his order and then he called an order to empty rigging. Coltman had come aft, and he caught Rattlebags' eye. The boatswain at the helm, too, observed the silent exchange. And Rattlebags stumbled below, too shaky to walk right.

Walters ordered me to fetch gasket ropes from the boatswain's locker – oh aye, my favourite spot on board. Dark down there. Coltman heard Walters and darted below through the charthouse, taken with belly cramps, he said. Orders being orders, I made my descent, nearly gagging with dread of it. Some days I wished Coltman would just use me quick and honest, spare me the waiting, but that torment did be part of his game. I had great trouble picking up loose gaskets, because one day Coltman had hidden there, knowing I'd soon be along, and grabbed me, sounding like some great big crow. Only a bit of fun, he told everyone after, a bit of skylarking. I knew Captain Walters would get impatient, and as his step neared overhead I grabbed any old loose length and climbed the ladder. By then, Walters had knelt down and stuck his mess of a face into the locker hole, blocking out the light. I cried out and nearly lost hold of the ladder, and he called me twitchy thing. Said 'I shouldn't need to chase after you so, Kit. I tell you, time and again: the devil don't stalk you, for your soul's too small.'

As he gave life to the word 'devil,' I smelt something like burnt blood or salt water set afire. Gust-borne, it passed right quick, but it sickened me.

Captain Walters smoothed my hair and tightened the bit of rope Atthey had used to tie my plait. 'Tis like walking on wool, Kit,' he said. 'I am lost without you. Count paces to my cabin.'

Maybe an hour later, Coltman lowered his spyglass and sniffed. I caught the odour, too, that burning stench again. Fog quick as a dream took us then. Fog at sundown, great long fingers and cliffs of it, hiding us from one another and playing merry hell with our voices.

The men cursed. 'Young eyes,' said Coltman, his voice coming from starboard when last I'd seen him larboard midship. 'Kit, take this.' He pressed his spyglass into my hands and spoke to me as he spoke to the other men, all of a cause he needed my small size for a task more important than his shaking jollies. 'Climb aloft and tell me what you see.'

I slowly climbed the ratlines. I could only see my own hands and feet and the lines I grasped.

Coltman's voice came at me in pieces. 'Speak, for the love of God.'

'I see naught but the fog,' I called down.

Calm water slopped the hull. I wanted Atthey.

Coltman ordered me down out of it and then grabbed me by the ears. He twisted them before I could reach for my knife. Then he bade me listen if I wished to survive the night. 'Get below,' he said, 'and get Rattlebags. Now.'

Childish loyalties and standing orders compelled me to wake the captain instead. He'd been deep asleep, but he climbed the companionway and charged through the charthouse like a whipped horse. 'Morris, the rung! Where be Kit? Ah, Coltman, more foolishness. What mischief drives you to ruin me sleep? What do you see?'

'I see naught, sir,' said Coltman, glaring the promise of a hard smack at me. 'Be what I smell that bothers me.'

Captain Walters snorted hard enough to snot up his chin. 'A clot of squirmin weevils. From what biscuit now did God tap ye lot? Rattlebags suffers visions of skewed charts, and Coltman smells the stink off his own clothes and calls it hazard. What next in this Bedlam pageant, Christ Himself stretched on a spar? Be my kitten the only one of ye with any sense? God damn the lot of us if Kit be the only one who can see.'

The men laughed a bit, nervy. They playacted relief and settled back to work, and they may have convinced themselves all was well, for they did be long practised at such spliced thinking. Walters walked fore, and he disappeared so fast I expected a splash, but he spoke. The fog split and dragged his words down starboard, down larboard until his voice surrounded us. 'As for the smell,' he said, ''tis just trickery of fog. God alone knows what the fog carries in itself. Ghosts and spies and the stink of far-off lands.'

Coltman dug his fingers into my hair. 'Rattlebags,' he ordered me. '*Now.*'

I found him on his knees, sighing, hammock out of reach. I helped him stand, helped him walk, and his lips cracked and bled when he asked me the course. I told him I knew naught of the course at that moment, only that the men on deck worried about a smell.

Rattlebags stopped walking and held my shoulder hard. Then he asked 'Burnt seaweed?'

'Burnt something," I said, tired now, and damp from the fog.

'Sweet Christ Jesus,' said Rattlebags, 'what be the course?'

We sneaked on deck. The fog parted a moment and revealed the boatswain at the helm, sweating freely. Walters stood behind him, quite content, and called the bearing. Rattlebags listened, then tugged me gently so I might help him back to the charthouse. There he retrieved and unrolled a different chart, spreading it over the table and tacking the corners with rocks. 'Latitude,' he muttered, 'latitude, take your departure and sail straight on, never a glance spared for the sky. You proud and poxed-up stunned bastard, you can't see. Christ, for a backstaff and a clear sky. Burning seaweed, God, my God, storms we cannot avoid, but this... fogbound in the Isles of Scilly. Damn you, Walters.'

Captain Walters had entered the charthouse. 'None will damn me, only God. I passed no word for you, Mr Rattlebags.'

Rattlebags stared at the man who could not see him. 'Please, sir, can you not smell the burning kelp? It be a warning, sir. I be afraid –'

Walters mocked him. 'You be afraid?'

'Aye, sir, for I've got the sense to be! God's not deafened you, so listen. Our course hauls us too close to St Mary's and Peter's Rue. The water here hides rocks of the devil's own design. You know this, sir. We must change course. I can plot it, and you can call it, but we must change course.'

Captain Walters spoke about cargo due in Harbour Grace and cargo waiting. Then he reminded Rattlebags how he'd restrained himself but could do it no more. 'You be troublesome, but you be no Atthey. I will beat you down with one blow.'

'Sir,' Rattlebags pleaded, 'alter course!'

Captain Walters had already turned his back, and now he looked over his shoulder, stretching out the word almost past meaning. 'No.'

Bon Wally rocked harder as the winds picked up. On deck, Walters got jovial and told a story about calenture, a fever that struck in great heat. He giggled. 'And the poor man,' he said, 'gazed out on the grey sea, grey as dug-up gravecloth, and he described it all as the most vivid blue. Called it one of the blues God must see when he decides how to paint the sky. He went on about greens, next, green like grass in the brightest sun. Then he got stuck, trying to tell us about a little dimpled sun he'd once held on the palm of his hand. He meant an orange. We dragged him below, tied him to his hammock and spoke gentle words, but he only babbled about colours.'

Rain spattered, and Walters finished his story. 'He strangled himself in his own hammock.'

The captain ordered me below to fetch his greatcoat. I passed Rattlebags, half-asleep on the charthouse floor. I wanted to ask the captain permission to get Rattlebags a drink, but Walters called me to count paces. My eyes, tired and strained, kept seeing little flames on shores not there. A common enough fault of sight on a night-watch, except those flames looked different. I told the captain, and he ordered Coltman to check through his spyglass. Two points off the starboard bow: flames as real as ourselves, and I asked about the burning kelp. Walters and Coltman promised me I'd seen no such thing. I forced myself to believe them, they being more experienced. I swayed a bit on my feet after that, and Captain Walters ordered me below to hop in my crib and sleep. And I slept.

I remember little of the rest. The water roared, or perhaps the nennorluk did. Whatever roared, we just got in the way. I jumped out of my crib into water up to my waist, and rising. I got numb and drifted, trying to swim to the companionway. Somewhere I lost all bearing and spun underwater. I hung off a rock for a while. I remembered Coltman's certainties and made a deal with God.

13) PETER'S RUE

SUMMER 1720, ISLES OF SCILLY, AS TOLD JUNE 1734 TO LIEUTENANT JOHN KELLY, RN, BY CAPTAIN CHRISTOPHER MATTHEW FINN.

Gulls woke me. Crying like that. I felt some heavy weight on top of me and rough sand working into my hair. Sand already up my nose, which burned and burned. Jammed down like a chart, I was, pinned. Waves broke. Hardly afraid. Long past that. Every bit of me hurt, and the more I awoke, the more it hurt. Even just to breathe.

Wrecks no novelty in these waters, those living on Peter's Rue made quick work of the salvage. A gull waddled over the weight on top of me and peered at my face. Not brazen enough to pick and eat, not yet. I took a breath, and the pain of it made me scream. A very salt and dry scream: no one heard it. I rolled my head. The seagull landed on the beach, next to my head. Fish and rot wafted off it. I tried to blow the gull away, but it hopped closer and darted its beak close to my eyes. Feet shuffled on the sand, and a man reached down to shift what pinned me down. The gull flew just beyond reach, patient. Finding me with a moving chest, the man called out 'Live one,' picked me up and hoisted me over his broad shoulder. I spewed and spewed down his back as he slowly climbed, and I took a departure, just like I'd been learnt. Lines and sail all tangled in themselves. Rocks and seabottom and this jagged shore. The charts amply warned us, but we'd made right for it. Women laid out corpses gone graceless and stiff and shooed gulls. I recognized some clothes but no faces, marks of the soul being scoured away by one night.

The man bearing me up the small hill said 'Like as not the one washed over you trapped the warmth what kept you alive.'

God rest Ki Rattlebags.

Gigs skimmed out and around the wreck, and I took my final look at *Bonaventure Walters*. Larboard sundered, starboard cocked, rigging heaped and mast defeated. Beautiful once but violated now, and deserving of it.

I took a fine catarrh in my chest and head out of it, slept, fainted sitting up. A constant fire burnt high, low, and a man muttered complaints about the use of fuel. A woman pressed me back and tucked blankets tight round me, over and over. Broth, gruel, then goat's milk. For days I lay there, scoured and dried out but too numb and too weak to stand. Bored. The woman fed me off a spoon and told me how pleased she was that her dead boy's clothes fit me. I ate, dozed, and tried to speak, to explain, but the salt water had damaged my voice. You can still hear how it's right hoarse. The first time I stayed awake, she studied me, patient but vigilant, too. We met eyes, and I wanted to ask her questions and thank her for the food and clothes and say I was sorry for her dead boy. I think she understood, all of a cause she just patted my knee and said 'Only I tended and saw you.' Then she showed me the little pile of clothes I'd been wearing, complete with the canvas jacket and lanyard and knife. Most pleased to see that knife, and I held out my hands for it, but she passed me the jacket instead. 'Stranger things than you have washed ashore,' she said. 'The others expect you be a boy, and I've not righted them. We see what we expect and want in this world. Otherwise tis all too frightening.'

Christina Foote, her name, an ancient twenty-six. A grand little conspiracy we had going, like a hidden fire. She'd tell her husband, Jem, how I did be weeks away from enough strength to help him with the fishing, why, I'd nearly drowned and had the man no sense? Other women came visiting, and they all cooed and fussed over me, one even reaching out to finger my hair, saying it rolled in a lovely curl and didn't I look just like a girl? I took a coughing fit at that, and Christina chased them all out. Jem, for his part, eyed me like some weird living flotsam and often asked when I might work my keep.

Christina and Jem both stood about middling height. They kissed a fair bit, though Jem sought something from Christina she could not give over. Jem fished, like most of the other men. The islanders collected seaweed, dried it out, then burned it in pits. A man called Hicks owned a ketch, and he would take the ashes to St Mary's and sometimes the mainland. He'd ferried back the only other survivor of the *Bon Wally* wreck. I've heard people curse the Scilly Islanders for ruiners and thieves, but those curses deceive. Aye, they salvaged wreckage. What else can you do when a ship runs aground, especially when no one survives? Those shores chewed wood and bone with equal ease.

Jem Foote wore an odd plait. Christina had woven a black ribbon through his hair. 'Mourning,' he told me, catching me stare at him. 'Seems we're always burying some mother's son. Your lot we buried nice and proper in the high ground, all in together, that great bloated man with the horrible face on top. With the rings on his fingers, we figured he be commander.'

Still I did not speak. Jem harassed Christina about it, and she answered him hard. 'The boy just lost all he knew. I should like to hear you telling poems after so much death.'

Jem made a harsh sound and demanded to know why their boy and the other youngsters on Peter's Rue died after the Bad Salvage, while I survived a wreck that killed all the grown men?

Christina had no answer for that.

As I got better, I took to mending clothes, and then nets. Hoping, at least, that Atthey's distant ghost might be pleased. All my sharp teeth – ahhh, still got most of them, though Martin Sikes knocked loose a few that night in Salem – helped me cut thread and cloth. You need a good few teeth for mending nets and coats. I tried to mend a wig once. Stinking failure. That net I mended for Jem Foote: I made that better than it had ever been, except for in some dream of perfect nets. I sat outside on an upturned bucket, watching Jem and the others come ashore, windburnt and famished. Salt and fish-scales glittered all over them. Jem took the net from me, held it against the sun, called it serviceable. And so I finally earned some keep.

I dreamt far too much on Peter's Rue. Afterward I hardly dreamt at all. Not until we met *Kindly One* off Harbour Grace. I dream again now, vigilance and sweat, a long watch no other can relieve. You nod, Mr Kelly? Then you know I dream of monsters who look like ordinary men?

Early in September, Christina pronounced me fit enough to help unload the gigs. I'd been helping her with the house, and she told me secrets over the washing. Maybe a dozen families had left the larger island of St Mary's for Peter's Rue. The fishing seemed better, and the ground grew bigger vegetables. Her parents and others had rowed over with their children, some still in bellies. Then, one by one, they got sick and died. They blamed the first well. It gave sweet water, but they all got bloodshot eyes, stiff joints, sore guts. They dug three more wells, all reeking of brimstone. That saved the children, who shat out flux and blood and flesh but healed. Their parents languished, wore themselves out, working sick. A few of them got to see their grandchildren. The ones growing up married young, as soon as paps and blood announced themselves, and within a few years the rocks echoed with the racket of infants. Those youngsters suffered bad wind and hard bellies, screeching, drawing up their legs, beating their heads off their mothers' breasts and shoulders, Christina said. But only two of them died, and life on Peter's Rue got sweetly predictable.

A bad wreck came, bodies washing ashore for days, but also crates of beautiful fabrics, lace, candlesticks and wine, pretty things tumbling out of stories about royalty. Most of the youngsters played in the salvage. Kings and queens on the beach that day, lords and ladies, fevers by nightfall and black flux at dawn. All dead in a week. The islanders burnt the fabrics and the crates, buried the candlesticks and wine. No baby got born after that. Some got started, but they only bled out before five months. The Bad Salvage, they called it.

That September, I studied the shore all of a cause I wanted to determine the precise line where the salt water ate the sand so I might imagine a boundary for the nennorluk, should he have crossed the sea. I felt the first crooked winds. Rough weather coming. I slept badly – we all did – waking up a dozen times, dreading the thing that picked its way toward us. See, I knew that, and I knew it different and apart from how I knew mending and compass points.

Voices in the rain. Not children's voices, as we often heard, but strange men's, hoarse and cracked, calling to one another, calling to God. One voice pricked through that racket to complain of a broken ankle. Bracing their doors ajar, the islanders took lanterns and got to the shore, hoping to find and guide the wrecked. I stayed behind to renew the fire and help strip off and dry them, the Foote cottage being the first sanctuary and closest to the sea. Richard Noy eventually took master and mate, and the Carews sheltered two seamen. Hicks found the lame gentleman crawling the shoreline, groping at seaweed. He pleaded for his wig. 'Fetch it,' he said, losing patience with his new underlings. ''Tis blasted expensive.' I got him warm and immediately bound his ankle. This act impressed him. Lamplight flashing over his eyes showed an unusual light blue-green, like icebergs. The left eye wandered. He spoke like a king, but fear shook him nonetheless. He made some observations, and then he looked at me as though he saw the truth of me, right down to my bowels. And still that wandering eye strayed. Hicks invited the gentleman away, saying the Footes already housed one survivor, me, from an earlier wreck. Accepting

Hicks's arm, the gentleman stood, sat down again, and stood once more in what I'd learn was a rare bit of indecision. Hicks finally persuaded the gentlemen to lean on him, and as they passed through the door, the gentleman asked my name. Hicks explained I could not talk. The gentleman looked back at me as Jem closed the door.

By dawn, the rain had thinned out but the winds kept kicking up. Just at the northeast point, where the rocks met sand, leaned a little sloop called *Honour*. Right sweet and complete, canvas neatly furled and quite thoroughly aground. Fallon Carew put his arm round the sad captain's shoulders and remarked he'd once got his gig caught in the very same spot, so he knew precisely how the captain felt. Someone muttered that it took only a hair's breadth of error to let in disaster, and someone else said that this is what comes of gentlemen and secret plans. *Honour*'s master cuffed him, and he stopped up.

I mended torn shirts while the women cooked a feast. Wrecks usually forced corpses on the islanders; this fine occasion of not burying strange dead must be celebrated. The gentleman's ankle proving sprained and not broke made him easier to bear. High tide swamped *Honour*. Then, walking to Hicks's house, I spied something I've wished over and over that I'd missed. Tangled in seaweed, pushed and dragged, loose strands swirling out of the sodden grey mass: the gentleman's wig. It looked like a cloud trapped in water, shifting like that. I carried it with me, thinking the gentlemen very stupid to have gone looking for it in the storm.

He sat in Hicks's best chair and invited all to admire his ankle, now propped on a crate. He'd wound some linen round his stubbled head so he'd not catch cold. He noticed me immediately, though he affected otherwise. One of the women called out: 'Look, Mr Reynolds, the dumb boy found the wig.'

'Mercy unfettered,' the gentleman said. 'Rejoice with me, for I have found the coin which you have lost. And I thought he carried a drowned cat.' He studied me once more, and I didn't mind it, because his gaze made me feel worthy of something. Then he looked at the women, eyes lingering on their chests. I heard the rigging of his mind work.

The men arrived, rowdy and joyous, and we ate an extra meal, some very fine carrots and potatoes, fresh fish and small beer. Reynolds took Jem aside and asked him to thank his son for the wig, and Jem explained the Bad Salvage and how I did hardly be his boy. Reynolds asked Jem if he sheltered me because his own son had died. Jem said 'No. We shelter him because he survived, and we know not what else to do with him.' Mr Reynolds did need be satisfied with that response, for I answered naught to his repeated questions of my origin.

Later in the evening, Reynolds beckoned to me and Jem, saying he must relieve himself, a tricky procedure when hobbling. Between the three of us, we mutely reasoned best angles. Outside, a little way's off, I could hear Christina speaking softly to someone about love and confusion, and a male voice answered. Jem begged leave of us, so Reynolds leaned all the harder on me, remarking I stood a better height for this purpose than Jem. 'I am a coward who fears pain,' he said. 'I put this off much too long.' He pissed mightily. Jem returned, angry and distracted, and Reynolds asked if he might borrow me. 'Just until your Hicks can ferry me to the mainland.' Jem granted me to Reynolds as long as he needed me. He warned Reynolds that he could not guess how much I understood. Reynolds grasped my jaw then, his hand very strong, and forced me to meet his gaze. 'Oh, he understands. Quite well.'

Reynolds' favourite pastime over the next few days was trying to make the dumb boy speak. He seemed to think of naught else but prying loose my voice, and I thought of naught else but screwing it in tight. Some days I felt sure Christina would burst out and scream the truth of me at Jem, all of a cause she needed a weapon in the battles between them. But she kept my secret, tucked it away with her other ones. So, me and Reynolds, mute boy and gentleman, went out a-walking the shore together like a pair in some song – oh dum-dilly-dum-dum – and as he leaned on my shoulder, bracing himself against the wind, his makeshift turban unwound. Linen trailing off him, he spoke as though the turban's failure was my fault. 'What manner of creature are you? I beg you, boy, before I take it in my head to bash out your brains with a heavy rock, tell me of the knife and lanyard you finger, and tell me your name, for I'll not be indebted to the anonymous.'

I said naught to that, my firm habit by now. Then Reynolds stopped, bent over with some difficulty, and picked up a likely rock. He slipped and cried out against the pain in his ankle, going right pale, and bowing his head to hide his tears. Stubble matted his scalp, stubble with bits of silver in it, and no hair grew at all near his temples. His wig lay drying in the sun outside Hicks's house, weighted down with rocks like a chart, but it grew stiff and stank worse each day. Hicks had strenuously offered to bury it. I wondered if he'd place it in the burying ground or throw it down the poison well.

'This,' said Reynolds, making sure I got a good look at it, 'will do it. Do not bother to run. Where on this small island might a lost soul run?'

'Lost soul' confused me.

Then Reynolds dropped the rock, and the noise of it rang in my teeth. 'I did ask Mrs Foote if you've ever talked in your sleep.'

I waited.

He scowled. 'But she said she'd not heard a sound. A pretty mystery, when I know you are no foreigner and no born mute. Come, sit with me.'

Reynolds interrogated me quickly and furiously and showed no surprise when I finally answered. I felt then as I do now, with you, Lieutenant: burdened. My voice startled me, all dusty and harsh, as I told him of *Bonaventure Walters* and how many men sailed her. Details spilt out me, cargoes, ports of call, the scent of Coltman's brass spyglass. Then Reynolds asked which man on board I'd called 'Father.'

'None,' I said, limply, hoping he'd not ask how I got on board.

He teased some useless facts out of me, such as what we ate noon Wednesdays, in what direction lay Harbour Grace, the colour of the first mate's eyes. That question hurt, and I described Rattlebags as if the right words would drag him back to life. Then Reynolds set me to repeat a little speech, which I mostly got on a few hearings:

A ward, and still in bonds,
one day I stole abroad;
it was high spring,
and all the way primrose and hung with shade;
yet it was frost within,
and surly wind blasted my infant buds,
and sin like clouds eclipsed my mind.

Reynolds quickly demanded where I'd heard Vaughn before, and I asked, 'Who is Vaughn?'

He praised me then, called me intelligent. I asked if that meant the same as useful, all of a cause that I liked being so. 'It can be,' he said, 'with education and good handling.' Then he asked if Captain Walters has been a good man. Twice more he asked me, voice hard, and I did need apologize for not being intelligent enough with words to answer him. Finally I got out 'We were so afraid at the end, though none said so. Except Rattlebags. And the captain mocked him for it. The captain, blind as worms, made a mistake giving the course, and so we wrecked.'

We sat another few moments, and my arse got cold on the rocks. Reynolds turned his gaze from the water back to me. 'And what of all the details you've not told me?'

I expect he'd guessed how I ended up on board a merchantman, ships not normally known for employing boys, though tis not unheard of. The navy in wartime be different, your ships packed with midshipmen and little powder monkeys. How do ye look after all those boys?

Shame gnawed me, all of a cause of this man with the strange eyes, grand captain of the human heart despite lacking one of his own. He saw each of my darknesses writ out on my forehead. I needed a drink, small beer or even salt water, just to swallow that shame back down into my belly. Surely this Reynolds smelled the usage off me, figured me like many linkboys a tool of corruption. Ruining a man's soul, or at least giving him a rash on his prick.

So I thought on the wreck and told Reynolds of my deal with God. Coltman tried to teach me plaindealing, and the good half of that makes your lies plausible. Except I hardly lied. The night *Bon Wally* holed and water flooded us, I made tallies and exchanges against my past bad usage and begged God to damn me as He pleased, only take Coltman and drown him. To Reynolds, I said 'I hated a man on board, and I begged God to strike him from my life. The only man on board who'd asked me my true name died after saving the man I hated, and the hated man lived. I promised God I'd be right thankful and quiet and meek ever after if He'd take the man I hated.' I pointed to where pieces of *Bon Wally* still lay. 'See how God did it.'

Reynolds seemed to understand. He asked my age, but we both had to guess at it. Then he praised me again for being intelligent and possessing capacities I knew naught of. 'These qualities need guidance to make them useful,' he said. 'Should you like to come with me?'

No dull voyage. I leapt up like a fawning dog. 'Please sir, I'd work hard,' I told him.

He smiled back at me, not entirely happy but at least pleased. 'So many teeth,' he said. 'Now, we need a story.' I offered to tell him of the sailor man and the shells and the boatswain, but he held up his hand, demanding silence. He said 'Injured in the wreck, flesh bruised and gone mortified, necessitating removal – no, I can do better than that. I need a good reason why you squat to piss.'

I ran. Ducked past his grasp and lit out. Forgetting his ankle, Reynolds made to stand, bore full weight and fell. He greeted the rocks with his hands and knees. I stood out of reach. He ordered me back to his side, and I refused. He said he should strike me, and I thought again to run, but where, Peter's Rue being sandbars crammed against a rock and some soil. I could criss-cross the land, but, though it might take all night, Reynolds would find me. Turban in hand, picking his way on a bad ankle, he would limp and fall, curse and rise, never losing sight, and he would catch me. Pick his way over the rocks, like Appolyon in that long story Pilgrim's never finished telling me.

Dread being worse than punishment, I let him catch me. He grabbed my shoulder hard, harder than Walters ever did. 'I demand obedience,' he said. 'I will care for you, but at the simple cost of obedience. Else I shall cut you loose to starve in the cold, and such a waste that would be.' He palmed me between the legs then, his hand very warm. 'Disguise and memory, boy.' He gave that word only subtle weight. 'I should strike you so hard your ears would ring for days, but I shall not. Because we each need the other. You may trust me, for I promise you no bad usage. I've got work that might only be done by a young one with tough legs, sharp eyes and an excellent memory. More than all else, I need your memory and your disguise. Consider your deal with God, and then get to your knees, for you are saved. So long as you work for me, you shall suffer no want beyond that necessary to the task, and you'll be warm and fed and a good sight safer than your sisters. Decide and say, will you come with me? Will you plaindeal and obey?'

A very pretty rescue.

Plaindeal and obey. You understand. Aye, you know how Reynolds lied. For a start, his true name was Phillip Runciman.

14) *RARA AVIS*, COMMON CURS
MARCH 1722, PORTSMOUTH, ENGLAND.

In the private home of Captain Sir Alexander Dunton, a visitor from London peered through the curtains, tugged them shut, and snorted. Dunton winced as his friend, Phillip Runciman, swallowed wine and bile. Runciman felt grateful to Dunton for hosting this private meeting, this tiresome reprimand, but he cursed Dunton's presence in the room. Runciman's humiliation here stained them both.

—Shall I explain again?

The visitor, a royal advisor and Runciman's superior in the intelligence service, pretended to make a toast. —I beg you, Mr Runciman: make the attempt.

Runciman lifted his own glass. So did Dunton. *To hour three.* —My plan, or my 'wisdom,' as you kindly termed it a moment ago, depended on one simple courier job. On the advice of my colleague, Captain Dunton, I tasked one Lieutenant William Cleasby to carry a message and money to a contact a child might have spotted. Instead, Mr Cleasby announced himself to another man, presuming this man to be correct simply because he expected him to be. Mr Cleasby has difficulty separating desire from truth.

Sir Alexander Dunton studied his wine. He'd recommended Cleasby, under pressure from a commodore who seemed overly concerned about the undistinguished lieutenant's career.

The royal advisor poked spots on the tablecloth as though they were places on a map.

—Then we should fear for the navy. Your underling's failure means some local sheep-shagger now owns the cipher key and the gold, while the real man now stands unprotected and impotent! And how, sir, shall he get to Benvolio now?

—If I may point out, sir, the real man missed the sailing, and the rendezvous with Lieutenant Cleasby, of his own negligence.

—Indeed he did, sir! Truck with Irishmen and boys and bankrupt gentry. Do you see why I despair? Two of your men, each failing, Cleasby even giving away codes and cash.

—Cleasby fouls everything he touches, I grant.

—And Benvolio. We've not done discussing His Majesty's interests on that fair isle. And you sent an Irishman. No word for months?

Runciman shook his head, mouth tired and sore with *No, sir.*

—Michael Farr, another Runciman man entrusted large amounts of money, not to mention the hotter currency of intelligence. Do you think him killed?

—It would be easier, sir, to kill a kraken. I've got reliable sightings. Of Farr.

—Mr Runciman, I must ask: for whom does your exceptionally well-trained, well-paid and well-stocked Michael Farr work? And precisely what does he work at? Can you answer me?

Runciman almost traded *No, sir* for *Not at this time.* —He works for me, and I work for His Majesty.

—Yet you've lost contact with him. Do you control none of your agents, sir?

—Intelligence, my lord, is not got freely as fish in a basket. It needs worrying. I am confident that Michael Farr –

—What words might he trade for food?

—I do not know.

The royal advisor leant forward, knocking over his wine. It flowed rapidly toward Runciman, dripping off his end of the table and onto his breeches. —Retrieve your man Farr from Benvolio, or stop his mouth. The precise methods, sir, I leave to your discretion. Then, perhaps, we may salvage your position.

Light thinned and shadows grew as Phillip Runciman strode over a muddy common, and a flea leapt from his collar to edge of his ear. Wreckage of a day – fuckery, Michael Farr would call it. Not that Runciman could claim the reprimand surprised him. Between Farr and Cleasby and two lesser cock-ups, he looked laughably incompetent. And he'd not got much means – or time – to fix this. His prestigious task, the supervision of Benvolio and the Genoan interference there, was a test. European politics in the Mediterranean dearly mattered to England, and Farr's handy, if nominal, Catholicism justified the means of using him. But if Runciman failed this test, he would progress no further in the service. He might even meet with an accident; failed spymasters knew too much.

Michael Farr would be masterless. So he thinks. Let him starve a few mercenary years, and then he will come rapping on my door.

The flea leapt into Runciman's ear and bit him. Runciman kicked a bony dog, not caring that it snarled.

Retrieve Farr, oh, easy. My best agents already tasked, and most overseas. Headaches of foreign policy. Migraine preyed on Elizabeth's spymaster, Sir Robert Cecil – small wonder.

One of Runciman's predecessors had died of a stroke; Runciman had reported to his office, found the man insensible and bleeding from the ear. Quiet and middling deaths for some spymasters. Cecil took several days to die, wracked with pain and guilt, apologizing over and over, begging for mercy...

Death – ha, death. Not the issue. Not my death.

Send whom?

The flea jumped further into Runciman's head, stopped at the eardrum, leapt out.

Overhead, a kittiwake called. Runciman stared up at the belly of the bird; behind him, something snuffed. *A final tempering.* Black lips, grey teeth and slobber, growl expiring on a high note beneath Runciman's hands. Throwing the strangled dog's carcass to his left, the permanent observer in him noting the speed of his own pulse, Runciman sighted five other dogs, one of them dirty white, the others grey and brown, waiting. They stood as if balanced on the edge of something Runciman could not see.

The dead dog's fur stirred in the wind.

The white dog growled.

Dusk took the light, and Kit's eyes burned. Portsmouth muttered beneath the window; somewhere, dogs barked. Belly cramps clenched her. Kit scowled and wrote the date – *Thirtieth of March 1722* – the quill wretchedly delicate. Kit preferred to mark paper with sharp lead, annoying Runciman one day with a series of big-eyed caricatures. —Is this gratitude? How many of your station learn to read and write, and you would draw me a fool?

Runciman's displeasure was a short path to exile past his doors. Never back to sea, no. The street – again? Squatting to shit out rotten scraps of food, or relishing the bursts of fat and meat in her mouth from Runciman's plates? So, please him: study, clean, draw, recite, wait. Venture out with older agents and learn how to listen and how to hide. Dread Runciman's moods.

Outside, men yelled, and dogs howled.

Kit sprinkled sand on the wet ink of a chart drawn from memory: the Mediterranean Isle of Benvolio. Teeth clenched, fists right, Kit struggled to keep her anger pent. Being angry with Runciman made no sense; she paid him nothing. Runciman kept his promise, no usage, and he sheltered, fed, taught and studied her. Kit the gift. Thin, even bony, hair tied at the neck with a new black ribbon, hips square with her waist, broad shoulders, heavy forehead, green eyes feverish and raw. An enticing accident, he once said, drunk. A freak prize, a gift. Blurred roughwork of God.

Telling Runciman of her early life, Kit had put words in her dead mother's mouth.

—She said to Robert Pike, 'Take her from this trade. Teach her something else.' Maybe he loved my mother. Maybe he owed her something. I owe him. Another girl born to be split for pleasure, and he tried to keep me from that. Warned me about bawds and how kind they might be, because the shaking virgin could bring in good money.

Kit would feel rage, some greasy fire that and hissed and flared. Sometimes she ignored it. Other times, it took command. She'd yell. Kick the wall. Throw the ink. Gouge the floor with her knife.

Runciman would observe these outbursts carefully.

Kit shook the paper clean and placed it on the far side of the desk, where it joined earlier work: England, Ireland, more Benvolio, the New England coast, Newfoundland. Then she laid her head down on the desk and closed her eyes. *Kitchen-maid late with the bread and cheese?* Runciman had forbidden Kit and the maid to speak to each other, but sometimes they stole conversation. A scrap such as *Good morning* packed a potent thrill. Once, Kit's hand brushed the maid's, and each hesitated before drawing away.

At the moment Kit noticed her absence, the maid, a five-minute-walk away, was babbling for her mother. A handsome bird-monger who often called on Runciman's kitchen buttoned his breeches, glanced round for witnesses, kicked the maid in the pelvis, and rejoined the marketplace traffic. He nearly turned and ran when he saw Runciman himself hurrying towards him, clothes askew and dirty; instead, he walked normally, eyes down, brushing Runciman's elbow. Runciman irritably flinched and strode faster.

Kit dreamt of correcting charts and needing more light. A hand bore a candle –

Eyes suddenly open so wide they hurt, she leapt up, knife ready. Lamplight flickered onto Runciman's hard face beneath his wig.

—Easy, easy. Tis only me. Breathe slowly, slowly. And put down that knife before you do me a murder. I just beat off stray dogs with a stick; do not inspire me to repeat that. My aching head. I must review your sea-charts. England and Ireland are passable. Coastal Massachusetts is excellent. This peninsulaed rhombus – quite unrecognizable, new-found-land indeed. Draw Benvolio again. Tomorrow, mushbrains. Now I'd have recitation; give me Rochester. Stand up. Are you ill? Blood? Oh, God, this day! I may tell you now what a woman once told me, she carrying much extra cloth for such times, and within that, on my behalf, cloth packets of letters. She bled two or three days and was done. Some bleed a week. Sshh. For a woman I could trust who might teach you better – Kit, for the love of Christ, settle down. Tis just blood. But we must hide it. Do not get splenetic with me. I'll have you go about my tasks as a young man or not at all. Later, when – starve, then. Go. You are free of me. Be used, be fucked and be killed – wait. Stay, my useful one, my *rara avis*, stay. Stay. Where would you go? I'll get you cloth. I've new breeches and a shirt for you. We've each need of the other. Wait. Wrap this between. No little wonder females wear so many layers; you lot must hide so much. Ridiculous, aye, but you were so born, not me. New breeches, black, hide all manner of dirt. Turn. Bind those down. When came this new growth? Luckily they're still small. Wind the linen so. Tis good linen. I bought it years ago to use as my gravecloth. Shirt. Turn. Turn again. Good.

Runciman stepped back, his gaze threaded not with desire but evaluation.

—Give me Rochester, 'The Maim'd Debauchee,' from 'bearing arms'.

Breeches too large, shirt untucked, confused, Kit recited lewd verse. It helped her master think.

I'll tell of whores attacked, their lords at home.
Bawds' quarters beaten up and fortress won,
Windows demolished, watches overcome,
And handsome ills by my contrivance done.
Nor shall our love-fits, Chloris, be forgot

When each the well-looked linkboy strove t'enjoy
And the best kiss was the deciding lot:
Whether the boy fucked you, or I the boy.
With tales like these, I will such heat inspire–

Runciman held up his hand, smiling. *An Irishman and a boy.
Now all I need is the bankrupt gentlemen. Matthew Johnson.* —That
slut of a serving girl is not coming tonight. We must find supper
elsewhere.

—The blood, sir. Is it an old wound just now cleansing itself?

The dull light did not warm Runciman's face; it only
emphasized his pallor and bones.

He glanced once more at Kit's seacards of Benvolio and
Newfoundland, tucked the awkward islands into a warped drawer
and then walked around the desk.

—No. All females bleed. Eventually you may work for me as a
female. A woman can transport quite a few documents within
stockings and skirt. For now, we'll work with your young man's
body and young man's story. Who are you?

—I am called Christopher, sir, or Kit for short. No parentage
to speak of. I did be stolen off the street, sir, and hard used, and
afterwards traded to a papist priest, with whom, as servant, I
crossed the sea to Barbary. There we made to ransom and rescue a
French hostage, but our mission stumbled. Soon we found
ourselves muted by unknown language and unknown faith. In
Barbary, men must go circumcised. I, sir, being a young boy and
frightened, jumped and screamed, and – I still feel the slice, the
stab. The knife slipped and took far more than intended. My
wounds refuse to heal. My voice remains trapped.

Phillip Runciman took Kit's hands in his to rub them warm.

—I must send you out. Away. You'll travel with an agent of
mine, Matthew Johnson, to – aye, Benvolio – and find for me that
which is lost, a man called Michael Farr. I will give you orders that
you must pass only to Farr. Mind he sees them.

*And should you come to be harmed, I'll see Johnson fucked with
a spike.*

Kit smiled back.

So many teeth.

Runciman never saw that smile again.

15) LITTLE *HONOUR*
CANNARD'S LEDGER.

At Afterson's coffee shop in Bristol, in April of 1717, Runciman's wayward eye took in the world over my shoulder while his good orb stared me true. He said, 'I consider us a company of monetary adventurers, Cannard. A company, not a society, for we are not so stuffy; monetary because of the economic interests pulling stops and strings; not merchants, for we are not merchants – though merchant you might have been had I not got to you first. Adventurers, sir, not soldiers, not mercenaries, but couriers, agents, risk-takers: men who get things done. Excellent coffee, is it not?' I said I found it second rate, that I had tasted better coffee in the gutters of London. Runciman replied, 'Oh sir, witty yes, witty indeed: second rate, second best, Afterson's, Bristol second to London.' One of Runciman's eyes wandered off to the right, and I would swear now, in my mature hindsight, Runciman did stretch the socketed orbit to take in the entire room. He said, 'Cannard, I'll give you this: I have tasted none finer in Bristol. Tell me of your father, that excellent businessman and fine companion.' I should have suffered no surprise at what Runciman knew. Unfolded and laid out end to end, his brains would make a great reckoning, for Runciman, one of those unhappy freaks of God, possessed such capacious talent and ability one could only pray he put them to good use. He could recite Homer's *Iliad* in English, memorizing Pope's translation as a new volume appeared each year: *in what ill-fated hour sprung the first strife?* His purpose, truth and reason: being one of the controlling minds of England's intelligence networks, the names, assignments, maps and charts, talents and aliases of God knows how many men hidden and tucked within his memory. He will receive no credit by history for this, titled as a clerk to another civil servant, one not remotely connected with intelligence. Silent and profound, then, the loss of Phillip Runciman. When he sank deep into conversation, one eye wandered, and this defect compelled one to look at him harder. Those blue eyes could woo a man to any task, and if the eyes failed in courtship, the voice would elicit submission. How the weaker sex responded, I do not know, though I imagine seduction came easily. Other than his eyes and his monstrous wigs, affected to fool observers into thinking him a cockahoop dandy, Runciman stood unremarkable. Given the nature of his work, this more than sufficed.

I asked Runciman how long he had known my father. Runciman said, 'All Bristol, well, all Bristol business knows Will Cannard – but you conjugate the man in the past tense?' I explained that my father had died a few months before, the doctor suspecting a stomach cancer. 'Dreadful,' said Runciman. 'His father died the same; knew you so? Eaten out. Then I did miss the funeral. Do forgive me, sir, for I had work in London. Take care to your own stomach. Eat food neither pickled nor brined, but do consume plenty of onion, an humble herb, much underrated. How does your brother?' When I replied my elder brother did well, Runciman protested, 'Well? Is that all you have to say of your brother, sir, heir to Cannard and Son?' I added that my brother did 'well enough' and hoped Runciman would change the subject.

He did. 'When last I spoke to your father,' he said, 'Cannard and Son supped on a tidy profit, particularly for a company of its size, the ships' co-owners and backers quite content. I expect your elder brother runs Cannard and Son exceedingly well, for I do hear much of him since arriving in Bristol. Indeed I heard commented just last night *Why is it we see Tom Cannard boozing and whoring*– forgive me the diction, sir, I but repeat what another man spoke – *yet never the younger?* Given your elder brother's wealth, am I to presume Cannard and Son does well enough? Sir, you flinch at my questions, my indelicate probes of a wound: I find pus. Would you soothe the soul of a troubled man who knew your father? By your silence I am to know I have offended you. I plead patience, sir. I often offended your father, but he became accustomed to me and such offences as I gave him would he flick off his sleeves like flakes of snuff. I am an offensive man. Your father thought very highly of you, do you know that?'

I spoke foolishly. 'Then why did he send me away? To my mother's people in Wales and then of course to school. Do excuse me, sir: my schooling was a gift, and by its denigration I do my father dishonour. Is it the heat in here?'

'He sent you to Cambridge eventually, where you prepared to take Holy Orders,' Runciman said, faint amusement in his voice. 'To return to adventure, sir.'

From this digressive preface did Runciman's stray eye rejoin its fellow, disquieting me. Those eyes conducted no sign of emotion,

125

only fierce intellect and reason. No, I do Runciman a disservice: his eyes betrayed a contained glee, a delight, not at coffee-house discourse with me, as I first supposed, but at spreading me open before him and plucking the juiciest and most useful bits. The memory of a tale told to me while I still wore leading bands and frocks, of the old pagans sacrificing boys, Abrahrams absent or delayed; Maypoles and bonfires, strange dances, old ways: I could see Runciman there, kicking and bending and not once slipping his wig nor his well-heeled shoes.

'Adventure, Cannard, taking risks, getting things done. Your father took risks; his greatest risk now sits across me. His firstborn he did groom for the business, but Tom will shortly prefer, or perhaps need, his games of Ruff and Honours even to the denial of women. How is it a card game can suck a man dry? Now you, his second son, he sent to school with the keen desire to make him a better man than his father. No, you did not gall him with your disdain for Holy Orders, for are we not all botched divines? Not even your sullied romps with Jane Wilkes, a commoner track not trodden this county, dismayed him. No, sir. You hurt your father with your sulking, your shrugging off all he tried to give you as though it were worthless. No small sacrifice made he to send you to university.'

Here I did protest that the happiest time of my life was the summer I travelled with my father when he sailed as supercargo, and that I wished… but I could not complete this sentence.

'You wished what?' asked Runciman. 'To return to a handful of sennights now bleached pure by sunlight that shines only in your head? Spare me, sir. You got sick and cried for your mother.'

I drained the last of my coffee and placed the cup on the table before him, thereby causing a drop to fly into the air. It arced and then splattered across the tip of Runciman's nose. Returning to itself, the drop was about to fall onto the table when Runciman sniffed. I leaned forward so as to ensure none else in the coffee shop would hear, and I informed Runciman that my good mother had long lain underground, and that he had given me great offense, not so much by what he said but for the reasons he had said it.

'Sit down, John,' he said, his voice loud and friendly enough to carry to the doorway, so that several men glanced about with interest. A hesitation on my part would cause them stare longer, raise eyebrows, take note of younger Cannard; and who be that, addressing him by his Christian name? I sat. 'Now, I can see you'll brook no wasted time. I am myself part of a company of monetary adventurers, but there's more to it than that. Discretion, sir, is my greatest need. Recovery, sir, is yours.'

Recovery from what, I enquired, and Runciman smiled as though at an old joke. 'Your brother, sir. According to my estimates, Cannard and Son might last the six months left to it or fail within three. After that come the long debts to merchants and co-owners and backers. Within a year, insolvency. Ruination. I will not stand idly by and see your father's toil melt away simply because one of his sons soaks up more liquor than air and the other lacks the will God gave a louse. Keep your seat, for you *will* hear me. Are you a prudent man of money? No. Employ you a prudent man of money? No. According to your records – you do have a fine hand for clerking, at least your education shows there – you have sold one ship already to cover losses and have plans to sell two more. That leaves you with the little sloop *Honour*, which is the talk of this shop at present: last night, your brother wagered the sloop. And lost. *Honour*, named for your mother? How did I see your records? I paid a young man to break into your offices, bring me your books and then return them an hour before first light. A company of monetary adventurers, sir: leasing spies is easy and cheap. A dockside brat could have accomplished the task. But I need not docksiders, sir: I need men of capacity. I need adventurers. And you, sir, need recovery.'

I bade him good day in a jolly manner and, abuzz with coffee and allegations, returned to my offices in the late afternoon light. Aye, he might easily have invaded our offices, or employed a careless ruffian to do so. A few mornings before I had blamed my brother for the spilled ink.

Seasons changed, bills mounted, and I caught sight of Runciman twice more in the next year, always at Afterson's, where we each feigned ignorance of the other. He stood quietly at my brother's funeral, and he walked me back to Afterson's when the burial was done. I knew where Runciman wished me to go, and, being too worn to argue, I suffered myself to be led. His arm about my shoulders, so warm against the damp Avon fumes, he said, 'A hard death for your brother, lung fever. Out all night in the rain, swooned against the office door.' I wept, not for my father, his death a blessing and release, and not for my brother, his drunkenness a comical damnation, but for myself, quite alone and ignorant of my best chance at succour.

'Recovery, Runciman.' I now looked him in the eyes, pleased he kept the wanderer checked. 'I ask you, sir, you as a friend of my father's: how might I work recovery?'

Inheriting Cannard and Son, I dealt mostly with captains and merchants. My offices neighboured those of Captain George Walters, that fine Bristolman then flush with coffee profit and once much interested in acquiring Cannard and Son. When I was a boy, Captain Walters would ruffle my hair as he spoke to my father in a blunt manner I much liked, but which my brother mocked. Father sometimes invited Captain Walters to dinner, and I remember best a dinner in 1709. Father permitted me to remain at table, and I was most pleased, for I counted Captain Walters the only one of Father's friends who did not assume that my brother nursed a love for the sea and a head for shipping and that I, the indulged schoolboy choked with Latin, did not. Captain Walters looked me in the eye as he did Father, and then they'd discuss business.

I woke with my face crumpled in the tablecloth. The racket of my own snoring shook me to see, through blurry candlelight, past dirty plates and heaped-up napkins, the linen, bones and forks now set like little buildings, that the Captain and my father had moved to Father's study, their voices lower now, more serious. Father had spoken of selling Cannard and Son. To Captain Walters, then? Spluttering about birthright and hairy arms, I made for the study over the unsteady floor to halt the proceedings right there. I stopped when I heard my father's voice turn sympathetic, like Mother's had when my brother or I shook out a fever. Then Captain Walters spoke again. 'Cannard, I wouldn't wish it on a Sallee Rover. Not even on the snotty what first whacked me on the head. It burns, this thin flicker of hell, this reminder. Years ago, some dirty cunt, I should have gone up her arse, would have been cleaner.' Here the Captain hiccoughed a few times, damning the wine. My father murmured something Walters having years left to him yet.

'But tis now, Cannard, me sight's going now. Cock and balls next, swoll up like beach rocks. You hire captains all the time, Cannard, but tis *my* ship. Mine. My money. My rotting pizzle.

And there be naught I can do but wait for the darkness to overtake me.'

The truth, or the dream, overtakes me in daylight, the hauling on frozen ropes, sleet dripping down the line to coat my numb hands, sleet cutting my cheeks and squinting me blind, so vivid still after forty-one years. I am brought back to the worst moments of the wreck with no more warning than when I bring myself to my next breath, and even if shaken about the shoulders by Lacey or Aurelius Jackman, I would give no answer. Not until my dreaming self sights the fire rocks through the rain do I escape back to Port au Mal, to my true senses. The hatred, the fear and, above all, the tedium I have suffered here, particularly during Lacey's days, seem preferable, Gilead balm, to these paralyzing bad dreams.

As sayeth the one who ran: the waters compassed me about even to the soul; the depths closed me round about; the weeds wrapped about my head. I had but late changed from stocking and breeches to more sensible tarred trousers. Once, in the wardroom, I found four of the men intently studying the table: encouragement, abuse and cheers. Their bent heads touched. Two tapped biscuit, saved from a previous meal, and out fell weevils. The confused creatures undertook travels, sometimes away from and sometimes towards the finish line, which had been determined by the gnawers of biscuit. Winner decided, losers despised, cracked and dirty thumbs squat the weevils, and the men stood up to go on watch.

In 1719, some years after my father's death and my departure from Cambridge in disgrace, I put to sea. My vessel: *Bonny Jane*, a brigantine, new-built and fresh out of Bristol, this time with John Cannard, second son, as supercargo and majority owner. Runciman found new co-owners and gave me a destination: Harbour Grace.

This ledger book and ink I did lately buy in Harbour Grace. To be sure I have much to do, cataloguing stores and provisions, credits and debits. My one companion in such matters has been dead these seventeen years: Robert Lacey, late and so-called fishing admiral of Port au Mal – no companion but an adversary, a tyrant of strange order. But at least, conversations scarce enough, I could speak with him.

A certain quality here, perhaps something in the rock, skews a compass. An experienced master, armed with local knowledge, good weather and God's grace, could manage the narrows; the skipper of Lacey's ketch put in safely twice each year. Should a larger vessel, as chanced with my *Bonny Jane*, lose her course and, in ignorance, desperation and dusk make for the narrows of Port au Mal, her compass will go dumb, deviate, and babble like an idiot, jerking east sou'-east on heading northwest, tip west, east again, perhaps loll from west to south, as did ours for seven consecutive minutes; I did count those seconds, dumb myself. Eventually the hapless officers will try needle and cork and thereby waste more time before venturing on deck, without the wit for words. Wind drove us through the narrows larboard first, and only as we strained in that passage did we hear the waves smashing against the fire rocks. The men screamed it. 'Rocks! God!'

That first impact gutted *Bonny Jane*. Loosed cargo shot up to the surface. A tossed hogshead hit Captain Wren in the chest and crashed him over the starboard bow. Rats and foodstuffs tumbled about the deck with us, the rats' squeals blending with ours and just as blunted by the wind. Curtains of rain and sleet would briefly part, allowing us to glimpse the fire rocks. All my inheritance invested in *Bonny Jane*. I imagined the rewards of government service would pay it back; tokens of that government service were locked in my strongbox: papers. A courier, and expected shortly in Harbour Grace, I was to deliver these papers to a particular set of men who would engage me in matters theological, remarking, when I referred to *Matthew* chapter 26 verse 73, do you not, sir, mean *Matthew* chapter 27 verse 6? I'd tucked that heavy strongbox beneath my right arm and slung the key to it around my neck. I stumbled back on deck; fire rocks surrounded us now. Several of the men turned to me, mouths identical holes, and one of them pointed. I did not feel the lurch that threw me overboard. I knew the thrill of descent, the taste of salt water, and, detached suddenly, I asked 'So then, Lord, shall I freeze, or shall I drown?'

My mind flitted like a moth in front of a light. My last sight, a wave, persistently returned as Behemoth cracking open his jaws and then diving to engulf my delicate brigantine. Darkness, ignorance and incomprehensible voices. Perhaps I would die and go to Wales. My mother's family had land in Wales. When I awoke from that, no dark Welsh beauty graced my sight, only a fair ordinary woman with a promise of jowls and three white hairs poking out of her chin. She helped me sit up enough to drink, uttering words in rhythms I recognized, but by God, the storm in my ears stole the meaning. 'Not dead. Be not dead.' I finally understood. 'You be not dead. Stay in bed now, until I gets the Admiral.' I tried sitting up, could not, and asked of admirable girls and islands. The woman said, 'Newfoundland.' I lunged up once more, saying, 'The *New* Found Land? John Donne's blissful kingdom: *O my America, my new-found-land...*' Here she laid her hand on my shoulder to ask if I meant John Dunn. 'He be two houses down. Fetch him, I shall.'

I shut my eyes a moment and opened them again to dusk. Just over the screams of rats and rigging, just beyond the wall, two men spoke. Smelling salt and rot and human filth and determining I would escape it, I got out of bed and stood up, quite carelessly, forgetting I had not eaten properly since before the wreck. The cook had extinguished the fire and came on deck to fumble in hope and terror with the rest of us. I stepped towards the voices and found two men. The taller, the size of a grenadier, gawped as though I stood horned and hoofed as well as naked, while the older man studied me calmly, saying 'Nancy, give the man back his clothes. He has need of them.'

More tedious dreams, days' worth, until I suddenly felt well: I could see, I could hear, I could think. The smell of death so thick upon the place was only superstitious nonsense that rises like fumes from the sickbed – just the odour of the sea. The house was perched on stilts to keep it rooted in the thin soil and prevent it from sliding down the face of rock. That quirk of architecture, combined with the drying fish outside and the moist remains of codfish on Nancy Truscott, indeed, upon the persons of all the inhabitants of Port au Mal, all save Lacey, had conspired to stodge my nose until I could dream of naught else but shipwrecks. I sat up. Someone had dressed me in a shirt of most excellent linen, softened by another man's wear. I did welcome it. A pair of breeches lay at the end of my improvised bed. As I stood and dressed, I recognized the props from my fever terrors. The empty hogshead, salvaged from my wreck and now used as a table, and the basin atop it: so often had a vision, like steam from hot water, risen from it and scalded my eyes. Rats, my brother putting a wager on my recovery, a whore I'd jostled once at the Bristol docks, fellow schoolboys, Wren, captain of my doomed *Bonny Jane* – all brought to life by my fever and that hogshead and basin. Captain Wren I particularly

131

wanted to see. If I had come through that icy salt death, that truer hell than flames, then so had he. Despite our differences, I did much enjoy the company of Wren, coming eventually to respect him. Hardly a good man; I could not then call him a good man. Some five bastards had he on his ledger. A whip scar marked his neck and jaw. He told me he'd killed a man. I had not the wit to cull details, waiting instead for him to offer up the story: he did not. From the cook I did hear how the man who'd whipped Wren died in a Bristol alley, throat cut in a manner very similar to Wren's scar. The cook would give me no date for this story.

Beneath the breeches I found stockings. I wondered idly if I might find a wig and waistcoat yet, for someone, presumably the jowly woman, had shaved off my hair and beard for fever, just as I had done for my father in his illness. His razor I kept in my strongbox, reasoning I'd not need it until landed. The thought of the strongbox, rather its absence, caused me a nearly unbearable pang, exacerbated by the useless key I still wore around my neck. The weight of the strongbox alone should have drowned me; clearly I had abandoned my duty so I might live. Runciman would learn of my wrack as he learned of everything; for all I knew God Himself whispered in Runciman's ear. He would then wipe me from his mind and file my name in a dusty corner of that great Alexandria housed beneath his wig. Not even a simple courier job could I manage; damn my stupidity, my losing the chance to repair if not my compact with God then at least my reputation amongst men. I failed to hold the strongbox.

I looked to the rude floor and there discovered not buckled shoes with a good heel but good boots, high and brown, boots a squire might wear for inspecting his fields. A precious gift, one of some sacrifice. I hauled them on, the leather pliable and still retentive of another man's feet, and recalled a particularly muddy day when I'd insisted on stockings and shoes. I resolved when next I saw Nancy to pass mildly by.

Feeling much improved, I descended the muddy slope to the shore, landing on slippery beach rocks that clattered beneath my feet like so many petrified grey eggs. The settlement of Port au Mal had been built backwards from a puddle off the main harbour. Beyond the offreach: a jagged sheet of rock, dull red smudged with black. The harbour itself stretched out into the narrows, while behind me, the settlement's houses dotted the land. About halfway up the cliff, perhaps the last reachable point, lay a flat and fertile piece of ground, yellow with last summer's grass, the closest thing to greenery apart from the conifers. The woods to the west reached the horizon. The cliff, high but blunt, seemed to have suffered an axe blow to the face: a wedge-shaped cut, out from which the upper rock sheared, under which gravel crumbled but did not fall. Calm water in the narrows and harbour, chop enough beyond.

To my right I suddenly saw people – just women, but even women might speak and tell me where the rest of the men from *Bonny Jane* convalesced. The women stood at a rickety table, on which they had laid out pieces of whitish flesh. Knives glittered in the obscured sunlight. Stages, I reasoned, stages and flakes. The women were curing fish. Those long shacks there, propped up stilts upon the slope behind the stage, those are fishing rooms. Spotting the woman Nancy, I hallooed and picked my way towards them.

'Nancy, tell me, tell me, good lady, where are they?'

Nancy there commanded me to call her Mrs Truscott, for she'd long risen above the rank of servant. I did indulge her, and she said 'Admiral's Hall. This be his stage, behind be his rooms. Go to the Admiral's Hall.'

I nearly clasped her hands, her gut-stained and maggoty hands. I pleaded 'Take me there. I must see them, by God, what we've suffered. How fare they?'

Nancy Truscott said naught. The other women, about a dozen of them, looked directly at me, and one toddling brat, young Aurelius, rubbed his nose. I glanced about for a building grand enough to be the Admiral's Hall, sheltering a dozen near-drowned men. As Nancy made to take me, another woman muttered, quite clear enough to hear, 'Lacey's slut.'

Nancy led me up over the rocks and onto some thin wet soil towards a house built comfortably at the edge of the woods, prompting my sensible question of why did they not all live up here, back from the water, considerably less cold and damp? She answered, 'Cold and damp got longer legs than that. Go on in. The Admiral likes no women here.'

Perhaps not in daylight, I said to myself, displeased with her insolence. But a larger neglect concerned me now: none had told me that my shipmates, my countrymen, were housed in this Admiral's Hall. My lucid moments had been few enough, but a word of my countrymen's presence, a whisper of their survival, and my fever might have run less bleak.

Overcome by a fit of wheezy coughing, the like of which still haunts me in winter, I pulled open the door, then leaned against the doorjamb and squinted. I eventually discovered the bearded man who had studied me in my nakedness. Now I studied him: handsome, in a heavy way, his body compact and strong, profile fetched of strong features and no doubt a strong mind, though his nose did be fleshy. Truly, a man untouched by doubt. He wrote in a ledger. I stepped towards him.

He did not turn, instead held up a hand, and said, 'A moment.' I waited. Then he pushed himself back from his table and stood to face me, still eyeing his entries, his question nearly finished before he looked on me full. 'The Englishman. Now then, sir, what can I do for you?'

His bearing confused me. When last I had seen him, he'd commanded. Just then he had kept me waiting, as he might a servant come bearing trivial news. Now he stood before me in courteous respect, hands clasped before him. But a habit of leadership moulded his face, for even now his muscles and nerves relaxed into a confident stare. White shot through his fair hair and beard, yet the skin, while lined by the sun off salt water, looked plump and young. I guessed him to have no more than ten years on myself, putting him at thirty-five. He looked me up and down in an insolent manner and opened his mouth to speak but stopped. His silence irritated me even more than his stare. Angered by Nancy's discourtesy, perhaps excusable given her ignorance, and now by this Lacey's blunt way, I came directly to my question. 'Where are they?'

He looked at me, asked me to repeat my question, which I did, though he hardly answered it. 'It seems the breeches fit,' Lacey replied, calm as fog. 'I had to dig hard to find those old clothes of mine. Shirt's a good linen, too, better than anything you could ever find here. The razor was my father's. I've given up on it over here.'

I did repeat my question, and Lacey's answer clarified nothing. 'Resting in the rooms, I expect, mending nets.'

'*My* men, not yours. Where are the men from *Bonny Jane*?'

Lacey glanced up under his strong brow, curious now, contemptuous. 'The drowned? You might just catch sight of them beneath the waves in certain moonlight. Go out and look. *Bonny*

Jane, I shall write that down.' He did this, adding, 'Were they really your men?'

I'd hired them, with Wren's good advice. I'd paid them, or would have done on return to Bristol. I'd provided food, beer and rum for them: truly then, my men. Admitting it deepened the loss. Not only had I lost my inheritance and the chance at redemption it had brought, but I had lost all outward signs of that inheritance. And I had lost lives, lives on loan to me. My loss was deeper than any of my brother's gambling debts. I'd need pay a heavy reckoning upon facing God.

I asked once more. 'All of them, sir? Not one other man from *Bonny Jane*?'

'Look there. Only the shadows of crates and barrels, not men. I shall show you where we buried the ones that came ashore. I expected you to die of that lung fever, but then I doubt God would spare you drowning at sea only to have you drown in bed. I am Robert Lacey. Are you a religious man? Were I a religious man, I would consider why God saw fit to grace me. What good act earned your survival?'

I do not recall what all else he said as he led me to the burying ground, that boggy meadow halfway up the mountain. A knotty wooden plank marked my men's grave, and gouged into it with a marlinspike was WRACK 19. Lacey stopped speaking and finally departed. When I rose, stiff and cold, to return to my stale sickbed, dusk had come. The water lapped the fire rocks. Not one answer rose from the grave of my men. Not one answer rose from the sea.

At table with the Truscotts, that evening, I ate with them for the first time not as an invalid but as a guest, and this change called for an entirely new chart of manners. Gritting my teeth against their scrapes and slurps and licked fingers, I looked at them, made conversation with them. After the exercise of the day, the climbing down to the beach, then up the hills, I would have much welcomed one more night curled in bed, mashing tack with my tongue against the roof of my mouth. However, I had bolted back to civilization, so my plaster self must be made to smile. Properly witty conversation, however, lay beyond me. It mostly certainly lay far beyond Tom Truscott, who began with, 'You met the Admiral today.'

I chewed and swallowed with more delicacy – codfish, codfish, codfish – then asked if he meant Lacey. Truscott said, 'Admiral

Lacey. There's none calls him by his surname alone, sir. Offends him. Best remember that.' I remarked how this Admiral Lacey seemed young for his rank and asked when he'd retired from the navy. From there, Truscott offered a treatise on the venerable office of the Newfoundland fishing admiral, a tawdry arrangement of migratory convenience, power, and, sometimes, surrogate judiciary. Before settlement, the strongest fishing captain would take control of an area, reserving the best ground and facilities for himself and his ship. He might be called Lord as well as Admiral, these titles seasonal but weighty. He might then delegate authority to second-in-command, a captain crudely called Lady. These admirals had charters and necessity supporting their authority, but as Truscott told it, authority was an expedient, law a nuisance and profit the goal. Like men anywhere, the admirals could be benevolent, incompetent, or cruel – it was business. Should a man not enjoy life under a particular fishing admiral, there was naught he could do except wait for the next season and hope for someone better, or at least someone else; woe to the conquered. Even today, writing this note, I care naught, fishing admirals being neither of my time nor my concern. Besides, I believe the seasonal despots helped settle the island. Lacey had even arranged to bring women over to Port au Mal. Very cunning man, Robert Lacey, and quick to adapt.

'So Admiral Lacey,' continued Truscott, 'still be the fishing admiral, in his way. He arrived first three years in a row, young man, too. And he gave passage to our wives. One year he said he'd take only married men, so we double-hooked the hammocks and only married men crossed. Cramped days, til we landed. Back and forth to the ship then until the houses got built, the Admiral looking after us, food and all. We owe him. He got us across the ocean and through that first winter. There's much to be said for the devil you know, Englishman. Cannard. We called you *Englishman* for so long tis hard to remember you got any proper name.'

'But you're English, Truscott. We're all English. Why do you mark me out?'

'I'm Cornish. English was shoved down our throats when ye forced us to eat the Book of Common Prayer. Now we belch it out like the rest of ye. And what of you, then, John Cannard? Bristolman?'

'Very good, sir. Did my name give it away?'

'Nay, your accent.'

'No Bristol speech leadens me, sir. Cambridge has seen to that. My education – I am an Englishman. Indeed, sir, my lands are widespread. I've small holdings in Kent, tenants in Ireland (God help me), and aye, land and houses in Wales. Granted to the family by King James, sir. That is good enough for God and good enough for me.'

I told the lies comfortably, for how would the likes of Tom Truscott ever discover my deceit? I could not claim a blade of English grass. Even those miserable Irish farms had been sold to shore up Cannard and Son and to build my *Bonny Jane*. One hundred feet of dependable brig. I'd specified plenty of room for the men to sleep so they might rest without jostling one another. *Bonny Jane*: graceful, pretty, mine.

The following morning I begged to take up work. Lacey would not hear of me going out in the dories, and his command there suited me, for I'd sworn my next taste of salt water would be my last, would be my voyage home. But I needed to make some small gesture of thanks before leaving Port au Mal for Harbour Grace, where I would arrange my passage to England. I told Lacey of my clerking and accounting work for Cannard and Son, of my religious background.

Lacey nodded and gave me an axe. I cut firewood.

Humiliating and exhausting work, this, and very slow, but it drove the last scraps of fever and dreams from me. One afternoon I decided to take a walk and ease my shoulders, so I ventured into the woods behind the Admiral's Hall. Nancy spied me from the stage, bundled up her skirts and ran towards me. I ignored her as long as I could. As she stood next to me, panting a little, asking if I had done with the wood, I wondered if she'd dare bid me to go work at the stage. Unlikely, I reasoned, as dressing fish took delicate hands. Deciding I must begin to set things right, I interrupted her litany of tasks awaiting me and demanded Lacey's whereabouts.

Most helpfully: 'Admiral Lacey be not here.'

'I know that, woman, and so I ask you where he is.'

'He's got business in Harbour Grace.'

At this I felt such a rush of passion I feared apoplexy. My papers and strongbox rotted at the bottom of the sea, but I knew some of the contents. I could at least sketch the contents to the men awaiting me. And after that, start for England.

'Harbour Grace? Is it near here? How far is Harbour Grace?'

137

'Dark flush taking you. Will you sit down?'

'*How far?*'

'Days. The Admiral's been gone two weeks now. Sometimes he's gone more than a month.'

'For Christ's sake, Mrs Truscott, how does he get there? He cannot fly. Truscott will take me.'

'Tom be out fishing. And he be the Admiral's Lady. He does nothing without Lacey's command.'

'Talk sense. See now, see my plight. I did be voyaging to Harbour Grace when I got wrecked. I have King's business there.'

'You said that in delirium.'

'Then does it not stand to reason it is true?'

'I got work to be at. If you want to go to Harbour Grace, talk to the Admiral.'

'When does he return?'

'I know not. But I can tell you this: he will not take you.'

Disgusted, I turned quickly from her and strode to the grave of my men. Fog and rain already marked the plank. In another few summers the gouged words might be quite worn away. Of course I would be long returned to England. Who would remember *Bonny Jane* then?

That night, I asked Truscott directly to bring me to Harbour Grace. 'It is my true destination. Truscott. You must, in the name of the King and all that is right, take me there.'

'How do you see that?'

'See what?'

'See I must. Our charity not enough? You receive comfort like cold porridge. Thrown out of the sea, breathing and sound, not even a broken bone.'

'I lay feverish sick for months.'

'Hundreds of miles of broken coast, and you drifted to the shore of an English settlement. See that first. Second, you need see with mine and the Admiral's eyes. This be a new settlement, and delicate. The Jackmans' boy be the first child born here to live his first year. Good lungs. Could hear that one cry a mile off. God suffers our presence here. But we've seen no decent catch for four years now. Tomorrow we might catch more than the whole season. And when we catch naught, it is time to set traps and haul wood. Winter is a few days from now.'

'You exaggerate, Truscott. Tis but the end of August.'

'A few days to work what remains. A day's work undone now means a week's famine this winter, and you will not see that. Did you think you could sit and stare at the sea all day like a blessed mooncalf? Wag your Bristol tongue and lord over us? No. You shall work for every bite you swallow.'

'I have been working, Truscott, and for very wretched bites and swallows. Could we not just sail on Sunday to Harbour Grace?'

'Sail? Born with a caul on your face? Still there. Hitch that to a mast. Get out. Go weep at the sea. I be sick of the smell of you.'

I departed, equally sick of him, and as my eyes picked out the fire rocks in the dark, I saw I had been arguing with the wrong man. Only Lacey could help me. I petitioned him promptly upon his return, so promptly that his boots still tracked water from hauling a laden dory ashore. Men and women made quick work of unloading that dory as Lacey heard me out. His ketch, *Boyne*, lay at anchor safely past the fire rocks, and, wading a few steps with him, I fell into the dory. I explained myself further as he rowed back out.

Boyne lowered goods by block and tackle, and I quickly found myself in the way.

Lacey gestured to the men on *Boyne* and watched the cargo descend. 'Take the spare oars and help me row us back. I need your help on shore. We'll discuss this once we've unloaded.'

Back on shore, both of us soaked, Lacey waved at Boyne, and the ketch made moves to depart.

'Admiral Lacey, have you heard naught? I must get to Harbour Grace. Please, sir, you must help me row out to *Boyne*. At once.'

'Absolutely not. That ketch is due elsewhere. Mind that fatback!'

'Then give me a boat, a chart, and a compass. I'll row to Harbour Grace myself.'

'Mr Cannard, please. Each dory is used each day by a fisherman. A compass, if I owned one, would be useless. Myself, I think tis the rock here sets a compass to dancing. Likely now it played a part in your wrack. How long would you last in a dory, pray? And a chart? Do you think this is the Admiralty Office? I am but a landed fishing admiral, and one of a vanishing breed at that. I have no way of getting you from here to anywhere else. Flour, one hundred pounds –'

By now we'd reached his Hall. 'Then I am your prisoner.'

'No. Necessity's. And necessity calls out work only a lettered man may do. God, man, you've gone death pale. You see those barrels there against the wall? You'll be leaching from them soon enough. *Boyne's* skipper knows when to come fetch me. He is indebted to me, like all the fishermen here. I sell their catch, then buy food and gear and dole it out accordingly. How much they eat correlates to how much they catch. But there be a year's gap, for I buy in advance, the spring before they go out, then pay last year's debts with this year's catch. Precise calculating, I can tell you. Keeps me up many a night, figuring fair. Not one bite more than they're worth, unless they wish to lengthen the debt. Indebture, I call it, abeysance and indebture. Now I would think, John Cannard, that lists and figures is work more fit for your talents than chopping wood or catching fish. I'll be blunt: I'd be mighty feared to set you out on the water, for you'd slip overboard in no time, if you weren't shoved. So I invite you to be my clerk.'

My voice caught on the necessary speech. 'You are very gracious, Admiral Lacey.'

'You can sleep here now, in the Hall. I'll need you to start with the cataloguing of what I have brought back from Harbour Grace and what we salvaged from your ship. When you have finished, we can work out conversion tables from the catalogues of what food exists and what each man caught. Then there be the advances I spoke of. By God, I can't tell you how much I need the help.'

If invisible Newfoundland lies pinned to my table, then Benvolio hides, far off the edge and part way to my wall. Runciman's interests in Benvolio, revolution's warp and woof, might have been directed by that hushed foreign policy kings did not acknowledge. Wren, my unfortunate captain, told me four days out he could smell Runciman off me. When I asked how Wren knew Runciman, Wren hesitated. 'By his trade. Some men call him *Owl*. It will work as a strange reference for you, this task, for it will be only men of Runciman's cut will hire you from here. Tis thick money.'

Here in my telling one winter's night in 1754, Aurelius Jackman interrupted, asking me, 'What be an owl?'

I sighed. The first child born here to survive his first year, the man grown from the snotnosed brat hovering with the women at the stages my first day on my feet, and he did needs ask me what is an owl. 'The bird of Pallas Athene. A night bird. Great staring eyes that nictate. It calls hoo, hoo, like the question. It – there must be owls in the woods here?'

Jackman looked at me slyly. 'Gulls cry out like people.'

'Fine, fine, like a gull then.'

'Yet how is it a man – that Runciman – might look like a bird?'

I could have recanted the Apostles' Creed. 'He simply did!'

'A scavenger then?'

I banished Aurelius Jackman. 'Out, out! You have sucked my patience dry. Begone, man, until I might stand the sound of an idiot more.'

I will not resume that story.

16) MENHIR
LATE SUMMER 1723, ISLE OF BENVOLIO, AS TOLD JUNE 1734 TO
LIEUTENANT JOHN KELLY, RN, BY CAPTAIN CHRISTOPHER
MATTHEW FINN.

'Owl Runciman,' they called him, for his watching and his
night-hunt and the way he asked *Who*? Tightwrapped in damp
disguise, I'd touch my face and ask the same question. I sailed to
Benvolio with Matt Johnson. A second son, debt up to his tits, just
smart enough to be useful and easy prey for Runciman. Me
following along to learn the trade – 'learn the trade,' 'tis all a trade!
Johnson travelled as a passenger, sick and useless most of the way.
I worked the ship, to keep from going mad with boredom and
found I liked it. Runciman tasked us to find his precious Michael
Farr and then coax him back to England. I suffered much doubt
we'd accomplish this. But Farr surprised me. He wanted to be
found so he could gloat and refuse.

When Runciman needed to persuade, he would talk. Incessantly.
Incessantly. Morning and night, over food, while pissing. He even
got me to sketch Farr's face from his descriptions. But it was Farr's
value Runciman tried to press into me. Hoped I'd take Farr as a
model. An experienced courier who could handle papers, cash,
arms. Intelligent and efficient, vicious and cold. Violent when
angered – Farr had beaten two men to death. A useful capacity,
when harnessed, Runciman called that. Farr also spoke four
languages. His speech came wordy and decorated and hid a deep
coldness. He looked melancholy, but he would bark laughter at
brutal misfortune. He hurried with his food.

Runciman studied my sketches. —Very good.

Christ, what a crooktback lame story Runciman came up with.
Did he want us to fail? Matt Johnson, pretending to be a Jesuit
with me playing the mute servant-boy so as to gain entry to a
monastery on Benvolio and wait for word of the missing Farr.

That long table where we ate with the Franciscans, their brown
eyes, green eyes, blue eyes, fine noses, fleshy noses, brown hair,
black hair, white hair, Johnson speaking to one or two of them in
Latin – Runciman's training keyed my senses to a weird pitch where
I knew things before reason could explain them. Those monks
knew why we'd come, though they might never say it. Finally he
arrived. Through a tunnel, he later said, a tunnel blocked with a

mighty stone. I found him while sweeping a hallway. Be sure, I got much practice walking silently. All you heard was the sigh of the broom. The abbot's rooms were nearby, so I handled the broom to sound as though I moved farther off, not closer. Then I leaned against the abbot's heavy door and listened.

A man prayed. An Irish voice rattling through words as though they were tasks, as though he must speak many more before sleep. I listened for a long time, but the mumble slipped into silence, then a snore. The abbot's steps came to the door, and I flattened myself against the wall, barely breathing. When the door opened, it hid me. But then the abbot closed and locked the door behind him, catching me. He abused me in his own language, then smiled a bit, boxed my ears and shoved me so I fell. I knew I must find and advise Matt Johnson.

At table that evening, in the dim gold light of sunset without candles, I recognized the face I'd sketched. Details I'd missed: a broken nose and a cloth bag, slung over his chest, left shoulder to right hip. He called it a nunny bag. I tried to avoid his eye, but he caught me looking. He stared me down. I stared back. Johnson missed the entire exchange.

The three of us left the monastery the following morning and travelled hard across scrubby rocks and hills. Like Norway. Like Newfoundland, but much warmer. Speaking little, Farr got us to a strange cave. It reared up forty feet, all cracks and dents and dust, all delicate menace like a cobra. I saw an engraving of a cobra once – that hood. Yet the cave also looked like a cottage, if one warped by a fever-dream. The steep roof gave slide to hundreds of rocks, fallen and piled against the east wall.

So. Sunburnt and standing as far from England as from heaven, Johnson and Farr argued.

First, the tired question dropped out Farr's mouth as he mauled cheese and licked the whey that leaked between his fingers. 'Runciman and his plots, aye, on who else's charge would we three hug the edge of Benvolio?'

Johnson compared Farr to someone named Ahab, and Farr grinned.

'Runciman hides what makes a man gurgle in an alley, hides behind policy and reports, but he sees, like those menhir staring out, staring down. When I cast my thoughts back to this damned rock, all I shall ever see is those tall squinting statues, all neck and face – Christ, they unnerve me. Did they burst up through the ground, shrugging off soil and smaller rocks to glare down on us and judge? Spine of a whale, a piece of it, what are they called? I saw the same face in scrimshaw once. Who is it? Like someone we have all seen but cannot place. Ferocious. Taller than we are, the head growing out of stone. Christ. Look behind us. Naught but more empty land. Higher ground, that's what we need. Johnson. Wasting your thoughts on prayer?'

Johnson met Farr's eyes with some fear, as if expecting to be struck. He'd looked at me suchwise the night we met. I'd rolled him out of a puddle and exposed his beaten face to the night air of a Portsmouth alley, and I'd said quietly, 'My master Runciman would know if you still refuse.' As on that night, Johnson rose from his knees like a foal. He studied the Irishman, studied the crumbs of cheese at the edge of his mouth, and said, 'When, Farr? When can we leave?'

Farr ate more cheese and said 'Been away long?'

Johnson lied, as Owl instructed, and then took it on himself to lie further. Said he'd been gone four years on a fool's errand to Barbary, to find word of another agent who'd disappeared, but that he'd arrived in Barbary with wretched timing – the land shook with revolt – men fixed to crooked crosses – and the Sallee Rovers stole him for ransom. He'd met an interpreter, handily, a Spaniard, hair and beard in long plaits to his waist, each plait of his beard knotted off with a tortoiseshell bead. The beads clicked as he moved. The interpreter spoke passable French and primitive English. He decided, so Johnson's story went, that Johnson threatened the emirate. He'd not got the wit or the knowledge to puzzle out how this was so. To find out, he put Johnson to the rack.

Farr laughed. He had been sitting on the ground, his chin bowed, his eyes on the horizon, nibbling cheese. He held up one hand, so graciously, to indicate he meant no insult.

So Johnson continued his tale, saying the interpreter racked the English out of him and then left a time. He returned with 'this pup' (meaning me), a ship's boy made prize by plundering Sallee Rovers. Said he tried three days to make me speak, but I loosed not one word. Then Johnson described his discovery of my injuries, of how I'd been utterly unmanned while still a boy. Happily, the interpreter returned, plaits knotted so his beads would not click, to lead us aboveground. A Benvolian trader waited in the harbour.

The interpreter leaned down at Johnson's feet and drew a fish in the sand, just where a wave would soon melt the impression away. From there we sailed to the abbey on the western shore.

Farr rubbed his itchy back against a rock and said, 'Horseshit. You travelled dead straight from England to find me. Runciman did not even expect you to last out the voyage, so he sent one of his boys, that one there, to coddle you along. And to give me instructions in cipher. Did you not know the boy had instructions to give this to me, and me alone? Hard to know if passing the cipher was more to test him or test you. Now there be the odd fleck of truth in what you say. I believe in the boy's old injury. I even believe Runciman sent you on an errand. The Owl has figured out at last that I've had enough of him and wish other employment, but you see, Johnson, I'm too valuable. I know the land here, I know the people, I know the policies. But by Christ, for a chance to get off Benvolio. I did once. But that damned Owl found me, sending in two redcoats to bring me back, if you please. Fuckery. All of Europe, or in your case all of Barbary, stretches in front of us like some tantalizing fat woman, and we're set to hide in her until he plucks us back, wet and squirming. Myself now, eight years on this island. I've been back to England twice, should have been three times, but I missed a rendezvous. That ghoul always knows I'm coming and sends agents to meet me. And they take me back to the next ship sailing for Benvolio. I tell you, this is no life but a sentence.'

Each man stared northwest. Johnson took in a breath but said naught.

Then Farr nudged him and asked if he would rather be back with the Franciscans. 'Hide amongst your own skirts at the abbey. Go papist. Runciman will never find you there.'

Johnson still said naught. I tried hard not to stare.

Farr tore into him again, saying, 'Johnson, my man, you're not afraid to return to England? You're not the same Johnson that Runciman had beaten half to death in Portsmouth? Tis all in the ciphers the boy gave me. I believe Runciman tried to do you in. Consider it: if you return, will Runciman pay you enough to even dent your debts? Creditors and bully-men: will not you be beaten again? And again, until you bleed to death some night? No need to turn your back, Johnson. I have asked you some simple questions. I err now and then.'

Johnson said, 'You err now. Is this some further test of my loyalty?'

'No, no,' Farr said. 'You are unwell. You should be retired, put on half-pay like some naval officer in peacetime. What may I do to help you, Matt Johnson, and make certain Runciman never finds you again? Why? Because I am tired, too. What would your dream be?'

Johnson shut his eyes, and a breeze stirred his hair, and he said, 'Freedom from debt. And freedom from this work.'

Farr said, 'Agency is a young man's work. But freedom won't come without a great deal of noise first. You can't go back to England. You're not fit to go to the colonies, working the fishing boats or the coastal traders. I have no proposal yet, only the desire, and this is the loyalty I want to test: will you forsake Runciman and work with me to get off this damned rock and become our own men? Will you join me in the knowledge that should we separate and Runciman catch up to me, I should say naught of you? Will you do the same for me? God will not protect you, but I might. Once Runciman pins you to a spot on the chart, he will catch you. He does not let his dogs stray so easily. Think you I am still Runciman's man because I wish to be?'

Johnson said he thought Farr enjoyed the work. Then Farr demanded that Johnson tell him about me, and my uses. Johnson said, 'At the abbey he swept the floors, mucked out the pigs.'

I arranged stones, all the good little witless mute, but when I happened to glance up, Farr was staring at me. I stared back, and Farr said my eyes burnt hot as a forge. 'Now then, Johnson, back to your safety. I'll be some time yet arranging our disappearance, for it must be done in secret, and my funds come by way of Runciman. Eventually. Where shall we hide you in the meantime? And how will you pay for it?'

Johnson said, 'Take whatever you want. Take my soul if it stop your mouth.'

Farr laughed. He said 'I see no candle, bell and book, no *homo fuge* throbbing on your forearm. I don't want your soul. What use would that be? I'd have to be hauling it back up through the dirt while the devils would be hauling it below, and the screaming would keep me awake.'

Then Farr rose suddenly and strode to where I'd arranged small rocks so they resembled a leafed vine. Briefly taken with the image, Farr grabbed me under the arms, hoisted me up, and said for payment, he'd take me.

He staggered as I wrenched myself out of his grasp. I aimed a kick before he could get up, but he caught my foot and upended me. That fall knocked the breath from me, but I gasped in enough air to call Farr a dog-fucker.

Farr laughed and compared me to a pig that squeals at sight of the knife. I kicked him properly then, right in the stones. He fell, and I rolled out of reach. Farr vomited cheese and said 'Not mute, then? I'd as soon break that one's skull as trust it.'

Johnson stood over Farr, looking happy. I didn't like it. He commanded Farr to stay on his back so they might bargain. 'Get me to safety, keep silence, and keep the boy.'

'You care not what happens to him, then?' Farr asked.

Johnson said I belonged to Runciman, who would see him dead, so any bad turn for Runciman would be reason enough. Farr said he'd witnessed more cleverness in a sheep getting penned for the night and advised Johnson to choose a line of deceit and stick with it. Johnson kicked Farr in the ribs, and he said, 'Will you get me safety?'

'Chainshot fuck you in darkness.'

Spittle flecking his lips, Johnson kicked until Farr gave assent to the ground. He wiped them clean with the back of his hand. Then he sat down near Farr, straightened the robe over his legs, and stared northwest. Again.

After a time, Farr managed to stand. He called me over. 'Bristol boy, if so you be, tell me your name.'

I told him 'Kit', and he said, 'No surname? Finn will do. I like it. I'm not accustomed to assault from servants, Kit Finn, so go at me once more, and I'll bind and dump you a mile from the crossroads. Leave Johnson. Leave your thoughts of Runciman, too, for this is Benvolio, and you are mine.'

Farr grasped my wrists and forced them together, most painfully. I refused even to whimper.

I woke up alone on our last morning in the cave. The fire had gone out. The fire being my responsibility, I feared a few good smacks from Farr if he returned to dull embers, so I hurried it back to life. I had fallen asleep the night before to the drone of discussion between Johnson and Farr. Johnson deciding, questioning, deciding different. Farr muttering of changed minds and treachery and how he now understood why anyone who knew Johnson would try to beat him to death.

Beautiful sunrise that morning as Farr picked his way back to the cave, blood on his hands and clothes. I did not ask after Johnson, for I did not want Farr to utter aloud what he'd accomplished. Runciman's orders, or Farr's desire? No, I did not ask, but Farr somewhat answered me. 'Because he kicked me when I was down, my head rattling in the rocks. Could not be trusting that. I need to know whom I can trust. Did you let that fire go out?'

I ran from Michael Farr the second chance I got, as much because of blood as gold.

We'd just delivered a sack to a woman of about twenty. She'd risen up from the high grass and held out her arms. She did not take the sack; Farr placed it in her hands. Then she calmly walked towards the high rocks. I asked Farr how long he had lived on Benvolio. 'Too long. Better to answer this: how shall I get away from here? Policy. Interests. It rests on this, Kit: who will own this island, England or France? And meanwhile, how do I please the locals enough to get away?'

We met a goatherd and his companion a few weeks afterward. By then Farr could no longer hide his emotions from me. His disgust and fear in the goatherd's cottage – all in the neck with Farr. I hoped that neck would get wrecked in a noose some cold morning, joint by tingling joint. The goatherd embraced and kissed Farr, who was slow to return the greeting. When Farr hesitated, the goatherd pointed at me as if to say, *Am I the only man bearing new faces?* The second man looked like he might be the goatherd's brother. He kept his large eyes fixed a way off, as though he spied demons over your shoulder but could not say. He made the request, or gave the order; Farr and the goatherd scratched maps in the dust. I figured it out. Farr must kill a man. A murder. For money. Disguised as a bad debt, or revenge. Farr agreed, and policy rose off him in a stink. The goatherd turned to his flock. The second man departed into the darkness, invisible after three steps, silent after four.

Farr said to me, 'Test by fire, salamander.'

I slept next to him, as I often did, and soon he rubbed at me, and I smelled animal blood and dirt off his nails. I let him do what he wished, for he'd long since found out. Handily, though, he carved me a sort of open pipe from wood, wider at one end, so I could safely piss standing up, provided no one looked too close. He kept me warm. By then I'd gone two months bloodless. I woke up sick. Then I bled heavily, and it hurt very much. Farr struck me twice across the face for it, and I knew I must run. Yet Runciman said I could trust Farr. The much-safer Owl. Me and him walking in Portsmouth in our guise, gentleman and trusted servant. I'd carry Runciman's heavy leather bag, and he would say, 'Farr may be trusted. You'll be safer with him than many, but watch yourself, as always. And come back. More tasks await, and I much value you, my *rara avis.*'

As we travelled, delayed by my bleeding, I asked Farr directly, 'Whom were you asked to kill? What if you get caught? Do you not fear a trial?'

And he answered, 'Aye, as I fear I'll go to hell for stealing, so I shrive. Christ, I'll need join the Franciscans after this. I fear a trial as I fear the menhir. I have as much chance of actually going on trial in Benvolio as I have of growing wings and a cunt. I'd claim vendetta if caught, but I'll not be caught. Know you how the accused are decided in Benvolio, Finn? 'Tis near as humane as English policy. *Ex informata conscience.* The judge's conscience informs him. Angels whisper to him in his sleep, tickle his ears with their godly tongues. Bribery, idiot. The judge might interrupt a trial gone on weeks after an imprisonment of months, and cry *O, ex informata conscience!* Me, the foreigner? The judge's conscience would inform him of my shining innocence. Then I'd be released into the open arms of the men who wished me dead in the first place. Vendetta is more efficient. These people have no government but foreign meddlers, Venice, France, England and Spain, of which I am one cracked and dirty finger. But I like the cash. I still carry some of the Owl's gold. The goatherd promised coins and rings, all of it likely stolen. Cash, not promises: with gold I might escape. Reach the coast and secure passage as far as France. I can make my way from France, work my passage, haul lines again. By Christ, Finn, I could do it. *How many miles to Babylon,* did you ever play that? *Marlow Marlow Marlow bright, how many miles to Babylon?* And one stands over there, and one stands over here, and there needs be a third standing blinded in the middle. *Threescore and ten. Can I get there by candlelight? Aye, if your legs be as long as the light, but take care of the old grey witch at the roadside.'*

149

I prayed to God: make my legs as long as the light.

Farr kept fingering the string of the nunny bag and looking at me. Absent-minded sometimes, he'd call me Melitta as we travelled to kill. We got stuck in soft ground. Thought I'd drown, or worse, die trapped in mud past my hips, the earth sucking at me, washing away the old blood. Farr hauled me out. We rested on dryer ground, and when I brushed off mud, I brushed off old blood with it.

Brain-rotting gold. Farr whispered in my ear as though reciting prayers, steady in memory if uncertain of meaning. 'Gold. I expect the abbot has already written to Runciman, and that, Finn, is why we need the gold. Only gold will stop men's mouths, and then only till they swallow it. It warms to the touch. Flamed, it becomes more malleable than flesh. Come with me. Owl will hunt my glittering trail, but this time he will not find me. Be good to have you along. But naught without its price. Before we see a glint of the gold, the gold, the one way off this weird rock before we harden into menhir – my knees feel already stiff – we've got a simple transaction.'

All part of learning the trade, this learning to kill on demand. Runciman intended I study such a lesson from the start, because Michael Farr, rogue or loyal, would teach it.

We walked for days, finally reaching a house Farr knew well. A girl flitted from a back window and descended to open the door, beckoning us up a stairway. She held no candle. The walls felt cool and bumpy. The girl locked us in a high room.

Farr worked his whispering on me. 'Be silent. Not one thump, not one whimper.' Hearing that threat again, my belly got cold. Farr kept whispering, explained in quiet detail and with much repetition just how to kill a man. Like a beating, only with words, always striking the same spot. 'The setting first,' Farr said. 'He shall come walking past this house tonight. He is slow and weak, very thin, hardly living. Another man will call out a window and distract him. The distraction is essential. Then you shall pull a dagger from the boot and stab him in the heart. The simplest thing. The heart, the heart, it must be quick and it must be the heart, dagger's sharp enough, stab these sacks of seed, the heart here, here, here, stab here, it must be the heart. It will seem the work of a faction, a cadre, local policy. Some youth none's seen before and none shall see after, ghost in the night, that shall be your part. Run quickly to the back of this house and come up to this attic, where I shall be waiting. And I shall be watching. Set time, distraction, the heart. All rests on you so we might earn the gold coins and chains and dust and race to the western shore to meet the ship. The gold is essential. Buy passage, work passage, stop men's mouths.'

Thin light pried past the roof, and it made us look like shades. I shook. I cried. Farr kept telling me all his useless experience, his easy kills. He set up boxes and a sack of flour, marked the heart, and politely bade me practice. I stared at the sack of flour. Farr struck my face. I stabbed the flour sack. Again and again, until I stained myself white.

I dropped the dagger. 'Why? Why can't you do this, your own God damned work?'

Farr struck me again and asked would I not kill if attacked, and what did this matter, for, this being not our feud, the specifics of it touched not our souls? Indeed, this transaction would service a greater need. I cringed at his 'indeed.' Any time he used that word, I'd best bring the discourse to quick end with obedience and rightful awe. But he sniffed out my hidden thoughts and little promises to myself to run away. He darted behind me and jerked my jaw up and back, saying, 'Recall how easily I might slit your throat. As quick as that, and in silence. Did you hear Johnson cry out?' He let me go, and I turned quickly to face him. He took the dagger from the floor and pricked his fingertips with it. And he said, 'I could not let you live, not knowing what you know. And why have you do the work? Because it pleases me.'

I'd not felt so cold since Coltman broke my finger.

I wore Farr's boots. I kept the dagger by my right calf, and I waited in the dark, outside the house. The wheeze, the pace: I recognized the noise of the target. My heart slowed, and my sight sharpened. No torch tonight. All emotion and memory dried up, and – who, who? – Kit Finn stabbed a stranger. Hard shove, clothing and skin rasped. The wet dagger slipped easily back into the boot. The man collapsed, thin and weak, just as promised, and I ran back to the house. Got to the high room and retched at the door. Heavier steps plodded behind me, and their owner reached around to unlock the door and hand a quantity of gold coins and figurines and dust to Farr.

We descended once more and slipped out the front door. I kept spitting because my mouth felt polluted, and we mounted the same horse. The girl who'd first let us in spoke quietly to the man who'd paid Farr, and this man turned on us with ferocious words. Farr jabbed his bare heels into the horse and grimly translated. 'You stabbed him in the arm.'

I'd failed. Useless. And now Farr would kill me. I'd no doubt of that.

Once the houses were behind us, Farr shouted curses at me over his shoulder. 'Galloping like this,' he said, 'we'll need to water the horse as soon as we're at the river. I will give you a fine reckoning there.'

Oh, he reckoned me at the river. I screamed my little pleas, and he pounded my head and mouth, kicked my ribs and hips. The horse drank noisily. But then my heart slowed again, and Farr suddenly restrained his hand in mid-air as we both recalled just who walked barefoot and just who still had the dagger. Crouching away from the blows, I slipped Farr's dagger from the boot and attacked low, cutting his Achilles tendon. A trick he'd learnt me himself, but I never thought it would work. I stabbed him next. Thigh and upper arm. Then I slashed his face as though roughmarking a map. Almost justice. I loved it. 'A scar-ruint spy,' I said. 'Earn your bread now, dog-fucker.'

Those marks would never heal. Each man setting eyes on Farr would learn and remember that face.

I cut and yanked the nunny bag from Farr chest and got his blood all over it. I tucked the dagger back into the borrowed boot, and rode hard for the abbey and the western shore to rendezvous with the Benvolian trading ship. Farr screamed after me, voice fraying: 'I shall hunt you. Hunt! Seven days, seven years, I shall hunt you.' And some more about slicing off my tits and ripping my womb straight out my cunt, til he choked on dust and his own tears.

Dread? Not this time. I laughed. Being of no parentage to speak of, only Runciman, Johnson, and Farr – dangerous names I must discard – I held on to the more useful bits of my stories and worked a passage to Massachusetts colony as Matthew Finn. One name given me, the other I stole, some little memorial so I'd not forget the dangers and needs of gold and spymasters. I enjoyed the joke.

17) 'IF YOUR LEGS BE AS LONG AS THE LIGHT'

Aurelius Jackman asked me many troublesome questions. Lacey discouraged young Aurelius from speaking much in the time he lived with us, after his widowed mother traded her son's labour for extra food for the younger siblings. So, after Lacey's death, Aurelius spewed questions at me like a stogged river just freed. A particularly vexing one: 'What are the correct forms of prayer?' I had just unwisely confessed my time at Cambridge for Holy Orders, and now we careened towards a pit of heresy. Some papists had always lived in Port au Mal, Irish of course, indebted somehow to Lacey. Jackman did not care about this. He said, 'Speak to me of the best forms of prayer. Please.'

I smiled, recalling how it had been Lacey's task to tend to the souls of Port au Mal, when he felt like it. 'I am no minister, Aurelius, not like the man in Harbour Grace.'

Aurelius always sought even a whiff of a clergyman when we voyaged to Harbour Grace on business. Once, accompanying Lacey, he found one preaching in the street. 'Tall and blond and voice on him deep as the water out the bay, speaking of pilgrims.' Then that slyness came to his eyes again as he said, 'Did not Admiral Lacey keep a Bible here someplace?'

I doubt Aurelius remembered the day Lacey read a lesson; perhaps his mother told him of it. That lean spring, just gone 1721, around the time Lacey's ketch *Boyne* should have come due. I slept badly, waiting for a voice to cry sight of *Boyne*'s sail. Hunger clawed. Sleet had been falling for days, coating the trees until they bent double, crowns frozen to the ground; and then the sleet would melt and the trees slowly rise until the sleet would storm again. All that summer the trees would struggle to straighten; some never did. Ground treacherous as grease, yet sometime in the night a man had come, slipping and falling, wet and cold and thin. Water flew from his hand when he struck me. The door to the Hall blew open, its warped edge caught by the wind and pried back to slam against the outside wall, and our wet intruder leapt inside, breathing hard. I lay on my bed dreaming all this until I knew the step at my side was no trick, and I woke and rolled over. Only the absence of light. Out of that came a fist. Then weak daylight, pain, and Lacey shaking my shoulder: the stores had been upended, pillaged, any noise of it obscured by the banging door. Our remaining fat and flour: gone. Slipping, cursing, slipping again, we visited the shacks, one by one, until we found lips glistening with fat, fingers white with flour: Michael Riordan, one of the indebted papists Lacey had brought from Harbour Grace, huddled on his pallet, crouching near the wall. Housemate Eamon Gate stared at him.

Riordan turned pale; Lacey said naught.

Lacey and I returned to his Hall. It happened to be a Sunday morning, and along the way, Lacey pointed at the bowed trees. 'Not one left upright. How will I fix him? Cannard. Go door to door, now, tell everyone to gather in the Hall. Gate and Riordan, too.'

Stiff jaw warping the message, my words caused some surprise, and no little resentment, but all did as their Admiral bade, and soon enough we did crowd into the storeroom of Lacey's Hall. The sleet melted to a cold rain, drenching everyone. The inhabitants, even Riordan, gathered in front of Lacey's rough table, which he also used as a desk. I stood to one side, facing the door; Lacey stood behind the table, leafing calmly through the Bible he had taken from his chest, acting as though his congregation did not exist.

Then, without looking up, he opened to *Luke* and he read, quite badly: 'It is impossible but that offences will come, but woe unto him through whom they come. It were better for him that a millstone were hanged about his neck, and he cast into the sea, than he should offend one of these little ones.'

I thought this a very odd choice of lesson after the work of a thief and waited for the commandment to forgive. Instead, Lacey rode hard for the mustard seed. 'And the Lord said, If ye had faith as a grain of mustard seed, ye might say unto this sycamine tree, Be thou plucked up by the root and be thou planted in the sea, and it should obey you.' Then he calmly closed the Bible and covered it with his strong hands. In the dimness of the Hall, he seemed to look us each in the eye, one by one, and then he said, 'A thief stands among us.'

Truscott cleared his throat and glanced at the faces around him, seeking guilt. He found it in Michael Riordan.

Lacey continued, saying, 'A thief who would steal from your mouths what we've all hoarded through the winter. A thief who has stolen from our shared future.'

154

Riordan spat before addressing Lacey. 'We run out of food on two accounts.' He pointed to the water. '*Boyne* is late.' He pointed to me. 'And we got an extra mouth.'

Lacey nodded and said, 'An extra mouth with a near-broken jaw. A mouth belonging to a man who shall pay his debt. Now, who among us has not been hungry? Who among us has not lain in bed all day, cursing the wind for waking us, then struggling to get back into sleep, only to wake in the true darkness, staring, alert and hungrier than before? And cold? Who has not felt the cold?'

Young Aurelius, the only walking child present – we did not expect the two infants to survive the winter – spoke high and clear, 'I'm cold.'

Jackman cuffed his son on the ear. 'Shut that. Admiral's talking.'

But Lacey nodded again, gesturing with his hands for Jackman to be gentler with the child. 'We are all cold. We are all hungry. And Michael Riordan would steal flour. At least when Prometheus stole fire, he shared it.'

The inhabitants turned to look on Riordan, now stepping back and stumbling against an empty barrel. Truscott had come forward and conferred with Lacey, pointing to the door. Wind drove the rain against the walls, and more sleet hid within the rain. Aurelius took advantage of this pageant to pick up a torn net and play with it, pretending he stood in a dory, casting out. The inhabitants stepped towards Riordan again, studying him in the dim light, squinting at him. Lacey questioned a suggestion made by Truscott, and Truscott shrugged, indicating he had done his best. Lacey nodded his assent and then showed his palms as though helpless. Michael Riordan remained at the back of the Hall, guarded by a group that did not speak, only stared. Aurelius tried to cast out the net, but it tangled at his feet. Truscott, always graceful despite his size, strode to where Aurelius played and took up a small wooden box. From that he removed a massive nail, more a spike, and a heavy hammer. Riordan looked from Lacey to Truscott, back to Lacey. Truscott returned to the doorway and reached as high as he could above the doorjamb, to the split log just beneath the ceiling, and drove the spike through the wood. Then he opened the door, letting in some blessedly fresh air, and sleet, and hammered again, beating down the end of the nail against the wood outside. I wondered this stress did not crack the wall. Coming back in, wet but determined, Truscott eyed the placing of the spike, measuring. Once more he strode to the back of the Hall, picked up a line and returned to the doorway. Still, none spoke, and still, Aurelius played at casting his net. Truscott bowlined one end to the spike, tugging hard to test the strength of his enterprise, then called the accused. Riordan did not move. Truscott spoke then with heavy contempt. 'Must I come fetch you?'

None argued hunger. None argued for Riordan.

Riordan walked quietly to Lacey and Truscott. Looking to each in turn, Riordan scowled and removed his shirts, peeled away layers of fraying grey and yellowed cloth. Loose skin sagged off his bony arms and back. Truscott tied Riordan's wrists together. Rain and sleet rattled against the walls.

Lacey looked it over. 'Truscott, open the door, or I shall drive him against it.'

Leaning around Riordan, Truscott did so, while Lacey rummaged through his chest, carelessly moving some objects, treating others as fragile treasures, until he retrieved a three-tailed cat. He studied it a moment, as if to read something written on the knotted-off ends, calmly positioned himself behind Riordan, and swung.

Aurelius's head jerked round at the dull slaps of first blow, and he dropped the net. He saw the second blow, and the third. Riordan cried out at the fourth and ran out of breath on the seventh, and he swayed through the doorway to meet the sleet. Lacey stopped, his face red and sweating, and Truscott released Riordan, supporting him to Lacey's own chair. Riordan's breath came hard round his teeth.

Lacey gave benediction. 'Go on. Go home. Mind the ice. Cannard, get the water from the kettle there, see if it be cool enough to bathe his back.'

Gate did his best to tend Riordan's back. One day, late May, when the rotten snow melted so quickly that all footprints deformed, both men left. Lacey pronounced them 'Masterless, with legs long as light.'

We did not see Riordan or Gate again.

Grown Aurelius snorted and frowned at me. These memories of a flogged thief hardened into anger and something akin to contempt in his eyes. He said 'If you will not answer me, then you be no better than Admiral Lacey.'

A bitter comparison. 'No better than Lacey? That man confided in me he'd stand between ye and God, aye, he'd make himself obstacle and ye'd never see round him. You compare me to that? Get out of my sight.'

'Yet you'd control me with those words, Cannard,' said Aurelius Jackman before gently closing the door.

Open the door, Lacey had said, *or I shall drive him against it.*

Aurelius felt grieved, I later discovered, by an illness of his wife, who indeed died a few days later in a fever so high, said her oddly subdued husband, so high he feared hell and not bones burned up through her. True to himself, Aurelius laughed graveside. He grinned at me, eyes hot like I never saw them again, as I dutifully recited blunt words of dust. Then, still grinning, Aurelius recalled aloud the day she agreed to be his wife. 'And she says to me, Is it so long as it looks?' The wind blew colder and harder here up the side of the blunt cliff, in the only bit of high ground we had, and this strained ribaldry did not warm me. Aurelius chattered still, and now his sons smiled as their father continued, 'I promised her it was and that it would find her happy coin. And she said, Well, I suppose, but let me test the goods. And as God be my witness, that woman squeezed my codpiece so as to know herself whether I'd stuffed it not, and then I proved it.' Snorts of laughter then and high giggles from the women. 'And soon after that came Tobias here.' Whereat Aurelius Jackman, newly bereft of his wife and best companion, led the duped mourners back to his crooked shack.

18) THE WANDERING EYE
MAY 1733, THE PRIVATE HOME OF ADMIRAL DUNTON,
PORTSMOUTH, ENGLAND.

—I like not your colouring, Mr Kelly. I beg my old admiral friend for shelter where I might meet with capable man of intelligence, and look, God dumps a redhead at the door. I like your name even less. You smack of Judas and the Irish, sir, of passionate treachery.

Lieutenant John Kelly kept quite still. Abuse like this from Phillip Runciman was hardly unknown, but it was always unwelcome. Kelly half expected a sympathetic glance from Runciman's secretary, a bitter-looking man on a crutch, face heavily scarred, but no look came.

Dull daylight, further blunted by heavy curtains, played across Runciman's slob-ice eyes, and the left one wandered. He cracked his knuckles. —Reports on your conduct in the Navy are pleasing. Sir Alexander – Admiral Dunton to you – tells me you were an inquisitive but quiet boy, and you stopped smiling after your father was lost at sea. Dunton, I fear, is not long with us. You noticed his wasting, his high and fruity breath? He drinks water constantly, is somnolent. I have seen it before; soon he shall take to sleep and not wake up. However, I did not beg for a capable man so we might mourn a death in advance.

Lieutenant Kelly waited.

—Gold, Lieutenant. The gold stories are spat in the coffeehouses. Men laughed first, added lascivious details. The gold was taken from a ship en route to Boston. The gold was stolen from a woman of means taking secret passage on a frigate.

Runciman stood up and walked out around Kelly, who studied the vacated shadow. Then Runciman's voice came from below Kelly's left shoulder.

—John Kelly, second lieutenant. Is there anything more useless than a second lieutenant?

—Only a third or fourth lieutenant, sir.

Runciman stood in front of Kelly now, eyes cold and fierce and, somewhere, laughing. Little hands dwarfed by his large wig, he passed that wig to Kelly and exposed his naked head. —Do me the service of holding this.

158

Behind the desk again, Runciman reached to the back of his balding head and plucked out a grey hair, then laid it on a seacard that his secretary had just weighted at its four corners with small rocks. Runciman dismissed him, adding a command he lock the door.

The secretary stared and sneered at Kelly as he passed, and Kelly took a slow breath. Once the lock clicked, Runciman shook his head. —Keep my enemies closer, aye. Would you come study this, Mr Kelly? The seacard was privately sketched for me in 1722.

—Tis the Mediterranean, Isle of Benvolio.

—Aye, you'll make midshipman yet. Pry past the gold stories, and you may find Benvolio and the Finn stories.

—Who is Finn, sir?

—Truly, I should like to know. I hear Finn is a wicked pirate. Tales to frighten linkboys. A sloop called *Kindly One* crashed ashore in the Isles of Scilly a fortnight ago, bows scorched, master and boatswain long dead, murder done. One Matthew Finn named, Bristol-born by the accent, but also sounding of other lands. And I also believe Finn has stolen gold rightfully belonging to His Majesty, gold I needed to complete a transaction abroad. Do you grope at my meanings yet?

—I believe you speak of spies.

Runciman touched the hair on the seacard, sad, or made so by a trick of the light.

—Lost, taken or killed? No, this one ran. Others longed to go masterless, but this one ran. A description from Massachusetts colony, Captain Matthew Finn, master of the sloop *Kittiwayke* out of Salem, a Bristolman distinguished from his fellows by having escaped the Sallee Rovers at Barbary but there suffering an injury that prevented his full growth to manhood. My Finn, the one I knew years ago, also bore such injury. Botched circumcision, a lot of it about. No doubt Finn said something to anger those with knives. My Finn, just Kit then, also lamed my secretary and carved up his face. A little thing, 'Kit' or 'Matt' Finn, but tricky enough. Stole the Benvolian gold, too, coins, figurines and dust that rightly belong to the King. Windows demolished, watches overcome, and handsome ills by your contrivance done. Ha! Finally pinned you wriggling to the chart. Murder, no less, though also a matter of time. What hauled the maddened fury out of you?

159

Kelly's fingers sweated under the wig as he waited for Runciman to speak sanely.

—Consider Finn my prodigal, Mr Kelly, my *rara avis*. Consider Finn cunning and dangerous. Consider yourself Finn's escort back to me, alive and in good health, for I need and I will have Finn's especial usefulness. And the gold. Pass me my wig.

—Please, sir, with respect –

—Why you? Why the useless second lieutenant for this desperate task?

Kelly nodded. Draught stirred the curtains, and his fingers quickly cooled.

Wigged once more, Runciman poked the lieutenant's belly.

—Because you get hungry. You're newly assigned to *Dauntless*, a frigate under the command of Captain William Cleasby. Cleasby, unfortunate but unavoidable. I believe his patrimony to be an old admiral's, surnames notwithstanding.

—Sir, I must ask–

—Because *Dauntless* is ready to depart, that's why. Even Dunton can only pass me so much grace. Captain Cleasby is charged with protection of your life. He has also been ordered, in my most fawning and complimentary manner, to leave the interrogations of Finn to you. Success will not go unrecognized.

Kelly swallowed. —A delicate situation, given command.

—I cannot help you there. Captain Cleasby is stained by stupidity and disagreeable habits, but captain he is.

—To know more of the mission than my captain –

—At least on *Dauntless* you shall be first lieutenant.

—Sir, you have surprised me today.

—You are quick to anger, Mr Kelly. Learn to hide it.

—And you, sir, ask too much.

Phillip Runciman stepped out round the desk once more, avoiding the light. —Do you not understand it yet, Mr Kelly? This work is not new to you. I *ask* naught. I demand.

19) THE CRITCH AND THE NUNNY BAG
1731-33, SALEM, MASSACHUSETTS.

Coat unbuttoned and flapping loose, Newman Head peered downhill towards the waterfront. The early November sun still gave heat inland, but at the waterfront the air would be cold. The fog had burned off, and the water near the docks looked especially foul. In the burying ground, leaves still blazed yellow and orange; elsewhere they'd gone brown or fallen.

Newman Head stood in the doorway of Morrow's Tavern and tried to will friend and business partner Jericho Gosse to be on time for a change, and perhaps even sober enough to talk sense. As his neck chilled, Head decided he'd accept Gosse's turning up at all. Then he caught sight downhill of Gosse's fine coach.

The sun had bleached the muddy street to soft yellow dust that winter would soon make dark and wet; for now, dust flittered and floated up at the horse's hooves. Hallooing, Gosse waved at Head but did not alter his speed. Head waved back. Head's business enterprises relied on credit and freight with Gosse Shipbuilding, and while Gosse also relied on Head, Gosse stood superior, and he never discouraged supplication. Lately, however, he'd favoured Head with long repayment terms and low interest. Business be damned: he'd not watch a fine old friendship fall captive to mere money.

Jericho and his widower father James had arrived from Boston when Jericho was nine. James Gosse, distantly related somehow to Newman's merchant father, Catch-the-Hope Head, settled in a small house. He quickly got work with Catch Head, keeping his accounts. Jericho and Newman became like brothers, or the way brothers are supposed to be. For years, people shared rumours of James Gosse's hiding a good amount of gold. No one ever saw this gold, and the Gosses behaved and dressed with fierce respectability. Father and son also both took a taste for the stronger liquors, James insisting frequent doses of rum were the best medicine for his rheumatism. Certainly he'd nothing else to ease the pain. As boys, Jericho and Newman once spied on James, delicious fun until James tried to straighten his swollen knuckles to pray, until James cried out when he grasped a large goblet with both hands and lifted it to his mouth. Rum dribbled. Jericho told Newman to go home. Neither boy ever spoke of it afterwards. James Gosse died a few years later, in bed; his rheumatism had turned his skin to leather and his joints to stone.

Catch-the-Hope Head took Jericho in, and he soon had to lock up the stronger drink. Thirsts aside, young Jericho Gosse proved himself an able shipwright and even better draughtsman: he could see finished work in the very air, he said. Apprenticed to shipwright William More, Jericho worked happily. Once Jericho came of age, Catch Head put the young man into contact with an uncle in Boston and gave him the family gold, which he'd been holding in trust since James's death. Family contacts and melted gold financed a new business: Gosse Shipbuilding. Now William More worked for Jericho Gosse.

Gosse Shipbuilding turned out three fast sloops, *Apple Bough*, *Oak Leaf* and *Kittiwayke*. Up to one-quarter freighted by Gosse himself, with the remainders rented out to Newman Head and various other merchants, these sloops traded along the colonial coast: the West Indies to Newfoundland, with Salem and Boston in between. Salem's fish might be carried anywhere, but acts of Parliament dictated what she got for it, and when. Salem's sugar and molasses, bought from the West Indies, must be shipped back across to England for inspection and duty payment. After inspection, the cargo would then be loaded onto different ships sent back to the colonies – at predictably inflated prices. Merchants like Newman Head felt that the sugar and molasses already belonged to the colonial market and did not need to be sent anywhere. But Head played it carefully, shipping some of his sugar and molasses to England. Some. The rest he kept and traded as the market demanded. Newman Head and Drinkwater Gosse partnered in what Head called 'cocksure ingenuity' – never 'smuggling' – and both men profited from a common taste for something sweet.

Then reports of *Oak Leaf* being overdue arrived from agents in Boston, St John's, and Harbour Grace. *Oak Leaf* had disappeared. Gosse declared the sloop lost, guessing at a hurricane, the day the shipwrights laid *Kittiwayke*'s deck.

At Gosse's news, William More dropped his tools. His two sons sailed on board on *Oak Leaf*.

—Gone, sir?

Gosse nodded. His luck and finances had never taken such a blow. He ordered *Kittiwayke* be leadbummed, delaying her completion by a good year and angering More.

162

—Lead will slow her down, Mr Gosse, and the first hurricane she's in will beat that lead off her.

—I right well conceit you on the storms, but leadbumming will keep her swift. Weeds can't grow on lead.

—And how will you pay for it?

—As I pay for all else. Shipping rates.

Apple Bough's rates jacked sharply. Newman Head and his fellows submitted – all speed for molasses, and all speed for re-scheduled payments. William More left Salem, signing his considerable skill to a rival shipbuilder in Boston. Gosse lost some respect and business after More's departure but had nearly regained it with the quick and profitable shipping runs of *Apple Bough*.

When Gosse entered Morrow's, Head was ordering flip for them both. Goody Morrow had mixed the flip in a large pitcher, blending old rum, ale, raw eggs, sugar, pumpkin, cinnamon and cream. Rather than heat the drink over an open flame, she dunked into the pitcher a red-hot iron ball dangling from a chain. The drink frothed and hissed. Goody Morrow removed the ball and poured the flip into two large goblets. Gosse and Head toasted each other and then moved to a table.

—Gosse, you're late.

Wiping his nose – it always ran in the cold – Gosse took his spyglass from a pocket and placed it on the table. He drank quickly, burning his mouth and throat. Flip was good as a meal to Gosse; he could work the entire day on this goblet.

He poured another. —Am I?

—I've little time. I thought we were to discuss money owed –

—No fear, I've not forgot that. Take that spyglass and go outside. Peer out the harbour and tell the name of the ship coming in.

Head returned quickly. —*Apple Bough*. She's over a month early and should be on her way to Newfoundland.

—Aye, so she should. Still want that one-quarter ownership?

The two men travelled in Gosse's coach down to the waterfront, Head soon buttoning his coat as the wind chilled. They argued schedules and finances, and then took shelter in one of Head's warehouses. Head often felt the foreigner at the waterfront now, walking like a landsman. He'd made captain himself, but on marrying he promised to stick to a desk.

163

Apple Bough sailed steadily closer. Finally, the sloop anchored in a spot that would keep her free of dockside congestions, and lowered a jollyboat. A small man stood in the boat, holding a davit line. Gosse and Head walked out to Gosse's dock and waited for the boat to reach them.

Gosse swayed a bit. —Not come in to the dock? Has Captain Button gone cracked?

Head figured it out. —More to the point, has Captain Button gone to God?

Apple Bough's short and ropey mate, much tanned and lined by the sun off the water, secured the boat to the dock, a rough coffin the cargo.

Gosse frowned. —First mate Matt Finn and a coffin. You've guessed it right, Head.

Gosse extended his hand to help Finn up to the dock. Swaying on sea legs, Finn muttered about kindness and high tide and then delivered the unwelcome news. Head studied Finn but could not guess the mate's age – skin rough but firm, squint lines at the eyes and scowl lines around the delicate mouth.

Finn's voice was throaty, a bit high but hardly sweet. —My apologies for this delay, Mr Gosse. Captain Button died less than two days ago, and we being so close to home port, I thought it fit that he get a dry burial.

—I right well conceit you. Properly done. Come with me into Mr Head's warehouse, and I shall write you up as new captain of *Apple Bough*. If you will accept, that is.

Once done with paperwork, Finn stopped to talk with some men who had known Button. Head and Gosse waited. Then Gosse caught sight of someone he needed to speak to and walked straight into a tall man called Pilgrim, who carried a barrel on his shoulder. Gosse and the barrel knocked Pilgrim off balance, and as he tried to correct himself, he fell into the water. The barrel slammed onto the dock but did not break. Matt Finn slipped off a heavy coat and a cloth bag worn crosswise over the chest and jumped in, swimming for the rings that marked Pilgrim's descent. Finn dove. Bubbles rose. Gosse and Head jostled to the edge of the dock. The water almost revealed the shapes of arms and a face, and Head thought Finn had pushed Pilgrim upwards, but that made no sense, Finn being so much smaller. Pilgrim's head broke the surface, then Finn's. Gosse and Head both tossed dock-tied ropes to Pilgrim; he caught one, slipped under, rose. Finn caught the other. Sailors and dockworkers quickly helped Pilgrim and Finn out of the water, offered jackets and flasks. Gosse hurried them into Head's warehouse, out of the wind, while Head broke open a crate of woollens.

Teeth rattling, eyes red and raw, Pilgrim stared at Finn. —How did you know I cannot swim?

Finn, shaking just as hard, could not immediately answer.

—Couldn't just watch you sink.

Head got them sitting back to back and then wrapped new blankets round them. Then Gosse got the idea to take them to Morrow's in his coach – a spectacle, perhaps, but also a necessity. At Morrow's they could get close to a fire.

He did this, returning some time later, offering Head cash for the blankets.

—Keep your coins, Gosse. Are they well?

—I rented them each a room and paid for a new suit of clothes. I cannot speak for the fit.

—Take this back to Finn.

Gosse accepted the coat, which he laid out carefully on Head's chair. Then he picked up the cloth bag and held it up to the light.

—Heavy. So be the coat.

—That hardly concerns us, man. Tuck the bag into the sleeve and bring the lot back.

—Jumped straight in. You doubt me making Finn captain now? I'll have him master of my beauty, *Kittiwayke,* yet. He's travelled for the edges of the charts, let me tell you. Button always spoke well of him.

—Poor John Button.

—Poor Matt Finn, you mean. John Button died with his manhood intact. Finn got – injured in Barbary. Captive into Sallee. Button told me most of it, but I heard Finn mutter it once: still a boy, a capture at sea, red tapestries, defiance, a brutal cutting away. You can hear it when he's angry; that voice rears up like a mad colt. Passes water with a wooden pipe. But I must go. I'm sure you right well conceit the reason: a new investment to attend.

Until late in the autumn of 1732, Jericho Gosse thought no serious difference of opinion existed between him and Captain Finn. Gosse had looked after Finn, giving bonuses for fast runs, and Finn had shared the bonuses with the men. Head put down

Finn's popularity as a captain to three things: plaindealing, hard work, and an exotic history. Men who worked *Apple Bough* and then *Kittiwayke* described Finn as a good listener, if somewhat melancholic. Gosse warned them not to ask Finn anything of Barbary.

The dispute between Finn and Gosse began after Gosse insisted that his *Kittiwayke* must be considered the finest sloop ever to sail from Salem. Finn, inspecting *Kittiwayke* after a hurried voyage home from the West Indies when wintering over would have been more sensible, declared the sloop unfit for firewood. Newman Head tallied cargo piled on the dock – sugar and molasses – while half-listening to Finn and wishing Gosse would hurry to the waterfront. Cold wind, biting with the promise of snow, tormented everyone.

Finn's strained voice screeched through the din. —A streel. A scow. That useless fool Gosse expects me to sail something that would sink in a puddle.

First mate Con Pilgrim spoke, his low voice rumbling, but Finn's voice cut through his words.

—Tell me not what shape she's in when I got my own eyes, Pilgrim. Lead bums be all fine and wonderful when the wood of the ship be strong enough. I still thank God we did not drown this voyage, *Kittiwayke* leaking like an old man's eyes. Barely a year in the water.

A sailor appeared on deck, limping; he'd injured his ankle on a weak rung of the companionway.

A dark red flush spread up Finn's neck and face. —Fuckery! Rotten splinters now, tearing at his flesh, planting pus and inflammation. How was that rung hewn, with milk teeth? I'll 'right well conceit' Jericho Gosse. Whose kiss decided this lot? Tis no hard deal to see William More had little hand in *Kittiwayke*. I'll not have my men injured for no good reason. I've paid enough out of mine own purse to keep *Kittiwayke* seaworthy. And she could be a lovely thing, graceful and quick. Now look on her. Precious lead peeling off, that lasted three hurricanes – luck, naught else. She needs a proper careening. Blocks are in good shape. I paid for those. Canvas, too. Think you I've seen a half-penny's recompense?

Newman Head looked up from his tally, embarrassed by this spectacle. —Captain Finn, I ask you to consider that you are hard on Gosse.

—No. Easy, now that I stand on dry land. I was hard on Gosse during that hurricane.

—Tis wear and tear and all speed for molasses, sir. Parliament will almost certainly pass the molasses tax next year.

—All speed for molasses? All speed for repairs, or ye'll have no molasses all of a cause of my patching leaks and tarring coats withal. Sir.

Head stepped closer, lowered his voice. —Gosse may not possess the cash.

—I be not stupid. I know ye lot owe him money. And he owes his own creditors. Ye're merchants; all is owed. But Gosse? A majority owner delaying repairs on his one and only vessel? It don't tally. I apologize for drawing you into my anger, and for the profane language that bothers you so, but take comfort in what Pilgrim believes: the sin of cursing taints me, not you. Tell me, sir, may I get some of that clover balm your wife makes for that man's ankle. I need – hie!

A rotten line thumped Matt Finn in the head, falling from a spar above. Part of a footline, Finn saw, a splice of badly rotting rope probably discarded in Roger Conant's day. The topman's feet kicked like a hanging man's until he hauled his belly over the spar. Bent over at the waist now, he grinned and called down. —Line's gone, Captain. Shall I splice it anew?

Finn sniffed the rope and then threw it in the water. —Get yourself down, and lock the hatches. We shall see neither splicing nor delivery nor departure nor even daylight to count by until this ship's dog-fucking majority owner hauls his arse down here!

—Captain Finn, surely you cannot blame Gosse for one bad splice. Your boatswain –

—Then whom? Hey? Who else oversaw and approved rotting rope for *Kittiwayke*? Mr Head, that man could have fallen and brained himself as we discussed clover paste, all of a cause of Gosse's neglect. I am sorry to catch you in this, but your cargo will sit until Gosse gives *Kittiwayke* a proper going-over and full repairs.

Gosse did not come that day, nor the next. Finn walked to Morrow's and entered so quietly that none saw. Steady, land-legs back, Finn threw a hat down on Gosse's table – a hat that had been a gift from Gosse. The hat just missed the pitcher of flip. Gosse looked up slowly. There followed a conversation that even the discreet Goody Morrow described as *storming like the kettle*:

excuses and promises from Gosse, disgusted refusals from Finn. Finally they agreed to meet again, at Gosse's home this time, better for privacy. Gosse would then present a detailed plan for repairs. Finn, still too angry to wish Gosse as much as *Good day*, left Morrow's hatless, cutting through a children's game of 'Marlow, Marlow, Marlow bright' in the street outside. Gosse then beckoned over one of the other customers in the public house, a tall and muscular shipbuilder, repeatedly fired for his unsteady temper, one Martin Sikes. Gosse bought him a drink.

The following night, after departing the decaying home of Jericho Gosse, Finn visited Newman Head, who often sat up late, and then set out for *Kittiwayke*. The sloop was tied up near Head's warehouse, and, on this tide, only her rigging would show over the dock. Smiling at this, Finn hesitated. Someone rattled a locked door to Head's warehouse. Finn slipped into the nearest shadow to check on the door – and could not breathe. Dazed: pain and tears after a stiff blow to the face. Vision focused: a large man, that mercenary lout, Martin Sikes, held Finn up against the warehouse wall by the throat, one hand just under her jaw. The other hand groped under her coat, fingers hard and rough across her chest and upper neck. Air hunger hit, and Finn struggled hard, aimed a kick. Sikes, dodging Finn's knee, let go her throat but slammed his other hand into her collarbone, forcing her back against the warehouse. Finn tried to reach the dagger she kept in her boot, but Sikes leaned on her, groping now at her shoulder. Finn gasped air. *Walked right into this. Pike would be ashamed.* Writhing, reaching into her left coat pocket for a rock, she screamed – a short scream, given that she couldn't take in much breath, and given that Sikes whipped his hand back round her throat. He stared. Then he took up the strap of the cloth bag. Finn slammed the rock into Sikes's groin. His grasp weakened, and she slammed again. Dagger in her right hand now, she cut him as he fell. She stumbled off a few steps, breathed in deep, and ran for *Kittiwayke*. Con Pilgrim's head appeared over the edge of the dock as he swiftly climbed the rigging, startled by the scream. Finn leapt to the high ratlines over him and hung on, looking like a youngster splayed out against a net.

Finn and Pilgrim scuttled down the lines, Finn coughing and retching. Pilgrim watched as Finn vomited over the side and then darted below.

168

A week after this incident, about which Captain Finn told any man who asked, and several who did not, pointing out bruises on face and throat and then asking loudly where Martin Sikes might be, Gosse visited Head at his home, greatly surprising Head. Dust had settled, and Rachel, twelve and tired, tended her to mother. Mistress Head sat in front of the fire, scowling in pain and clearly too weak to stand. Unaware of Head's growing irritation, Gosse stared. He'd known nothing of this strain.

—Gosse. What is it you want?

Mistress Head vomited something black into the bowl Rachel held. Rachel stared into the bowl. Bottom lip wobbling, she stood up smartly and strode past Gosse to throw the mess outside.

Gosse licked his lips. —I've come to warn you away from Captain Finn.

A short dispute, Gosse's voice soft and wheedling, Head's barking louder with each sentence, until Head shouted: —I care not if you think Captain Finn is Satan himself! Here is truth for you: Captain Finn was the only thing keeping us to you. He came to me last week to advise he'd bought you out and become majority-owner of *Kittiwayke.*

Gosse took a step back; Head had never dared name the devil before.

—And as Matt Finn is now majority owner of *Kittiwayke*, it is with Matt Finn I shall book cargo, not Jericho Gosse. Coward and liar. All Salem knows what you tried to do to Matt Finn by way of Martin Sikes. And now all Salem will know what you tried to do here tonight! No, I owe you naught. My debts cleared when Finn took your ownership. Lend you? What? Money? With Parliament discussing more molasses tax to keep those bloody West Indies merchants happy at our expense? 'Right well conceit' this: you are ruined, and it is of your own doing. For it is not only bankruptcy that haunts you now, but your blackmarked reputation. None trusts you. None will do business with you. Sully my house no more, Gosse. You'll give my child nightmares.

As new majority owner of *Kittiwayke*, Captain Finn directed repairs and re-payment plans for the merchants. Head uncovered irregularities in Gosse's arithmetic and reduced the other merchants' debts accordingly. He buried Gosse's financial records, which also detailed precise amounts of molasses, in a spot behind his house where Rachel had once buried a dead fox.

Creditors seized Gosse's house, and he moved to the edge of the town. Some children told stories of seeing a wild man on his hands and knees in the woods, and their parents beat them for it. Stories of strange business in the woods had already proven dangerous. It was Gosse. Goody Morrow took pity on him, permitting Gosse to supp on strong flip once a day in her kitchen, out of sight of the others. Tacitly ignored, Gosse sheltered in the hollow trunk of an ancient tree as he built a fragile shack for winter. He often spent the first hour after dawn crawling on the ground, picking through mounds of earth.

—Do you ever curse those who harmed you?

Con Pilgrim had asked that question before; now he slurred it. His breath helped heat the blankets he'd tugged up to his nose.

Feathers poked through the pillow and scratched Matt Finn's face. Not as drunk as Pilgrim, and in a considerably fouler mood, Finn wanted only to sleep. Pilgrim, when he got liquor in him, wanted only to talk and smoke, and they'd sat up late, Pilgrim sharing much of his past and his desire to do something good with his life. Winter cold had forced them ashore, them and half of New England. Finn had, with luck, obtained the usual room at Morrow's, but Pilgrim could find nothing better than Head's warehouse, Head himself being away on business. Finn invited Pilgrim to share the room. Any man would.

They'd slept in the same bed before, Pilgrim showing all courtesy and respect for his captain. This night, however, Pilgrim asked repeatedly about the Sikes attack, about the scream he'd heard. Finn kept changing the subject and finally just pretended to be asleep.

She listened to Pilgrim's breathing – settled now. Snoring. Fully clothed, as was Pilgrim, she peeled back covers and stepped into the cold, rattling teeth preventing a good curse. She blew on an ember in the grate, but the ember quickly cooled to black. Delicately, brown plait heavy down her back, Finn retrieved a chamber pot.

Pilgrim's snores stopped, and the mate turned over, patted the bed. —Wound paining, sir?

Finn said nothing.

—But do you ever curse those who did that to you? You must work to forgive them. Not the stories, I mean, can't curse stories. The ones who did it.

Finn gently got back in the bed. —Pilgrim, tis late. And you be drunk.

—But do you hate them?

—I hate chatter when I want to sleep.

Pilgrim lay on his back, tears on his face. —I would protect you. In all your black moods and odd manner. Little Barbary sacrifice, that be what Jericho Gosse called you. He says you told him all. Would you tell me of it someday? Now, coward. Tell me why you squat to piss, hey ho?

Because it's too damn cold to fuss with the wooden pipe. —Shut it.

—Gosse be not worth the breath. Tell me. Gosse weaving the promise of some great tale. I get none of it. Why am I the hungry cur?

—Pilgrim! Surfeit. Else, sleep on the floor.

Con Pilgrim lapsed into whispers. Snored.

Back to back then, like under the horse blanket. Just for warmth.

Finn turned over, cuddled into Pilgrim's warm body, wept. *Just for warmth.*

Thoughts straying to buried books and fox bones as he worked late one evening in June 1733, Newman Head knew nothing of the arrival His Majesty's frigate *Dauntless*. He did, however, look up from his work as a Royal Navy lieutenant and some red-coated Marines swayed by the window of his warehouse. Curious but busy, Head returned to his accounting. Half an hour later, he upset his inkpot as he jumped in fear at the sight of Marines and the lieutenant dragging Jericho Gosse towards the waterfront. That this happened in fading sunlight disturbed Head even more: uniforms at dusk, uniforms and bored faces – except Gosse's.

Held fast by a man on either arm as they pitched towards a boat, Gosse spat dirt and projected his voice like a minister. —Ye can't press me. I'm a colonist. Queen Anne's rule. Head! Newman Head! Get Newman Head and tell him I'm pressed. Sweet God, help me, I want to die on dry land. Head!

Newman Head stood by his warehouse, hands on his hips. The lieutenant ordered the jollyboat away.

The following morning, the lieutenant returned to shore. Newman Head, coming back from a business meeting at Morrow's, found the lieutenant banging on his warehouse door. He had fine bones and thick red hair, and his plait reached the small of his back.

Head stopped a few yards away and called out loudly enough that others might hear, though his voice did not carry as well as Gosse's. —Have you the courtesy to knock before pressing a man? Who are you then? I can't hear you, sir, do speak louder. Lieutenant Kelly of His Majesty's frigate *Dauntless*? Am I Newman Head? Aye. Know I Jericho Gosse? It pains me to say so, but aye. Accompany you back to *Dauntless* and help clear up a few difficult matters concerning Jericho Gosse? If I must. An order? Oh, you can't order a colonist, but you can request co-operation from an Englishman? Lead me to your boat, then.

Head counted guns. *Dauntless* was a sixth-rate frigate, then, ship of the line if need be, but also small enough for swift errands. She'd likely carry a commander rather than a full captain in wartime; a full captain might consider the posting an insult or a step backwards. Men worked repairs on high masts and spars, and a dozen red-coated Marines drilled in the stern. Head declined the sea-chair and instead climbed aboard, impatiently explaining he'd sailed from age nine to twenty-four and made captain himself, thank ye, glancing back a moment to the frail Salem docks. Polished and holystoned, *Dauntless* gleamed.

Kelly took Head below through brown shadows to the captain's day cabin and bade him wait inside.

Already there: Jericho Gosse, hands folded in front of him on the table, his face greasy and disturbed. His jaw hung slack, and his nose ran freely. His bright and darting eyes set upon Newman Head.

—I knew you'd come and get this all straightened out. Head, they're after *Kittiwayke. Kittiwayke.* I own –

The ship's captain entered, the lieutenant following.

—I am Captain Cleasby, commander of His Majesty's ship *Dauntless.*

Cleasby carried himself with not only command, as did Kelly, but with a blatant sense of entitlement to that command. Impatience, anger and desire marked his face. Head immediately knew he'd no wish to please this man.

Gosse got to his feet, but Head leaned his arse on the table and folded his arms across his chest. Kelly goggled at him a moment, nearly dropping the charts he carried furled under his arm. He made to speak again, but Cleasby got a word in first.

—You've met Lieutenant Kelly.

Kelly pointed with his free arm. —Captain, this is the colonist Jericho Gosse, former majority owner of *Kittiwayke*. It turns out –

Cleasby gave a slight sneer.

—It turns out that Gosse has sold *Kittiwayke,* in part to this merchant, Newman Head.

Captain Cleasby nodded at each of them in turn. —His Majesty thanks you for your help in this matter. The charts, Mr Kelly. Head, I will be much in your debt if you would show us *Kittiwayke*'s routes.

—Why?

—Because I ask it.

—But why?

Jericho Gosse tried to laugh and managed a yelp. —Because they think Matt Finn's a pirate.

Captain Cleasby pointed to the chart. —Please, Head, *Kittiwayke*'s routes.

—Folly. Matt Finn is as much a pirate as I am.

Pretending to study the chart, Lieutenant Kelly looked up.

—Stolen some gold, have you?

Gosse yelped again. —Molasses, more like. I'll show you. *Kittiwayke* runs Salem to St John's, Newfoundland, stopping sometimes at Boston first, then Harbour Grace – also Newfoundland. Then tis all speed for the Indies.

Head rolled his eyes; how had he ever called this cur his friend?

—Captain Cleasby, if you've got Gosse to show you, why do you need me?

—To confirm it.

Gosse tried leaning back in the chair, forgetting it was bolted down.

—You think me unreliable? But I have no reason to lie and deceive you gentlemen. Head does.

Captain Cleasby looked to the merchant. — Know you of the stolen gold, Head?

—Tis 'Mr Head,' I thank ye. And I am no liar and no pirate. Nor have I truck with suchlike. The only thief with whom I've suffered intimacy sits right here with dirt beneath his nails and leaves stuck to his hair.

Lieutenant Kelly looked to his captain, who nodded. Kelly then spoke to Gosse. —Share with Mr Head the facts you have shared with us.

Gosse stretched as though waking from a sweet nap to a sweeter day. —Matt Finn bought *Kittiwayke* from me. Cuntspliced me to be sure, but he paid with gold – gold, Head – small papist idols, medallions, coins and dust. Mark me, I know not whether that gold was stolen, but I also know not where a man such as Matt Finn gets that amount of gold, and that after already spending some for repairs to *Kittiwayke*. No, I am not saying Finn stole that gold. I am saying Finn stole my reputation. And reputation here is like currency, can't do business without it. Matt Finn does not understand business. Expenses. Balances. The tricky flow of money. When Finn offered to purchase *Kittiwayke*, he showed me gold. That was the night I proposed I cut him a share of *Kittiwayke*'s profits. Finn and I disputed. See, I fear not to admit it. I could just deny it, but no, I own up: Finn and I disputed. I owned *Kittiwayke*. Well, majority-owned her. I designed her tidily and saw her built well, at extra expense. But I ran into trouble. Finn never understood that. Pestering me for repairs when *Kittiwayke* sailed sound as my heart. We'd already lost *Oak Leaf*, and she took payment for *Kittiwayke*'s lead bum with her. Then *Apple Bough* disappeared. With only *Kittiwayke* left, I'd debts so high I could never see over them. So it needed be that I borrow against the merchants. As I said, Captain Cleasby, tis all out now between Head and me. He knows I did borrow from him. Short shipment here and there. I would pay them back, and that right quickly. Finn fussed about repairs and what he'd paid for. Then he threatened me. Won't sail without repairs, said Matt Finn. Then he said he'd sail *Kittiwayke* to Boston and take out a bummary.

Well, no man's going to mortgage *my* sloop, never mind repairs, so I said 'Come visit me. I will propose a plan to you. See if we cannot square up?' So he came to visit, and I explained my inner arrangements and offered him a right fair cut. Do you know what he said? He said 'No.' He said he'd buy my share of *Kittiwayke* off me first and only, that being the price of his silence about me borrowing against the merchants.

174

I named him a ridiculous price that included what the merchants owed me. Finn cut it in half. 'Tis all to buy my silence,' said he. We dealt a little more, and then Finn said 'Surfeit.' Then, delicate like the spider, he worked loose that ancient cloth bag he wears over his chest. Called it a nunny bag. Never did I suspect he carried such a treasure in it. He opened that bag and poured out some of the gold so it shone like fire on the table. 'Draw up the papers,' said he, 'and meet me at Morrow's at noon.' I nodded, and I could not stop myself from reaching for the gold. Finn blew out the candle. By the time I got it lit again, Finn had gone. Deserted me. And took his gold with him. Next morning, too sick a sudden to rise from my bed, I could not meet Finn, nor send him any message. I got down to the docks the next day, to set things right with Finn, only to hear the tale of how I hired Martin Sikes to throttle him and then steal the nunny bag. Matt Finn might be a little weed of a gelding, but he is no man to anger, for he scolds like a maddened bluejay. Most of Salem knew his story afore I'd even shaved.

I got to *Kittiwayke*, but Finn, who liked to live on board her even in home port, refused to see me. I left word with Pilgrim that I should await Finn at Morrow's, with the papers. Seemed every man in Salem frowned at me that day. Even the children ducked away. Finn gave over the nunny bag and the gold and took ownership of *Kittiwayke*. Excepting my creditors, I did little more business after that day.

Kelly and Cleasby glanced at each other, and Kelly asked it:
—Finn owns *Kittiwayke*?

Newman Head frowned. *Gosse, you viper.* —Quite a yarn you've spun for the Royal Navy, Gosse. And where lies all this wondrous gold now?

—I'm coming to that. Remember the cloth bag? The lieutenant there, he's much interested in that bag, so I gave the rags of it back to him. Creditors were asking me to melt the family gold, but I'd long since spent that. So I had the nunny bag treasure melted instead: rings and figurines and coins. Then the creditors came, someone telling them I had enough gold to pay my debts, and they divvied it up. But the dust, the dust in the bag, I kept that. I know now why Finn wore it.

I walked early one morning, the bag sweet and heavy in my hand. I cupped it, sniffed it. I tripped. Easterlies that day. Being

175

much rotted by old blood and sweat, the cloth burst. The easterly took the gold like it was dust from the ground and swirled it afore my eyes, whereat it glittered and blew away.

Head let out a long breath.

Gosse sniffed again and glanced at Head as though expecting a kerchief. None came. —As I said before, Lieutenant, I am prepared to swear this in a court. And think on this. If Matt Finn wore just that little sack round his neck, what all else has he stashed on board *Kittiwayke*? He rarely leaves her, not even in port. Tis said he'd almost rather freeze come winter than take a bed on land.

Lieutenant Kelly looked now to Newman Head. —Finn stole that gold. A young man then, short and high-voiced, called Kit, said to have been eunuched in Barbary. Green eyes and a heavy brow. Indentured to a man in England who desires both the return of the gold and the return of his servant. Have you anything to add, Mr Head?

Silence.

Lieutenant Kelly ducked and rounded the room until he stood beside Head, who still leaned on the table. —Mr Head, I am now telling you far more than I have direct leave to do. In effect, the prize was stolen from the King, and it must be recovered, even a portion of it. The prize is more than currency, sir: it is essential to the King's business abroad.

Gosse leaned forward now, all polite attention. —Isle of Benvolio, is it?

Lieutenant Kelly interrupted Cleasby to answer Gosse. —How knew you so?

Cleasby frowned. —Mr Kelly.

—A moment. Sir. Gosse, give over. When did –

Captain Cleasby spoke as he might to a fierce child wielding a candle. —Mr Kelly, I will remind you who commands here.

Gosse wiped his nose with his sleeve. —Sure, all Salem right well conceits Matt Finn's been to Benvolio. Or is it Barbary what matters here?

—Barbary. You hear, Captain Cleasby? How much more proof of my mission do you require?

—One man's words prove naught, Lieutenant.

—My orders come directly through the Admiralty.

—Your orders, sir, surely include discretion and submission to my authority.

—No, sir. My orders –

—Stink of policy and will not be discussed before talkative landsmen!

Head's stomach clenched tight. Witnessing such eroded discipline between captain and officer chilled him. *Avert your mind, man.*

Cleasby turned to Head. —Can you share anything at all useful regarding Matt Finn?

—I can share with you that which you do not know. Captain Finn is a conscientious and fair man, much possessed by the cocksure ingenuity that gets things done. He can read and write and navigate. Unlike certain others in Salem, Captain Finn enjoys a rich reputation and much respect. He pays up on time and tells the truth, even when tis unpalatable. Being much concerned with fairness, he sees his sailors get a bonus when warranted, which is frequent, they being eager to please their captain. He has never harassed a female, nor has he staggered about drunk and fit to be stocked. It comes to this, Captain Cleasby: Captain Finn works hard, squares up, hurts none. What more is required of a man?

Neither Cleasby nor Kelly answered him.

—Now I'll be obliged to both yourself and the lieutenant if you could see to row me back ashore.

Head and Gosse, sitting back to back in the jollyboat, returned to the docks. Head walked directly to his warehouse, shut the door behind him, and sat at his desk, unable to work. Gosse slowly walked back to his unfinished shack.

Molasses dribbled over the lips of the critch on Head's table the September evening Finn and Pilgrim joined him for supper. The invitation to Pilgrim and Finn sparked a frenzy of cleaning and cooking, and, on Rachel's part, dedicated supervision of the servants. Rachel ran the house with an efficiency even Head found fearsome, and he'd tried to find a way to tell Rachel her dead mother would approve. Instead, around four in the afternoon, he requested she be at her liveliest tonight, for his guests needed happy company. Sweaty and limp, Rachel glared at him.

Finn and Pilgrim arrived pale and thirsty. Head blamed their state on being greeted at the docks with the news that the Royal Navy sought *Kittiwayke* and Captain Finn. Rachel did her best to stir laughter, and all behaved merrily throughout the meal, but when Finn, Pilgrim and Head moved to the merchant's study, the three dropped their smiles like masks.

Con Pilgrim spoke first. —Where did *Dauntless* put in for supplies?

Newman Head sat down heavily and clicked his tongue. —I know not. I should have victualled him out, made some money. Finn, tell me, what is so important that the Navy has come to Salem seeking you? Why do they say you've stolen from the King?

—Everyone in this house has stolen from the King.

—How dare you, sir? God save the King!

Finn pointed at Head's mouth. —Molasses stuck to your lips. Will you suck it off?

—Aye, but that's Parliament. Molasses be not thievery but protest.

Pilgrim spoke softly. —Has not first the King stolen from us with unreasonable taxes?

—Not another syllable, Con Pilgrim, not in my house.

The mood chilled.

Finn sighed, sounding very tired. —These Navy men will not steal my freedom from me. Will they steal yours?

Newman Head could not meet Finn's hard gaze. He looked instead at Pilgrim, who in turn studied the floor.

Squinting in the candlelight, Head considered how shadows changed a man.

—Who is 'Kit' Finn? Your brother?

—Is this all of a cause of Kit Finn? Tis a name I heard on Benvolio.

—And was he – were you both – the injury –

Finn made a great show of standing up and backing away until blocked by the study door.

—Speak *not* to me of Barbary.

Voice still calm, Head got to his feet. —This is not about old injuries, Matt. This is not even about two naval officers arguing over stolen gold. Did you take it? And what work be Benvolio in all this?

Finn scowled. Pilgrim looked at the ceiling.

—Did you steal the gold? Matt, know you what I risked? Me lying to the Navy, and Gosse hinting about molasses?

Finn said nothing.

Head took a step toward Finn and seemed about to touch the captain's face. —Who are you?

178

—Surfeit!

Finn punched the oak door. Skinned knuckles quickly bled.

—I'll thank you not to mention this conversation to anyone else, Head, just as you thank me not to mention molasses, conny? Pilgrim, to *Kittiwayke.*

They gave Head no time to see them to the door.

Past midnight, Con Pilgrim rattled his fingers against Newman Head's study window. The merchant stirred himself from his chair before the dormant fire. Neither man showed surprise at seeing the other still awake and dressed.

—Pilgrim. Come in. I'll stir the fire. Sit here, tis warmer.

—Leave the fire. I prefer none see my shadow.

Head chuckled and quietly pulled up another chair. —Won't be seen with a loyal Englishman? Oh, Pilgrim, I jest with you. You are too valuable a man to quarrel with.

—I've not come to quarrel.

—Speak plainly, then.

Pilgrim sat, staring at the embers. He leapt up and blundered towards them, blew them to angry orange, jabbed the grate with a new split. Ash clouded up the room. Leaning against the chimney, still clutching the poker, he turned to face the merchant. His large body blotted out much of the revived flame.

—I've known Matt Finn a good while, some years now, and I am the only man he calls friend. Twice now Finn's saved me from drowning. I cannot swim, as you know.

—I remember. Sweet God, Pilgrim, you sank like you'd leadbummed your feet.

—And Finn jumped in right quick. Knew naught of me, only that a man had fallen in the water.

—Only what any decent man would have done.

—But no other man did. Not Gosse, not you, not any of the dozen or so of ye.

Head frowned. —Aye, Finn jumped in before anyone else.

—Patience, Head, for I haul lines bound to strange ends. I've seen Finn act thus many times. Not so spectacular a stunt as the rescue of a drowning stranger, but nearly good as. Little decencies, courtesies and kindnesses easy to miss. Sometimes he keeps back pay from some of the men until we return home, and then he pays the man's wife. He attracts children, which bothers him. I call him

179

the Pied Piper of Bristol, though he's asked me not to. My point is this: strange self and stranger history aside, Finn does be a good man.

—I'll not dispute.

Flames crackled.

—Goodness in him. Works through him, like someone weaves it there.

—Our Lord God works at a loom? Not an idea our old fathers would –

—Head, please, help me reason. Help me understand. I sailed with Finn on *Apple Bough*, and then he bade me follow him to *Kittiwayke*. A more solitary and Godless man, I have never seen. He carries a rock twice the size of his hand in his coat's left pocket. Knew you that? And a dagger in his right boot. He be not Godless by design, but Godless he be, Godless and seeking. He recites but one prayer: 'God grant me a full belly and a dull voyage.' We talked of God when Finn wanted. I have had many more proper Sundays than Finn and so chinked his gaps the best I could. I –

Pilgrim put down the poker, turned from Head and squat down, his eyes to the flames. He looked at once much younger than his twenty-five years, young and frightened, and much older. For a moment, Head saw how Pilgrim would look as an aged man: white hair, pouchy cheeks, deep lines.

—August there I finally recognized the salt desert Finn wanders. The omens were out. Omens be what my aunt called them. Sudden blue flashes, flames they be, gone as quick as be seen. High in the night sky. Best seen on first watch. I was the watch officer, and *Kittiwayke* cut along fine, all quiet and counted for. Captain Finn came on deck. Scowling a bit, but that be how he often looks. And fit to disappear within his greatcoat. The night did not be cold. Finn's head bobbed out of the greatcoat like a head out of water. Stayed aft, arms well within the coat, head back, staring at the omens. Beautiful things, quick flames in the sky.

First dog watch, we'd been discussing Lucifer. The last sermon we heard afore departure had been about the deadly sin of pride. Finn asked me later if murder were not worse. I said aye, but pride usually played a heavy part in any murder. Then he asked if the angels had committed murder before God cast them out. That haunts Finn, God casting out the angels. The reflection of a blue flame shone across the wet of Finn's eyes. He pointed upwards and said to me: 'The angels fall.' I saw only stars and omens. Another blue flame, gone quick as we saw it, and Finn said again: 'The angels fall. Watch, Pilgrim.' And I did. Finn said: 'So many angels, God casts them out still.' Some of the flames fell low in the sky, on the horizon. Into the sea.

Then Finn turned to me, right quiet: 'I dreamt of God tonight, Pilgrim. An old man limped along the shore, made dark by the setting sun. With one hand He picked up rocks, shook them in His palm and tossed them away, where they mingled with other rocks and the water. In His other hand, fit to shake on wet ink to dry it: dust.'

That frightened me, Head. I cannot tell you how that frightened me. I be no cleric, so I could think of no words. Finn leant on the starboard bow. Omens flamed in the sky, and the waves glowed. Believing the angels fall still, Finn reasoned so: if God had cast out the angels, and cast them out still, what punishment yet awaited men?

Head knew he should offer the mate a drink, for his mouth must be dry. But he stayed silent, suddenly feeling he had no right to speak.

—Then *Kindly One*. In April. From Bristol. Just coming out of Harbour Grace as we voyaged in. The sun and the wind beat on us from all sides. Fair beating winds, Finn calls that. We could scarce hear one another on *Kittiwayke*, let alone the calls from *Kindly One*. Sky gone light to dark blue in a head's turn. Clouds blew across it and raced the whitecaps. *Kittiwayke* full and by, and Finn laughing. We hailed our fellow English ship, all of us inclined to skylark. Each captain hallooed and traded news, Finn of Salem and Boston, Tilley of Bristol. Finn declared he'd been born in Bristol but not seen it sixteen or seventeen years.

Our two sloops being close enough, Finn and I swung aboard *Kindly One*. Captain Tilley welcomed us again. I made our two lines to belaying pins when Finn gave a start and softly called on Christ. *Kindly One*'s boatswain, bent and bald and spotted by the sun, some of his ear gone, looked on Finn with much surprise. Clearly each recognized the other, and the old boatswain took breath to speak.

Finn smashed the boatswain's face with a belaying pin. I hear that wet crack now, ash on bone. The boatswain's arms twitched about his head all sickly and weak, fox in a trap. Finn struck again, and again, and the boatswain fell dead, face wrecked.

This happened in much less time than it takes to tell.

Then Tilley cried out: 'Mark, sir, you've killed him,' to which Finn replied, very flat: 'He's fortunate I did not shove the pin up his arse first.' And with that he fixed Captain Tilley a blow across the head, enough to knock him bloody. Tilley fell, insensible. I tried to pry the pin from Finn's hand. I am much larger, but I could not move that pin without breaking my captain's bones. Finn looked for a moment set to bash my head with it but then he threw the thing overboard, blood and flesh stuck to it. He looked like a man in mortal pain.

I unmade a *Kittiwayke* line, yanked it tight and got it into Finn's hands. Finn swung over to *Kittiwayke* and called for grease, rags and flame. Just as I set to swing myself, two men from *Kindly One* hauled me back from the gunwale and called over insults and threats. Finn lobbed back quick work of a ball of rags and rope ends set alight. The ball landed heavily in the bows, and the flames caught. The men let me go. *Kindly One* shuddered in the changing wind and drifted a short way. My line gone short and tight, I had to jump. I saw the pit between our two sloops, the black water lit on top by the glow of flames. No rescue from drowning this third time. *Kindly One*'s men scrambled for buckets and water, and *Kittiwayke*'s men stood behind Captain Finn.

He watched the flames in *Kindly One*'s bows as though watching a sailor furl the jib.

I swung over, fell hard against the hull and hauled myself on board.

Finn ordered we wear on to Harbour Grace, said we must resume our duties. No man spoke an unnecessary word. Finn retired below, and I did not see him again until well after dark. Finn said to me, 'Pilgrim, I hope you are not badly hurt.'

I answered no, and we stood side by side then a while. The clouds still raced across the sky, grey against black now. We could see them only when they got in the way of the stars.

'Come with me to the charthouse,' said Finn, and I did. And the wind beat fair. Finn made correction on a chart. He dipped his quill in the inkpot with much care. I asked, 'Who was he?' Finn said: 'Ned Coltman. Killed my one friend, smashed my head against a wall, used me foully, sneaked me on board his merchantman, and locked me in a sea-chest, waiting the best time to use me once more before I smothered and he'd have to throw me and the chest over the side.

'But, Pilgrim: I plaindealt with God. Coltman crowed about God a lot, about me being a gift to him. So I made my deal: God would rid me of Coltman, and I would accept what all after came my way, blessing or offense. God, or perhaps just that blind old madman, Captain Walters, wrecked us in the Isles of Scilly, and most of us died. I and one other lived, but I never knew who, all of a cause that he returned to England while I lay sick with salt water in my lungs. Many things since came my way, and I accepted them all. God and I had a deal. And then today I see him. Atthey warned me my worst enemy would strike in daylight. And I struck.'

The names made no sense to me, but I understood Finn. A sudden madness, a random encounter neither Finn nor this Coltman expected. And so my captain fell into hell. All the men on deck had witnessed the act. All the men, like me, suffered a decision that passed through us like some spirit. It might damn our souls, but we each to the last man chose not to speak of *Kindly One*. I did be trying to say this to Finn as he shook sand on the wet ink, then picked up the chart and blew the pounce dust away. Motes floated in the lantern light, and grit fell at our feet.

—Dear God.

Pilgrim turned to look at Head over his shoulder. —Revenge, Head? Murder? Or long-buried defence?

Head sighed. —The unswerving punctuality of chance.

—Myself, I dream of fire. I followed and did naught to stop Finn.

—You'd no time. And you said Finn was as like to bash your head in next.

—But I did trust him. That without thought. Trust him, I mean, not just follow his orders. I'd stand by my captain even if he'd said he killed the boatswain because the sea tastes of salt. And I'd have followed him and protected him. I be guilty.

—Twas not you who beat a man to death! And with a belaying pin. Sweet Christ Jesus.

Pilgrim stood up, slowly. —I fear this will make the navy business worse. Will you give Finn over?

—Do not insult me. Captain Cleasby does not want Finn for murder but gold. And as I know little of any murder and even less of any gold, I cannot help Captain Cleasby.

—How can you not know what you know?

—By the lateness of the hour, is how. You take care of Finn at sea. I will look after the questions on land. And I shall keep this story close. Now go, before your captain who needs you finds you gone.

This time Head saw his visitor to the door. He held the doorframe and peered into the darkness that had swallowed Con Pilgrim.

20) CHASING WORD
Mostly at sea, spring 1734.

—I should like to see my sister.

Captain Cleasby looked over the top of his hand of cards at the ship's surgeon. He hosted card games in his day cabin; his night cabin lay on the other side of the panel wall. The panels could be moved, and the deck cleared, for battle. —Where is she?

Pollard played a card. —Harbour Grace, Newfoundland.

Cleasby studied the faces of Dr Pollard and Lieutenant Penney and guessed their hands as easily as if the slush lamp light rendered the cards into glass. Kelly's secrets eluded him, which made for better games of Ruff and Honours than he'd played for years. But this also irritated him. Cleasby kept that emotion checked, for now; he relied heavily on Kelly for the daily tedium of staying afloat.

Lieutenant Kelly, partnered to Pollard and playing opposite Cleasby, re-arranged his hand. —Surely, Captain, you could consider a short side-trip for the surgeon. Harbour Grace is one of our ports of call.

Penney played badly, costing the game, and Kelly winced. Cleasby gave a hard sigh and stood up. —Mr Penney, never mind your lieutenancy, how did you ever pass the midshipman's exams with such a poor comprehension of probability and mathematics?

—I apologize, sir.

Pollard split the winnings with Kelly and got ready to shuffle the deck. —Rods and spheres and orbits, Penney: all in its time and place, and elegantly at that. Another round, Captain?

—No, gentlemen, and I beg your pardon. Tomorrow evening, perhaps. Mr Kelly, could you stay a moment?

Lieutenant Kelly watched Penney and Pollard disappear behind the closing door. Then he faced his captain.

Cleasby sat down again. —I see you looking around. You covet these quarters.

—Your quarters are most pleasant, sir.

—Did I ever tell you I once took up work as an agent? Intelligence agent, I mean, not shipping. Aye, me, Will Cleasby. Seemed a tidy job; I was already sailing, so I sought it out. An admiral of my acquaintance put me in touch with this fool who could not even fix both eyes upon me as we spoke. He looked for someone more interesting or important the whole while. He gave me a task a boy could do in his sleep, and I got it done quickly, very quickly, to show him my capabilities. I gave a message to the wrong man, however, but the intended man was late, and the man I saw in the appointed place fit the description. For that I got a kick to the arse. The intelligence man ordered me never to cross his path again. Look at me now, captain of a frigate. I suppose he must be dead, or else setting up other young men for betrayal and abuse. What say you to that?

—I say tis a most unfortunate story, Captain.

—Drop the pretence. You reek of spies as a whore reeks of men. We're months and months at this now. I read Runciman's work in your face as easily as I read a winning hand in Pollard's. Are we chasing a ghost? Who is this Finn, really? Speak, man.

—A murderer and a thief.

—Oh, pretty. The master as deaf to purpose as a powder monkey.

—Sir, I did answer your question.

—You parroted back the contents of my sealed orders. Protect your life, is it? How can I protect you if I know not the truth?

—Sir, the truth lies with Finn's answering to stolen gold and murder.

—Fine words on fine lips. You think me a fool.

—No, sir.

—Then tell me, Lieutenant, whom I must not only protect but cherish as my very compass, why do we now wear on to the West Indies?

—*Kittiwayke* works the molasses trade, sir.

—Barbados, by the devil, bright sun and fever. And if no success in Barbados?

—Massachusetts, sir, Boston and Salem.

Cleasby rubbed his forehead. —Boston and Salem again. And if no success once more? May we at least winter in Portsmouth, sir?

—As you please, sir, but Newfoundland be closer to Massachusetts.

—I like this as much as losing at cards. Such fuss and expense with no return? Does your Runciman cherish these secrets against me?

Kelly's stomach fell away. A delicate situation, as he'd told Runciman. Delicate as navigating high rocks and sunkers, and, if Cleasby's foolishness did not abate, as navigating fire at sea.

186

—Let me tell you what I carry in my name, Mr Kelly. Remember when we put in to St John's and got the new charts for Conception and Bonavista Bays from the Governor? I ordered us through Bay Bulls afterwards. Know you why, sir? Any inkling? That other Captain Cleasby, losing to the French, burnt and sank his ship *Saphire* in Bay Bulls rather than let the French capture her. Honour there, aye, and a mark on history. But for this Cleasby? Spies and diplomats, sir, cipher and murder. And this secrecy – is it punishment? Runciman would sit in judgement of me? Shake your head, aye, and give the excuse: Finn, Finn, Finn. To that, sir, I say gold, gold, gold. Finding that stolen gold, the credit of it will go to me. It must. I command this vessel. And your task, a secret from me, shall remain a secret to all. How like you that, sir?

—Tis no matter how or what I like, sir. By guess or by God or by the devil himself, we both stand bound to our orders. Take credit as it pleases you, sir. I shall make do with the truth.

Cleasby squinted. —You, sir, are naught more than a redheaded lying Judas. Get out.

Once Kelly shut the door, Cleasby slid the panels, strode into his night cabin, and opened his sea chest. Lifting a folded blanket from his hammock, he exposed an intricate and heavily worked merkin. This unusual variant, custom-made, boasted a tube of soft pelt and long leather thongs which allowed the user to lash the merkin into place. Today, he did not bother, using it quickly. The pelt was getting stiff.

Kittiwayke anchored once more in Harbour Grace, Con Pilgrim worried about souls. Raised by a devout aunt who'd taught that he must not only earn his livelihood by the sweat of his brow, but also earn the hope of his birth's redemption by difficult voyages, Pilgrim believed deeply in hell and divine punishment. He also believed one need not die to be in hell: not a destination, he told himself a particularly cold night on watch, but a state of the soul.

His aunt read him Bunyan; she had plucked the lost boy's surname from *Pilgrim's Progress*. She had advised him when praying each night to ask himself if he'd yet earned the right to be a pilgrim.

Working, he often sang verses of Bunyan's song:

Whoso beset him round
With dismal stories

Do but themselves confound;
His strength the more is.
No lion can him fright,
He'll with a giant fight,
But he will have a right
To be a pilgrim.

This day in Harbour Grace, ashore, Con Pilgrim swatted away large flies, the kind that landed on split fish to lay eggs. Spontaneous generation, his aunt called it. Although maggots and flies come from eggs, some creatures just appeared. Like Adam.

As did I? Con once asked, reasoning he must be spontaneous, lacking mother and father. His aunt said something about there being no reasoning we might see, save our faith. Then she called him by his full name, Constant John Pilgrim, kissed his forehead, and begged him to remember *Matthew*, chapter seven, verses sixteen to nineteen: 'Ye shall know them by their fruits. Do men gather grapes of thorns, or figs of thistles? Even so every good tree bringeth forth good fruit; but a corrupt tree bringeth forth evil fruit. A good tree cannot bring forth evil fruit, neither can a corrupt tree bring forth good fruit. Every tree that bringeth not forth good fruit is hewn down, and cast into the fire.'

So many things I do not understand.

Kittiwayke bobbed lightly on her moorings. Pilgrim eyed the little sloop proudly and waved to young Seward, who stood watch. Seward would get his turn on shore.

The lad should get his turn immediately. He looks sad and pale. Was Seward's pallor born of guilt? His captain killed two men and set their ship on fire, and calmly sailed on to Harbour Grace. The idea of righteous mutiny or a crewman reporting the attack did not appear to bother Captain Finn. Harbour Grace to St John's, St John's to Boston, Boston to Salem, then back to Harbour Grace. Any one of them could have deserted in each of those ports and sought justice for the murders. No man did so, not even at home in Salem. Well, how much could a man clearly see from *Kittiwayke*'s deck? And what else could a man do at sea but tend to his duties and follow his orders? Secrets in all hearts – some later revelation for an incorruptible time. A much later time. God's forgiveness, meantime, was a private matter.

Pilgrim signalled to a boy in a dory, then climbed down into it. He paid the boy to row him to *Kittiwayke* and row Seward ashore. In the boat, Pilgrim swatted again, this time striking the insect. Fly? Hornet. Pilgrim grimaced and swatted at yet another pest, this one hovering over a healing gash on his forearm. Hornets and wasps, proof of the devil, he once told his aunt. God made the bees, and bees made honey, but God would never have created wasps and hornets. His aunt twisted his ear, forced him to chant 'great whales and every living creature that moveth' a hundred times, and then fed him bread and water until he had memorized the entire book of *Genesis*. Sometimes he murmured it to himself when he could not sleep. *In the beginning, God created the heaven and the earth. And the earth was without form, and void; and darkness was on the face of the deep. And the Spirit of God moved upon the face of the waters.*

Pilgrim glanced over the side of the dory but saw only rocks, some ways down.

—Mr Pilgrim.

—Seward. Quiet watch?

—Aye. Only me and the captain on board. Captain's resting. Does he never go ashore?

—Rarely. But you go on. That dory is waiting for you.

Pilgrim inspected lines, adjusted a few belaying pins. All quiet and fine, just as Finn liked it – and just as he liked it. He leaned his forearms on the larboard gunwale and clasped his hands together. One day, his own master, but command for command's sake, for the title of captain... no. Content to stay on board *Kittiwayke*.

Compelled.

Pilgrim hardly trusted the supposed certainties of this world – Polaris and bad weather being about all he counted on – but he was certain Finn needed him. Finn gave no sign of this; since *Kindly One*, Finn had hardly spoken beyond orders to Pilgrim. But the privilege of old confidences meant that Pilgrim recognized the marks of nightmares on Finn and felt guided to hold Finn somehow, protect the much smaller man with his height and bulk. Be a shield. And he would earn the right.

Pilgrim had dared open the subject a few days before. Finn had been busy with the charts.

—Make it quick, Pilgrim.

—I fear for you some days.

—Stay out of the rum.

—I speak plain.

—So do I. Three extra tots, by the smell of you.

—Two, aye, but only to get the courage to ask you.

—Ask me what?

—What is it that darkens you?

—Naught. I shrug off darkness as I do a coat. Now, please –

—Even in winter at Morrow's?

Finn looked up. —What do you want, Pilgrim?

—Our last voyage, we spoke easy and free, and we ate together, and we'd go ashore and drink together.

—And tis a failing of mine that I cannot hold much drink.

—Not every man admits that.

—Not every man bears my failings.

—This voyage, you are sour and solitary. I hear you suffering in your sleep. The whole ship hears you, but no one has the courage to speak of it, not even amongst ourselves. Tis a rotten silence we keep for you.

—Foolishness.

—Cries. Pacing. Those shadows around your eyes.

—I do fine, Pilgrim.

—You lie.

—I should give you the back of my hand.

—You'd need to leap to reach my face. Captain, all of us bear the weight of original sin. You be no different, save in degrees of pride.

—You be getting Godly on me?

—Tis no jest. Captain, if redemption bothers you – put down the knife.

—Do you know what I hold in my hand? Hey? Poor, sad Pilgrim. You laboured so hard to persuade me to throw my dagger overboard, and I refused. So for you, I dug this treasure out, and now I bear it around my neck. This knife the sailmaker gave me. Attend, Pilgrim, my friend, my concerned and Godly friend, and – get out.

—Matt.

—Go.

—Your voice –

—Cracks on knowledge of sin. Con, get as far away from me as you can. Go!

190

A slash meant for Pilgrim's face cut his forearm instead. Finn had pulled back, but Pilgrim's arm bled briskly. He stared at the wound, not yet aware of the pain. Then he stared at the knife, which Finn had dropped. Shaking, Finn took Pilgrim's arm and examined it; he allowed this, not sure why.

Telling Pilgrim to sit down, Finn unlocked a sea-chest and brought out a new shirt. She retrieved the knife and cut the shirt into strips, and with those strips she dressed Pilgrim's wound. Pilgrim's anger curdled in him, and he tried to remember what he said that night at Morrow's. Something salt dripped into his cut, and he flinched; Finn did not look up from her work.

—Con, I wish I might sail thousands of miles away and start again. But I've sailed my thousands. Christiania, Benvolio, Barbados, America, Newfoundland. What remains? The Northwest Passage? New Holland? Sail one more voyage, change my name one more time, then go ashore. No, let me be. Do you understand? You do not. We'll put turpentine to this tomorrow, once it dries some. I am sorry.

Now Pilgrim examined his forearm; the scabs itched but smelled clean, and they'd gone red and black, not yellow and green. Some said pus meant healing, but he doubted that. Anger still smouldered in him; he'd done naught to deserve the cut, which could have ruint the strength of his forearm. And Finn had not even asked how it healed. Finn who now hid.

Tis a rotten silence we keep for you.

Pilgrim descended noisily to the master's berth. He called out to Finn, voice well able to reach past the habitually locked door, but he got no answer. Leaning his cheek on the door now, he called again. He rattled the knob, pounded on the door, rattled the knob again. No sound came from within. Pilgrim got an axe and chopped a hole in the door near the knob. He carefully reached through, caught the key and brought it to his side. Then he unlocked the door.

A stink of sweet rum and corruption hit him as his eyes adjusted to the dark. He strode to Finn's desk and chair – not dead, dead drunk, limp and drooling.

Christ.

Slumped in the chair, knife in hand, shirt open, Captain Matt Finn snored. Gouges, slashes and nicks marked her chest. The left breast, once a pretty mound, bore additional scars around the

191

nipple, while the right dandled, red and swollen. Freshly clotted blood, green and yellow pus, ancient white lines, newer brown scabs: an indecipherable course. The stories of Sallee Rovers, abduction to Barbary and a circumcision gone broad – Finn's flesh-dug scrimshaw gave it the lie. And Pilgrim had known it for a lie, known it a long time, yet he had not known it.

Pilgrim swatted flies from the wounds, desperate not to touch Finn. Hornets and wasps, sulky with the heat, hovered over spilled rum. Sweat and tears grimed Pilgrim's face. *Oh Christ, oh Christ, a woman's hand on the belaying pin. Not responsible. Cannot be responsible.*

So many things I do not understand.

...something to read, dim light and grey, grey, grey, from the mould on the pages to the ink in my pot, once afforded me a reverie: I stood in the Library of Alexandria, or, at least, in my Library of Alexandria. Hot sun streamed in through high windows, motes of dust and sand lightly dancing there. Books and scrolls reached to the high ceiling, books confiscated from any ship that docked in the harbour, yet there was no stink of calfskin or mould, for a single hair bound each roll of papyrus. And that ceiling was higher than a mast, higher than Canterbury, broad as Albion. Many men populated the library, scribes all, winding cloths tight about their chests, bare feet shuffling, goose quills behind their ears. They all sought ink. Yet why? Why, when already so many scrolls reached to the sky, to God: maps and history, poetry and medicine, the knowledge of hundreds of years, hundreds of men. To prove my point, I did take down a scroll to read to them, but the scribes noticed me not, shuffling on, intent. The edges crumbled, and as I tried to make out the Greek so as to read it to them, the sweat of my hands darkened the papyrus, weakened it, and the single hair binding it paled from black to white. I dropped the scroll before it should be completely undone, but it had already decayed to dust before it hit the floor and my own suddenly bare feet. I took in breath to cry out, but something tight about my chest ensured my silence, and then I recalled there might be a copy of that scroll I had just destroyed, and if not that, perhaps I could copy it out from memory. If only the letters had stayed still. Hundreds of years of knowledge, and then, fire. Seeking the chief librarian, or failing him, his daughter, the mathematician Hypatia, or, failing her, ink, I shuffled away from those shelves, trying to shake the binding hair from my fingers.

The night in 1719 upon which I tried to get Runciman drunk so he might tell me more of his business, he removed his wig, and plucked out a matted hair. He had come to my rooms, which were behind the offices of Cannard and Son, most pleased to have gotten the invitation. 'My men, sir, the men with whom I have truck, aye, *my* men, well, few of them are in a position to invite me to their homes, and those who are, would not. Should they invite me to cross their private threshold, then I would not go, for invariably a house also shelters women and children. Both these creatures observe far more than we generally credit. But you, sir, alone as you are, your house is safe, and indeed I shall come for supper.'

I had hired a woman to cook, and the aromas of roast fowl, boiled potatoes with butter and dried fruit, now stewing, teased me the entire day as I worked the accounts. It being a winter day, the dark came quickly, and when I did need a candle to read the figures, I put the ledger aside. Finding dinner all in order and laid on the table, I dismissed the woman and waited by the fire, where I considered my earlier visitor.

Late that morning, I'd been standing in front of my father's desk, staring out the window at horses, men and women, mongers and workers, merchants and sailors, brats and fog. Sad suddenly, I dropped the curtain and stepped back from the window to lean against Father's desk, briefly my brother's, and now mine. Bills piled here, correspondence piled there; I could write until Bristol ran bare of ink and still not clew up. Father had worked long hours by candlelight, and I'd often found him asleep amongst his papers.

Then Father was standing behind me. I almost smelled him, his presence so close and large, as though he'd grown seven feet tall and might wrap me in massive arms. I dared not turn to look. We stayed like that some minutes, until the presence scattered. Outside, the noon sun broke through the low clouds.

Runciman sent me a note by a dockside brat, indicating he'd become delayed by the details of an enterprise he could not at that moment neglect. I fell asleep on the couch, letting the fire go low. A chill arrived with Runciman, who, letting himself in, for I could keep no servants, found me dozing.

'Cannard, Cannard, I do thank you. This smells excellent. Shall we sit to it?' Runciman ate, and Runciman drank, for I repeatedly filled his glass, being careful but to top my own, and the demolished short-legged hen between us served as the common island over which we spoke, or rather, Runciman spoke, and I listened. Tedious stuff, most of it, observations of deeds, ponderings on motives, and a short discourse on an underused section of the population, that being females. 'Ah!' Runciman had grinned, showing long teeth. 'That gets your attention.' He drank some more, the glassful at once, his Adam's apple jigging. 'You see them as nothing more than warm holes, bodies to clutch in the

194

dark. No question, they are good for that, made from the rib to comfort. But I, sir, I see more than most men, and I can see how better to put those bodies and whatever minds they house to use. But enough of that. Will you help me, sir, to the couch, for I find that my bones have gone heavy.'

I stood up and rounded the table to give this service, but Runciman suddenly took off his wig, lifting it ceremoniously and dropping it on the table. It slid to the floor. He'd not shaved his head for some weeks, and his matted hair swooped back from the temples. From the back of this head he plucked one dark hair and laid it on the tablecloth, where it was almost lost in the shadows of fire and candlelight. Runciman's wandering eye took in my presence, but still he did not gaze on me full. 'This,' he said, 'is one lost agent.' He plucked another hair. 'And this is another. This is a third. Killed, taken, deserted: I know not.' Then he picked the hairs up, struggling a bit to pinch at them with thick and drink-numbed fingers. Finally, he tucked the hairs in his waistcoat pocket. 'I wear them, I shed them, I hide them, but each one, Cannard, each one I know, and each one I remember.'

He fell quite asleep. I tried to stir him, to guide him to the couch, but I could not shift that muscular body. I left him, first taking care to replace the wig on his head so he would not catch cold. Then I went to the couch myself to look upon the fire and think, but I fell asleep, and when I awoke in the cold before dawn, Runciman had gone.

Of my various attempts to escape Port au Mal for the apparently mythical Harbour Grace, the September 1724 run is most illustrative. The wind tugged at *Boyne*, skipper and ketch both eager to depart, but Admiral Lacey tromped through the hold, making to him a most satisfying racket with his new boots. These he called God-walkers. When I asked him why, he said that it is simply a name.

I'd gotten aboard *Boyne* that year, being tasked to follow Lacey and count empty barrels. Then I hid with the cargo, near choking on the stinks of old rope, rancid seawater and salt cod. Lacey yelled my name. Then he cursed very quietly.

'I must keep this settlement alive, Cannard, and I will. And if to keep this settlement alive, I need to trap you here, then that is what I will do. You are too valuable. Can you not see that?'

He coaxed me next, iron under silk.

'Now, I do understand you, John Cannard, I do, for you be a conscientious man. You finish each task I set with the persistence of a dog with a bone, and with that persistence you pay your debts. Right now you suffer an obligation to me, and the weight of it chafes your neck like a chain. I understand that. However I also understand something greater. When Truscott and I leave for Harbour Grace today, most of the marks of order, the signposts at the crossroads, go with me. Your ship, Cannard, is gone. Your men are dead. Your strongbox rots at the bottom of the sea. You are part of Port au Mal now, and Harbour Grace has no more meaning for you. Now get your sorry arse ashore before I kick it there.'

Despot or no, he and his pleasure held my best chance for Harbour Grace. I did as he commanded.

The spring that Michael Riordan and Eamon Gate left the settlement, tearing into the woods at night – 'Be dead in a day,' Lacey sneered – I discovered several errors in the arithmetic of merchants. At least, I thought them errors, until I totalled them. Too many to be accidental. Lacey and I were working in the Hall that day, reviewing last year's catalogues, credits and debits. I showed Lacey how he had been cheated. All this time I considered my strongbox and Runciman's papers within. Surely I could still offer some of their content, even now, should the men tasked to await me in Harbour Grace still be there. I added and subtracted, multiplied and divided, made notes, scratched figures in the dust – we'd long run dry of ink – memorized lists, correlated in my sleep, did all I was bade, for I knew that Lacey's ketch would soon arrive, must arrive, and Lacey's ketch would carry me to Harbour Grace. And from Harbour Grace, I might get home.

Nancy Truscott sighted *Boyne*'s sail and ran to the Hall, screeching the news.

My very guts jumped with the hope. Merely a ketch, of course, smaller than my *Bonny Jane*, but mast and sail. This time I saw her myself, and soon I would touch her myself, my salvation, my transport to Harbour Grace. This wayward interruption would end. Steps, go in steps, first accompany Lacey to Harbour Grace, then find work clerking for a merchant or at the garrison or fort until the next ship going to England took her departure.

Truscott soon joined us, luckily, as hunger had rotted us all, rendering Lacey an especial subject to giddiness. Lacey had lost a good two stone that winter, but he remained a heavy man, an alchemist's failure, his soul aspiring to gold, his bones made of lead, and a difficult burden when his knees gave way.

Eye to his glass, Lacey studied the ketch's careful passage through the narrows. Truscott remarked he thought *Boyne* looked fine, but Lacey heartily disagreed. 'She looks like a drunken streel. My God, she needs work. Here, Truscott, look how dull she is, her lines aren't even coiled. What has he done to her? What drooling fools has he got sailing with him this time? I'd flay him if I could find another skipper I trusted. Cannard, I shall sorely need your help over the next weeks.'

Weeks! Weeks with Lacey in Harbour Grace! Plenty of time to arrange passage, even arrange my working the passage. I may yet find the learned men, complete a shadow of my errand; do you not, sir, mean *Matthew* chapter twenty-seven, verse 6? A shipwreck, they would understand and even forgive a shipwreck, the papers' loss; *why, tis enough, Cannard, you floated along to tell the tale.*

Lacey spoke again, smiling this time, rare thing, 'Glad to see you looking so pleased. Cataloguing agrees with you. I'll be back in a fortnight or so, so make certain the ledgers are correct. I shall also need you to correlate the credits with the catches from last season and then copy them over into the new ledger, which is in my trunk. Here is the key. Now there is another complication, for I shall have to bring Truscott with me. Keep Nancy in victuals, but not one bite more than she got last year. Do you understand me, Cannard?'

I understood I would not be going to Harbour Grace.

Lacey continued, 'Now, I'll be returning with stores for the year, and new bills and records from the Harbour Grace merchants, so be prepared for some extra figuring when I come back. Until then, tis you in charge of the stores.' More quietly he added, 'I'm sorry, Cannard. I must leave someone at the Hall.'

'Why then, sir, do whatever it was you did before my fortunate arrival.'

'Tis all different now. I cannot leave Port au Mal undefended. Bad enough I'm removing Truscott.'

'Admiral Lacey, I might fall to my knees in despair as much as in hope. You must bring me to Harbour Grace. I have prayed for you to bring me to Harbour Grace. It is the only hope I have for England.'

'Cannard,' he repeated, 'truly, I am sorry. Not this year. By next season you will have worked for me enough that I will owe you passage, not only to Harbour Grace but all the way to England. But this year I must beg you to remain. There exist masterless men, and they bring trouble. Gate and Riordan, should they come back, come to steal, come to burn – there is a pistol and shot in my trunk. Wear the key round your neck, what, do you wear one there already? Go to the Hall and start the correlations, while you still have daylight. Truscott, if you please?'

I barely ventured outside the Hall during Lacey's absence. I did not shave. I tallied in my sleep. I dreamt that seven demons came to visit me, changing shape and voice, stroking me, and while they danced and sang and so distracted, they prevented me asking after the eighth, the one for whom I waited most, but it turned out he could not be bothered to come. I unlocked the trunk, loaded the pistol and for three days sat at the desk and considered shooting myself. Instead, I persevered, hardly my intention but apparently my fate. Outside: fog and soft rain as the capelin rolled in. We gorged on fresh fish, Nancy bringing me my portion.

Lacey and Truscott returned after twenty-three days. As Truscott rowed Lacey to the shallow offreach, the inhabitants assembled themselves in a ragged line. We lacked only boatswain's pipes. Lacey waded to the shore, and Truscott began calling out orders. After bellowing out that I must take charge of unloading instead of Truscott, Lacey said 'The beard suits you, Cannard.'

Fatter. God's blood, Lacey and Truscott had eaten well, and their fuller cheeks brought to mind the pig's head an employee of Cannard and Son had given my brother and I after Father's death. The pig's white cheeks, bristled and gently rounded, and we threw the thing away, failing to recognize that the man had liberated the head from the worm-eaten table of his own large family. Now I'd have gnawed on the ears. Now I'd clerk whatever obscene list Lacey or Port au Mal needed if it meant a bite of cheek, for with the strength given by that repulsive meat, I would be on that ketch to Harbour Grace.

I failed.

Nancy Truscott came to see me in Lacey and Truscott's absence, a stale habit of hers. I had spent some time that afternoon on the burying ground, staring up at the crumbling cliff face, staring down at the rocks sloping away beneath the tide, considering how at the fire rocks the bottom fell away, how an island defied the ocean: desperate and beautiful. Grace. I'd tried to force grace when I must wait for grace to find me. Fine then, fine, I would wait, my patience an article of faith, I would wait for God to send rescue. Yet the bottom fell away. Frightened, I returned to the Hall. Nancy Truscott had been watching me. We discussed a list she wished to see made, a list which would become increasingly important as time passed: a tally of who birthed whom, who behaved as if married to whom, which children had whose eyes. She'd brought dried bakeapples, golden wrinkled things, that when placed in hot water and permitted to plump released a scent of elusive sweetness. She gave me water with berries in it, and in the odd firelight, if I did not squint, I might believe I sat in Bristol, in the rooms behind the offices of Cannard and Son. I might even believe I had a wife.

On June 16th, 1734, I sat on the high ground where Port au Mal buried its dead, once more wearing Lacey's castoffs, once more peering through Lacey's glass. My belly half-sated with Lacey's food, and my fingers stained with Lacey's ink, I looked first at the wretched collection of houses on stilts pretending to be a settlement, then at the harbour beyond. Fog at the narrows seemed to cut us loose; our world ended in white. I tried to escape the sticky effects of that morning's dream of *Bonny Jane* and her manic compass. Two distant crashes came, as if especially violent waves were destroying themselves against a cliff. Sweating and suddenly afraid, I did feel at my neck for the cord from which dangled keys to my lost strongbox.

And at that moment, mulling these thoughts and singing to push away the dream of the wreck, I sighted a tidy sloop, making steady and sure through the fog, through the narrows of Port au Mal. The sloop sailed so nimbly I thought it could only be the skipper of *Boyne* sudden come with a new vessel. Only three men on deck, odd for calling on a new port, but then I cared little for the sloop's complement just so long as she could get me home. Some man of sense must have heard of the Englishman in Port au Mal, some man of sense had found me. God had finally seen fit to recognize my now fourteen years' worth of prayers.

I believe I screamed as the sloop tacked to avoid the fire rocks, heading for the teeth of the sunkers that had beaten open *Bonny Jane*. Rocks and hull collided, and the three men fell. I read the sloop's name: *Kittiwayke*.

'Wrack!' Nancy Truscott, emerging from the Hall and tugging down her skirts, cried it. 'Wrack!' Lacey bolted out behind her, buttoning up. One *Kittiwayke* sailor rushed to the bows and nearly fell overboard, while the second, a tall and fair man, ducked low, ran larboard and peered over the side. The third, whom I thought was the ship's boy, skittered up the ratlines to view the damage from above. Even now, writing this, I feel the wide-eyed waking dream of myself in the ratlines, screaming in that sailor's ears: 'There! That shadow: my wreckage!'

Kittiwayke did not sink. Little sound escaped her, the fog muting everything. She listed as much as ten degrees, and once enough water flooded aboard she would slip beneath the surface amidst foam and a roar, but right then she seemed stable enough. The fair man had disappeared below and now came back on deck to heave cargo over the side. I wondered why neither of the other two helped him, but it became clear that *Kittiwayke* carried next to naught. Truscott and John Dunn launched their dories. Another cry from the women on shore, and from myself: 'Topsails!'

A small frigate came into existence out of the fog. She was dangerously close to the shore, tacking in through the narrows on a violent angle. She flew the Red Ensign: Royal Navy. *Dauntless*, bearing down on the ruined *Kittiwayke*. A Royal Navy frigate, here! In my excitement, a long-forgotten state, I threw Lacey's glass against the plank that marked the grave of the men from *Bonny Jane*. I quickly retrieved it, unbroken. *Christ, Christ, Son of God*, I prayed, *by all, by all, by all that is holy, by all that is right, guide that frigate past the sunkers. Grant me pity: grant me hope.*

Christ listened. There came no more yelled confusion down at the shore; the inhabitants stared in silence at the second ship. *Dauntless* picked flawlessly through the narrows, past the sunkers, until she set to anchor near *Kittiwayke*. Grappling hooks bristled out, but *Dauntless* heeded the protests from *Kittiwayke* and disturbed the hazardous sloop no further. The wind picked up, parting the fog slightly and carrying to us a confusion of words. Captain Cleasby of *Dauntless* addressed Matt Finn of *Kittiwayke*, for that ship's boy stood the master, demanding that Finn come

200

aboard the frigate with his strongbox. In Truscott's dory, Lacey chose that moment to rise to his feet and introduce himself and offer his assistance, whereat a red-haired lieutenant bade him wait. The last few fishermen now returned home, rowing one by one around the two vessels. Lacey and the lieutenant parleyed a moment longer, but a sudden cry from *Kittiwayke* interrupted, a brief cry but bodily deep. *Kittiwayke*'s captain, I saw through the glass, had fallen to his knees and now tried to beat his head against the fiferail. The large blond man hauled him back, whereat the captain struck him. The large man turned his face aside, resigned to something, and *Kittiwayke*'s master rushed belowdecks. *Dauntless* floated ever closer, near crushing Truscott's dory for his refusal to move, until *Kittiwayke* lay near enough for the red-haired lieutenant to swing aboard, followed by a small boarding party, armed. The remaining two *Kittiwayke* men surrendered, palms raised, heads down, there being naught else for them to do, and the *Dauntless* lieutenant ran below. He returned a scant moment later, with *Kittiwayke*'s master shouting protest, voice shrill enough to furl canvas.

The complement of *Kittiwayke* transferred to *Dauntless*. The lieutenant and captain conferred briefly, then the lieutenant and *Kittiwayke*'s master went below with two Marines, while more Marines escorted *Kittiwayke*'s two sailors elsewhere, the brig most like. A midshipman called down to Lacey, accepting his offer on the captain's behalf. A party would be coming ashore presently, so would Lacey see to the accommodation of officers and a prisoner? Lacey bowed, a hazardous move in a dory. Truscott rowed him ashore quickly. Lacey's face and voice lit up with delight as he ordered everyone about and demanded from me explanations I'd no hope of giving him.

They came ashore at dusk. The prisoner stared straight ahead in fury and met no man's eye; the lieutenant, suffering from catarrh, kept his pistol fixed on the prisoner; the captain scowled at the settlement in disgust. 'Which one of you is Lacey?' he asked.

Our fishing admiral stepped forward, beach rocks clacking beneath his God-walker boots. 'I am.'

'Good day, sir. I am Captain William Cleasby, commanding His Majesty's ship *Dauntless*. My first lieutenant, Mr Kelly. And that is Matt Finn, common pirate.'

Finn snorted as though dismissing a paltry bet. 'I am the master of the coastal trading sloop *Kittiwayke*, harried down into this harbour whereupon my vessel was wrecked. Captain Cleasby, you shall answer to Newman Head of Salem.'

Captain Cleasby did not even look at Finn. 'Newman Head answers to His Majesty, the King of England, as do the settlers here.'

'Pirate?' said Lacey. 'That little weed? What knows he of savagery?'

Matt Finn met Lacey's eye. Lacey took the step back.

'I be no pirate.'

Captain Cleasby still did not turn his head, addressing the rocks now. 'Pirate, murderer, thief. Now stop your mouth, or I'll stop it up for you.'

Lacey looked Finn, Kelly and Cleasby up and down in his insolent fashion. 'Captain Cleasby, I be confused. Why is a murdering pirate standing free on the King's own land? Does he not belong in irons?'

'Parley, Lacey. Alone, if you please.'

'Aye, sir. My Hall and rooms stand ready. This way. Cannard, with me.'

'Is there a plague of deafness here? I said, alone.'

'John Cannard is my clerk, Captain Cleasby. What you say to me, you may also say to him. Besides myself, he is the only lettered man in the settlement. We may need him. I vouch for his discretion.'

'On both your lives, I'll accept your good word.'

Lacey nodded.

'Very well. Mr Kelly.'

No one spoke again until we stood at awkward angles to one another inside the Admiral's Hall.

'Where is it, Lacey?' asked Cleasby.

'Where is what?'

'Finn is a pirate,' Cleasby began, but Finn interrupted to protest he was the captain of a Salem coastal trader. Cleasby's hands twitched as he barked at Finn. 'You are His Majesty's prisoner and will conduct yourself accordingly. Lacey, this murderer fled to this settlement – what do you call it?

'Port au Mal. After Utrecht –'

'I expect Finn has sailed here before to deposit prize, prize which rightfully belongs to the King.'

Lacey chuckled. 'Buried treasure? Captain Cleasby, I can assure you –'

Whereat it came my turn to interrupt. 'No, Captain Cleasby, *I* can assure you. I am John Wesley Morgan Cannard, and you must listen to me. My father was Frederick James Cannard originally of London and then of Bristol. He owned Cannard and Son Shipping. I was sailing to Harbour Grace when my brigantine was wrecked here, in 1719. My *Bonny Jane* is strewn on the same rock that captured *Kittiwayke*. I have prayed, sir, prayed until I no longer knew I prayed, for an English ship to come, for any ship to come. Had Finn arrived before now, believe me, sir, I would not be here to argue with you.'

Kelly studied me now, quite keenly, but Cleasby carried on as though I'd said naught.

'Lacey, you can give me your word Finn has left no prize here?'

Lacey glanced from Cleasby to me as if asking if I could believe what I heard. 'Aye.'

'One detail troubles me, Lacey, and it is this: I do not believe you. I have it on good authority that somewhere in this settlement is buried King's prize – gold – which we must recover.'

'Then you got it on the guess of a madman or an idiot.'

'You are Irish, Lacey, and that is enough to make me doubt your loyalty. What else is it you pretend?'

'Irish? I'm orange as King Billy himself. I own a ketch called *Boyne*, man. I collude with neither papist nor pirate. By God, sir, this insult, and we have given over salvage rights to you.'

'That *Kittiwayke* jetsam already belonged to the King.'

Finn could stay dumb no longer. 'Captain Cleasby, there be no prize here. I could have died happy never hearing of Port au Mal. Tis not even named on my chart.'

'Be silent! Lacey, you will accompany us back to *Dauntless*, where you will remain on board until the prize is uncovered. We will dig up every grave and burn down every shack if necessary.'

Lacey crossed his arms. 'I will do no such thing.'

'Then I shall shoot you where you stand.'

Lacey uncrossed his arms and showed his palms.

Cleasby nodded. 'It is well you insisted on bringing your clerk.'

For three days *Dauntless* tars dug up the ground and found only stones, rummaged through beach rocks and found only water, tore through the shacks and found only wood. So orderly: a polite and disciplined sacking, almost tedious. They near dismantled the Admiral's Hall, upending barrels of food; one midshipman even ordered the tars to sift the flour for gold dust. The second and third lieutenant questioned us all, relentlessly: had we seen gold, coins or dust, little figures, battered rings, Virgin Marys, foreign kings? Mounds of soil, piles of rocks and broken spades impeded passage through the settlement. I supervised the disturbing of the graves myself, pleased to recognize Wren's clothes – a dry burial, all this time. No gold shone in the cold rocks and mud. We found only the stouter remains of adults and infancy's soft bones.

22) CALENTURE
As told June 1734 to Lieutenant John Kelly, RN, by Captain Christopher Matthew Finn.

So, now you know the most of how came I to this fuckery of wreckage and rocks. Aye, no doubt I screamed and fought. Possessed? You need to ask Con Pilgrim about demons, lieutenant, for I got no Godliness to me. I know only what I feel. Do you not see the marks on me? Your captain's inquiries have no courtesy. No, sir, I shall not rescind my words. Ask him yourself. He ordered me tied to this chair for a reason. Not that he need fear I'd take a belaying pin to his head. I be spent there. Tilley, the fool – he'd not got the sense to let me be. None of you did. Sweet Jesus, Kelly, I gave you the truth of me, and I gave you the truth of the gold. I spent the gold buying *Kittiwayke* from Jericho Gosse. I stole it – no, I earned it, earned it off Michael Farr, because he meant to beat me to death.

And the best kiss was the deciding lot: whether the boy fucked you, or I the boy.

I've naught left to say. No. No.

Just let me be. Can you not just let me be?

23) BLURRED ROUGHWORK
JUNE 15, 1734, ON BOARD *DAUNTLESS*, AT ANCHOR IN PORT AU
MAL, NEWFOUNDLAND.

—Ash on bone.

Con Pilgrim licked his lips after saying that. His tongue rasped
over flattened bits of skin that felt like charts laid out. He bowed his
head to the creaks and rattles of the navy frigate *Dauntless*, creaks
and rattles very like those of *Kittiwayke* and yet utterly strange.

Kelly's freckled hands disappeared as he lifted his arm and
coughed into his elbow. Pilgrim heard wheezing. *Odd thing, me
being the prisoner but sitting down, him the man in the right and
standing.*

Trying to catch his breath, Kelly coughed again, and again.
Wet spasms.

—Mr Pilgrim, would you repeat that?

Staring at the table, Pilgrim divined patterns in the oak beneath
the varnish. Bright airiness of the lieutenants' mess. Too much
light, after the brig.

—I said, ash on bone, Mr Kelly. A noise I shall not forget.

—Belaying pin to a human skull, aye, dare say you'd not. The
fireball?

—Afterwards. Likely a rock at the core of it.

Head pounding, Kelly shuddered beneath his coat. *Now, of all
days of this wretched voyage, now I take sick?* —Tell me more of the
belaying pin.

—Loose. No lines made round it. Finn took the pin –

—Murder, then.

—I said no such thing.

Hands still clasped behind his back, Lieutenant John Kelly
walked a tight circle around the table. Con Pilgrim wished his own
hands were smaller. Nails like coins. Knuckles like knots. Palms as
hard as the table.

—Mr Pilgrim. I need your faithful accounting of events. Trying
to protect Finn will only delay –

—Where be your captain?

—Captain Cleasby shall look to the final justice. My unenviable
task is to muck out the details.

—And the devil?

Kelly said nothing.

Pilgrim sniffed. *Certainty of disease. Not just the brig.* —Wide is the gate, and broad is the way. Finn is my captain. As Cleasby is yours.

—I commend your loyalty. Ships would stink less if all captains deserved such loyalty. But to whom will you give your final reckoning, Pilgrim? Your captain, or God?

Pilgrim's face burnt red. —To God, sir. But I might ask the same question of you.

—You spoke of ash on bone. Finn took the belaying pin, a fierce club by any measure –

—A belaying pin is merely a tool, sir. It holds lines.

—Answer me, Pilgrim, for the sake of your captain's neck. Consider me your interlocutor as you give your account to God. Speak we of murder?

Ash on bone. Face – Coltman's face –

—Mr Pilgrim!

—Can you not see it, Lieutenant? Guess it? Smell it? She is not responsible.

Kelly thought Pilgrim meant *Kittiwayke*. Then, in Kelly's memory, Runciman at Admiral Dunton's house: *Consider Finn my prodigal, Mr Kelly, my* rara avis. *Consider yourself Finn's escort back to me, alive and in good health, for I will have Finn's usefulness.* Trying to hide his anger, his disgust, his sense of gutting betrayal at being made an ignorant tool – *ha, a very agent* – Kelly spat. Unbefitting conduct for an officer, that glob of saliva, but at least it gagged the curses.

—*She?*

—Aye. She.

Runciman with his wandering eye knew. Of course he knew. An agent who could disguise herself and not only sail but command – for Christ's sake – *she!* A fine prize. Runciman would treat the murders on *Kindly One* as an inconvenient mess, quickly mop it up. No spymaster would permit sacrifice of such a one to the nuisances of the law. Finn would stand no trial but instead conveniently disappear and be made once again an agent. A tool. For the good of England.

—'She' be damned. Speak we of murder?

Pilgrim looked up from the table, his large face wet. —'But if thine eye be evil, thy whole body shall be full of darkness. If therefore the light that is in thee be darkness, how great is that darkness.' Aye, Mr Kelly. Murder. But Finn – my – my friend, til I did see, and again after I chose not to see – Matt Finn – she be not responsible. Cannot be.

—Do you truly believe that, Pilgrim?

—I believe in order that I might understand.

—Man, woman, or demon, did Finn swing that belaying pin?

—Aye. At the head of a man long thought dead. The falling stars I tried once to explain to Finn: was it Wormwood?

—Enough Scripture!

Kelly suffered another coughing fit, spitting phlegm into a handkerchief this time.

—How came we to this?

Defeat tugged Pilgrim's shoulders down. —I do not know the full story. Some I've heard at night, some by day, and the rest I've guessed. Consider this: the *Kindly One* boatswain Finn killed, he did badly use her when a youngster. Repeatedly. The sight of him, so unexpected after a long respite, inspired some buried rage. I doubt Finn even thought of what she did. The speed of it, sir: heartbeats.

—Murder is murder, but here at least I see some reason. Explain the death of Captain Tilley.

—He got in the way.

Stiff silence.

Pilgrim tried to smile. —Newman Head calls it the unswerving punctuality of chance.

—I call it sickening. Pilgrim, do you understand the punishment for murder?

And the Spirit of God moved upon the face of the waters. —I do.

Short of breath, Kelly almost fell into the bolted chair opposite Pilgrim. He tightly crossed his arms. *How in Christ's name will I keep this from Cleasby?*

As Pilgrim quietly prayed, Kelly struggled not to cry and not to laugh. He nearly coughed his lungs out instead.

Then Pilgrim spoke. —Mr Kelly. I got a proposition.

24) CUNTSPLICED TO THE BUMMARY
JUNE 16-17 1734, ON BOARD *DAUNTLESS*, AT ANCHOR OFF
PORT AU MAL.

Rehearsing a conversation with Cleasby that demanded privacy and therefore might never happen, Dr Hugh Pollard designed his sentences to sound scientific and abstract. Perhaps cold reason would influence the captain.

I must caution you, sir, as I would caution any man, and indeed as I might caution the angels in my prayers for the stability of the universe: appetites need balance and order. Justification will not suffice. No, sir, I do not object to interrogation and truth, nor to following orders, and certainly not to acting for the good of the service. I merely point out the dangers in thoughtless exercise and indulgence of the baser appetites of man. How careful must be the man who exercises both authority and law, careful to sidestep the seductive and corrosive pleasures of being right.

Pollard's hypothetical conversation with Cleasby caught on another hazard: Pollard deeply disliked his captain. Disliked him, distrusted him, feared him. As their tedious and apparently pointless mission found few triumphs – and as the ship's surgeon detected a stink of politics – Pollard increasingly felt little emotional shoves from Cleasby. One expected friction at sea, just as one expected good sense to mellow it. But Cleasby exploited the friction and played games with his officers. His blatant hatred for his first lieutenant stained almost every word and action; the men joked of the day Cleasby and Kelly would finally go shirtless and bare-knuckled, or the day Kelly would die with his arm twisted behind him as he tried to pluck a knife from his back. *Whatever it takes, hey, my man?*

Foul, this man, a captain who slurped and gnawed his power. Coward, his lieutenant, who hid and disputed with the prisoner Pilgrim.

Dislike being a luxury and Pollard being a subordinate, the untended good patch in the doctor's soul shrivelled while his anger festered. It would burst – only one prick needed – the prick of certainty – Pollard suddenly knew he'd never see his sister. Less than a day's sail away, a few hours...

Dreaming he flew at the captain with his fists, almost hearing the thud, Pollard knocked on the door of Cleasby's cabin and announced himself.

A Marine let him in. Cleasby stood with his back to the door, gazing out the windows. Blood and bile stained the floor. Finn, bleeding from the nose, rolled over and tried to get on hands and knees but gave up. Saying nothing, Finn looked at the surgeon. Pollard reached for his patient.

Blocking the light, Cleasby crouched beside Pollard. —Sir, did you trip?

—With respect, captain, I object –

—You object, sir? To what?

—To your treatment of the prisoner.

—Sergeant, help the surgeon to his feet. Can't have you down in the muck, sir. I shall note your objection, if you wish. But, sir: this is no brother officer, nor even half the man you are, and I count you a limp and soggy man. This is a murdering thief. And I will have that thief's prize for the King. How does Mr Kelly?

Pollard tested the grips of the two marines who held him – no, who helped him. One on either arm. He could break free, but that meant lunging into the captain.

The sergeant whispered him a warning: —Sir.

—I do not like his cough, Captain. But if he rests, he should avoid a lung fever.

—Bring him my compliments, and advise him to carry on his interrogation of Pilgrim.

Finn mumbled.

Suddenly disgusted, feeling gifted with new sight, Pollard wanted to kick Finn himself. *Down there in bile and shit, like a fucked pig: stand up, man. Desserts, this, for naught else makes sense. Rods and spheres and orbits.*

—Captain, I remind you I stand by in sickbay should my services be needed.

—Very good, Dr Pollard. That will be all.

In the passageway, Pollard leaned a few moments against the cabin's locked door as Finn spat and begged for a moment's peace and Cleasby argued peace carried the price of truth.

—I will elicit confession if it takes all night. Gold, Finn. Where lies your prize?

—Innocent.

On deck, and despite the impediments of a smashed nose and

a close guard, Finn's throaty voice carried. The wind stirred, and the dangling weight very slightly bent the yardarm.

—Con Pilgrim killed no one. You just hanged an innocent man.

Men muttered. The midshipmen and the second lieutenant looked to Kelly. The corpse slowly twirled. Captain Cleasby bawled for silence.

Lieutenant Kelly strode to Finn, and the two stood close enough to whisper. Finn shook. Kelly clasped his hands behind his back and murmured Runciman's name. Captain Cleasby joined them and clapped his hands down on Finn's shoulders.

—See that rope round his neck? A bitter end. You're cuntspliced to the bummary now, Finn, and that mortgage must be paid.

—I paid with the truth.

—Where lies your prize?

Finn tried to point to *Kittiwayke*, but, arms and shoulders stiff with bruises, failed. —Prize? There! All I possess is on board her. *Is* her! Take *Kittiwayke*, for all the poxy good it might do ye. Give *Kittiwayke* over to the King! Pry her off the rock, dog-fucker. I'd be glad of it.

Captain Cleasby did not strike Finn. He looked instead to Lieutenant Kelly, strange emotion tugging at his jaws, then back at Finn.

—Mr Kelly, it seems our mission is near complete, and seeing you understand the mission better than any man on board, being trusted and favoured by the admirals, guided to soft chairs by the hearth of ease when I must whine at the door for food, I say it is your deserved task to board *Kittiwayke* with a party and retrieve the prize.

—Tis fraught with hard risk, Captain. She lists the further as we watch.

—Duty is fraught with hard risk, sir. Would you shirk duty and orders? Do take care to your answer.

Finn snorted, starting another nosebleed. —Stout discipline.

Kelly spoke calmly. —I will certainly not disobey you, sir. May I ask to take but a small party, as I've no wish to bear the burden of wasted lives?

—You will bear the burden I set, Lieutenant. Take the third man from *Kittiwayke*, Seward, as incentive for Finn, and two of our own to guard him while you go below and retrieve the gold. And you, Finn. I've torn your bluffs, exposed your folly. Were this a game of Ruff and Honours, you'd be pleading bankruptcy. I hanged your Constant Pilgrim! Hanged him, in the King's name, and I will hang young Seward, too, to squeeze the prize from you.

Blood dripped off Finn's lips. —Gold is essential. Buy passage. —Speak up?

—Stop men's mouths; the sailmaker failed. The gold, the gold, the gold. Nennorluk.

Then Finn smiled.

Seductively, Cleasby decided, as though daring him – to see? *I'll be damned. Whatever it takes, hey, my man.*

Kittiwayke squealed and groaned.

Kelly, Seward and two men readied themselves to swing over from *Dauntless*. The fishermen had rowed well clear of the wreck, fearing the sloop would collapse onto them as they passed. Sunkers had holed *Kittiwayke*'s hull, just past her famous lead bum. Lines streeled out on the wind, thumped against hull and masts. Sail filled and snapped.

Kelly, Seward and the men swung over, landing badly. Kelly limped when he rose.

Cleasby's order carried well. —Get below, Mr Kelly. The captain's cabin, you fool! Where else would the gold be hid?

Pushing Seward out of his way, Kelly stumbled below. *Kittiwayke*, finally breaking, slid off the sunker and rapidly sank. The water foamed round the sloop, sucking at men, timber, canvas and line, and the wake of it rocked anchored *Dauntless*. Captain Cleasby ordered a boat lowered, while from the shore of Port au Mal, Tom Truscott and John Dunn rowed out. One of the *Dauntless* tars broke the surface with his face and tried to float upon his back; Truscott got him, sighting the other sailor far below – the water so clear – struggling, spinning, unable to right. Near him, pinned and torn, Seward drowned. His bones lie there still, and tiny fragments of them would wash ashore for many, many years, mistaken for shells when noticed at all. Kelly surfaced, slipped under, surfaced again, fighting the weight of his coat. Dunn grabbed for Kelly's long red plait and caught it, nearly falling overboard. Helped by Dunn and the tars and sobbing for breath, Kelly hauled himself over the gunwale of the boat from *Dauntless* and fell to safety against the bottom. Captain Cleasby leaned hard on a *Dauntless* rail, scowling, and ordered Finn to be taken below. Men and officers helped Kelly climb aboard; Cleasby only snorted when the saluting lieutenant collapsed at his feet.

25) BOOKING PASSAGE

When the *Dauntless* tars returned Lacey from an interview with Cleasby and came asking for me, in the evening after they hanged the sailor Pilgrim, my hard despair fell away. Had God's deal with His humble servant, John Cannard, come due? Had grace arrived in the shape of a navy frigate and a red-haired lieutenant? Surely, once Kelly heard my tale of accidental settlement, of my being cast away, he would convince his captain to grant me passage back to England.

Lieutenant Kelly met me on deck, his plait still heavy and wet, coughing. He suffered in the evening wind, which, despite the calendar insisting June, cut to the bone. We stayed near the bow, speaking rapidly. The strong *Dauntless* deck rocked lightly beneath my feet as we came to risky and allusive understanding, he asking me if I knew a man with one wandering blue eye. The men on watch did their best to ignore us, only giving away their anxiety with sudden efficiency at the watch officer's announcement, 'Captain on deck.'

Kelly stood to attention, and I copied him. Cleasby came towards us, squinting and angry yet somehow satisfied of something, and speaking in a jolly manner that hardly fit. 'What, sir? Will you invite landsmen aboard without my knowledge?' Kelly attempted explanation, but Cleasby talked the louder, saying, 'Shipwrecked? Him? No, Mr Kelly, he is a settler here, and he will return to his settlement and his obligations. I will brook no further dissent, you see. I've just come from Dr Pollard. The prisoner has suffered an injury.'

'An accident, no doubt,' the lieutenant remarked.

'Exuberance and zeal for the truth. Now, Mr Kelly, you will return this landsman to shore, and then you will accompany me to the sickbay.'

Captain Cleasby returned below.

Kelly, pale, said only 'Undone.' Then he placed a hand on my shoulder. 'I am sorry, Cannard. You must return to shore. I will do what I can for your passage.' He clouted a hovering midshipman on the head. 'So long as you're eavesdropping, you know to get Mr Cannard ashore.'

Watching tars ready the jollyboat again, watching Kelly go aft to the companionway, watching my chance at England disappear, I sagged against a fiferail. Belaying pins poked at my back.

Debt laws' intricacies lie beyond my knowledge, and the laws themselves are, I fear, bent like trees beneath snow. I can say that all of the men in Port au Mal, and at least one in Harbour Grace, probably more scattered about Conception Bay, were indebted to Robert Lacey. That is to say, the men of Port au Mal owed Lacey not just their livelihoods but their lives, for he not only acted as their agent with merchants, he fed them in winter and advanced them gear and other necessities against the next season's catch, as the merchants advanced Lacey. A bad season's catch delayed repayment, and the poor seasons of the 1720s had indebted the fishermen yet more. By Lacey's take on these laws, the debtor could work nowhere else, until he paid his debt, whether in money, goods or time served. The fishermen here, few of them had ever seen money, and they could spare no goods. Their currency was time. Therefore, I suppose, Cleasby had reason enough to believe what he did and to send me back to Port au Mal, to what the captain called my 'obligation' and what Lacey called 'indebture and abeysance.'

The following day I helped Lacey tidy his Hall and rooms. Footprints in flour and heaps of disturbed earth pointed to the odd pageant of the past week. *Dauntless* had departed in the night, and I viewed the empty harbour at dawn. Fog loomed. Lacey bade me pour him a drink and said 'Do you know I should have had you flogged?'

Even after all my years of serving Lacey, of learning to expect his offensives, this jarred and galled me.

'All those times you tried to run away, on my own ketch yet, I laugh when I think about it; all those times when you tried to get to Harbour Grace, you challenged me. You undermined me. This is my settlement. You know that. I know that. The only reason I did not bring you to justice was that I respected you, as a man of your station. And you respected me and my station. And with that respect came my promise that if ever I heard while in Harbour Grace of transport to England, I would tell you. I heard naught, but that be hardly what matters. The laws are that this is my settlement. I am the obsolete fishing admiral, yet here I stand, right here. Right now. Both Lieutenant Kelly and Captain Cleasby asked

215

if you knew anything of Finn's gold.' He fingered his cheek. 'I protested your innocence and did my damnedest to prevent them taking you on board for useless questions.'

The thrill of descent: will I freeze, or will I drown?

Lacey sighed and said, 'As I made clear to Captain Cleasby, one cannot transport a debtor from Newfoundland back to England, no matter what he wears about his neck. Help me scrape up the flour, Cannard, there's a good man. My God, how much did they waste?'

Horribly, *Dauntless* returned the following day, some bad dream. They lowered a boat, which swayed and crashed against the hull. It carried Lieutenant Kelly, much weakened by a catarrh and a fever on his lungs. Sailors and midshipman rowed Kelly ashore, and the midshipman explained that the Lieutenant Kelly must wait in Port au Mal for a rendezvous. Stunned, we said no word to the midshipman. The tars regarded us with a sullen hatred better placed in our own eyes.

I cared after Kelly myself during his last few weeks, assuring him that *Dauntless* had indeed departed and promising I would carry his news to Runciman, for Kelly possessed much knowledge of the truth of Captain Matt Finn. I said many things to calm him down.

26) FINAL REPORT
AUGUST 17, 1734, HOME OF ADMIRAL SIR ALEXANDER DUNTON, PORTSMOUTH, ENGLAND.

Death, sirs. That and bad weather. Mr Runciman, Lieutenant Kelly did press me to get you the message that we did indeed apprehend the Finn you sought. But the enterprise ended badly. Finn confessed to all accusations but denied possession of any prize and indeed was quite ill. The surgeon suspected kidney troubles.

Sirs, I wish you to know that Lieutenant Kelly died bravely in the line of duty. On his second foray to the wreck of Finn's sloop *Kittiwayke*, he nearly drowned. Lung fever finished the job. My ship's log indicates his grave's latitude. I always regret the need to bury a man at sea.

I am sorry to grieve you, Mr Runciman.

Utmost secrecy, Admiral, I understand. For the good of the service. Whatever it takes.

27) THE SURRENDERED PLAIT

John Kelly, lying in my bed, fingered his plait, which we had shorn against his fever, and which Lacey had instructed me keep: a heavy plait, thick as three clews braided together, but the sight of it unsettled me. Kelly sat up, first hefting the weight of the plait in his hands, then fingering the smooth bumps, and finally plucking out three hairs, burning red, almost orange, like bog grass in autumn. He laid out the hairs on the sheet before him, in idle play, it seemed. But I knew. And Kelly knew that I knew, for he would not have plucked out hairs so for Lacey or Nancy Truscott.

'I wear them, I shed them, I hide them, but each one, each one I know, and each one I remember. Did he say it to you, too?'

I nearly dropped the water Kelly needed.

Kelly drank, then said, 'When Cleasby and I brought Finn here to the Hall, for Cleasby to speak with Lacey and ask after prize, you spoke of being shipwrecked here.'

I agreed I had. Kelly tried to sneak a breath past his cough.

'Runciman asked me to keep an ear out for news of you. Harbour Grace? *Bonny Jane?*'

I nodded.

'He'd be pleased to see you return, even these many years too late. For on occasion, Cannard, he will seek out the lost. If the lost carry something he deems important. He sought hard after Finn. Do you know the prize, Cannard?'

'Gold. Captain Cleasby asked repeatedly after the Benvolian gold.'

Kelly smiled and looked more deathly ill than before. 'I heard of the gold before I'd even touched ashore. Pirates and murderers.' He got wretched with his cough and rested a while, then said 'But this pirate, sir, so little truly known, save Benvolio and gold. Then the stories cragged off: Finn took the gold from a ship of English passengers en route to Boston, or stole the gold from a rich woman who took secret passage on a navy frigate, she being an admiral's mistress, on and on it went, as many versions as tongues to tell.'

Runciman (said Kelly) tasked me to bring back his prodigal Kit Finn, his *rara avis*. Runciman quickly told me he valued the lost gold, but he valued something else the pirate Finn carried much more, and by the blood of the angels, I must find and bring back Finn. I did point out the holed logic of this enterprise, for how might we arrest the pirate Finn if we'd found not even a hair of him? Here Runciman corrected me: that master of the Salem sloop, *Kittiwayke*, the sloop *Kindly One* that had run aground at Peter's Rue in the Isles of Scilly: murder and fire on board *Kindly One*, at Finn's hands. More stories: this Matthew Finn, like Runciman's Christopher Finn, suffering an injury as a boy that prevented his full growth.

Runciman plucked a hair from his head, and he loomed over the chart. 'Lost, taken or killed? No, this one ran. Others longed to go masterless, but this one ran.' Fury. And something else. I might have sworn an oath that Runciman felt some affection for this Finn.

Master or pirate? *Rara avis* or common cur?

Kelly slept nearly two days after telling me this much, slipshod as it was. His fever broke, and he coughed in long wheezy spasms, his lips tingeing blue. New hairs poked out his scalp, and I prompted him to resume his story.

I took a sharp risk (said Kelly) getting you on board *Dauntless*, but I had to speak with you. The balance tipped away from me, and Captain Cleasby took great offense at your presence. Cleasby and I stood at such blind and bitter odds. Our duty had boiled down like flip left too long on the flame, boiled down to but two things: Cleasby and me.

He abandoned me here. He showed me the supposed orders, knowing full well I could not read them, fevered like this. There is no rendezvous, Cannard. He abandoned me.

Kelly coughed again, the wheeze and struggle pathetic, for he could draw but little enough breath in, and that air got trapped in the water on his lungs to bubble and spin like a drowning man desperate to surface. His fever quickly rose, and I got only babbling pleas from him.

Admiral Lacey looked in and shook his head. He beckoned me to him, quietly asking, 'What has he said?' I responded that the lieutenant had said very little, and Lacey observed, 'He's closer to your size than mine. When he dies, you can make use of his clothes. Be a warm coat, if it ever dries out. Tend to him, now. Aurelius be due back in from the water. I'll have him bring more firewood.' And Lacey left.

Kelly's fever broke in the dark. My bones ached from sleeping in a chair, and the tedium of fetching the water, bringing the pot, washing the face, bore through me like a deepening hole. I resented Kelly for evicting me from my bed, for mumbling nonsense when I wanted the rest of his story, for being sick. At times, as he gazed up at my face, as he felt me pound his back, as I shook him awake so he could finish his story, he resented me. But the story came.

A long chase. The enterprise maddened Captain Cleasby. The surgeon, Hugh Pollard, spoke to me about the captain's state one night. First Pollard mystified me with a treatise on rods and planets, mechanics of orbit and refraction of light. Then he came to the point, saying, 'The captain hardly sleeps, and he speaks – I think he becomes fearful of you, Mr Kelly, dark fearful. What can you tell me so I might ease the captain's mind?'

I thanked Pollard for his conversation, it being a pleasant diversion, but begged my leave as I had work above, apologizing for there being naught I might do to help him. Then a midshipman came to the door, squeaking of a brawl between the men, so I left the surgeon, who called after me about discipline and duty.

Not far from Harbour Grace, early in the afternoon watch, in poor winds and the pestilence of fog, we encountered a New England sloop, *Seraphim*. Heavily manned and loaded, *Seraphim* sailed low to the water. I had just thought to muse on the ties of trade between New England and Newfoundland when *Seraphim*, sighting us, veered away. I recommended we give chase, for only a guilty master would avoid the Navy so, but Cleasby would have naught but *Kittiwakye* and Finn – *whatever it takes, hey, my man.* Cleasby even speculated on Finn's stolen gold in the hearing of the men and the Marines. I changed the subject as best I could. *Seraphim* remained in sight, though shrinking; she should be making for St John's or Boston, but she tacked east as though heading for England. *Seraphim, Seraphim,* the name bothered me, for I'd seen it scratched in ink: *Seraphim,* out of Boston, Newman Head of Salem one-third owner.

I wondered if *Seraphim* had got word of our pursuit through Head's agents and took *Kittiwayke*'s cargo and crew so that newly-lightened *Kittiwayke* might race ahead.

I did explain this to Captain Cleasby, even whispering that Finn's prize might be stashed on board *Seraphim*, but Cleasby shook his head, saying to me, 'You can be sure that neither Finn nor his prize are anywhere near *Seraphim*, and *Seraphim*'s master goes nowhere near England. He won't cross weighted like that. Mark me, Mr Kelly, Finn and *Kittiwayke* are near. And it is with Finn and *Kittiwayke* we have concerns, not with goods due in Salem.'

Kittiwayke had just departed Harbour Grace as we came to sight her early in the first dog watch. She beat northeast, unladen, high and quick. Captain Cleasby gave his orders smartly, we taking every breath of wind we might, and though *Kittiwayke* did dart far ahead in the fog, we kept her intermittently in sight of the glass.

Then *Kittiwayke* slowed, finally stopped, caught in irons. Clews had come loose, and the larboard sheets flapped. We bore steadily down, and Captain Cleasby ordered the Marines to be at the ready. Then he said, 'Make Finn damned certain we wish him heave to. Ready the bowchasers.'

We closed in, soon near enough to see shapes moving on deck through the fog.

Cleasby bellowed through his speaking horn. 'This is Captain Cleasby of *Dauntless*. You will heave-to.'

Kittiwayke gave no reply.

My captain gazed on *Kittiwayke* as she slipped in and out of the fog and ordered we fire broad across *Kittiwayke*'s bow, the custom of warning. Then *Kittiwayke* shuddered and caught the wind. She was coming about, this being madness. We fired, deliberately missed. *Kittiwayke*'s sails filled, and now she picked her course southeast. Spittle threading after his words, Captain Cleasby ordered we aim the guns at the *Kittiwayke*'s headsail, where one good hit could slaughter the rigging and cripple the sloop. It risked injury to Finn, whom I must bring back unharmed, but at that moment my concern mattered for naught. As *Kittiwayke* dragged herself into the fog, we fired again The ball fell into the sea.

Captain Cleasby called me aft and, smiling, ordered that we now hug the coast. 'Go check the notations for sunkers, man.

We've harried him down to Port au Mal. We'll have him, Kelly, me for my reasons, you for yours, and we'll yet see who comes out taker of the prize.'

We pursued *Kittiwayke* hard and smart though the narrows, and we heard her drive into the rocks. Almost all of us sighed at that, for tis a sickening noise. Cleasby ordered grappling hooks out but changed his mind on better seeing *Kittiwayke*'s perilous angle. He could not risk *Dauntless* sinking with her. There were only three on board *Kittiwayke*: Matt Finn, the mate Con Pilgrim and a boy of fifteen, Edward Seward. I felt certain Finn had offloaded crew and cargo to *Seraphim*. Fog impedes hearing much as it impedes sight. Your Admiral Lacey rowed out and demanded parley at the same moment Captain Cleasby yelled across the gunwales to Finn, demanding the presence of himself and his strongbox. Lacey hallooed again, and as Captain Cleasby turned to ask for silence, tall Pilgrim stood behind Finn and hauled his captain back by the shoulders. Finn struck Pilgrim, and he staggered. Then Finn rushed below, very foolishly, and Cleasby ordered me to board *Kittiwayke* and arrest all aboard. Our party easily took Pilgrim and Seward. I hurried below to seek out Finn.

Matt Finn, fugitive, murderer, prodigal, thief. Matt Finn, who knew *Kittiwayke* when I did not, who like myself now stood ankle-deep in cold water, fearful to step heavy to one side or the other, yet descending further, further. A slush lamp still burned where I passed, very low. Silence impossible, I splashed to the captain's cabin. The door, previously damaged by axe, hung partially open. I opened the door quickly, staying well behind it and fearing a shot. None came. I peered through the gap near the hinges; Finn, hands shaking, crouched against the sternmost wall, struggled to hold and fire the pistol but dropped it in the water. Black rocks darkened the windows. I thought of an engraving once I'd seen of an adder cornered before a barrel of apples and ready to strike. I ran through the doorway, eyes fixed on Finn's hand, which darted into a coat pockets and came out with a fair-sized rock. Armed now, Finn flew at me like some devil fresh thrown out of hell, slipping in the water and falling hard. Only then did I draw my pistol, reasoning I must return Finn unharmed but could never obey that order if Finn killed me first.

I managed to grab one arm, and by that I yanked Finn close. Our feet numb and awkward as blocks, we danced slowly towards deck, Finn cursing me out as I'd not been cursed before, inviting me to copulate with a dog at one point. Seeing Pilgrim and Seward under guard, Finn quieted, and I eased my grip. Pistols can misfire, and I had the additional worry of the frizzen getting damp, which would render the weapon useless. Captain Cleasby called across an order, and suddenly Finn broke loose of me, reached for a boot and brought out a dagger. Pilgrim yelled something, and only with me holding Finn from behind and a Marine working at Finn from the front did we get that dagger loose. It fell somewhere, and another knife, hanging off a lanyard, flew off from round Finn's neck.

Marines behind them and Marines before them, Seward, Pilgrim and Finn swung over to *Dauntless.* Cleasby ordered Pilgrim and Seward to the brig and Finn to his own quarters for questioning. Finn struggled at this, very strong, like something possessed, Cleasby said. The Marines took aim, and Pilgrim begged Finn to stop. Separated from Seward and Pilgrim, Finn seemed to understand something mighty, and all fight departed. Cleasby ordered Finn bound to a chair. 'For the safety of all,' he told me.

I interrogated Finn alone, and I kept my questions short and direct. Finn answered some of them, very watchful, confirming facts. *Kittiwayke* sailed for Newman Head's cartel. Finn came from Bristol and was taken captive into Barbary. Men and cargo had been transferred to *Seraphim.* But when I asked why Finn had forced the chase, my prisoner grew sullen and would answer naught more.

I got called away, deliberately, so Captain Cleasby might ask of Finn his own questions. Then we came ashore, and I saw more sad proof of gold prying my captain apart. I took notice of as much as I could, for I would need report these events to the Admiralty. My reports would ruin Cleasby.

Throughout the night I tried to reason with Captain Cleasby. I tried sense. I tried orders. Naught would budge him from the damned gold. I questioned Finn repeatedly on the matter of the Benvolian gold in Cleasby's presence, but Finn kept mute. My words blended around us like threads of fog; I heard my voice and wondered who spoke. Finally, Cleasby needed to go on deck. I dropped my voice low and spoke of Runciman and the old Barbary wound. Finn still said naught. Captain Cleasby returned, refreshed by the air above and a draught of rum. He ordered me to rest, noting my long watch and mounting phlegm, adding I would need my energies in few enough hours. I had to leave. I could not at that delicate time risk inflaming the captain, nor risk my own freedom.

So I left them, hearing Cleasby's voice as I shut the door, 'Now, sir, there remain two matters: murder and gold. Where shall we start?'

When Captain Cleasby gave the order to hang Constant Pilgrim for murder, I knew my enterprise had nearly come undone. Captain Cleasby did think correctly in one thing: whatever my agenda, whatever my policy, there remained the question of justice for the murders on board *Kindly One*. We should have transported Pilgrim and Finn back to England to stand trial. Indeed that had been Runciman's desire and final firm reason to haul Finn home. But in Captain Cleasby's gold-rotten mind, these two were murdering pirates. He'd been told so. We kept Finn and Pilgrim separate, and I could read in each face not just fear but their need to talk to each other. I played their minds and loyalties with different scenarios of punishment and freedom, but neither betrayed the other.

I joined Captain Cleasby in the lieutenants' mess. He was alternately cajoling and threatening Pilgrim about the gold, but Pilgrim said naught, did not even look at Cleasby, only sat at the table, hands out in front of him, palms down. Then Cleasby struck Pilgrim with the back of his hand, knocking the man out of his chair. We waited, for Pilgrim stayed a moment crumpled on the boards before he unfolded his long-boned body and got back up into the chair, where once more he sat, hands on the table in front of him, bleeding from the mouth, silent. Then Cleasby tacked away from the gold towards *Kindly One* again, reminding Pilgrim of how pirates may be hanged from the yardarm of the capturing vessel. Still Pilgrim kept silent, blood marking his shirt. To my relief as well as Pilgrim's, Cleasby left the mess and did not order me come with him. Now I could ask the colonist what he knew.

Pilgrim said naught to me for almost an entire watch. Bells marked the beginning and bells would mark the end of four hours of us sitting together. I told him, gently, how I knew of Finn's history, of Benvolio and the stolen gold, but no reaction surfaced in Pilgrim's face. I tasked him on the murders, on responsibilities and duties to the law and to God. He became very angry, arguing with me that Finn has committed murder yet was not responsible. Evasion, I thought. He surprised me.

She is not responsible, he argued. She had killed a man who'd attacked her some years before, and the luckless Captain Tilley. Finn was female.

(Here Kelly became angry with me as I hurried to cool his forehead, I arguing delirium, he promising he'd come to the proof and demanding I let him be.)

This complicated everything. Then Pilgrim said 'About the murders on *Kindly One*, Mr Kelly. Finn was not responsible. They happened at my hand. The first did be an old quarrel, the second an accident, but I killed them.' He cocked his large head just the slightest bit and asked, 'Do you really think someone as small as Matt Finn could kill one man, let alone two?'

I found Cleasby on deck. 'I am weary,' he said to me, turning away from Pollard, the surgeon, who was leaning on the starboard gunwale and gazing out the narrows. 'I am weary of strange demands made on me by inferiors. Have you gleaned anything useful, sir, anything at all, from the colonist?'

I asked if we might discuss the matter in his cabin. Cleasby said, 'Another demand,' but to his cabin we went, and there I told him how Pilgrim had confessed.

'A knotty enterprise, this,' Cleasby responded. 'If the man confessed, then the man must hang.'

I protested vigorously, saying we must transport Pilgrim and Finn to England, where any matters of trial and piracy would be settled, adding that I did not trust the confession.

But Cleasby chose his own course. And mark me, Cannard, he chose, as clearly as he chose whether first to eat biscuit or pease. 'You do not trust his confession,' he said, passing me a fresh handkerchief. 'Yet he has freely made it. And he is not the man we needs pressure, for it is Finn and Finn alone who knows where the prize is kept. No, no dissent, I know there is prize still, as much as I know there are bones beneath my flesh. Let us assume for the moment Pilgrim did kill those men, as he has freely confessed, we putting nothing harsher to him than questions. If he killed those men, and savagely at that, then he must hang. Justice concerns us this voyage as much as your secret policy, Kelly. If Pilgrim did not kill those men, and we hang him, then the pressure upon Finn will crack his mouth. Even if Finn be so cold and unmoved to confess, at least fear might chafe his neck.'

Cleasby's plans chilled me, and I asked 'Sir, did not the Admiralty request we find and detain Finn and return him to England for trial on piracy?'

Cleasby said, 'Aye. But the orders say naught of what to do with Pilgrim.'

I spent what time I could then with Finn, coaxing and teasing out the story, coming down over and over to the prize, the prize, the prize, assuring Finn that once we had the prize we might depart. Finn stared at me as if I was mad and asked why she should be so eager to return to England. I told her a fatted calf might be waiting for us, but she did not recognize this reference. I finally reached Finn by saying, 'You possess abilities and talents much desired by your former master, a certain cunning and a capacity for disguise. Your recent actions on *Kindly One* only increase your value. The knack to kill he considers useful. I am to bring you greeting from the far-marked man.'

She flinched and cursed at that. Then she asked 'If I give you the truth of the prize, will you plaindeal with me?'

I told Finn I could promise nothing, but I would hear the proposal.

She met my eyes and said, 'Let Pilgrim go. Take me back to England, to Runciman – tis him, then? One wandering eye? Let Pilgrim go, for he's done naught wrong, naught, and I shall show you the prize you seek and then turn it over into Runciman's own hands and return, I suppose, to Runciman's work.'

I knew not if the little discretion Runciman had afforded me covered such pacts, and Captain Cleasby had already ordered the boatswain to tie a noose, but I knew not what else to do. And there remained the troublesome matter of murders. So I asked, 'Who killed the men on board *Kindly One*?'

'I did, you fool' said Finn easily, almost absently, 'though I only intended the one.'

I reported to Cleasby that Matt Finn also confessed to the murders. Cleasby gazed steadily at the wall opposite, finally saying, 'I cannot hang Finn without the gold. Are you not the officer of the watch, sir?'

On deck, I prayed. I stood very still, officer, agent, pawn. Heaviness everywhere, settling on us, pushing us forward, frightening some, pleasing others. At this, the butt-end of a long chase, some climax now, some release, sweet anticipation of whatever relief might come from seeing a man die. It darted from officer to officer, man to man, like light in the rigging at night.

Captain Cleasby came on deck with Finn under guard and installed the prisoner under my care. Then he surveyed the boatswain's work for the yardarm. Pilgrim and Finn had still not been permitted to speak together, and I had not been able to speak to either of them, Cleasby keeping me busy with choosing a dozen men for the hanging party. I tripped in a sloppy coil of line and bawled out the boatswain, who in turned called back to me an apology, adding he 'be a mite busy this morning, sir, with other rigging.' I went below as if to cool my temper. Cleasby did not call me back. So I descended to the hold, where Edward Seward and Con Pilgrim sat, in dampness and in irons.

Seward came near the grate immediately, fetters dragging, telling Pilgrim he heard the key. Pilgrim looked up at me slowly when I knelt at the grate and called down his name. He'd not slept, predictably, nor had he eaten. His fair beard coming in gave him sunken cheeks. 'Pilgrim,' I said, 'Captain Cleasby will hang you for your confession, but you and I know it is false.'

'If your captain wills to hang me, then your captain will hang me,' said Pilgrim as he shifted a little against the irons. 'There be naught I can do about that.'

'Recant, you stubborn ass!' I knew excitement would only seal Pilgrim's will, but I could no longer speak quietly. 'This is no easy death, Pilgrim. Do you know how long a hanging takes? What is it that makes you willing to die for Finn?'

Pilgrim stared at something I could not see. 'Willing to die? No, sir. My will means naught in this place, at this moment. But someone must die for *Kindly One*. And Finn be not responsible.'

I discarded discretion and told Pilgrim that Cleasby would hang him to force something else from Finn.

Pilgrim's absence of concern may have come from fatigue, strain or some detachment I could not sound. He said, 'Your captain will get naught from mine that my captain does not wish to give. If I recant now, your captain will be forced to hang my captain, and what prize will be got then?'

A quick despair revealed itself in Pilgrim's face; he fought it down.

I wanted to shake him. 'Damn my captain! Damn the prize! Are you not afraid to die, man?'

'I should not be.'

I knew then I'd interrupted something private. I wished to say one last thing to him – words that meant something. I managed 'God have mercy on your soul.'

Pilgrim answered me: 'And on yours.'

I returned above, Seward's pleas for freedom scattering behind me.

Disputing with Cleasby might be useless, but I did dispute. He tried refusing me entry to his cabin, but I entered, speaking quickly now. He ordered me to the sickbay, citing my cough, my leaking nose, but I would not go until he heard my plea for Pilgrim. I spoke to Cleasby's back until he turned and said, 'Your mouth flaps like a loose sheet. Need I clew it up? Make no mistake, I can put you below the rest of this voyage, in the same irons now on Seward and Pilgrim. I can justify this to the Admiralty as insubordination. Your orders be damned, Lieutenant Kelly, for no matter whom you serve, you remain but the first lieutenant. And I remain captain. Now. I just ordered you to the sickbay. Why stand you here?'

In the sickbay, Dr Pollard gave me rum and I-told-you-so, as well as bitter dry leaf to chew, and he must have guided me into a hammock, because there he woke me some hours later, *Dauntless* gone oddly quiet. Lieutenant Penney stood in the suddenly distant sickbay door, piping my name. When had *Dauntless* bloated out so? The moment my fever stoked, that is when.

I managed to get on deck, which wavered before me. I took my place and stood as steadily as I might.

All men, officers, idlers and prisoners stood where they must, for now not even Captain Cleasby could stop what he had set in motion. I caught Pollard's eye and thought again of his talk of rods and orbits and spheres. Pilgrim stood, hands bound behind him, watching the boatswain bind his feet. He balanced with some difficulty, and a fine trembling took him. The boatswain fixed the noose at his neck, and Pilgrim shut his eyes. The order given – *Handsomely, handsomely* – the men in the hanging party hauled in silence. Pilgrim struggled, a spasm waving from his head to his feet, lashed through him by the force of many arms and one rope against his breath. And Finn watched, utterly silent. The wind gusted a bit, and Pilgrim looked down past his own feet at us. Then, as he twisted, he looked on wrecked *Kittiwayke*, then he twisted again and looked on us once more. I know not how long he saw us, or when the red and black came over his sight, for I could not point to the moment he died. He'd calmed, but now he shook himself as though throwing off a coat. Eyes open and bulging, neck stretched, his face flushed red, purple, blue: the man became a bruise. A great release blew through us, sickness following in me.

Then Finn accused us of hanging an innocent. She promised she'd see me drown for this, and I tried to explain that Runciman commanded us both.

Cleasby, much red in the face, strode towards us and jerked Finn round, giving insult and demanding prize. Finn told him once more the only possession of value sat trapped on the rocks. Cleasby ordered me back to *Kittiwayke* to find the hidden gold. Finn smirked. I'd no choice but to go, for even if I refused and there risked insubordination, cowardice and arrest, he would send someone else, he would risk another for gold that was not there, and I would not, could not, allow another man's life to be risked for this fable.

Gulls cried, attracted to the yardarm. Finn mumbled about gold and mouths.

As I stepped away from Cleasby, readying myself to follow orders, Finn spoke again, but in different tones. 'Kelly, no. Captain Cleasby, I appeal to your good sense and your conscience. Surfeit. Please, sir, send no one over. Enough death. There be no gold. Please.'

Captain Cleasby had walked away, too, and my last glance at Finn as I readied to swing over was of a little body nearly lost within a greatcoat.

Kittiwayke slipped. I fell onto my arse on her deck, and then her deck vanished. The cold water, thick salt death, took me from behind. I broke the surface enough to suck in air, but I can't swim. Deaf and gone under a third time, I tried to twist out of my coat. Someone got my plait and nearly tore it out of my head, hauling me up. Then hands everywhere, hands and air. Someone held my nose and forced me to swallow rum. Pollard and Penney rapidly stripped me in the sickbay, and then I spewed, rum and salt and gall, Pollard the while wrapping me in blankets and bidding me remain in the chair and not dare lie down while Penney fetched my spare uniform.

I sent for you a few hours later. My last chance? I suppose you were, but my last chance at what? What I needed from you was some sense of what had just happened, some confirmation that all

I had witnessed was real. Then I recalled Runciman speaking of you and your *Bonny Jane*, ordering me in an aside to keep an ear for word of you, and there you stood. I had much to ask you, for there was a good chance you were whom you said. And now I am dying in your bed, and I've still asked you naught. Captain Cleasby interrupted. I will be facing final judgement, and that ass will bellow that my orders and soul be damned, he will face judgement first. Do you know I dream of him first and last? The moment I drift to the moment I wake, his face, his voice, Cannard, interrupting my dreams. Interrupting my dreams!

Captain Cleasby ordered you ashore, and me below, to discuss, what was it he said? A strange matter. Oh aye, very strange. Strange as a captain in His Majesty's navy ordering a prisoner to be beaten for questioning. Strange as Finn the murderer, Finn the pirate, Finn the thief, and Cleasby the captain, Cleasby the judge, Cleasby the hero, taking the musket butt himself to Finn in grossest perversion of office. Naught had dug up the gold to now, no threats, no death, naught, for no gold existed here. Finn spoke true. The only prize was Finn herself. And Cleasby must not know.

Finn lay insensible, bloodied from injuries to the head and face. Yet these injuries did not fret Pollard as much as the blows to Finn's back and the odd swelling on the right side of Finn's chest.

I asked how these injuries had come.

'The prisoner angered me,' said Cleasby. 'Pollard, tell the lieutenant what else we have uncovered.'

Pollard took a quick breath; he might speak more boldly to Cleasby than I, and he did, looking like a stiff actor. 'I am most concerned with injury to the kidneys. These blows are unnecessary. And I know not if I can treat them. What in hell possessed you to strike this prisoner so?'

Cleasby grinned like a snotty midshipman after his first whore. 'Handsomely, Dr Pollard handsomely.'

Finn grunted.

'Dr Pollard,' said Cleasby, 'tell the lieutenant just what you discovered when you looked to the injuries.'

I did not need to be told.

Finn looked at us now, pain hardening that already hard face, the same face I'd studied for three days.

Captain Cleasby laughed.

Even smaller out of the greatcoat, Finn moved with slow care.

Dr Pollard had removed Finn's shirt to treat the blows to her back, and of course he had unbound that tiny bosom. One small breast suppurated. Many scars marked her chest, as though someone had taken a knife to her. The blanket clung to a form almost without curve, waist and hips near on a straight line. Rough and ropey flesh. Accidents and a boyish body. The cunning and tutelage of a spymaster. Stolen gold. Bitter knowledge late tempered by the friendship of Con Pilgrim. A person at once used and refusing: a murderer, a thief, a captain, a spy, a *rara avis*, a female.

Dr Pollard asked, 'How hide you the bleed?'

I asked, 'What is your name?'

Cleasby asked, 'Where is the prize?'

She spat at us. It landed on her arm.

Captain Cleasby ordered Pollard and me from the sickbay. Pollard said, 'The captain's wrath, long a prisoner, is now released. Kelly, a jar is shattered at our feet.'

I coughed. My plait, still wet and heavy, soaked my back. Hearing noise from the sickbay, I recalled the Portsmouth dock and the half-dead tar who picked me up as though I weighed no more than a doll. I had but five years that day, out walking with my mother, though now, looking back on it, I cannot say what she was doing with me in hand on the fogbound docks. The tar, missing an eye and most of his teeth, leaned against a barrel and seemed asleep, mouth slack. I peered at his gums while my mother peered somewhere else, and then she tugged my hand to move me along, but the tar picked me up, his hands immense and tough as rope under my arms, and he seemed set to fling me above his head, very happy. My mother screamed. And he put me down, almost dropped me, mumbling something about the colour of my hair, and he ran off, slipping easily into the fog. Years later, at the house of my uncle, for we lived with my mother's brother, I sneaked into her bedroom and found the box she tried to keep secret. She'd shown it to me once when I suffered a fever. She'd tried to tell me something. Within the box lay a letter and a lock of red hair, darker than mine. I tried to find that box again, view that lock of hair. My father, she'd said, had died at sea, and his name had been John Kelly, too. I promised her I'd never go to sea.

Cleasby opened the door and ordered the surgeon to tend to his patient. To me, he said he'd get us on course for England, but I must submit to the surgeon's care.

231

I followed Pollard into the sickbay, where he said he'd find me something for the cough, when my knees gave way once more, a most annoying weakness. Pollard got me to a hammock, prying loose from my fingers what I'd found on the floor when I fell: a fly-button, thread ripped. Another sound, of hard breathing, and Pollard hastily took covers and placed them around Finn, who leaned heavily against the wall, and who, under this one gesture from Pollard, suffered herself to be helped back to a hammock.

It mattered little, Pollard said to me as he tucked covers round me and a paper in my breeches in preparation for my journey in the jollyboat back to Port au Mal. It mattered little that Cleasby ordered Pollard to sew Finn's corpse into canvas and dump it overboard with neither recognition nor ceremony, for Finn could not have lived much longer. Injury to the kidneys meant blood in the pisspot, then no piss at all. Pollard added 'She may not have known what happened.' Murderers will be hanged. And ships will sail home. I felt confused as Pollard helped me up to deck. England already? Fever so long as that? Then I took in the meaning of the jollyboat, of Cleasby's refusing to meet my eyes as he spoke of my duty done by *Kittiwayke*, of new orders to wait in Newfoundland for a rendezvous with another agent. Fever, I told myself, it must be the fever, for what tale would Cleasby tell the Admiralty? Yet here I lie in your bed, you bitterly watching. Pollard so gentle, tucked covers about me, muttering of the danger of chill, and I asked him where *Dauntless* was bound. He said, 'I wish for Harbour Grace, so I might see my sister.'

Yet even then, with his telling me so much, Kelly hid other truths – within his breeches, inside a false pocket: begrimed papers. Kelly being protective of his clothing and Lacey declaring he would know the reason why, I stole the papers. At Lacey's next absence from the Hall, I hauled off Kelly's breeches and much disturbed his lungs, but I must get the papers before Lacey did. In Kelly's secret pocket rested notes towards a report addressed only to 'My dear and honoured SIR' and topped with 'Rejoice with me, for I have found the coin which you have lost.' I peeled the sheets apart, deciphering with difficulty the secretive hand. Folded with these notes lay a short letter in yet another man's marks, some medical gibberish. Thankful for my foresight and large pockets, I kept the papers, for Kelly, despite his ravings about duty and his need to

232

confess, would never freely give the papers to me. What man would?

I place the papers here.

Rejoice with me, for I have found the coin which you have lost.

My dear and honoured SIR:

Your task and my voyage being most difficult, and I fearing I may not return for reasons both beyond and within control of mortal men, I hereby collect my records of conversations with F—, who did come to trust me as a tired traveller might trust a sudden innkeeper and so did speak with some freedom.

Oedema at ankles, wrists, and face. Stoppage of urine. Gross injury to kidneys?

Body shows recent bruising and swelling.

Body shows many knife scars on the chest, the tops of the thighs, and within the hairs on the *pudendum muliebre*. One breast swollen, recently knifed in an attempt to drain a large sac of pus. Body shows some emaciation about the ribs and the deconditioned leg musculature somewhat typical of the seaman. Buttocks flat and firm like a boy's. Shoulders broad. Arms strong, well-developed. Hair brown with some grey at the temples and over the ears. Eyes green. Age difficult to ascertain as many teeth remain. Cause of death: exhaustion. H Pollard, MD.

28) DUST ON WET INK
CANNARD'S LEDGER.

As John Kelly lay babbling in his fever, I suddenly called to Lacey, startling us both with my tone. 'Admiral Lacey. Do you believe in the sacred trust of the deathbed?'

'What of it?'

'I must get to Harbour Grace.'

'You've not made that demand a while, Cannard.'

'Not for me this time, but for Lieutenant Kelly.'

'And how do you intend to get there?'

'Why is it, sir? Why? Why have you, year after year, prevented me leaving this settlement?'

Lacey said, 'At each moment, I needed you.'

'Yet you had no understanding of what I needed. You deliberately interfered with my tasked work. All those years, spring and fall, I tried to get on board *Boyne*, because, sir, I needed to get to Harbour Grace and get my news, if not myself, back to England. Why did you prevent it?'

Lacey smiled, almost fondly, though his eyes stayed cold. 'See the splinter in my eye? Be a good man now, and remove it.'

Passion left me. 'Was it simply because I wished it?'

'You give up too easily, man.'

After a few moments, I walked where he'd walked and stood in the open doorway. I watched Aurelius Jackman wade ashore, late returning. Beyond him, the offreach and the harbour, the narrows and the fog, vast water. Behind me, blunt cliffs and conifers; above me the old spike used to hold Michael Riordan. The fog rolled in quickly; I would see no stars that night. *You give up too easily, man.* Kelly mumbled behind me, and I stood before and within all this presence, understanding naught.

234

ACTS OF FAITH

So bitter, so courageous,
at times I think you may just
need to cry.

Wake up...

Madison Violet, 'Wake Up,'
Worry the Jury, 2004.

29) 'FRET THY SHORE'
August 29, 2009, Orange Lodge, Port au Mal, Newfoundland.

—Jesus, Nichole! Couldn't you make it any more tourist-friendly than *that?*

—Evan!

Evan Rideout pointed in mad dismay to his copy of Nichole's play manuscript. —How the hell is anyone gonna show the Royal Navy diggin up a settlement on stage? 'Infancy's soft bones'? And don't get even me started on your Captain Cleasby character. No way, *no way* would a naval officer behave like that. You are *never* gonna get TCR fundin if you don't make this more realistic.

—No, I am never going to get TCR funding if I tell the truth!

Seth Seabright knocked on the open door. —Sounds like I got the right place.

Nichole made introductions. Evan politely complimented Seth on his last book while looking at him pretty hard; Seth thanked him.

Then Seth gave a long study to Nichole, as though trying to decide whether to strike her or hug her. He finally sat down, slouching with restrained drama. Hideously conscious of the weird silence he'd caused just by turning up, Seth scrambled for words.
—TCR's programmin content now? Didn't take you for a policy-wonk there, Rideout. Thought you had a pair.

—B'ys, it's government. The way they see it, it's their money, and –

—It's our money. We pay the taxes.

—*Everybody's* money, Seabright. Government's the steward.

Seth changed tack. —So everyone involved in this today lives in St John's, yet we're all after drivin out to Port au Mal for this meetin?

—The Rural Business Schedule Quota. All departments need to hold so many meetins a year outside St John's.

—Rural BS is right. Fine stewardship of our money. Right up there with goin out on the fuckin north Atlantic to suck oil out of the seabed. I don't know which money is gonna be after ruinin us first, tourism or oil.

Evan stood up quickly, scraping his chair hard on the floor. *I'm just gonna keep quiet now about Jackman suggestin Nichole throw a*

236

few Beothuks into the script. —Move your legs there, Seabright. I'll go find a kettle.

—Find some balls, while you're at it.

Nichole rolled her eyes. —Seth, give it up. Evan's a nice guy.

—We're all 'nice guys.' You haven't asked me how I'm feelin.

—How are you feeling?

—Like a drink.

—What happened with the stings after?

—Slept for three days, they pumped that much Benadryl into me. Woke up from that hung over like slut on Sunday mornin. Then they kept me in there for a detox.

—Are you okay now?

—Told ya, I feel like a drink. Or like somethin fuckin drunk me and pissed me out against the wall. Listen, Nichole, I – here he comes, tourism's Sir Galahad.

Evan passed Nichole a steaming Styrofoam cup of stale Golden Pheasant, its malty sharpness almost an assault —Found a few tea bags and one of those hot water spigots. Sorry, Seabright, I couldn't carry back three.

Seth stared out the window. If he jumped out of it, he'd fall on the whitecapped water. He heard bells.

Nichole took a thick envelope from her backpack and slapped it over her copy of the script. —So tell me, Evan, is all this null and void? Hey? Are you going to tell me that the narrative in Cannard's ledger doesn't matter?

Evan put his copy down and carefully, slowly, opened the envelope. Discovering regular white paper, he rapidly flicked through the sheets. —You photocopied Cannard's ledger? You stuck an early eighteenth-century document on the fuckin Xerox machine?

The shock, anger and little spark of glee in Evan's voice caught Seth's attention.

Nichole smiled sweetly. —Every page. Before I handed it over. Before I even showed it to you. It's not a great copy. Bits didn't come out. And where's Cannard's ledger now, Ev?

—In a climate-controlled case in the Rare Documents collection until Thomas Wright formally presents it to Chris Jackman on September 19.

—Locked up in Rare Docs, wherever they are this week, where no one can see it! *And* where it will probably catch fire.

—Nichole, I can't believe – all the curator trainin I've given you – the potential damage!

—Desperate times, Evan. What's happened to you? When I first started at the Admiral's Rooms, you kept telling me about the responsibility we had, not as arbiters or gatekeepers but interpreters of history.

Evan heard his grandfather complaining about the whiskers he grew for the Tattoo. *If it's history you need, my old man's straight razor's up in the attic.* He said nothing.

Seth drummed his fingers on the boardroom table. Driving out around a particularly grim bay for a Saturday afternoon meeting in a stuffy old Orange Lodge to discuss a play that now looked like it wasn't even going ahead? Stuck listening to a couple of academic townies bitching about history while they all waited for a board of directors' meeting to start? *Yes b'y, fine way to spend the day. Fuckin grand.*

Seth tried to interrupt. —Your Lieutenant Kelly character. Have you thought about writin this from his point of view?

Evan spoke before Nichole could. —Nichole, I also told you and told you and *told you* about responsibility to old documents! Jesus, anyone finds out you put a Rare Doc on the photocopier – tell me you at least wore the white cotton gloves.

—I cut the fingers out of them. You know what I photocopied? Yeah, you know. Proof, Ev, quill-scratched, ink-blobbed, bloody *proof* that Port au Mal had settlers before 1760. Well before. Sure, it was you who showed me the matching correspondence from Salem.

Evan very nearly remarked to Seth about the hazards of literate women but chose instead to swallow some tea. It scalded his oesophagus. *God, I hate tea.* —Nichole, you're like grapeshot at close range. I'm already stressed to the nines with my grandfather, and Jackman tryna fuck with the *Peril on the Sea* exhibit, and now you pull this stunt on me?

Embarrassed for Evan and Nichole, Seth tried again. —You mean John Cannard in the play, right? That ledger: are Kelly's notes still there?

Nichole showed him the photocopy of Kelly's notes.

Pleased and impressed, Seth nodded. —Very good, then. Can I take a look at that? And what about those letters from Newman Head?

Evan spilled tea all over his chest. *Sealskin packet hidden away with Pop's ammo. I fuckin smuggled history.*

Seth, digging in his pocket and then passing Evan a wad of fraying tissues, noticed, but decided not to comment on, Evan's developing erection. *Takes all kinds.* —B'ys, I got to ask you about this Lieutenant Kelly – that air conditionin's got some cold.

Evan sneered. —No AC in here, Seabright. Can't retrofit a Heritage Buildin. Who the hell is that?

Reverend Elias Winslow was playing with the dart scoreboards as though dialling up a launch code. The door clicked shut, despite being out of anyone's reach. The cool air collided with the stuffy sunned-up air, and threads of fog coalesced round Winslow's head.

—Ms Wright, Mr Seabright. Back again?

Nichole introduced Evan to Reverend Winslow, each recognizing the other's name from correspondence between HARC and TCR. Nichole had not seen nor heard from Winslow since the night he told her the Finn story she'd used for her play. She had no certainty that visit actually took place. An escort of coyotes? Puked bezoars and stolen knives?

Winslow straightened his robe. —Dorinda Masterson and the rest of the ACHE board will be late. I need to speak to you three before they get here, because I just remembered something I need to do.

Softly, softly.

He gently blew cold air at them. Evan, Seth and Nichole tried to stand up, but those hard plastic chairs felt as warm and soft as beds. As though Nan had just placed her homemade afghan over your shoulders as you sat near the woodstove, as though fever imprisoned you and forced you to keep still.

Eyes sad, Reverend Winslow raised his hands in benediction and exhaled again. —Please. Tell yourselves the truth.

Pop with the gun and Pop won't go to the doctor and Pop courtin Mrs Dunphy, Pop raisin me from age six and teachin me the old songs and stories and down to the Folk Festival every single summer and out round the bay every chance we got and bringin me up to Signal Hill for the Tattoo performances and then takin all those pictures the first time I came home in Tattoo costume and then takin more when I came home in the proper costume, the late eighteenth-century one. Not sayin boo when the girlfriend spent the night, and now can't drive, can't hardly see. Jesus. Can't remember. Jackman keeps

promisin me he'll fast-track Pop into one of the good Homes, and I love
him, owe him, want him looked after, but I can't stand havin him in
the house. First time in my life, I'm afraid of him. Get him out, get
him out –

  One of those Seabrights? We knows all about you, my son, yes, we
sees ya up there. Your mother and your aunt there tried to make a go
of dinner theatre in the 60s and 70s, gave it up when the youngsters
came along. Both of them stunned enough to get tangled up with Pete
and Ricky Seabright. The manly art of cheque fraud, now, and where
are those two big men these days? Both women gone skinny and grey –
still got those scarves round their heads? Your aunt still wearin curlers,
never takin em out, and your father? Don't be talkin. If you even
amounts to half of him – that's what he always said: You'll never be
half the man I am, Seth. Think you're gonna climb down from that?

  Foxe hardly the worst. Foxe just sniffed me out. Damaged goods.
Grandfather softened me up, groomed me photo after photo, every time
a new camera came on the market I'd get excited, and damn it, there's
the fuckery: I'd get excited. Special special special, all grown up if I'd
just pose right and then suck him off, and I know now, I know I know
I know all wrong depraved and shameful ho ho ho shame, you want
shame, wrap my throat in shame and pull taut, because I felt kicked but
loved at the same time. With Foxe I didn't like it, no, can honestly say
that, not one shard of pleasure in that numb time, just that gnawing
need for – what, to make sense of the past? Love? Sins sins sins –

  Nichole struggled against her tight throat and jaw, forced
words out: —Sins of the fathers?

  Winslow's knees buckled. Nichole tried to reach over and help
him up, but she remained trapped in her chair.

  Winslow panted, looked up at Nichole. —I stole the secret
knife.

  Nichole tried to respond, if only to ask *What the fuck?*

  —I stole it. I started off singing, and somewhere, I stumbled
and fell, and then I knew cold. And watched a father abandon his
daughter to the cold ocean. He hacked off her fingers as she clung
to the kayak. One by one, he cut away his own daughter's fingers,
because he feared how much she might eat and what offspring she
might bear. But necessary, Nichole, do you understand? All that
suffering and love, necessary...

  Nichole wrenched her lower jaw down again: —I...

  It came out *Ah.*

240

Winslow crouched, shoulders rippling, and showed his teeth.
—You do understand.
—Ffff-ray well.
—Free will? When senility, addiction and abuse gnaw and tear
at the three of you? Currents and decay. I was sure this world would
end in 1974, quite certain. I dreamt it, you see. I should have
dissipated years ago. Died. I flitted round Port au Mal, darted in
and out of groundwalkers' lives. I love to watch, but I am created
for something else. Nichole, my dear, keep struggling like that and
you'll have a stroke. I stole the knife from that obscure woman in
1734. Now you know. I could not quite walk, could not quite be
seen, but I swear she felt me, knew I lifted the knife from around
her neck, and I fed off her anger. A poisonous meal, to be sure,
but her anger, hatred and guilt enlivened me for another two
hundred and seventy-five years. It drew me back, Nichole. Back to
what? Forgiveness? God? My own bones warped the goodness.
Being human. Like Sedna's fingers, knife wounds in salt water, all
that pain for a reason... surely, there are reasons? Nichole, keep still.
God, I had so much to tell you, but it just seeps out my skull and
dries up. I've forgotten. Wait – history damns us, but you must
fuck your history. No, that's not the right word. Be fucked by
history. God, no! What am I trying to say?

Nichole rolled her eyes left and then right. Evan and Seth both
sat forward, elbows on knees, staring at the floor. They breathed
softly, as though asleep.

Winslow pried open Nichole's clenched fingers and placed an
ancient onyx-handled knife on her palm. —Deny it. No no no –
defy it. Fray well.

Nichole clamped her fingers round Winslow's, squeezing them
against the knife. Suddenly, she could stand, and she did, backing
away from Winslow, falling over her chair and barking her head off
the hot water radiator. No pain yet, just that horrid stunning, like
when a wasp first stings – that brief reprieve before true knowledge.

Allied Cultural and Heritage Enterprises
Board of Directors Meeting
Saturday 29 August 2009
Fisherman's Stop Motel, Cannard's Point, Port au Mal
Present at Fisherman's Stop Motel:
Dorinda Masterson, President

Lewis Wright, Secretary/Treasurer
Evan Rideout, Assistant to Mr Jackman (taking minutes)
Reverend Elias Winslow, representing HARC.
Present via conference call:
Linda Gillingham, Eastern/Central Representative
Cissy Dawe, Western/Labrador Representative

Regrets: Vice-President / Avalon Representative Johnny Malone, Government Representative Chris Jackman. Addition-al regrets: Nichole Wright, commissioned playwright for Settlement 250; Seth Seabright, commissioned actor for the Settlement 250 play.

Meeting called to order at eleven am by Dorinda. She notes that the meeting was moved to the motel because the Orange Lodge is not accessible for her, on crutches.

A motion was made to adopt the agenda by Lewis Wright. Cissy seconded the motion.

A motion was made to adopt the minutes from the last meeting by Linda. Lewis seconded.

SETTLEMENT 250
Dorinda delivered Johnny's latest report on the progress of the Settlement 250 project. The report stated that ACHE has received several e-mails and letters, as well as many comments on the ACHE website, protesting the mounting of a play based, however loosely, on Port au Mal history. Dorinda noted that Reverend Elias Winslow was in attendance at the meeting to bring the community's concerns directly to ACHE. As noted previously, Settlement 250 is expected to attract many ex-pats and tourists, and advertising material has already gone out, with follow-ups planned.

Cissy commented there has been absolutely no interest in Settlement 250 west of Trinity, and she reminded the Board that the initiative offers nothing to central or western Newfoundland or to Labrador. She asked if there was any talk yet of further settlement celebration initiatives.

Reverend Elias Winslow, on behalf of HARC, presented a list of "grave concerns" about the play. (List is cut and pasted below.)

Quality of historical research.

Subject and themes of play seem to deviate from the ACHE / Settlement 250 mandate.

Portrayal on stage of ancestors of people presently living in the greater Port au Mal area, which is still home to many Jackmans and Simmses, for a start. Does not the survival of surnames point to the need for thoughtful respect?

Finally, the moral life of an actor hired to take part in the play has already inflamed controversy. It is neither libel nor slander to note that profanity and pornographic imagery are staples of both Mr Seabright's written work and many of his performances. In addition, Mr Seabright's connection to known criminals Peter and Richard Seabright raises concerns. Can ACHE assure HARC of the suitability of the content of this play?

Lewis received a cell phone call from Seth Seabright, informing him that Nichole Wright is in Conception Bay North's Von Haldorf Cottage Hospital, waiting to undergo tests for a suspected concussion.

Dorinda asked Evan for the latest update from TCR. Update (Chris Jackman's memo) is cut and pasted below:

> While there has been unexpected and vigorous protest from the good people of Port au Mal, including many calls to VOIC Radio's Free Line show, TCR wishes to make clear that our discontinuation of funding for the Settlement 250 play project has nothing to do with these issues. TCR, like all other departments, is under a cabinet-wide fiscal restraint policy, and difficult cuts have to be made. Both playwright and actor will be paid for their services up to this time.

ACTION ITEM: Dorinda Masterson to inform Nichole Wright and Seth Seabright that the Port au Mal Settlement 250 play will not go ahead.

BUSINESS ARISING

Cissy stated that central, the west coast and Labrador feel neglected by TCR. Vigorous discussion.

Dorinda reminded Cissy that Johnny had urged her (Cissy) to submit a report on this matter.

ACTION ITEM: Cissy to prepare a report on her region's concerns. Cissy to add her report to the agenda for the next meeting.

30) 'I AIN'T GOT A TIME OR A PLACE'
September 15, 2009, Criminal Court, St John's.

Enough of this.

My name is Nichole Laika Wright. I am here today at the trial of Mr Foxe to read a victim impact statement.

Starting in late 2004, Mr Foxe seemed to turn up more and more often at places I frequented. I avoided him at the time, as he worked for a rival broadcaster. But he began to talk to me, and I expect he figured out I was not in a good state. I suffer from chronic post-traumatic stress disorder, which in my case often manifests as high agitation and clinical depression. When Mr Foxe approached me, my illness was impairing my judgement, making me particularly vulnerable.

My relations with Mr Foxe started out as consensual. He asked to photograph me in various states of undress. I complied. I cannot say I consented. I expect you find the difference difficult to understand. It is difficult to explain. Mr Foxe was not the first to take advantage of me in this fashion. When younger, I was made to pose for child pornography. I was groomed to comply with such requests. Believing myself loved, I posed for Mr Foxe.

Mr Foxe tried to use the photos to blackmail me for money. He presumed that, because of my last name and family connections, I had ready access to large amounts of cash. I tried to explain this was not the case, and I attempted to break off contact. Repeated e-mails and phone messages and, again, my own impaired judgement, persuaded me to visit Mr Foxe one last time at his house, ostensibly to pick up some belongings. Mr Foxe forced me inside his home, locked the door, and bound and gagged me in S&M paraphernalia. He sliced off my clothes with a large hunting knife, slowly. The blade was warm by the time he was done. Then he ejaculated over my back. My muscles cramped, and I tried to speak to him. He left me alone a while. Then he returned and took more photos of me. I thought I'd die. I wanted to die. My eyes got starry with the camera's flash. Eventually he untied me, and, as soon as I could move my arms and legs again, I left Mr Foxe's house in borrowed clothes, specifically, a pair of leggings another woman had left behind and one of Mr Foxe's button-down flannel shirts from LL

Bean. I remember looking at the tag, because I thought that flannel was one of the softest things I'd ever touched. I wore my own shoes.

I quit my job during this time. I broke off contact with my family. I could not sleep. I briefly entered a psychotic phase. While my symptoms are now better controlled, I still suffer from nightmares and hyper-vigilance. These nightmares are a blend of both childhood and adult experiences.

I hope I have communicated effectively, and I thank the court for allowing me the opportunity to speak.

31) FAMILY REUNION
September 18-19, 2009, St John's.

—You did good the other day, ducky.

—Thank you for being there.

Gabriel shook his head, steam from his tea wafting up his face. He'd nearly left the courtroom, but, hiding his sweaty fists in his pockets, he'd stayed and listened, Dory's presence beside him an anchor. Nichole had addressed Gabriel in the observers' pew, reading her statement directly to him. Once Nichole had finished, Gabriel quickly got to the men's room and threw up in a sink.

Neither he nor Dory had said a word the whole way home. When they'd pulled in the driveway, Dory had asked *It was just us and reporters there, wasn't it?*

Yeah.

Gabriel gazed out the window of Mahon's. Across the street, another busker, the fifth he'd seen since parking Dory's rig, sawed away on a fiddle dying for a good polish. —Young fellah's not bad.

—Seth Seabright. Is there nothing he can't do?

—Ducky, he's not buskin on Water Street because he wants to. Look at the face on him.

—I can't see it for the beard.

—Bit shaggy, no question. Where do you know him from?

As Nichole explained, Seth winced at a wrong note that cut his aching head like a blunt razor pressed too hard. He'd been drinking heavily since the meeting out in Port au Mal – *some fuckin vision now at the Orange Lodge.* Recurring dreams of the redheaded John Kelly trying to talk to him did not help. Seth wanted to swat him away. *A character, just a character.* Seth could always see Kelly clearly enough, but he could never quite pick out his words. Seth tried to change the dream's course one night, tried to tell Kelly what a fine role he'd make, and how much Seth wouldn't mind playing him, but Kelly shook his head.

Whenever dream-Kelly faded, Seth's father loomed, as he had in Seth's childhood. After the moratorium, after the family's collection of grocery and hardware stores dried up and blew away like dandelion seed off a mower, Pete Seabright thinned out and even shrank a bit in height, but back when undead Cabot hauled his undead baskets, Pete ruled Flannery Point. Big man, oh yes, big man up and down the shore, but a gentle giant, heart of gold, wouldn't hurt the proverbial fly. No, the only one he ever touched was his one child, the piece of squalling flesh with no understanding, no respect for a good night's sleep. The child that had forced him to marry a girlfriend he'd despised for a whore.

It got bad in 1980, around when Seth turned five and announced he didn't like boats and wanted a set of paints. His father considered the declaration and the request and then apologized to Seth for being busy with the stores and the fish plant. He said he'd take Seth out to the old Seabright premises and the woods on weekends. *Show ya man stuff.* After a few weeks of watching his father's cruel games with snared animals, Seth told his teacher he didn't like going in the woods with his father. He also mentioned it to his mother, who detected her own deep sadness in her little boy and distracted him with a long game of make-believe. Pretending to be someone else, somewhere else – always potent medicine. Seth's teacher, a local girl, had told her mother at dinner about the stuff the kids had said that day, adding in a lower tone what the little Seabright boy said about the animals and the woods. Her mother repeated it to a clerk at a crowded check-out in a Seabright-owned store the next morning, and by suppertime the whole point knew that young Seth feared his father. Laughing at the story – *Kids, right?* – Pete deflected any suspicion. Seth got the paints but hardly used them.

As Seth grew up he proved himself quite the handy troublemaker, only calming down after his father had taken to the premises or the woods. By twelve, Seth could experiment with fighting back, but the hard truth remained: Pete outweighed him by nearly a hundred pounds of muscle and could easily hang him off a length of fishing net he kept strewn up in the premises' high rafters. Two storeys, originally, those premises, second floor removed. Old net, weighted and tangly. Seth dreaded the net more than the tortured animals, the blows and Pete's hand blocking his nose and mouth. *Toughen ya up. Quiet now, or I'll give ya somethin to cry about.* Seth could keep the tears back until his father removed whatever saint's pin Seth wore on his jacket, pins put there by his Grandmother Clatney on the Friday nights he'd pretend to fall asleep at her house, on the daybed by the woodstove. She'd pin on St Raphael or, *God help me, that proper little pill, St Tarcisius,* lament about how he kept losing the pins, tuck a blanket round him. Come morning she'd give him breakfast, another fiddle lesson and a hard time about practising, never mind his playing by ear. The sound of one of those saints' pins landing in some dark corner of the premises always paralysed Seth, gutted him. Resignation, then: Pete shoving him up the ladder. Hanging fifteen feet off the ground, wrists galled with line – *Keep still, now, til I finish* – fingers hooked through the meshes, father and ladder disappearing in the darkness beneath. That mostly ended as Seth grew bigger, though he didn't come near Pete's size. *Never be half the man I am.* Seth asked his grandmother for medals instead of pins, those medals on endless chains. She happily obliged, eventually giving him a fine collection of the more obscure saints.

After Seth accidentally set fire to an overflowing garbage can in the boys' bathroom at school playing with a lighter, Pete hit him across the face – out in the premises. Seth flew at him, rage hauling him past sense, vicious and fast like the snake that did not even live on the island of Newfoundland, forcing Pete to defend himself with a split from the woodpile. Or so Pete told it. He'd hauled a stunned Seth up the ladder and, heaving for breath, returned him to the net, only without tying his wrists. *Stay there, now.* Refusing to cry – *no, not one fuckin sound* – Seth lowered himself, hand over hand, to the end of the net, and jumped, landing hard enough to damage his knees. He grabbed not a split but the axe and tore after Pete. Just as a Ranger pulled up, coming to ask respected community businessman Peter Seabright about his annual donation to the volunteer fire department.

Trying hard to root out whatever it was in him that so angered his father, and keeping to himself, Seth had spent his grade eleven year, the year the moratorium came down, in a reform school. In June, the school returned his wallet and explained they'd informed his parents he'd been released but had received no reply. The school gave him a bus ticket. An American schoolbus, bare of other passengers, ferried him home. Seth recognized the driver, friend of a cousin, but the driver said nothing until he announced Flannery Point. Stopping first at a bank machine and then the liquor counter of one of his father's stores, silently daring the clerk to ask his age, Seth returned to the old family premises. He got in through a door he'd damaged at fourteen; his father had either never noticed or never bothered to fix it. After three days, Pete came into the premises to hurl curses at the rafters and discuss a kiting scheme with his brother, only to spy Seth curled up in the corner where the pins had landed, half-starved, unwashed, holding an empty forty-ouncer by the neck. Pete had said nothing to his son, only clapped his brother on the shoulder and suggested they go for a drive. Rick Seabright agreed; he hadn't seen Seth.

Seth's mother and aunt fed him and washed his clothes in exchange for repairs to the fence, to the door, the roof, the walls, work now ignored by Pete and Rick Seabright. All that man stuff Seth had supposedly learnt. He actually could fix almost anything. Just give him an hour or so to study the problem and some half-decent tools, and then it was all best kind, less some grime, sweat and profanity. He'd lived in the premises while the summer held, hiring himself out. A handyman can't make much in a dying town, but he'd earned enough to finance working out his first major role: the town drunk. A bit young for it, maybe, but a man's got to start somewhere. Sometimes he wrote stories or letters to no one, jamming them into bottles and throwing them into the sea. Then, nights getting too cold to sleep in the premises, he disappeared. Escaped, really, to St John's, with the envelope of cash his mother had hidden in a box of maxi-pads. His father received a serve-on-weekends sentence for cheque fraud. That done, Pete left the island for work in Labrador, hauling his wife along with him. Flannery Point, steadily losing population and finally even the postal counter and last convenience store in 1999, fell in on itself, like Pete Seabright's too-big, cheaply built and neglected house.

Ten years later, Seth haunted the place. He'd been darting out for visits when he had the gas money, shocked each time, despite knowledge, by boards on windows, slowly collapsing sheds, caved-in lawns over septic tanks, tree-obscured driveways and overgrown graveyards. He broke into abandoned houses and woke the ghosts.

His father's premises. Empty now, rafters bowing, birds living near the ceiling and fouling the place with guano so badly that Seth's eyes burned. But he stood there. The population of his weird dreams since the meeting in Port au Mal stopped jabbering. Even Lieutenant Kelly fell mute beneath the filthy net.

One of *those* Seabrights.

It got so dark out home. Not like St John's, full of streetlights, though still dim by Google Earth standards. No: honest dark out here, proper night.

Seth departed the premises and returned to his Grandmother Clatney's house. Boarded-up windows let in only shreds of fading light. Rats scattered. A baby ghost cried, someone shouted, and someone else dropped a heavy knife. Spooked, Seth fled to the back yard, stopping at the edge of the woods.

Jesus, settle down, b'y. It's not like this is the only abandoned town the world.

He unscrewed a bottle. Drunk, sure. But that meant nothing. Explained nothing. Bit of local colour, that's all. Brown, specifically, dark rum in one of those gorgeous square old-fashioned glasses his father had kept set up and polished on the home bar. The colour of the old wooden frame round his grandmother's mirror, the one he defaced with a fine black marker and very small letters: S Solam S Tattler S Echongornder Gemataur. The priest knew what that meant and lectured Seth on the hazards of the occult. They made a pact never to tell Seth's grandmother. Great priest. Got transferred further up the shore when another parish's Father Diddler finally got arrested.

Where's that mirror to now?

Seth knelt, then lay face down in the wild grass. He dug his nails into the wet ground, knowing quite well he'd run off and drink and come back and run again. Regardless, he prayed for the strength to hang on, hold fast.

That was yesterday.

Today he prayed for enough change to buy something to ease his headache. So far, twelve cents taunted him from the fiddle case. Preparing to start 'Jack Was Every Inch a Sailor,' Seth looked up the street. He spied a woman walking his way, a bit thinner than the last time he'd seen her, a woman around whom way too much weird shit happened.

God, B'y, what are Ya at? I pray for relief, and you send me Nichole Wright?

Nichole stood before Seth and waited for him to finish his tune, her patience positively bovine. He watched his fingering by way of excuse not to look at her – he just did not have the strength, not today. He really, really hoped she'd just get the fuck away from him.

She didn't.

—Seth, I never got a chance to thank you.

—For wha?

—Going with me to the hospital.

—Was nothin. You look like hell.

251

—So do you.

Seth pointed his bow at her. —Keep that up, and you'll hurt my feelins. You know you're damaged, right? I mean, deeply and fundamentally cracked. Someone molest you when you were a kid?

Light refracted strangely and bounced around the thickening fog, and Nichole's patience abandoned her. —Charming, Seabright. And you are? Hey? Who the fuck are you to say that to me, you who grew up safe, because you were a boy?

—Yeah, that's right, safe. Because I was a boy. Listen, now. You need this.

And he played again, Apocalyptica this time, hauling a melody line up from cello to fiddle and squeal-out crucifying 'I'm Not Jesus.' Something fell in the fiddle case and made the pennies jump, and Seth shouted lyrics of abuse and recognition as Nichole walked away.

On the other side of the street, Gabriel Furey watched this scene play out in a store window as he pretended to study the souvenirs placed in the lap of a sou'westered mannequin. The mannequin had a Styrofoam head, eyes drawn with marker and mouth cut with a knife – someone had jammed a cigarette into it. Gabriel turned and crossed, getting angrier with each step. He tossed a twenty in the fiddle case. —You're a piece of work, my son. One of God's own fools.

Seth kept playing, kept singing, and drove off Gabriel, too.

Well done, Seabright.

Fuck it, fog's comin in.

Seth lowered his fiddle and bow and looked at what Nichole had dropped in the case: a knife, chipped onyx handle, decent blade, but old enough to get lost in a museum.

Cut loose one of God's own hungover fools?

The fog thickened and blotted out sunshine and landmarks. Each street seemed to be the edge of the earth.

Very good, then.

Gabriel, worn out, tried to take a nap on the floor near the biggest clay study for his *Sea Sentry* sculpture, but his dead daughter wouldn't let him sleep. He dreamt of beating great big gulls away from her with a broom and a chainsaw. Crows and ravens hovered further off. Not worried about the birds, Claire turned into her seven-year-old self, drawing intently in a sketchbook Gabriel had given her one day when she was sick and feverish. Claire tugged on Gabriel's sleeve and tapped the sketchbook, trying to show him something. He saw only a blank page. He finally figured out what she was saying.

—Daddy, go out. Go. Just go.

Only half-aware of petty details like crosswalks and cars, Gabriel turned sharp angles and wound through little private lanes to a residential area. Spent gardens bowed, limp, and the foghorn's warning echoed off rocks and buildings. He kept walking. The front yards changed, shrank to little strips of supermarket potted flowers or dying grass. People closed heavy windows; the temperature had dropped seven degrees in the last few hours. Rowhouses and dilapidated squares, and even the designated Heritage Buildings, brightly painted and well-kept by government subsidies, looked mean. Tired in a way a week of sleep would not soothe, Gabriel permitted tears to mingle with the fog on his face.

Seth finished his study of the Wikipedia article and then set to gathering tools. First he got the jerrycan. He'd followed a hyperlink to an article on jerrycans, too, grimly amused to learn that the practical and ubiquitous container was a relic of Nazi engineering. He also noted how a traveller might carry one jerrycan filled with precious gasoline and another with precious water. Say your Jeep breaks down in the desert. Which do you cherish: gas or water? Say your body roots to a rock in the north Atlantic. Which do you fear: oil or water?

He walked the short length to the nearest gas station, ignoring Dorinda Masterson as she filled up her SUV, pre-paid for twenty dollars' worth of gas, and with great care filled the red jerrycan. He darted back into the station to wash his hands. Figuring he had nothing left to lose, he acknowledged Dorinda, who was in the cash queue, and let her drive him home. She smelled great, like she had first thing in the morning once, before putting on perfume. She told him he looked terrible. He stared out the windshield, jerrycan on the vehicle's floor between his feet.

Out behind the decrepit rowhouse where he rented two rooms, Seth studied his Zippo lighter. Dorinda had given it to him last winter. Nice weight to it. Felt like a weapon, like something that mattered. In his right hand he picked up the knife from Nichole. *Why did I talk to you like that? And why, in the name of God, did you give me a fuckin knife?* Then he noticed a small hole

253

in the handle, good for threading a line. He took up a stray bit of soft rope, frayed it enough to pluck out a strand, and used that to tie the knife to the belt loop over his right hip. His own knife hung over his left hip, in easy reach. He considered using it to hack off some of his hair, but he didn't have the energy.

First he stood, but then he knelt, reasoning he'd fall otherwise. He removed the medal of St Jerome Emiliani from round his neck— *can't forget that* – and, broken asphalt galling his aching knees, unscrewed the cap of the jerrycan and hoisted the hard weight of it over his head. Arms paining as though he still hung from his father's net, Seth held his breath and poured the gas. Over himself. Someone called out from the sidewalk, a male voice he vaguely recognized, but no time for that now. He patted the knives, and he picked up the lighter. Flicked it open, the familiarity of the sound pleasing him.

God's own fool.

Gabriel Furey, that Zippo rasp guiding him, tackled Seth from behind. Roughly the same size, they rolled hard into the wall of the house, away from gas spill, but what soaked Seth soaked Gabriel. The Zippo, still in Seth's left hand, could spark any second, could ignite if dropped or if Seth moved his wet fingers quickly enough. The Christian Brothers had beaten Gabriel until he learnt to make letters with his right hand, but he drew and painted with his left. Now he pried at Seth's fingers with his left hand. Seth struggled, lashing like some huge and dangerous fish within Gabriel's embrace, and Gabriel nearly lost him. Seth thumbed at the switch; Gabriel reached over Seth's shoulder, grabbed two of Seth's fingers and broke them. Crying out, Seth dropped the Zippo; Gabriel caught it, not knowing how he did so, and flung it into the street. It clattered and clinked but did not spark. Seth slipped out of Gabriel's hold and made for the lighter, but Gabriel blocked him. Staggering, Gabriel wrapped his arms around Seth and held him hard, drops of gasoline raining down as Seth writhed and screamed. The screaming had a rhythm to it, almost a pulse, and, losing himself in it, Gabriel recognized that Seth was crying. Bawling, like a betrayed and violated youngster, choking on snot, gas and salt. He collapsed against Gabriel's chest.

At St Clare's hospital, Nichole took her hand back from just above Seth's hair as he said her name. She answered him quietly, looking nervous. —Morning, Seabright.

—What the fuck are you doin here, after the way I spoke to you?

She didn't answer right away. —Not sure. Gabriel called me – said you were in here. I know my way around hospitals, and I know these curtains. So I had to come and check on you. I mean, I didn't know what I'd say if your family was here. But it was just you, so I sat down.

Seth made to shake his head but barely moved. *Makin as much sense as ever.* He still smelled and tasted gasoline, but also the bitter disinfectant used on hospital sheets. An intravenous dripped calming glue into a vein in his right hand. Foam-lined splints cradled the two broken fingers on his left.

Nichole spoke again. —Can you tell me why?

—Where's my lighter?

—Gabriel's got it.

—The fellah who –

—Yeah.

—Very good, then.

He drifted into a dream of fighting cold salt water, of someone hauling him out by his long hair. And how much it hurt.

Her voice woke him. —Seth, I'm getting tired of this hospital yo-yo thing we've got going. I mean, for two people who hardly know each other –

—I know, girl.

—I've got to go to work. But I'll come back. If that's all right?

He thought it over. —I'll be here.

Nichole smiled. —Good.

Chatting with her cousins Lewis and Matt Wright and sneaking glances at their father, Thomas, who now walked quite stiffly, Nichole slowly ate some baked Alaska, putting down her plate after a few bites. Tonight she would not binge and purge. God knew she wanted to, but no, tonight she'd permit feeling and memory. Tomorrow – fuck tomorrow, she'd deal with tomorrow when it came. Tonight, she would not binge and purge.

Her parents sat at a bistro table not too far off, talking with other Wright cousins not seen or contacted since the late 1970s. They all looked unhappy and strained. Nichole found maybe four relatives just a few years older. No one younger. Beneath dull smiles and I-haven't-seen-you-since or I-remember-hearing-stories-about-you floated an unspoken agreement: this reunion was a bad idea. And whose idea, again? Why use this stunted gathering to give old documents to the government? No Wright seemed to know.

Wait staff threaded the crowd, bearing plates of fruit, cheese and sausage rolls. Suddenly, turning away from his sister, Thomas Wright looked ill.

Matt and Lewis quickly got to him, one on either side. —You all right, Skipper?

Thomas looked at his sons and Nichole with shame. —I forgot the ledger. It's back at the house.

They helped him sit down on a cushioned bench. Through one of the huge panel windows, Nichole saw a government limo pull up and Chris Jackman and Evan Rideout climb out of it. Jackman's hair defied his combover, and he seemed to dance a little jig. Evan scowled and pointed to the brightly lit floor above where the ceremony would take place.

Thomas moaned. —How much am I startin to forget?

Matt took over. —Lew, you and Nichole dart out and get the ledger. I'll stall Jackman if he finishes working the room before you get back. Don't worry, Skipper, we'll look after you.

Nichole and Lewis passed Evan, who stood at the coat-check accepting two tickets. He'd not invited Nichole out for sushi for weeks now, despite her peace offering of showing up for work wearing intact archivist's gloves. *Peril on the Sea* demanded serious overtime from them both, and seeing each other tonight at the Admiral's Rooms felt like just one more extension of the workday. Evan nodded at her, and Nichole tentatively smiled back before following Lewis outside.

Lewis sniffed the air. —Someone's got a backyard firepit going. I thought the city had bylaws against that so late in the year. This won't take long. When we get to the house, you check downstairs, and I'll check up.

They drove uptown. A few blocks from the house, sirens wailed, and Lewis pulled over to let the fire trucks pass. Neither he nor Nichole commented, both pretty sure what they'd find when they got to Thomas Wright's house. Flames. Already reaching out the windows, through the roof. Investigators would quickly determine that an old electrical fault had sparked. That knowledge would not soothe Lewis when he considered the loss of childhood books and toys, old photographs of his grandfather, the Ghostometer. Oh, and John Cannard's ledger.

32) 'WINTER'S STERN COMMAND'

—Why hollow clay?

Nichole smiled at Evan. —Because it's fragile.

Gabriel Furey had delivered his sculpture of *Sea Sentry* slightly ahead of schedule, giving the Admiral's Rooms an extra week to finalize setup. Evan and Nichole had put together something they both felt proud of, but Nichole still spoke rather coolly to Evan, blaming him, he thought, for TCR's axe falling on the Settlement 250 play.

What a weird day that was.

Evan noticed how Nichole's fingers did not end in gracefully shaped nails but in quick-bitten ragged stubs. That slight tremor in her hands seemed to have worsened. She'd dropped a good ten or fifteen pounds, but what really startled Evan was her hair: tied back in a loose braid, exposing her face and the lines and dark circles that aged her. Not sure why he'd ever found her attractive, yet still finding her so, Evan pointed to a skewed porthole on Gabriel's sculpture. —Do you think that's deliberate? Aw, shit.

Off down the hallway: the long stride and sharp jabber of Chris Jackman. —Yeah, I hear ya. I understand that right well, right well. Cost overrun – put in the diversion schedule – shag the news crowd, I haven't got time to talk about – when I get back – the PM's gonna have my balls – I know, I wish I still had that assistant, on my way to see him now – leave it on my desk. Bye. Evan, me ol cock. Where ya been hidin out?

I am in no mood for this today. No. Mood. —Right here, Chris. Been workin.

—How's your grandfather? I understand the missus didn't press charges.

This city is too damned small. Had a good laugh about that, did ya? —Mrs Dunphy? No, she's finest kind. She knew Pop just wanted to kiss her. Then he got confused.

Nichole cleared her throat. —Should I come back later?

Chris smiled at her but only with his mouth. He didn't like her eyes: sadness and some strange knowledge in there, what all those models and celebrities made up like crack whores and vampires tried to emulate. —No, that's fine. Ev, listen, I got more fundin. I really need you back. The Minister's got me drove cracked to get the museum review policy up to TFAT standards, and that friggin Seth Seabright is after workin up some rant about us havin no theatre. He's pullin some performance arts stunt now down by the cruise ships.

Nichole laughed. She tried to make it a cough, but she could not disguise that joyful noise.

Jackman turned back to Evan. —When can you start?

—I'm a little busy here, Chris. Nichole, do you think we should turn it so people see the porthole as soon as they walk in?

—Come on, don't let me down here. I need you.

—You need help, no doubt.

—Will you please look at me when I speak to you, Rideout?

Not until I find out if you fast-tracked my grandfather.

—Nichole, maybe if the porthole faced the window –

—Evan, stop fartin around and listen to me! I – what the hell is this?

Evan said nothing. Nichole fixed her gaze on Chris. —*Sea Sentry.*

—The rig that sank?

Nichole nodded. —Part of the exhibit. I'm sure I sent a press release about it to TCR.

—This is government-funded, is it?

Squinting a bit, Nichole studied Chris Jackman as she might a lost little boy. —Well, yes. TCR supports the Admiral's Rooms.

—The utter gall of ye. She left behind eighty-odd families when she sank. All hands gone. My father among them. And you turn it into arts and crafts!

Nichole glanced at Evan, but he was studying the floor. She tried to speak. Chris raised his arm and swiped at the clay *Sea Sentry* with the back of his hand.

The sculpture toppled onto the stone floor and shattered.

Evan's headache rivalled Dead Man's Pond for depth when he got home. The hired caretaker had just helped True Rideout back to his favourite chair and re-started the old VCR. The tape carried a decayed recording of an episode of *Shores and Tides*, a weekly Newfoundland documentary series that had run in the 1970s and 80s. Evan wondered how much longer the tape would last before it frayed and snapped.

—Pop, how ya doin?

—Sshh, me show's on.

The caretaker smiled sympathetically. Evan flipped through the day's mail. An envelope from the Department of Health. *Finally.*

Dear Mr Evan Rideout:

As to your recent and expedited request to fast-track TRUE RIDEOUT (relation: GRANDFATHER) into the Seniors Home System, we regret to inform you that your application was not successful. As you know, the fast-track system is new and still under development and at present runs on a lottery basis. We recognize that you do need to access the Seniors Home System, and so we have placed your application on a Priority Two Waitlist. You can expect to hear from the Seniors Home System within six weeks to confirm the placement of TRUE RIDEOUT (relation: GRANDFATHER) on a Priority Two Waitlist. Please contact us if TRUE RIDEOUT (relation: GRAND-FATHER) changes his contact information. If TRUE RIDEOUT (relation: GRANDFATHER) experiences any worsening of symptoms, please contact a doctor.

Evan put down the letter and stared at the strange caretaker, and then at the stranger, disconnected man who looked like his grandfather. The man who'd confusedly held a gun to his grandson's head and now la-laed with the *Shores and Tides* opening theme. For a moment, Evan's focus sharpened dramatically. The tear fell.

True pointed at the screen. —That's me favourite show, that is. Favourite show.

33) BLOWOUT
OCTOBER 9, 2009, AS TOLD BY CHRIS JACKMAN TO SOME WRITER AT
THE WRECKING BALL, ST JOHN'S.

Fuck, b'y, I'm after avoidin you for months, and you got to find me here. Got your little voice recorder, I see. Yes, take footage of me on your cell phone. Hang on now, I gives ya the royal wave. Hulloooo, hulloooo. Cheers. I, Christopher Lawrence Jackman, do hereby pledge allegiance to God, history, every greasy cent, every piece of dinosaur shit and every human bone in the oil fields, and thereby allegiance to the Republic of Newfoundland and Labrador. Orphan Basin forever, whooooo! Some fun, wha? Oral history? And what the fuck is oral history, my son? You're goin around collectin stories about *Sea Sentry* like they're seashells. Necklaces from bits of metal next. Be on sale at the Folk Festival in Bannerman Park. Drink? Vodka and lime. Ya got me cornered now between the stinkin little corridor to the urinal and the VLTs. Inside of two sunkers. Jesus, I can't get clear of that rig today. Yes, b'y and me after wreckin a sculpture of it. That can't be very good for an assistant deputy minister of Tourism, Culture and Recreation now, can it? Larry Jackman. Born today. Died on board that fuckin *Sea Sentry*, February 15, 1982. Had to be today I see that sculpture, had to be today. Right delicate it was. Looked like stone, sure, or concrete, and I took it out with one strike of my hand. Career's gone. Once again, history fucks Chris Jackman up the arse.

Cold, that night, so fuckin cold, wind drivin the rain and sleet and snow against the windows, and me all snuggled in bed with my hockey cards and great big Luke Skywalker action figure, size of a rag doll, thinkin how safe I was, because I was inside. Tucked in bed. Mom kissed me. And I knew Dad was safe, too, out on the rig. I just knew it. Sure, ya know it gets stormy. Weather's fuckin savage in February. But *Sea Sentry*, she could take it. Monstrous, pontoons and everythin. Be a rough night, no question, but nothin that rig couldn't handle. No more lanterns in the windows. No more women walkin the floors askin God if they'd been made widows. That Jesus wind. Soon as I woke up, I knew somethin was wrong. I'd overslept. Mom hadn't gotten me up for school. There she was, hunched at the kitchen table, VOIC playin some loud. The guys in the newsroom that mornin sounded right slow, like

261

they were listenin to somethin else while they read the news and were tryna translate all at once – vodka and lime – next thing I know aunts and uncles and Nan and Pop are all in the house, soakin wet, and I poured out a Jesus big bowl of Rice Krispies and heaped on the sugar and milk and ate the mess of it sittin on the good livin room carpet. And no one said a word to me. I couldn't believe how stupid they all were. No way Dad died. No fuckin way that rig went down. It didn't happen. Soon as we all wakes up and sees the sunny skies, we'll understand that, I told them. I wrecked that sculpture. Can't go makin arts and crafts out of somethin like that. Jesus. No b'y, I'll call me own cab. TCR's got an account with Bugden's.

Not callin no fuckin cab. Only a short drive.

Head to one side, Jackman, just the airbag. Windrose carved outta rock? Undo the belt first. Some foggy. Jesus, it's Casper the Ghost Real. Or Riel, is it? Who's after crashin into that?

34) 'BUT ITS TRUTHS ARE ALL BOUND TO THE NEVER-ENDING ESCAPE'
OCTOBER 11, 2009, VON HALDORF MEMORIAL COTTAGE HOSPITAL, CONCEPTION BAY NORTH.

Damp, chilled and wired after driving for almost three hours in drizzle and fog, Nichole drained the last of her cold coffee as she approached the nurses' desk. —Hi. I'm looking for Reverend Elias Winslow. I received several telephone messages saying he wanted to see me?

The nurse escorted Nichole to a room where someone had taped a handwritten sign reading 'Reflection Chamber' to the door. The nurse whispered that they hadn't been able to find any of the Reverend's family, that he'd only asked for Nichole, and that they expected him to die within a few hours. They'd moved him to this room where he wouldn't be disturbed. Nichole's eyes widened at that, and she almost snarled about cruelty and convenience disguised as dignity. Her anger startled her, and she tried to parse it out. Then she considered how she'd made such a long drive without hesitation. Closing the door, the nurse told Nichole to press the call button near the Reverend's bed if she needed help.

Hang on. I didn't agree to keeping any vigil.

Jesus, another hospital bed. Reverend Elias Winslow, one of thousands who fell.

And how did I get tangled up with you?

—Nichole.

She grasped the rails on his bed.—I'm here, Reverend Winslow.

—About time.

—Pardon me?

—It's important I speak to you, and those nurses kept hushing me. I wanted to finish this at home, you know. I tried to. I'd crawled under my bed and settled down with the dust, but Mrs O'Dea from Riordan's Back came by with a cold plate, and she found me. I can't move anything except my eyes and mouth. Intolerable! Take me home. Take me home right now.

—I don't think the hospital would let you go.

—But I can't move. It's not even dancing I want now, or those long leaps. Nichole, I just want to sit up by myself, not wait here like something beached, wait for the tide to catch up with me.

—I know.

Winslow wept like a toddler trapped at each turn, and his chapped lips bled as he spoke. —If I hadn't – in 1734 – I should have just faded out then, already thinner than drizzle, but I had to wait for you – too long stuck to flesh. Now I must obey the laws of flesh. This is all your fault!

Nichole poured him a glass of water and helped him drink it. Then she took a pot of lip balm from her pocket and gently rubbed some of it over the Reverend's lips.

—Thank you. Do you remember what I told you, the fray well part?

—Yes.

—And did you keep the knife? The sailmaker's secret knife?

—I gave it away.

—You think so? I stole that from history. Groundwalkers squabbling offshore, and I could not quite coalesce. All bad enough you wrecked my hold on history with your ledger and letters and proof.

Maybe I should buzz for the nurse now.

—Because it seems to me you are the one who must keep the knife. It's a good knife; it should protect you a bit. And you testified? Well done. So what you need to do now is digest all this history. Just don't purge it back out. I see those calluses on your hand, the delicate translucence of your front teeth. I know what you're up to.

—Reverend, I don't understand –

—I'm losing it, as the young people say. Lost it years ago, one seed at a time. Gnawed hole in the sack of my soul. Sow. Reap.

Reverend Winslow suddenly sat up very straight. Nichole could swear he'd shrunk in the last few moments.

Is he going to pray?

He bellowed. —Dementia! Deeeeeee-meant-CHA! Cha-cha-cha.

Nichole eased him back onto the mattress and smoothed hair off his forehead. —Ssh, Reverend, it's all right. You're safe, you're safe.

—Sea-snakes, Nichole. My brothers keep trying to teach you about blessing the sea snakes.

—That's Coleridge.

—The girl in the graveyard. Demon-demon-demon-ain't-ya. I don't like these flesh rules. They are hardly fair. Unaware.

—Of course, Reverend.

He shrank some more, as if being sucked inward. Skin wrinkled; hair fell out; accent changed. —Nichole Wright. I should have guessed. One of that green-eyed brittle arrogant crowd. All of ye three steps shy of madness. Took ya long enough to be born. Dost know how long I've waited for thee? One gets cold in Labrador. Demon-ain't-ya. Demon daimon. And Pythias.

Winslow's bowels released sulphurous gas, and Nichole could no longer read her watch. Once more she smoothed hair off his forehead. —Do you want another drink of water?

He vomited nails and pins but no fluid. The nails and pins fell to the floor and tolled like huge bells. Then he snarled. — Already? Frailty is for... for... that word, thingy... groundwalkers! Nichole Wright, you canny bitch, you stole the last breaths from me. In defying me, you've exhausted me; I haven't breathed for days. I am as much a part of creation as you, Nichole. You will always dream of the photos. Posing by the cherry tree. Posing for Foxe. Because I give you one last gift: bad dreams.

Nichole took Winslow's cold hand, tried to warm it.

—Nichole, is that you?

—Yes.

—I'm scared.

—I'm here, Reverend.

—In this mess? Of your own free will?

—This time, yes, yes, I am.

—And will you remember?

—Yes.

—Good.

Winslow's eyes dulled, and his breathing got shallow. Then it stopped. The room chilled. Nichole sat with the corpse for perhaps half an hour, the Reverend's hand still in hers, first too tired to move, then too confused. But she managed to gently lower Winslow's hand onto the sheets, unfold herself from the hard plastic chair, rise and rejoin the rest of the hospital.

The nurses must have changed shifts. Nichole did not recognize the woman furiously making notes at the desk. She waited a moment, loath to interrupt, but finally she spoke up.

—I think Reverend Winslow has died.

—Hmm?

—Reverend Winslow, in the Reflection Chamber? I think he's died. Do you need me for anything else?

The writing nurse looked up and made eye contact. —I'm sorry for your loss.

Nichole almost explained that Winslow was no relative, but the snot and tears in her nose choked her. *The fuck?*

The nurse got up and walked with quick gracefulness. —Poor old Reverend Winslow, he used to scare the whillikers out of me growing up, me and all the other youngsters. Funny how he never looked his age. I'm glad he didn't have to die alone. Oh, sweetheart, it's all right. You need a minute?

Nichole struggled to get the words out. —I hardly knew him. And he could be such a nuisance.

—Dementia's hard, my love. You never know what's going to come out of their mouths. Don't beat yourself up for getting angry with something he said.

—He told me a story.

—That's nice. Sometimes their memories come back just before they die, and they're sharp as nails.

I'm not getting through to you. —Yeah, nails. The mess on the floor, it's nails and pins. I don't know how it happened.

The nurse frowned. —Did you knock over a sharps container? The yellow bin, where the used needles go?

—No, he – I thought he –

Nichole and the nurse entered the Reflection Chamber. Winslow's corpse looked frail and small. The air smelled a bit sharp, sweet but mineral, like broken spruce needles and sun-warmed rocks.

—Nothing on the floor here, my love. I want you to go back to the nursing station and sit down for a bit, okay? You're shaking like a leaf. I'll see if I can get you a cup of tea in a minute.

Nichole heard scrapes and dings, as though the nurse had kicked –

Fucking get out of here before they hook me back up to sing the Thorazine blues.

Nichole backed out of the room, caught sight of a fire exit, and ran.

Safe in her car, Nichole dug to the bottom of her backpack for any stashed candy bars to binge on. *Got ya.* Just under a notebook, long and heavy. *Must be a king size bar.*

But no. Across her palm lay the old blade, the onyx handle: the sailmaker's secret knife.

—Did you like the lobster, Gabe?

Gabriel held the storm door open for Dorinda while she balanced on her cane and unlocked the main door.

—Best kind. Your sister's a good cook. But can ya tell that husband of hers to mind his own fuckin business?

—You're mad he kept trying to get you to drink the wine?

—That, too. But I am not suin Chris Jackman, and that's the end of it. Jesus lawyers.

Takin me aside and sayin I'm weak not to, now.

Dorinda smiled at him over her shoulder. —Come in, if you want.

Gabriel followed Dorinda. He'd been up here before, but only after repeated invitations. His tenancy of her basement apartment galled him more and more, yet her kindness to him – not noblesse oblige, not even the remnants of an old crush... Gabriel smiled at the thought. His ex-wife once accused him of sleeping with Dory Masterson. He hadn't. He'd never wanted to. And he didn't now. Right?

Several baskets of clean laundry on the sofa needed folding. Gabriel wondered if he should offer to help but instead just dug in, asking if Dorinda was sure she felt up to company.

—Cup of tea, Gabriel?

—Yes, please.

Nice bra. 36DD? You're a double D? Frig, are you tryna get me goin? Did you leave this out on purpose?

—Why are you looking at me like that?

Gabriel recognized that the sofa hid the sight of his hands in her laundry. He put the bra down. Tried to say *I can't. I think – I'm startin to love you. But I can't.*

Dorinda scooped tea into the pot. —Maybe I'm on too many boards of directors; I feel absolutely sucked dry. When will the insurance cheque come from the Admiral's Rooms?

—God knows. We're talkin government.

—Go to the media. Go on *Free Line* on VOIC. That'll speed up the compensation.

—Dory ...

—My brother-in-law's right. You really could sue Jackman's arse off.

—But what for? What the fuck for? All those bits of clay aren't gonna jump right back together again. And drivin his pickup into that statue – Chris Jackman's got enough to deal with.

—He walked away from that crash without a scratch. After destroying your work!

—My work, but his past. That's what he lashed out against, ducky. Don't get me wrong. I'm fuckin poisoned he ruint that sculpture. But that's – his reaction – I dunno, it's part of the risk.

Silence.

—Gabriel, you want a mug or a cup and saucer?

—Mug's good enough for the likes of me.

Gabriel stared at an old eight-by-ten photo behind the glass door of a knick-knack cabinet: Dorinda as a flower-strewn Ophelia from a 1979 production of *Hamlet*. Handwriting obscured her from the knees down. —Dory, what's this say?

—Oh my God, back when I thought I could act. That wasn't yesterday. And that perm. 'Lord, we know what we are, but know not what we may be. God be at your table!'

Gabriel kept studying the photograph. Dorinda's breasts had just brushed his arm and back – hadn't they? By accident?

She returned to the kitchen. Gabriel sat back down on the couch, feeling too big, too gangly for all this proper furniture. Clinks of the tea things then – he almost ran to the kitchen to take the heavy tray from her.

—You go sit down, rest your ankle.

Mortified at the sight of the laundry basket, Dorinda picked it up, hobbled and balanced, and hid the basket behind a chair. Then she sat down, trying not to watch Gabriel pour tea.

He made a toast. —Heard this one from a Scotsman who helped me out in a brawl. 'Here's tae us. Wha's like us?'

—'Damn few, and they're dead.'

Gabriel smiled. —Where'd you learn that?

Dorinda gave up trying to find the nerve to ask Gabriel to spend the night – just spend the night, be in the same part of this big house, because sleeping – or trying to sleep – got lonely. She wouldn't mind a good shag with him, couldn't help comparing his body to Seth's – *Jesus, Seth* – but she wanted something more. And she had no idea how to ask for it.

They parted, Gabriel sleepy from the big supper and the two warm houses. Dorinda fell asleep under two sedatives on the couch, breathing in Gabriel's scent. Downstairs, Gabriel wanted to kick in the studies for *Sea Sentry*, as though destruction might mean something. Instead, he walked carefully around them and got in bed. Maybe the caffeine in the tea, maybe the weird feeling off Dorinda, maybe the whole God damned last ten months – something made him dream the whole night long. Of gas and lighters, of St Raphael's, of a man who slowly spun, shouting at him through the wind.

Seth Seabright paced westward along the waterfront, knees and healing fingers aching hard in the damp. Cruise ship season might be finally over, small mercies. He felt run down, like he'd not eaten a proper meal in weeks – true. Like he'd not slept without the aid of some or another drug for months – also true. Like he'd kept a hard watch in the fog without knowing what he watched for, or why.

He'd met Nichole in a coffee shop line that afternoon. Mischief and joy lit up her eyes. *I'm turning that play manuscript into a novel. My publisher's really interested.*

He threw his cigarette butt in the harbour, weakly, with his right hand; the ember glowed as it arced up, then down. A seagull tried to eat it.

I got to start writin this shit down again.

—Nichole.

—Evan, good, I was looking for you. VOIC is on the phone. They want a comment on Jackman destroying *Sea Sentry*.

—Did you say anythin to them?

—Just told them I had no comment, but I'd be happy to put them in touch with a supervisor.

—I'm not a supervisor.

—I guess that's why they're still on hold.

—Nichole, you want to grab a coffee after work?

—Me?

—Anyone else here called 'Nichole'?

She swallowed, reached out for the stone counter behind her, gripped it. —I'd like to, but I need to get my loins respectable first.

—You need to what?

—Tomorrow any good to you?

—Tomorrow's fine.

She smiled at him, eyes crinkling up with pleasure – but still sad. Compassionate.

That, Evan recognized as Nichole spoke again, was what sparked her beauty, no matter how much she tried to hide it with tricks of shadow and light.

To Dr Miller, Nichole explained it this way. —I simply chose not to go. I did not comply; I did not respond like a groomed child; I chose. Spit, not swallow. Poorly chosen figure of speech, maybe, but it gets the job done.

Miller nodded, smiling. —So exactly what did you say to Evan?

Knowing Miller would eventually pick out the sense of it, Nichole cherished the truth of her reply.

—I told him, I can't go out tonight because I've got to fray well.

ACKNOWLEDGEMENTS

The woman-disguised-as-a-man storyline is an old one and turns up in several folk songs. The one that sparked me is 'The Handsome Cabin Boy,' as sung by Kate Bush. When I first heard the song in 1990, I knew I'd be running with the idea – but it turned out I had to write *Sky Waves* first.

The song that helped me finish this novel is 'Maid on the Shore,' as sung by The Once.

Special thanks to David Adams Richards for mentoring – and slogging through – an early draft of what is now *Acts of Fever* during a correspondence course through the Humber School for Writers.

Warm thanks to my husband, David Hallett, who reads nearly every word I write, to my parents, sister and brother-in-law, my mother-in-law, and to my daughters, my compassionate girls, Madeleine and Alexandra: I cherish you. Jeff Bursey, for a critical eye on earlier versions of *Acts of Fever* and a long friendship. Robin Martin, for years of ready history and ready kindness. My editor, Susan Rendell, for a thoughtful, close and very helpful edit. Phil Churchill. Creative Book Publishing. Cristin Fraser at True North Records. Anne Furlong, for helping this heathen with the saints. Blair Harvey. Joel Thomas Hynes. Madison Violet. Melanie Oates. The Once. Lee Thompson. Leslie Vryenhoek. Dave Walsh. Russell Wangersky. Kathleen Winter.

I crewed on Bytown Brigantine's tall ship *Fair Jeanne* in late October 1996, on the Halifax to Boston leg. Thanks to all of you on board then, particularly XO Chris Smith. I hope you're well, wherever you are.

The epigraph from Phil Churchill's host video, *Anything Is Possible*, shown at the 2008 Newfoundland and Labrador Arts Council Awards Show, is used with permission.

The epigraph and chapter titles from Blair Harvey's song 'Bury My Body in the Pines' (*GutterBeGutted* 2006) are used with permission.

The epigraph from Madison Violet's song 'Wake Up' (*Worry the Jury* 2004) is used with permission.